"That's becoming a habit."

Confusion showed on Jason's face.

"You insisted on doing the same thing last night after the wedding," Gin explained. "You carried me over the threshold."

"I don't remember that."

He shoved his hands in his pockets. "You should rest."

"That's why you brought me up here. To rest."

He nodded, but he refused to look at her.

"I told you I'm not tired."

"No. It's obvious you're wired. You should sleep it off."

"We both know that's unlikely."

She tugged his shirt from his jeans and ran her fingertips along his warm skin. "We both could use a shower."

She shrugged out of her jacket and let it fall to the floor. "Come on, Jason." Why wouldn't he make a move? "Come have some fun with your wife."

ABOUT THE AUTHOR

Debra Webb wrote her first story at age nine and her first romance at thirteen. It wasn't until she spent three years working for the military behind the Iron Curtain and within the confining political walls of Berlin, Germany, that she realized her true calling. A five-year stint with NASA on the space-shuttle program reinforced her love of the endless possibilities within her grasp as a storyteller. A collision course between suspense and romance was set. Debra has been writing romance, suspense and action-packed romance thrillers since. Visit her at www.debrawebb.com or write to her at P.O. Box 4889, Huntsville, AL 35815.

Books by Debra Webb

DEBRA WEBB

USA TODAY Bestselling Author

READY, AIM...
I DO!
&
MISSING

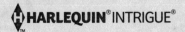

ISBN-13: 978-0-373-69716-8

READY, AIM...I DO!
Copyright © 2013 by Harlequin Books S.A.

The publisher acknowledges the copyright holder of the individual works as follows:

READY, AIM...I DO!
Copyright © 2013 by Debra Webb

MISSING
Copyright © 2011 by Debra Webb

Recycling programs for this product may not exist in your area.

Printed in U.S.A.

CONTENTS

READY, AIM...
I DO!

CAST OF CHARACTERS

Jason Grant—A Specialist and former military sniper. Holt has sent Grant out to assist an agent who has been compromised, but he finds himself the primary suspect when a sniper starts attacking civilians in the area.

Ginger Olin—A spy on the trail of a deadly new virus, she needs to identify the buyer, but she picks up an added assignment as authorities try to determine Grant's guilt or innocence.

Emmett Holt—Deputy Director of Mission Recovery. Holt took Lucas Camp's place when he retired. Some believe he will do anything to move to the top.

Thomas Casey—Director of Mission Recovery. Thomas is the consummate Specialist. He handpicks his people and is determined to protect his team.

Lucas Camp—Thomas's closest friend. He will do whatever is necessary to protect his friend and the interests of Mission Recovery.

Victoria Colby-Camp—The semiretired head of the Colby Agency. She and Lucas can't seem to stay out of the business of investigations.

Chapter One

You're next.

Jason Grant couldn't stop thinking about the note he'd received last month. So far he'd come up empty trying to determine the source. He wanted to write it off as a prank, but it wasn't the kind of humor any of his friends or associates indulged in. Although he knew he was considered the next in line for the deputy director post at Mission Recovery, it wasn't how his bosses would announce a promotion.

If this current assignment was any indication, the reality appeared to be that he was next up to either get fired or die of boredom. The sport coat he wore suddenly felt too warm; the tie he'd already loosened still felt too confining.

He looked around the hotel bar. Too early for a big crowd, but there were plenty of people coming and going and gambling. His deep well of training-induced patience was running dry. Not a smart thing in his line of work as a Specialist, but true all the same. Although impatience wasn't the ideal, he knew the value of being aware of his strengths and weaknesses throughout a fluctuating operation.

He signaled the bartender for another beer and thought about what he might have done to deserve such a low-level assignment.

Specialists were sent in to recover the impossible situations—not to sit back and watch for potential signs of trouble. Last month he'd been told to observe, and he had done so. Right up until the point when Director Casey needed hands-on assistance. This time it felt much the same, except he had no idea who might be in trouble. In fact, he had no idea what the hell was going on here.

All he'd been told was that the operative in place might need backup. He was supposed to hang out in and around Caesar's Palace, observe and make himself available to get her out if necessary. They didn't even tell him which *her* he was looking for.

It didn't feel right. A lot of things in Mission Recovery weren't feeling right these days.

Still, gut feelings aside, this was the job and here he was in Sin City. He'd found a cover story with a nearby convention on security systems and emerging technologies and booked an upgraded room in the Caesar tower, though he didn't expect to see it much.

He tipped back the dark bottle of beer but didn't risk drinking any more than the half bottle he'd already sipped away. Instead, his eyes scanned the constantly shifting crowd for any female who looked like a covert operative. Evening hours—really any hour in

Vegas from what he'd seen so far—meant women were decked out like there was a Bond girl audition nearby. It made for colorful and entertaining scenery, but Jason was ready for action.

This gig of sitting around watching was getting staler than the beer he pretended to drink.

He pulled out his phone and, per his habit, checked the police scanner app for any crime news. For the past two days, aside from a seven-car pileup on Interstate 15 the state troopers suspected had been started by a blown-out front tire of a limousine, it had been mostly routine stuff. Muggings, prostitution, disputes over money or lovers. Nothing that pointed to a spy in trouble. Certainly no high-speed shoot-outs involving high-end automobiles.

He turned his attention to the hockey game televised on the set above the bar. The odds were running like a stock exchange ticker across the bottom of the picture. If something didn't break soon, he might have to resort to the preferred entertainment and place a bet on something.

"Pardon me," the bartender said. "Is your name Grant?"

He nodded. The bartender slid him a shot of tequila with a salt shaker and lime. "Courtesy of the blonde across the way." He jerked his thumb over his shoulder to the other end of the bar.

Grant took a long look and smiled when the woman raised her own shot in salute. The hair was different, probably a wig, and from this distance in the subdued light he couldn't be sure about the eyes. But the dress.

He recognized the vibrant emerald dress that skimmed her sensual curves. A certain bold redhead had worn it when she'd crashed a wedding reception in Colorado last month.

At the time he'd considered her the prime suspect behind the cryptic *You're next* note he'd received. But the brief investigation and limited evidence disproved that theory. No one remembered a redhead or even a woman anywhere near the note. In the weeks since, he'd been looking over his shoulder and jumping at shadows, though he'd never admit any such thing. As much as he hated the wide-open, let-it-ride atmosphere in the gambling capital, the constant motion of Vegas was at least curing him of the jumpiness.

What the hell, he thought, and tossed back the shot. If Olin was the agent in need, the alcohol might dull the edginess he felt whenever he thought about the stunning redhead. Of course, tequila was better known for boosting the potential for trouble than preventing it.

Either way, this being Vegas, he might as well enjoy the ride.

GINGER OLIN SLID a fifty-dollar chip onto number twenty-five and considered herself lucky even before the croupier set the roulette wheel spinning.

Why couldn't all her targets have the good taste to conduct business in Las Vegas? The themes were over the top, but that was the beauty of it. Vegas catered to the bold and overwhelmed the inhibitions of the shy. It made for a delightfully level playing field.

As she strolled through the gaming rooms of Caesar's Palace amid the glamorous theme and thorough details, she noticed the atmosphere exuded luxury with an undercurrent of excited energy. One couldn't help joining in the fun. That energy drew like a magnet, made her feel alive in a way that only this kind of decadence could.

The ball dropped in, and she listened to it zip around the wheel as she scanned the nearby tables for any sign of the man carrying the deadly virus she'd been tracking all over the globe. Hearing the bounce and clatter as the ball landed, she timed her squeal of glee perfectly as the dealer called out the winning number.

"Twenty-five!"

Smiling, she accepted the congratulations and admiring glances along with the slightly taller stack of chips and stepped back from the table. Her target, a slick crime boss out of Europe, was on the move, but who was he here to meet? That was the million-dollar question, and she sought the answer.

She strolled along, just one woman among thousands dressed to the nines and looking for the next place to burn through her money. Waitresses cruised through knots of gamblers and hangers-on in an intricate ballet, trays held high, smiles wide and full of temptation. She supposed some people might find the glitter and glam overdone, but Gin enjoyed it. Here a spy could find the right background to blend with, no matter the circumstances. The perfect playing board for dangerous games.

She spotted her target, an older man with thick gray hair and wire-rimmed glasses, moving toward the craps tables and Gin shadowed him, wondering if he was enjoying the setting as much as she was. The virus wasn't with him, though. Her tracking tag showed it was stationary, probably in his room. Joining the growing crowd cheering on a lucky run at a craps table, she used the raucous, shifting party as cover while she tried to spot the buyer.

Her pulse stuttered when she met the hard, icy gaze of Bernard Isely. He was looking too closely, and not at her well-displayed cleavage. He preferred his women cheap, his vodka expensive, and those who betrayed him dead. He didn't know it yet, but she would soon fall squarely into the last category.

She felt an unprecedented surge of insecurity. Would her wig and contacts be enough to protect her? Her intent was not to dress the same way twice during her stay here. Her well-calculated costuming would, she hoped, be enough to keep her alive throughout and after this assignment.

She dragged her thoughts away from the edge of panic and focused instead on her extensive training and reliable intel. A few weeks ago while she was following a different lead, she'd been told this low life had entered the States, but he should never have been *here*. Not in person. He usually sent someone else to do the face-to-face work.

But there was nothing *usual* about this particular business. His appearance shouldn't have been a shock. She told herself it *wasn't* a shock. Everyone who should know believed his father had commissioned the deadly virus up for sale this weekend. It might not fit his profile, but then this particular exchange wasn't standard fare for the Isely crime family. The son might want to watch his father's greatest coup go out into the criminal world at last. Maybe that was reason enough to take such a high risk.

Regardless, she understood it was his abrupt appearance right across from her that could rattle her. Rattled spies didn't last long. Experience kept her reactions in tune with the excited crowd and her gaze averted from her enemy. Her heart might be in her throat, but there wouldn't be any outward sign of her distress. She had too much practice to give him that advantage.

Immediately she considered her options. This was one of the most wanted and most evasive men of the criminal underworld. They'd almost caught him last month by accident, but somehow he'd slithered out of custody before the right authorities arrived.

The player rolled again and won again, and in the subsequent roar of celebration, Gin slipped back and away, putting the other revelers between her and Isely.

She tagged along on the fringe of a group of women cruising out toward the slot machines. If he was on to her, it would be obvious right away. Unfortunately, her worst-case scenario was confirmed when she spared a glance over her shoulder. It was too late to make a preemptive bold move, but it was still too soon to panic.

There was always a way out.

Well, almost always.

She needed the right crowd or the right loner, she thought, turning toward the low lights of the nearest bar. And she needed one or the other right now.

The crowd was light and most of the patrons were

paired up or in small groups. Gin sought the solo acts. There was another blonde woman in a deep emerald dress, only a shade or so darker than Gin's, who might do in a pinch. Gin had the long-lost school chum routine down to a science.

But her first choice would be a man. Men were typically less suspicious and far less likely to admit they couldn't remember a hot chick from a prior rendezvous. She spotted a man in the corner sipping a cup of coffee and squinting into a book that was most likely a tutorial on blackjack. Too serious and sporting a wedding ring, she crossed him off her mental list.

Then she noticed the ideal candidate at the other end of the bar. She strolled right up to the only familiar face she could potentially define as a friend in this town and pressed a light kiss to Specialist Grant's cheek. "Oh, the whims of fate," she said in a flat Midwestern accent.

"More like the whims of my boss," he replied, signaling the bartender.

"Have you been waiting long?"

"A couple of days. What'll you have?"

"White wine," she told the bartender. Taking the barstool next to Jason, she swiveled so her knees brushed against his thigh.

He glanced down and then gave her an interested half-grin. "You don't have to bait me."

"I beg your pardon?"

He leaned closer. "I'm a sure thing, remember?"

She tipped her head back and laughed, playing along. "That's good to know." Studying him, she wondered how much he'd had to drink. Any alcohol beyond a

few sips to set his profile meant he was here for pleasure rather than business. Grant, she suspected, wasn't
the sort to bend the rules on a mission. His brown eyes
were a little unfocused, his pupils dilated. So maybe he
wasn't here on business. Still, even in the midst of tying
one on, he was her best bet to get out of here.

Using the mirror behind the bar, she checked for
Isely. He'd stepped just inside the doorway and was
checking out the milling crowd. He didn't come closer,
but she could feel his gaze land on her back. If he didn't
know for sure, he'd suspected she was trouble. Well,
Jason Grant could help her prove otherwise.

The bartender delivered her wine and she sipped,
rubbing her palm across Jason's knee. Isely had to believe she was involved with him, that they were simply
a couple here to enjoy a long weekend.

"Need a hand?"

"Why, Mr. Grant, that sounds like a wonderful start.
I think you're just the lucky charm that would be helpful to me at the craps tables."

He shook his head. "I—ah, don't gamble," he mumbled with a laugh that sounded almost drunken.

Alarms sounded in her head. A man who didn't gamble didn't do Vegas for pleasure. Something was wrong
here. "Sweetheart, are you feeling well?"

"Fine." He picked up her hand and stroked her palm
with his thumb. "Your hand is…is so soft."

And his was quite strong, but something was clearly
wrong. Careful not to break cover, she scanned the room
for whoever had drugged him. She needed to get him
out of here before he was too loopy to walk.

He started to slump to the side, and she signaled for the bartender to settle the tab. Jason managed a signature and she caught the room number he'd listed along with the drink tally. Two beers wouldn't have put him in this state.

"Why don't we take a walk?" she suggested.

"I'd like that."

"Good." She looped his arm over her shoulder and with hers at his waist she steadied him as they maneuvered through the bar.

The gun she felt in the waistband at the small of his back implied he was on the clock and only solidified her theory that someone had decided he was a target for something. As they exited no one seemed to care, not even Isely, but she couldn't be sure because it took all her concentration to keep Jason upright. His height of just over six feet and lean but muscular build were far more appealing when he was supporting both on his own power.

His hand slid down to cup her bottom and she jumped a little, surprised by his touch. She covered her reaction with a laugh. Maybe he was faking the drunk part. Was he taking advantage and hamming it up, or was there a real problem? It helped the cover, so she wouldn't complain. She guided him toward the main entrance, hoping the fresh air and surroundings would help revive him if this wasn't for show.

"What did you have to drink, sweetheart?" she asked. The crowded streets and traffic noise meant no one could eavesdrop and she wanted as much information as she could get.

"A beer. Not even. Oh!" He jerked a bit. "And you sent me a shot of tequila."

"Ah." As they walked, she checked his pockets. He had his wallet and his room key. She must have interrupted before whoever started this had finished the job. Well, luck was certainly a lady for Jason tonight. She would ask him later why he thought the person who sent him a shot was her.

"You aren't really blonde." He reached over and brushed at the blonde bangs of her wig.

"That's just for fun tonight, remember?"

"*Mmm-hmm.* Where're we going?"

Back to his room if she could manage it. She risked another glance over her shoulder. Damned if Isely wasn't still on her. What would it take to get rid of him?

She'd worn a disguise, stopped shadowing his seller and left the casino where the transaction was slated to occur. "Give a girl a break," she muttered, pausing to catch her breath. Her chosen method of distraction was turning into a serious problem.

Next time, she was going with the old school chum routine. No hormonal interference with that diversion. Running into Jason had looked like a fun, sexy ticket out of trouble, but now he felt like a block of cement dragging her down. She leaned him against a palm tree and kept him there with a hand on his hard chest.

She could leave him and call a cop to help him back to his room. Practical, but wrong. "Kiss me," she said.

"What?" His eyelids were droopy and his grin was that of a sweet drunk, and still it made butterflies circle in her belly.

"Kiss me," she ordered.

"In a minute." His hands were warm on her waist. "You hafta say 'I do' first."

She followed his gaze. They were standing under the bright neon lights of an Elvis-themed wedding chapel. To her left, Isely was only a few yards away. To her right, one of the brutal men she recognized from his personal security team was even closer and reaching into his jacket.

Damn.

Why couldn't these guys just believe the only thing she was into was her man?

Catching a glimpse of the shoulder holster, she made up her mind. Isely and his crew were known to act first and rationalize later. Drugged, Jason wasn't in any shape to help her. Maybe it was time to play the game their way.

"Well," she said to Jason, marching the fingers of one hand up his shirt while she reached for his gun with the other. She wasn't a great shot left-handed, but she only had to create a diversion if they tried to take her. Flipping off the safety, she kept Jason distracted with her body pressed against his.

Isely's thug had his weapon out now and his attention was locked on her. She didn't know who or what had tipped off Isely, but his intended method of problem solving was clear. As the thug raised his weapon, she fired through Jason's sport coat, aiming for the thug's knee and praying she wouldn't hit anyone else.

People on the street reacted predictably—a sudden flurry of motion set to the soundtrack of panicked

screaming. Isely's thug was hopping around in pain—
she must have clipped his foot—and people caught sight
of his gun. He was swarmed by determined citizens
yelling for police assistance.

Jason jumped, a delayed reaction to the sound of the
shot. He almost fell, dragging her with him. "Steady,
sweetheart. That's just a car back firing," she lied
smoothly.

"It's loud out here." He traced the shell of her ear
with his fingertip. "Let's get married so I can kiss you,"
he said.

She tucked the gun back into the holster at his back.
"If you insist, honey."

"I do." He sputtered with laughter when he realized
what he said. "C'mon." He pushed away from the tree
and wobbled toward the chapel entrance with the careful determination of a drunk.

She wasn't sure he'd appreciate her current opinion
of Specialist Jason Grant as sweet edging toward ador-
able, but there wasn't a better way to define him in his
diminished state.

Less than an hour later, to the tune of Viva Las
Vegas, they were newlyweds with the gold bands, a
champagne toast and a "Just Married" limo ride up and
down the Strip to prove it.

She wondered how happy her groom would be when
he woke up tomorrow morning?

Chapter Two

Emmett Holt steepled his fingers as he reviewed the detailed reports his assistant had sent to his computer. Apparently a sniper was on a killing spree in Las Vegas. Times, targets—hell, even the type of bullets—pointed to Jason Grant, the Specialist who would one day take over this very office. Director Casey had handpicked Grant for the deputy director's chair when Holt eventually moved up to Casey's post, but this development could change everything.

There was never a good time for an agent to go off the deep end, but in light of the recent scandal of false allegations and rumors against the director himself, this was the last thing Mission Recovery needed.

Specialists recruited to their covert agency were above reproach, but it looked for all the world like Grant was about to become the exception. That possibility didn't sit well with Holt. There was only one conclusion in light of this damning data: Grant, or someone who wanted them to believe it was Grant, was waging some sort of vendetta in Las Vegas.

If it was Grant, Holt wondered how he had secured the rifle. To date, their normal contacts in the area denied seeing Grant. Holt knew *someone* was lying, but that in and of itself didn't put Grant in the clear. All Specialists were well-trained in where and how to connect with a helpful associate when they were in the field. He may have purposely gone outside their usual suppliers.

But why? Had he lost it? Or had someone on the other side made him an offer he couldn't refuse?

In the past forty-eight hours the sniper—whoever the hell he was—had picked off a couple of irrelevant targets, caused one serious traffic accident and winged a major player in the drug trade. All of which had been kept out of the media. Considering the damper that kind of publicity could put on tourism, the local authorities had been only too happy to cooperate. The shootings looked perfectly random, but anyone with access to his personnel jacket would put Grant at the top of the suspect list.

The grim accomplishment was more impressive considering the Specialist hadn't missed a single status check-in call since his arrival. Holt suppressed his instincts on the matter. What he believed on a personal level was irrelevant. He had a job to do and no one could ever accuse him of failing to get the job done. He liked Grant as well as he did any of the others but that, too, was irrelevant at the moment.

"Shall I add this to the agenda for the next briefing, sir?" His assistant, Nadine, sat on the opposite side of the desk. Beneath the conservative suit she wore, her posture was particularly rigid as she asked the question. No one wanted to believe the worst. Not even the young assistant he had hired who willingly worked twelve- and fourteen-hour days in an attempt to keep him happy. He vaguely wondered if that was why she kept her hair in a sleek ponytail all the time. He didn't give her time to patronize salons.

He also wondered if she hated him as much as most who had the displeasure of working for him did.

He blinked away the concept. "No. I'll handle it privately." The less anyone knew about this situation the better. If he put it on the agenda for team discussion, Grant might hear about it. And if he knew they were on to him, he'd bolt before they could get a net around him. And if this was Grant, Holt needed to get a net around him as soon as possible.

"Any word from the agent Grant was sent to Las Vegas to support?"

"No, sir."

No surprise there. Everyone knew Vegas remained one of the easiest cities to disappear in. "Maybe the agent managed to get out without Grant's help." Holt said what his assistant expected to hear while his mind worked through the latest developments and numerous other scenarios.

"I'll keep monitoring the news out there," Nadine suggested.

Holt nodded. They both understood the harsh reality and the constricting time frame. He wasn't going to be able to keep the sniper issue quiet much longer. If and when the local police force connected the incidents to a single shooter, they would be obligated to call in federal assistance and warn the public about the threat.

Which meant Holt would be obligated to tell someone in another government agency there was an operative in the area with sharp-shooter expertise, and that would break Grant's cover.

If Jason Grant remained in Las Vegas, with his stellar career as a sniper, he would become a person of interest within the next twenty-four hours. By hour forty-eight, if he couldn't offer a valid alibi for the shootings, he'd be in custody or a wanted suspect. A pawn effectively removed from the dangerous game Holt was playing. No one, particularly his superiors, would be happy with his methods. But that had never stopped him before. It wouldn't now. And that was precisely why they had hired him. He would get the job done, one way or another.

The stakes were high and the risk-to-reward ratio bordered on irrational. But it had to be done, and he was the only one in Mission Recovery who could manage it. On days like this, the baggage of responsibility weighed heavy on his shoulders.

His assistant stood. "Shall I attempt to contact Grant?"

Holt leaned back from his desk and turned a pencil end over end on the arm of his chair. "No need. Until we know more, Specialist Grant's orders don't change. Get me the director as soon as it's morning wherever he is."

"But, sir, he's on his honeymoon."

That was right. The director of Mission Recovery

had gotten married last month, but work had prevented an immediate honeymoon. "The world doesn't stop spinning because he fell in love, Nadine," he grumbled. "As much as Thomas Casey would like to think so."

"Of course, sir."

His assistant left the office to carry his reports and orders to the Specialists currently on assignment and those preparing for assignments. Alone, he stared at the pencil in his hand.

He silently assured himself things were going according to the plan and it would all be over soon. Eager as he was to be done with it, he knew rushing the process now would bring the whole damn mess crashing down. On him.

He was the only one who could do this. Likewise, he was the one who would pay in spades if anything went wrong.

"Won't let that happen," he muttered. He'd come too far to bail out now.

Setting the pencil aside, he turned toward his computer and drafted the email his counterpart was expecting. He read it through twice more and then, taking a deep breath, he finally hit *Send*.

Chapter Three

Caesar's Palace,
Friday, November 21, 8:17 a.m.

Jason rolled to his back and squinted against the bright sunlight flooding into the room. His head felt stuffed with cotton, which, in any logical universe, should have dulled the incessant ringing in his ears.

"That's your phone, sweetheart. You should answer."

He knew that voice. What the hell was Ginger Olin doing in his hotel room? And why would she be aiming any endearments his way? He flung a hand out in the general direction of the ringing only to have the move stopped short by a warm, soft touch. He dared to open his eyes a crack.

"Careful. I've left you a glass of water." Ginger smiled down at him with a bit too much sympathy as he curled his fingers around the cell phone. "Take the call. I'll be in the shower."

Through slitted eyelids, he watched her saunter away, her body swathed in a hotel robe. He propped himself up on an elbow, struggling to clear the fog from his brain. What was going on here? What the hell was wrong with him?

The phone started ringing again, and he saw the number and stern face of Deputy Director Holt on his screen. Damn. This was one call he couldn't ignore. "Yeah." He cleared the rough edge from his throat, wondering how Ginger had managed to get him so drunk he couldn't remember squat. He never drank on duty. "Grant here."

"Where were you last night? You missed the scheduled check-in."

He opened his mouth to answer and snapped it closed again. He didn't know. Based on his nudity, the state of the bed and the woman in the shower, it wasn't a big leap to figure out what had happened. That still didn't explain this nasty hangover.

"I tried to contact you all night, but your phone was off. I learned this morning that you missed the recovery. If you have any sense of self-preservation, get your ass on the next available flight out of there or consider yourself relieved of duty."

"Sir?" How could he have missed the recovery? Agent Olin was safe, right here in the room with him. She'd been in trouble and he'd gotten her out of it. At least he thought that's how it had gone down. "Sir, I made the recovery," he insisted.

"You've dropped the ball somewhere, Grant, because the package is missing and Agent Conklin never encountered you or your support."

"Give me a second chance. I can meet with security and—"

"I can't. It's too late. Be on the next flight. We will debrief when you arrive."

The line went dead and for a long moment, Jason stared at the screen, utterly dumbfounded. If Olin wasn't the recovery, how had she known the code phrase?

She *had* given him the code phrase, hadn't she? She must have. He wouldn't have taken action unless he'd been sure. Although right now, he couldn't recall exactly what they'd done before coming to the room. It was pretty damn clear what they'd done after they got here.

He rolled to his feet, lost his balance when his vision wavered and landed back on the edge of the bed. He clutched at the mattress until the room stopped spinning. He'd been hung over a few times. Enough to know this wasn't the same thing at all. He'd been drugged. But why? And who would do that?

Carefully he looked around, taking in the view of his hotel room. Or at least a room that was identical. He spotted his luggage and wished like hell they hadn't upgraded him to a suite. The suitcase across the room might as well have been on the other side of the world.

Desperate, he entertained the idea of crawling over for fresh clothes when he heard the water stop running. He would not let her find him weak as a kitten on his hands and knees in addition to the troubling disorientation plaguing him.

Slowly he turned his head from side to side, then up and down until his dizziness eased off.

The shirt and slacks he'd worn last night were scattered across the floor along with a lace-topped stocking and garter. He half expected to see a bra draped over a lampshade. A memory teased him and he twisted toward the door. Yup. There was the blond wig he'd tugged from her head, eager to get his hands in her glossy red mane.

Something had gone down in this room, or at least she'd made it look that way. He wasn't sure which explanation he wanted to hear most: that it happened, or that he only thought it happened.

He reached for the glass of water on the nightstand and stopped dead. The wide gold band on the ring finger of his left hand glinted in the sunlight. He rubbed at his eyes, but it didn't go away. He was married?

His head and stomach protested as he took in the strewn clothing along with this new information. It certainly looked as if they'd started married life with a bang.

No. Impossible. No way in hell he'd forget his own wedding or the inevitable events leading up to it. No way in hell he'd marry a stranger—and Ginger Olin, CIA operative, fit that description. This had to be some ruse she invented to preserve her cover. Except Holt just said he should have rescued an agent named Conklin.

"Damn it all." He couldn't make sense of the vague scenes flitting through his mind. She owed him some answers. This time when he pushed to his feet, he kept moving forward despite the sudden tilt of the room. He was grateful when the wall kept him from hitting the floor. He pounded a fist on the bathroom door. "Get out here."

She opened the door and a steamy cloud of spicy

vanilla scent washed over him. It was so her: lush and tempting. He fought the urge to lean in and inhale deeply.

"Oh, dear," she said with a sly smile as her gaze slid over his body like a touch. He reacted as any man might when faced with the beauty of a gorgeous woman fresh from a shower. Whether his memory ever correctly filled in the details of last night, his body seemed convinced about what they'd done and there was no hiding the part of him demanding an encore performance.

Damn. In his determination to stay on his feet he'd forgotten to cover himself.

One long fingertip trailed across his jaw. "You're looking rough." She opened the door wider. "Come on in. A shower will fix you right up."

Was that a bit of Irish in her voice this morning? If so, was it real? He'd done a little investigating after their last meeting and knew she had a talent for accents. "What did you give me?" He looked past her, ashamed that he wanted to ask for her support to get him across the expanse of the luxurious bathroom.

"The time of your life. Or so you said."

Looking at the woman who'd starred in his fantasies since their one brief conversation last month, it probably had been the time of his life. How unfair that he didn't have full recall. "Not what I meant."

She tucked herself under his arm, keeping him steady as she walked him past the long vanity. "This way, big guy."

Something about the gesture felt familiar. "Did you do this last night?"

"We can talk about last night when your head's clear." She eased back but didn't quite let go. "Steady?"

Barely. "Yes."

"Cold or hot?"

"Pardon?"

"The shower," she clarified, her eyes quickly darting down to his groin and back up again.

"Cold."

"All righty." She reached past him and he saw the glint of gold on her left hand. What did it mean that she apparently had all her faculties and still wore a wedding band as new and shiny as his? Nothing good, he decided when she gave him a little encouraging nudge into the shower.

The cold spray against his scalp and rushing down and over his skin was a brutal shock, but it cleared his head faster than a pot of coffee and restored some measure of control over his lusty hormones.

When he decided he'd tortured himself long enough, he climbed out and reached for a towel on the warmer. The bathroom was empty. Her courtesy and thoughtfulness surprised him—and actually had him a little worried. What the hell was going on? For now he was grateful to find his shaving kit still near the sink closest to the shower. The other sink, which had gone unused since he'd checked in, was surrounded by feminine details, including a flowered bag, a pink toothbrush and a contact lens case pushed to the back of the counter.

Huh? When had that stuff gotten there? Was it his imagination, or was she planning to stay awhile?

Knowing it was risky, he decided to live dangerously

and shave anyway. Surviving the experience with only a couple of small nicks, he evaluated his reflection and thought he looked almost normal.

He opened the door to go find some clothes and nearly got rapped on the nose as her hand was raised to knock.

"Whoops," she said, her vivid green gaze direct and clear. "Looks like I'm late." She held out a stack of clothing from his suitcase.

"That was fast."

A small frown drew her brows together. "What do you mean?"

"Married less than twenty-four hours and my wife's already picking out my clothing."

She gave a little huff and shoved the clothing at him, but he saw the blush turning her cheeks a rosy pink. A small victory, but he liked knowing he had some effect on her. Being the one doing all the reacting was no fun.

"Get dressed. Room service should be here soon. Then we can discuss last night in a civilized manner."

"Yes, dear," he said irreverently, closing the door on her frown.

GIN PACED THE room while he dressed. Damn the man for being too handsome for his own good. Or hers. They were in the middle of a serious crisis. Attraction would have to wait. It had proved a serious challenge to ignore his impressive body and the instinctive way he responded to her, both last night and again this morning.

For a hefty tip, the limousine driver had extended the tour when Jason dozed off, then he'd been kind enough to find a drive-through for coffee. The caffeine perked up Jason enough that she could get him into his room. She hadn't counted on it being enough of a stimulant to have him put the moves on her.

The poor man had been so abused by the drug, and still he'd kissed her like it had mattered at the altar, but more specifically when they'd arrived right here. She brought her hands to her lips, remembering. She'd never expected his response to wedded bliss to be so enthusiastic, even if it had been his idea—albeit while under the influence of whatever drug someone had obviously slipped him. He was a test to her self-control, but she'd gotten him safely to the bed before he passed out again.

Once she was sure he would stay unconscious she'd dashed back to her own room and gathered what she needed to set the stage here in his suite. Then she'd returned to his room and searched it, looking for any clue as to why he'd been in Vegas, particularly in the same hotel where a deadly virus was about to change hands. She'd found nothing to point to his purpose or even a possible cover story. The easy explanation was this was just a quick getaway for him, but she didn't believe in coincidence.

Now, while he showered off the last effects of the drug, she cleaned up the mess she'd deliberately made and indulged in what was surely the most girlish moment of her life. She buried her nose in his shirt, remembering his hands in her hair and cruising over her body. The woman who married him for real would be one lucky, well-loved woman.

She shivered, squashing the reaction when the door

opened and Jason joined her. His step was steady now, his gaze clear despite the dark circles under his eyes. His thick, sable hair glistened, and even from across the room, she caught the fresh scent of him under the zippy mint of the hotel-brand body wash.

After sleeping next to him all night, making sure he didn't suffer nightmares or worse from the drug, she'd probably be able to pick him out of a lineup with only her nose. Good grief, what was wrong with her?

She twisted the gold band on her finger and searched for the right place to begin. "Could we, umm, talk out there?" *Away from the tangled sheets of the bed.* "I've brewed a pot of coffee, and breakfast will be here any minute."

He agreed with a subtle dip of his chin, and she knew he was evaluating her every move for a motive or a clue.

"Where's my gun?"

"In the closet safe. The code is your birthday."

His eyebrows lifted at that revelation. "Did we, ahh—" He finished with a tilt of his head toward the bed.

"You really don't remember?"

He looked away. "Just bits and pieces."

"Hmm. I should probably be offended," she teased. In reality, she was relieved. His lack of knowledge could work to her advantage. "It was a night *I'll* never forget."

When they were out of the danger zone most people called a bedroom, she poured him a cup of coffee, then slid onto the counter stool. She didn't want to do anything as intimate as sit across from him at the table as if they really were newlyweds. The thought made her chuckle. It didn't get much more intimate than tucking a naked, amorous husband into bed.

When he'd tossed her wig to the floor and pulled the pins from her hair so he could run his hands through it, it had been all she could do not to cave to the temptation he presented. He was handsome and quite striking when dressed. Nude? Well, artists would kill to paint him if they knew what treasures his clothing hid. His body, strong and sculpted, showed the results of his dedication to fitness and preparation. She had relished taking in every single detail.

"You okay?"

"Yes." She sat up straighter. "Thank you. Maybe this would go faster if you just ask whatever is on your mind."

"Are we married?"

"Yes." She handed him the documentation from the Viva Las Vegas wedding chapel. The paperwork was real and almost complete. The marriage license wasn't official, but he didn't seem to notice that. There was the added complication that the marriage wouldn't be considered valid if Jason Grant wasn't his real name. Her sources said it was, but mistakes happened. She still wasn't sure why she'd used *her* real name rather than the alias she'd prepared for this mission.

He tossed the certificate and marriage license to the table and the scowl on his face was enough to have her second-guessing going along with his convenient, drug-induced idea.

He crossed his arms and stared at her. "Why?"

The flippant remark on the tip of her tongue just

wouldn't fall. Neither would the truth. Fortunately, she got a momentary reprieve with the arrival of breakfast.

He stalked over to the door, gave a belated glance through the security peephole and yanked the door open. The waiter was all smiles, going on about the pitcher of mimosas and sharing the congratulations for the "happy couple" from the staff. To her shock Jason took it all with a smile worthy of any happy groom, even tipping the man on his way out, but as soon as they were alone, the scowl returned.

"It won't be that bad," she said as he lifted the cover from each plate. She'd placed the order last night when they'd returned to the hotel, but she hadn't expected the elaborate presentation or the mouth-watering aromas. Las Vegas might just become her favorite city, and she'd been all over the world—a few times.

A massive omelet, a plate of bacon and sausage, a stack of pancakes, two flavors of syrup, fresh berries and cream, along with all the other condiments and accompaniments, made for a remarkable display.

"Wow. This smells divine."

He replaced the cover over the omelet she was staring at. "Tell me why you did it and I'll let you eat."

"You don't want to go that route with me," she warned. "I'm hungry." Violence wasn't the way she preferred to have her hands on him, but she'd put up a fight if it was the only way to earn his respect. "You have reach and strength on me, but I have guile, training and a clear head."

"Fair point." He held out a plate. "Start there."

"Where?" She sliced off a portion of the omelet,

added a strip of crisp bacon to her plate and returned to the counter and her coffee. As much as she wanted a mimosa, she knew the clear head was a necessity.

"Start with your 'clear head' advantage. Why did you drug me?"

"*I* didn't." She'd merely stepped in and likely saved his life and possibly her own by capitalizing on the moment. "You don't have to believe me, but it's the truth."

His gaze locked with hers, then with an arch of eyebrows, he turned his focus to drizzling syrup over a pancake.

"Is your stomach bothering you?"

"I'm fine."

"Of course you are." And inexplicably she felt obligated to keep him that way.

Although she didn't believe he was the trouble in question, she didn't think it was coincidence that her morning email alert included a caution about a sniper in Las Vegas. From the little she'd been able to dig up on him, Jason had the background and qualifications, but even when he'd been drugged, his sense of right and wrong remained intact.

She'd searched his luggage and found nothing that indicated he had a weapon other than his handgun.

She knew he doubted her about the drugs, and she didn't hold it against him. People didn't join covert agencies for the transparency factor. They chose it for a myriad of other reasons usually starting with some noble concept of honor and duty. Suddenly she wanted to know his motive for joining, wanted to know how it might have morphed or changed since getting into the field, but this wasn't the time.

"What's the last thing you remember?" she asked instead.

"A shot of tequila." He closed his eyes. "I barely remember biting the lime. If you don't want to talk about that, tell me why you did this to us," he said, wiggling his ring finger.

"We'll get there. I promise." She swiped her finger in an X over her heart.

"Not funny."

She laughed. "Wasn't trying to be."

He grunted.

"Come on, Jason. What's the last thing you remember?"

"The wig. You were wearing a wig and I made you take it off when we got here."

She nearly choked on her coffee. "I meant the last thing you remember before we, ah, hooked up."

"You mean before we got married."

"I do, yes." She hadn't heard the poor choice of words until one of his eyebrows lifted. She stifled a laugh, knowing he wouldn't remember enough to understand the joke. "You know what I mean."

"The bar. I was hanging out in the bar waiting for the contact. I didn't expect *you*."

"Same goes," she muttered from behind her coffee cup. "How long had you been there?"

"A couple of hours. I was nursing a beer, keeping an eye on the odds for the hockey game."

"Did you win? I'm up about five hundred dollars since I hit town."

"I don't gamble."

"You're kidding?" Her surprise brought forth another scowl. It amused her. "Well, maybe you don't gamble with money, but clearly you enjoy some level of risk or you wouldn't be the golden boy at Mission Recovery."

"How do you know that?"

"Not because you broke protocol and shared anything. I have my own sources." She rolled her hand, signaling him to continue. "You're at the bar, watching the scores and odds and then what?"

She had to wait while he filled his plate with a slice of the omelet and two sausage links. Then he surprised her, bringing over the coffee carafe and refilling her cup.

"The tequila shot, like I said. The bartender brought it over and said it was from you."

"He used my name?"

"No." He returned to the table. "He pointed to you at the other end of the bar."

"Describe the woman you saw. Please," she added when he shook his head.

"Blonde. Emerald dress that matches a certain eye color."

"You said she was at the other end of the bar. When did she get close enough that you could see her eyes?"

He frowned at his plate. "Your eyes are green. The dress matched your eyes."

She shouldn't be flattered that he knew that, but she was. "I was wearing contacts last night."

"I noticed. And a blond wig."

"Yes." She was starting to really worry they'd both been set up by someone with too much information.

"The dress was just like the one you wore in Colorado last month."

"You're sure?" First of all, she would never wear the same outfit in an op she'd worn at a previous engagement. Men could get away with that kind of thing, but not a woman.

He looked up at her, his expression troubled. "That's the last thing I remember clearly. I was wondering what you were doing here and wearing *that* dress. After that the images are like snippets from a dream. I can't quite hang on to enough to put the pieces together. You walked up and gave me the code phrase for extraction and—"

"Oh, bloody hell."

"What?"

"We've been compromised." Alone but for her reluctant almost-husband, she gave in to the fidgets and started pacing the length of the room. "Something is dreadfully wrong. Yes, I joined you at the bar, but I didn't send you the shot. Drugs and sedatives aren't my style."

"Then whose style is it?"

"I don't know. No one I've been watching would have a reason to drug you." She pushed her hands through her hair, tugged just a little. "I saw lots of people, including a blonde wearing an emerald dress, who I followed to the bar. But once I got there I was focused on you." Because that's all she'd needed to see. She'd let

Isely's unexpected appearance rattle her more than she'd thought. A rattled agent fails and she sure had done so here. She swore, turned on her heel and came up hard against Jason's chest. He'd walked up right behind her.

He caught her elbows and held her in place when she might have bounced off of him. "You'll wear a rut in the carpet."

"I don't care. And, for the record, that green dress wasn't the one I was wearing the last time you saw me." There were similarities she had to admit now that she really considered it. It was comparable enough to have a guy thinking it was the same.

"Who's your contact? What's the signal if you need to be pulled out of your mission?" he demanded, dragging her attention back to him.

"I don't have a code phrase or a contact." She pulled herself free of his touch. It was too distracting. "I've never needed help."

"And yet they sent me to backup and offer an exit strategy for an agent in trouble."

"Then they sent you for someone else."

Jason frowned. "That's what my boss said." This he murmured more to himself than to her. "They sure didn't send me to get married. Of all the options to get us out of trouble, why did you do this?" He pointed to the ring on his finger.

"What's the big deal? Got a girl back home?" She wanted him to take the bait and bypass the bigger problem while she figured out a way to salvage her potentially compromised operation. Instead, she watched the storm brewing in his deep brown eyes.

"It doesn't matter." He turned away. "I wouldn't believe you anyway. But don't count on wearing the pants in this happy union, Mrs. Grant."

"Call me Gin."

He sank back into the chair where she'd draped his sport coat last night. "Now that you have a husband, Mrs. Grant, and I'm him, care to share your next move?"

Now he was just being stubborn. It seemed a shame to have so much handsome man at her fingertips and not be able to do anything fun with him.

"I'm here tracking a product and hopefully I'll get to oversee the sale," she admitted. "Sexy blondes in Las Vegas are everywhere. I thought it would be a foolproof disguise."

"The red *is* memorable," he agreed, eyeing her hair. "Too bad I forgot everything after that."

His eyes raked her from head to toe and she felt as if he saw right through her pale blue cashmere sweater.

If he ignored her barbs, she could ignore his. "It would be nice to get a look at the security footage from the bar. Maybe we can identify the woman who drugged you." Whether that would help with her mission or not was yet to be seen, but perhaps it would convince him that it hadn't been her who'd drugged him.

"Why? You just said sexy blondes are everywhere." He sipped his coffee and took another look at the marriage certificate. "Married by an Elvis impersonator. That is just not me." He shook his head.

"It was your idea last night."

"My brain on drugs." He shrugged, sipped more coffee. "Great. When you're finished with your mission are we going to do a drive-through divorce? I always thought those were an efficient concept."

"Give divorce a lot of thought, do you?"

"Enough."

She recognized a personal trigger point. She wanted to push for the real answers but, married or not, they weren't actually on personal terms yet. "Does the drive-through thing even exist anymore?"

He glared at her. "Guess we'll find out."

"We should be done here in plenty of time to qualify for an annulment.

"Same result."

"Does that mean you'll cooperate?"

"Sure. Marriage is all about compromise. Or so I've heard."

She didn't like the way he said that, and for the first time since bolting into the wedding chapel with an oblivious fiancé on her arm she questioned the wisdom of her rash decision. Well, the second time. Sharing a room with him had pushed her resolve to the brink.

"Getting married was your idea." Had she really needed a kiss from him that badly? She touched her lips again. If she were completely honest with herself she would admit that the kiss had been worth it. "I swear it was your idea."

"You knew I was compromised."

"True, and leaving you in a public place seemed like a really bad idea." She folded her arms over her chest.

"Let me get this straight. You didn't drug me, didn't see who did, but you thought it was okay to haul me into an Elvis-themed chapel and marry me?"

"Not exactly. My first suggestion involved you giving me some cover at the craps tables."

"I don't gamble."

"So you said."

"What else?"

"We went for a walk and I asked you to kiss me." She hurried on when he raised an eyebrow. "But you said we had to be married first. It was all rather gallant." If she didn't think about Isely and his thug flanking them. That was one part she could not afford to mention. Her mission was far too important to compromise for anyone, even the man she'd pretended to marry.

"Gallant?"

"I assumed it was a personality quirk. It fits your whole ex-military persona." She went to the table and pulled out a chair, sitting on her hands so she wouldn't fidget with the breakfast dishes. "But now that we're stuck together it could be an advantage. Just give me forty-eight hours to track this product and sale and then I'll pay the fees to grant you a speedy divorce."

It wouldn't be necessary because the receptionist knew he was intoxicated at the time of the marriage and because they hadn't filed the marriage license, but Gin could tell him the whole story later. No sense burning bridges and tossing away an ally right now. This might be her only chance to experience a marriage. Not to mention she'd been having fantasies about this guy for weeks now.

As a CIA agent, she wasn't the sort of woman a man brought home to his family. She didn't even resemble the sort of woman a man wanted to build a family with. No, she'd learned that hard lesson early in her life.

She was the sort of woman men fantasized about, the woman men liked to show off, but never the woman they kept around. They gave different reasons and it took her longer than she cared to admit to learn those reasons were a reflection of the men who gave them, not the reality of who she was as a person.

When he still hadn't given her an answer, she went for broke. "Please. I really need your help." There, she'd said it. Gin Olin rarely asked for help, but she was no fool and it was clear she couldn't finish this alone.

"Fine. I'll help. Holt gave me an ultimatum. Either I fly back to the office or consider myself fired. The suite is booked through the weekend. If I'm fired I may as well have a little fun with the last perk my job bought me."

"You're willing to risk your job to help me?" Was he serious? Would Mission Recovery really fire him? Emotions she didn't want to try and untangle were suddenly twisting inside her.

He startled her, tugging one of her hands free to hold it. "What are you doing?" she demanded.

"Do we need ground rules?" He raised her hand to his lips and feathered small kisses over her fingers. "Or do you trust me to be the best doting husband ever?"

She yanked her hand away. "Doting?"

"We might even enjoy ourselves."

That was her second biggest fear. Her first was losing the trail of that bio-weapon. "We need ground rules." That was a given. There was just something about this guy that got to her. As badly as she needed him, she also needed to keep her head on straight.

He sat back. "I'm listening."

"Whatever happens outside of this room stays outside of this room."

"Isn't that just the opposite of how it should be for wedded bliss?"

She ignored him. "I mean it. The 'doting' is for public consumption. Up here, we're just you and me—two covert agents sacrificing for the mission."

His brow furrowed. "Ah, sharing a bed, giving completely of ourselves." He made a tsking sound. "The sacrifices we make."

She rolled her eyes. Snagging another piece of bacon, she nibbled it while she resumed her pacing. What she was about to do was risky, but having a second set of eyes and a capable agent at her back in the casino was her best chance of spotting the buyer.

"Let me fill you in on why I'm here."

He leaned back, laced his fingers behind his head. "I'm all ears." He sniffed. "Wait. What is that smell?"

"Bacon?" She held it up.

"Not unless it's extra crispy." He looked at the dishes and then swiveled around in the chair. "Something smells scorched."

She sighed. "Probably your coat."

"Huh?" He pulled it off the chair and turned it until he found the hole. "Why is there a bullet hole in my sport coat?" He stuck his finger through it, but his eyes were on her. "An explanation, Mrs. Grant?"

"Technically that happened before we exchanged vows."

"Were they shooting at you or me?"

"Me. But I fired first." She paused, thinking it through again. "I was followed into the bar. I thought the disguise and chatting you up would be enough to dissuade him, but you were going loopy on me. So we left, but I was followed again." As much as she'd reviewed it, she couldn't come up with any reason Isely would be onto Jason. Isely shouldn't know her either, but she'd been following the virus for several weeks, and someone might have run a facial recognition that tipped him off. "They were definitely shooting at me," she said confidently.

"All right. Is there a police report?"

"Not that connects us because we ducked into the wedding chapel when people panicked. I fired the gun through your coat. Sorry, that's obvious, I guess." Why did this man make her so nervous? Maybe it was all those waking fantasies about him she'd relished.

He stared at her for a moment. "Did it work? Our marriage ploy?"

"You really don't remember?"

"Could you please stop saying that?"

"Sure. It worked well enough." She came closer and took the coat out of his hands, folding it so the bullet hole was hidden, then she draped it across the top of a different chair. "It made a great diversion."

"Good?"

"Sort of." She hesitated, balanced on the precipice of evading the truth or spilling it all in a messy rush of too much information. Unfortunately she was running out of time before the virus landed in the wrong hands. "Five years ago a European crime family named Isely acquired a lethal strain of influenza. A major sale was interrupted and the virus was confiscated by none other than Thomas Casey. Or so we thought. Testing proved the vials he brought back were fakes. The general consensus, if you assume Thomas Casey isn't a traitor—"

"Which he isn't," he cut in.

"Agreed and proven. But that means someone in the Isely food chain still has the virus. It's come back on the market recently and I've been following the tracking tags on the vials. One is here. I know the seller, but it would be great bonus points if I can identify the buyer."

"That was your assignment in Colorado."

"Among other things. Focus, Grant."

"Oh, I'm dialed in."

She met his intense gaze and nearly shivered in response. The man had an effect on her she could not deny. "Good." She cleared her throat. "I need you to help me identify who's who in this little drama. Two sets of eyes and gadding about in wedded bliss should be enough to get this done. I can watch the tracker tag and you can keep an eye on Isely."

"He's here? Isely?"

She nodded. "He surprised me. I guess he wants to oversee the transaction."

"Are these people I'm supposed to spot wearing name tags or carrying around steel cases with 'live virus' stamped on the side?"

She glared at him. "Lucas Camp gave me the impression you were a competent agent."

"I am."

"He also implied there was more to you than the few lines on your public résumé." She wanted to do a victory dance when she saw how that little barb dug into his ample pride.

"I think we both know résumés are always adjusted to suit the purpose."

Her confidence almost faltered, but she knew she wasn't looking at a hack or wannabe. Jason Grant was a Specialist, and how he got there didn't matter. He was plenty qualified to help her on this. He'd agreed and she should let it go, but she had the sinking feeling there was more to it than a fear of reprimand back at the office.

"Well then." He rolled to his feet and gathered the breakfast dishes, putting them back on the cart. "Let's go downstairs, play the happy couple and see what we see."

"Hang on."

One dark eyebrow lifted in response.

"You haven't explained why you're here."

"Right." He dragged out the word while he bobbed his head. "I don't know. What I gave you is all I have."

"You really expect me to believe that?"

"It's true. My orders were vague. I wasn't told anything other than the code phrase."

"What good is that?"

"Not much." He pushed the cart closer to the door then turned to face her again. "I'd think that would make you happy. I don't have anything to distract me from what you need to accomplish. Now, shall we?"

"Just let me check the status on the package I'm tracking." She pulled out her phone and entered the information. What should have been a simple, quick process felt like an eternity with Jason staring at her. Finally, the feedback came through, confirming the virus vial hadn't moved from the hotel room where the seller was keeping it.

She smiled at him as she tucked her phone away. "It's all good."

Chapter Four

Jason knew she was well-trained and talented—not just because Lucas Camp endorsed her, but because there was so little actual intel on her fieldwork. Last month his friend O'Marron at Interpol had given him the name to go with her stunning face, but beyond that there wasn't much to go on. Her passport records could have fit any number of cover identities, and they probably did.

But her sudden transformation into his blushing bride the very moment they crossed the threshold into the hallway unnerved him. Her hands were everywhere. Not groping, just the small, quick touches of new lovers who feel the slightest distance as an unbearable ache.

And which poet wrote that sappy line so it would get stuck in his head at the worst moment?

Alone in the elevator, she didn't back off. She grinned up at him as she pressed close and kissed him, nipping his lip ever so gently. It was for the cameras, he realized, struggling to keep up with her game and to keep his body in line. Mentally he understood her actions were about their cover, the mission, but physically his body struggled with the concept.

He wanted to blame the drug, but he knew it was out of his system. Lust was the source of his current haze. As much as his body might wish to play along with the marriage game, they had a job to do. And he had to keep things in line.

Still, he'd promised her a doting husband and that's what she would get. As the elevator doors parted, he tugged her toward the shops rather than the casino floor.

"What are you doing? I thought we were going to play some blackjack."

"In a minute." He wanted to put off the gambling as long as possible. "I haven't given you anything yet today." He draped his arm over her shoulders and pressed a kiss to the top of her head. "A doting husband always takes care of his wife first and foremost."

"That's silly," she said with a winning smile. "What could I need more than you?"

Oh, she was good. In a perfect world it would be exactly how he wanted his wife to feel. Contrary to any interpretation of his professional résumé, he'd spent enough time alone to know how he would treat the woman he chose to spend the rest of his life with.

In his line of work he didn't expect to find that forever sort of woman. In truth he didn't expect more than brief, superficial relationships. Not at this stage of the covert ops game anyway. Being a rather sad outlook didn't make it less true. Deep down, under the career accomplishments, he knew he wanted the stability his parents hadn't given him. He'd never so much as whispered it aloud, but he wanted the warm embrace his buddies had walked into after long deployments.

He wanted what his director, Thomas Casey, now had.

This marriage might not be destined to win longest running, but that didn't mean he couldn't enjoy himself for the time they had. Maybe that made him a glutton for punishment because this game would come to an end sooner rather than later, but he refused to allow that to deter him.

As they strolled down a wide corridor that felt more like an indoor mall, he silently commended the casino designers for putting everything within reach so no one had to leave. The clear blue of the fake sky painted on the ceiling made him a little claustrophobic, but it was evidently a system that worked.

"Here." He paused at the window display of a jewelry store. "We'll start here today."

Her hand clutched his in a strong grip. "No." She tugged him along to the next window. "If you want to buy me a present, why not something I need? I forgot my swimsuit."

He wiggled his eyebrows at her. "Fair enough." Not so surprising that she'd be practical, although he had no way of knowing if she really had or hadn't packed a swimsuit. He should have made time to search her luggage.

In the elegant boutique, he teased her, holding up bikini after bikini, each with less material than the one before. She didn't blush or protest—she just played along, dismissing some on color and accepting others. When she had a decent selection, she headed for the dressing room.

She spun around as he followed her. "You can't come in."

He didn't see why not. They were married and he'd certainly given her an eyeful this morning. Based on her ground rules, outside the room was his only chance to see her body. There should be some perks to the setup— besides those drummed up by his too vivid imagination.

"I'll be quick," she said. Though the words were light and the kiss sweet, he heard the steel underneath. She wanted to get out there and find the buyer.

He understood her dedication, appreciated it even. But she'd already gone so far as to marry him, so they could hardly waste the inconvenience and effort by not embracing the part fully. He sat back in the plush chair and checked the police scanner app on his phone for anything strange.

Currently things were calm in the area, so he skimmed the news sites for anything about the shooting last night. Scowling, he read the official report that stated a tourist from Germany had been shot in the foot with his own gun. Interesting way to spin it.

Being relegated to haunt this one casino hadn't been his idea of a great mission, but Gin was certainly perking things up, he thought as she shed her jeans and her bare lower legs appeared below the privacy curtain.

Knowing he couldn't stop the reaction, he went along with it, imagining what she looked like in all the places he couldn't see. If her toes ignited this slow burn of desire…well, it was no wonder he was trying so hard to remember last night.

There was a distinctive grace to her movements as

she stepped in and out of several different styles of swimsuit bottoms. Her toes pointed, her calves flexed. She must have been a dancer somewhere in her past.

He almost groaned in protest when she pulled on jeans and slipped back into her heels.

She whipped back the curtain, and a catlike smile spread across her face.

Caught, he grinned at her. "You made a decision?"

A tiny scrap of bikini dangled from her fingertip. "This one should leave you breathless."

He snatched it from her. "Can't wait, sweetheart." He went back to the sales floor, grabbed the first pair of board shorts in his size for himself and was headed for the checkout when she slowed him down. "We just need a couple of other things."

"Like what?"

She shook her head and exchanged a knowing look with the clerk. "My man isn't big on shopping."

"Few of them are," the clerk replied with a kind smile.

Jason regained his patience as Gin found a sheer cover-up, sunscreen and a pair of flip-flops for each of them. They were playing a game here, and just because he found her legs tantalizing didn't mean he'd ever get a look at the whole package. He had to maintain his perspective. This was a vast improvement over milling about waiting for something to happen.

When Gin decided they were set, Jason asked the clerk to add the charges to their account and deliver the purchases to the room.

"Of course." She tapped a few keys and as he was

signing the receipt, the clerk congratulated them both. "Congratulations! You do know you're entered in our wedding sweepstakes this month, right?"

Jason and Gin exchanged a look. "What does that mean?" he asked.

"Each month we give away a destination honeymoon, gift certificates to major retailers and cash. Each night's stay and every purchase you make in the hotel is an added entry."

"That sounds amazing," Gin gushed.

"Doesn't it, though?" the clerk agreed. "Did you have a honeymoon planned?"

"We're just taking the next couple of days here," he replied. "The plan is to do something bigger for our first anniversary."

"Well, Barbados or France would definitely be bigger. Good luck to you."

Gin clung to his arm as they exited the store. When he suggested more window shopping, she cut him off flat. "The seller just walked by. We have to tail him."

"Anything for you, love."

"Stop."

He assumed she wanted him to stop with the endearments, but she'd paused in front of the jewelry store display. Following her lead, he nodded and smiled as she pointed out various pieces.

"He's getting a coffee."

"Okay." That didn't help him much. Three of the five people closest to the serving counter were men. He gave her waist a quick squeeze. "Has the vial moved?"

She drew her phone from her pocket and swiped the

screen. "No." She said it with a smile, but he felt the tension humming through her body. "Let's get into the casino. He's a craps and roulette man."

"Not the biologist then."

"How do you know that?"

"I don't. Just seems like a smart man would favor a game with better odds."

"He's representing Isely," she murmured. "How smart can he be?"

Good point. They left the shopping area and passed groups of slot machines and the entrance to the twenty-four-hour buffet on their way to the gambling floor. Delving into the role she'd asked him to play, he matched her slower pace and pretended to look for just the right table to join.

"You've got to give me something better to go on if you want my help."

"Hmm." She drummed her fingertips against his forearm. "Let's try roulette."

"Sucker game," he said for her ears only as they walked closer. None of the coffee bar customers were nearby, but as Jason scanned the room, he spied a familiar face that filled him with dread. He didn't want to believe it. He couldn't imagine any benign scenario that would put the two of them in the same city.

Gabriel Frost had earned his forbidding reputation by doing the long-range dirty work for the side with the most money. In Europe the man was a cross between a ghost and an urban legend. Kill shots of all complexities were attributed to him. Jason only knew his face because he'd seen it once through a scope during the course of an investigation. It was the reason Interpol had brought him on board—to unravel the shooter's methods. Jason's efforts had brought them closer than they'd ever been, but still they'd been unable to make an arrest.

"Two chances and then I'd like to try some cards," he said, watching Frost head toward the blackjack tables.

She quirked an eyebrow in a silent question but didn't argue. She lost her first bet and lost again on her second. Smiling, she gazed up at him. "Love's better than money any day."

Her sentiment earned them a chorus of *awws* as they left for the card room.

"A kiss for luck?" he asked as they looked around at the various tables.

"Always."

When her lips brushed his, he held her a moment longer. "You're sure this vial originated in Europe?"

"Yes."

"That should do it," he said in a normal voice. He found a seat at the table that gave her the best view of the rest of the floor and him the best view of Frost.

He was up two hundred dollars when Gin whispered in his ear. Although it might have looked like sweet nothings to an outsider, she was telling him her target was on the move again. He had to assume so anyway because he had yet to single out the person she was shadowing.

Jason's newly acquired target sat in front of a growing stack of chips and appeared to be in for a few more hours of play. This wasn't the right place to share his concerns that Isely had brought a shooter to the party, and staying too close might jeopardize the advantage of surprise he knew he had right now. It was best to move.

Jason let her guide him with a deft touch on his arm or at his waist as they moved between tables. They lost a few more chips on a craps game before she declared she wanted to go for a swim. If it meant he got to see her in the bikini, he was all for it.

When they were back in the room, he stowed the chips in the safe with the gun. "When are you going to tell me who you're shadowing?"

"When you need to know." She was at the table admiring their purchases. "A girl could get used to this kind of service." She tossed the shorts his way. "I'm not sure what to think about Isely's absence." She pulled a tablet out of her suitcase. "Maybe they arrested him last night."

"More likely he's just lying low." And letting Frost do his thing. If she wasn't sharing her secrets with him, he wasn't about to mention the anomaly he'd noticed. He might need the information for leverage later.

"If they picked him up, they're not publicizing it." She sighed and set the tablet aside to pick up the swimsuit. "I'll change in the bedroom."

He pulled the price tags off of the shorts and waited until she was out of sight to strip off his khakis. There wasn't much point in modesty after this morning, but he meant to honor the ground rules. Besides, keeping his distance was the only way to regain his sanity where she was concerned.

"Where did you learn to count cards? Any chance you're undercover with the Gaming Commission?"

She laughed and he knew he enjoyed the merry sound too much.

His first instinct was denial, but he heard himself telling her the truth. "My assignments often involve long stretches of boredom. It was something to do."

"I'd think with a skill like that you'd gamble more often."

"I discovered a preference for other calculated risks."

She appeared in the doorway, and he whistled—couldn't stop himself. Her full breasts filled out the revealing cups of the bikini top. Tiny emerald-colored stones glittered on the matching silk. The sheer scarf knotted low on her hips left her midriff bare and did a poor job of covering her lovely legs. She was—in a word—gorgeous.

What were the ground rules again?

Maybe if he knocked his head against the wall, he'd shake loose the memory of those legs twined with his. Of all the things he'd seen in his life, why did his mind block the one memory he knew would keep him warm for the rest of his days?

She spun in a quick circle, hands linked at her back, and stopped with a wink. Playing along, he clutched his heart and pretended to faint onto the love seat.

"You'll cause more than a few heart attacks out there," he promised.

"I hadn't thought of that." She traced the stylized dragon tattoo on his biceps with her fingertip. "You'll leave more than a few hearts stuttering in your wake, too, I think."

"Nah."

She pulled him to his feet and into the bedroom and he had the inevitable hope that she was through with ground rules, too. "Look at us," she said, turning them toward the mirror, her arm linked in his. "We look good together. Like the perfect, newly married couple."

He agreed. Her rich red hair brushed his shoulder and her smooth, alabaster skin was a creamy highlight against his skin tanned from training outside.

"Let's go soak up some sunshine."

"So who are you shadowing, Gin?"

Her face clouded over as she stepped away from him. "Probably just a flunky since I bumped into Isely himself last night. I'd hoped he sent the virus here with someone he trusted, someone who could get us deeper into his operation. My gut says he's up to something."

Jason thought about the sniper. "Criminals usually are."

"I mean something bigger." She pulled a face. "It's not like him to micromanage a standard exchange. He blames that kind of behavior for getting his father killed. I'm just traipsing along behind the tracking tags on the vials." She held up her phone and showed him the status. "This one hasn't moved in two days. Our intel says the sale goes down sometime this weekend."

"Where?"

"Vegas."

"That's too broad a window for one agent to cover."

"Tell me about it. I've been following these little radar blips for weeks."

"How many are there?"

"Three tags that I know of."

"How'd you get the data for tracking?"

She winked at him. "That's classified."

He rolled his eyes. Considering her recent travels, it was a logical assumption that she'd managed that op on her own, too. "Why is it so important to expand your part of the mission?"

"It normally wouldn't matter, but this virus is worse than nasty. It's capable of wiping out a village in less than a week." She started pacing, her hips making the fabric of that scarf sway. "Biological warfare only hurts the innocent. I want to know why it's on American soil."

"Got it," he said, though he suspected there was a bigger reason lurking under the surface. "Any chance your flunky might like the pool?"

"Who knows? But I can watch the blip down there as easily as I can up here."

"Then grab the sunscreen." If they left the room, he could get his hands on her. If they were just killing time, he wanted to enjoy it.

Chapter Five

Gin's pulse fluttered all the way from his suite to the pool. She couldn't get over the reflection of the two of them in the mirror. Something had clicked for her in that moment. Something she couldn't afford to notice and would never consider acting on.

There was an ongoing mission here. Innocent people would die if she failed to follow that signal to the scheduled exchange.

The sobering thought was enough to keep her grounded through the nearly worshipful effort Jason gave to applying the sunscreen to her back. *Doting indeed.* Would he really spoil a wife this way? Would he take such care, or was he just going above and beyond to get under her skin?

Or her sarong.

She pushed her sunglasses up into her hair and squinted at him as he settled on the lounge chair next to hers. "What are you doing?"

"I'm just soaking up the sunshine with my gorgeous wife. As ordered." He skimmed a finger down her leg, leaving a searing trail along her nerves. "Would you rather we did something else?"

"Of course not." She replaced her sunglasses to cover her reaction to his touch. "This is fabulous." She even managed a contented sigh.

"Good." He was doing something with his phone.

"Problem?"

"Nope, just checking up on a friend."

She hoped that was all he was doing. In his position, she would be trying to figure how who had sent the doped drink and how to get out of an unexpected marriage. The thought was almost as sobering as the idea of a modern-day plague. She scolded herself for the errant thought and flipped over, the better to watch for the people critical to her assignment.

"Do you want to swim?"

"No, thank you." She patted his leg and enjoyed the view as he stripped off his T-shirt. "You go on ahead." His brow furrowed and she knew he thought she wanted to get rid of him. She would have made the same assumption if their roles were reversed. "I promise I'll stay right here. There's no reason to move."

He stood and dropped his sunglasses on the towel before diving into the deep end of the pool with enough grace to make her mouth water. Acting a part or not, she had to admit there was a mutual attraction here. A serious attraction she wanted to explore—time permitting. With every move he made in public, she forgot a little bit about why the ground rules for being alone were so important.

Although it had been fun teasing him that they'd shared something intimate last night, with every passing touch she wanted to see where those kisses might have led if he hadn't been indisposed.

And just where was the woman who had drugged him? It might have been a random con, but she just didn't believe it. Las Vegas and the general anonymity of the hotel scene, worked in the favor of people who wanted to skirt the rules. Gin was excellent with faces, but she had to admit that the constantly shifting landscape presented a challenge. Jason was right—they could talk to the bartender, but most likely they would have to reveal themselves to hotel security. The video record of the bar last night was the only hope they had of getting a lead on the woman who'd sent him the bad drink.

Because the blond wig and emerald dress had been so similar to her own disguise last night, she was more than a little concerned the woman who'd targeted Jason was also somehow related to her case. From behind her oversized dark sunglasses, she watched the other guests at the pool. It wasn't particularly crowded, but they were hardly alone. The staff moved here and there, ever present but never interfering.

No one seemed to care much about Jason swimming a few laps at an easy pace around the people relaxing and playing in the water. Well, no one but a few women with skimpier swimsuits than the one Gin wore. One of them—a blonde—caught at his ankle, and he pulled up short to talk with her.

Not the same woman from the bar last night. Gin could tell from here that the cheek structure was wrong.

Plus, she didn't think anyone would risk swimming with a wig on.

The easy smile Jason gave the stranger sent a tide of jealousy surging through Gin. Her toes squeezed the slats of the chair, and she thought going for a swim might be the right choice after all. Every second had that jealousy swirling stronger and stronger around her. It took all of her tremendous self-control to smother the urge to shout at him to show the woman the ring on his finger.

Except that's just what he was doing. The sunlight flashed off the gold band, and the smile he sent Gin's way was full of devotion.

And there went her heart again, doing a little tap dance of happiness. Keeping her head tilted as if she was reading, she turned the page of the magazine in her lap and mentally reviewed the projections of deaths that one vial of the virus could cause. She was in Las Vegas for a reason. She wasn't here to fall in love with an unattainable man like him.

She'd reached the secondary infection stage numbers when Jason's phone screamed out a Rolling Stones riff. Leaning over, she reached to mute it. If she happened to see the caller identity display *O'Marron*, that wasn't snooping—just an innocent accident.

Seemed like the right rationalization for a wife to make. At least it sounded good in her head.

But she must have leaned too far because her chair suddenly popped and shifted beneath her. Someone screamed and Jason shouted her name. She glanced over her shoulder at him and barely registered the horror on his face when another scream split the air and drew her attention in the other direction.

A lifeguard was on the deck, clutching at her leg, blood running freely between her fingers.

Following instinct, Gin scrambled to help. She was closest, but Jason suddenly was hovering over her, his body so close he dripped pool water over her.

"Go." He gave a nod indicating the nearest cabana.

"But she's hurt." Gin gestured toward the lifeguard.

"Your chair."

She twisted around and immediately understood his urgency. One of the slats of the chaise had a clean hole that hadn't been there when she'd taken her seat. A bullet hole. Someone had taken a shot at her.

"Go!"

There was no arguing with that tone even if she had been inclined to do so.

She raced to the cabana, Jason at her side, praying the whole way the shooter wouldn't tag either of them.

Knowing the trip was only a few yards didn't make it any less harrowing. She tried to catch her breath, but Jason spun her in a circle, his big hands brushing lightly over her skin as if he were searching for something.

"What?"

"I can't believe you weren't hit."

She wanted to peek out and check on the lifeguard, but Jason blocked her view. "Is she okay?"

"Looked messy but not life threatening. Lower leg. Probably hit by a ricochet of the first bullet."

"First?"

"Yes." He peered through a narrow break in the curtains framing the cabana.

"Can you see the shooter?"

He shook his head and turned back toward her. "Didn't you hear the second shot?"

"I think I missed the first shot. Your phone rang and I—"

"Shh." He pulled her into a quick hug. "We need to get out of here before the cops arrive."

She bobbed her chin in agreement. If they decided they had any helpful information, they could share it through official channels later. Sticking around now might just as easily get either one of them killed or worse—injure another bystander.

She let Jason carve a path as they slipped out of the other side of the cabana and joined the crowd getting pressed back from the scene as paramedics arrived.

He held her hand as they grabbed their things and then made their way back to their room, and she didn't think it was all about acting the part this time. His grip was too strong, just shy of painful, but she didn't pull away. She'd never admit it, but his touch was an anchor she needed after such a close call.

Someone had taken a shot at her.

Gin was well-versed in the physiological responses to adrenaline and fear. She'd trained hard to minimize those effects. Her increased heart rate and rapid breathing were normal, nothing to be embarrassed about. Those effects would settle and probably give way to shaking as soon as they were safely in the room.

But the shaking started in the elevator, and Jason

wrapped his arms around her, pulling her close, into the warm security of his solid chest. His heart beat strong and steady in her ear and she let herself cling, enormously grateful for the comfort he offered.

Tears stung her eyes, but she refused to let them fall. She couldn't recall the last time she'd wept, and she'd never done so on a mission.

The elevator car chimed when they reached their floor. By unspoken agreement, they walked in silence down the hallway to their room. She used the brief time to sort out what she'd heard and seen so they could effectively analyze the incident and potential reasons for such a bold strike.

But the truth was she hadn't heard anything…she'd been too distracted.

That was the most dangerous part of all.

Chapter Six

"Mr. Camp on line one, sir."

Holt scowled at the phone. The last thing he needed was Lucas Camp sniffing around and poking his nose into this situation. Holt had planned for every contingency.

Except Camp. Holt had been appointed to this post when Camp had returned to the private sector. A smart man would stay there.

After a quick mental rundown of current operations, he picked up the phone. "This is Holt."

"It's Lucas Camp. Thank you for taking my call."

Holt bit back a curt reply. He didn't have time to waste on distractions. "What do you need, Lucas?"

"I picked up word on a couple of shooting incidents in Las Vegas."

Holt rubbed at his brow. "Going slumming, Lucas, or are you planning your next vacation with the missus?"

"The details were vague, but I wondered if you had anyone in the area."

"No." Holt had to amend the outright lie. "No one I'm willing to discuss with you."

"I understand."

"I don't." Holt leaned forward and went on the offensive. "When Casey went missing last month, I understood your concern. But that's as far as my understanding goes. You're retired, Lucas, and I don't appreciate your interference."

"You were very cooperative in Colorado and I appreciated it," Lucas interjected.

Holt snorted. "Rest assured Thomas has made all his check-ins since he left for his honeymoon." There was nothing else about Colorado they needed to talk about.

"I'm glad to hear it."

Holt gritted his teeth. Thomas Casey and Lucas Camp went way back. After the trouble in Colorado, Casey had probably been checking in with Camp these past weeks, too. He told himself to ease up. This was just another wrinkle in the ever-shifting sands of his plan. But he couldn't shake the gut feeling that Camp knew more than he should about the problems inside Mission Recovery.

"What do you want, Lucas?"

"I want to know if you have someone looking into this thing in Las Vegas."

"Is retirement too boring?" When was this old man going to let it go? "The actions of this office are no longer your concern. Go find a hobby."

The other end of the line was so quiet Holt thought Camp had ended the call. He was about to replace the receiver when Camp finally replied.

"That's a good idea, Holt. I think I'll try gambling."

This time, he heard the click and knew the call was finished. He also understood that Camp's final words had been a warning he would be smart not to ignore. Holt replaced the receiver and sat back, tapping a pencil against the desk blotter. He checked his watch and pulled up a travel website to get an idea of flight availability.

Assuming Camp was in Houston there was any number of flight options that could put him in Vegas in time for dinner. Holt closed the search. It didn't matter.

Even if Camp got to Vegas, he couldn't possibly know where to look or who to look for—other than Grant. Considering the struggle his own people were having keeping Grant contained, he didn't think Camp had better odds.

Who was he kidding?

He broke the pencil he'd been toying with and tossed both pieces into the trash. What was the worst that could happen if Camp managed to interfere? Would one compromised link bring the whole thing tumbling down?

Holt pulled out his cell phone and made a call. A carefully phrased warning was all he could offer, but it would have to suffice.

Houston, 1:20 p.m.

Lucas Camp stared at the telephone. This was wrong.

"I take it that didn't go very well," Victoria Colby-Camp said from the counter where she was preparing lunch.

Lucas had a bad, bad feeling about what Emmett Holt was up to. He placed the phone back into its cradle and joined his wife at the kitchen island. "Holt is up to something. I can feel it. I think I should call Thomas."

Victoria gave him that look, the one that suggested he should rethink that strategy. "Are you certain you want to disturb his honeymoon? Thomas waited a very long time to take a wife. He deserves a proper honeymoon without interruption."

Lucas couldn't deny the validity of her point. "You're right, of course." He kissed his wife's cheek. "I waited quite a while to take a wife, too."

Victoria stopped preparing the salad and smiled at him. "Yes, you did."

He had been in love with Victoria since the first time he laid eyes on her when she was only twenty, but she had belonged to another—his best friend, the late James Colby. But Lucas had waited and now she was his.

"All right." Lucas relented. "I won't call Thomas. I'll just have to go to Vegas and check on this situation personally."

Victoria wiped her hands on a towel. "I think that's an excellent idea," she said to his surprise. "As long as you wait until Jim arrives tomorrow afternoon to pick up the children. He can give us a lift. I'm certain he won't mind flying back to Chicago via Las Vegas."

The Colby Agency jet would certainly make traveling considerably easier. "Very well, my dear. Holt gets a twenty-four-hour reprieve."

"One of these days we're going to have to actually retire," Victoria suggested.

Lucas grinned. "I'll remind you of that the next time an intriguing case comes across the desk of the Colby Agency or to you directly."

"Touché," Victoria confessed. Since they'd announced their retirement they'd been involved in as many cases as ever. The new Colby Agency Houston office had ensured they were never too far from the action.

As if they both needed a reprieve to remind them of what was really important in life, little Luke, their grandson, raced through the living room screaming at the top of his lungs. Eight-year-old Jamie was right on his heels. "Give me my purse!" she wailed.

Jamie had discovered accessories. Before they knew it there would be boyfriends and proms. Time had a way of flying entirely too fast.

Victoria laughed. "How could you possibly consider leaving me at a time like this?"

"What was I thinking?" He joined his wife in laughter as the two children argued over who did what.

Eventually Lucas played the part of negotiator while Victoria finished lunch.

His wife was right. *This* was the most important part of their lives right now.

The rest could wait.

Chapter Seven

At the door Gin let Jason swipe the keycard through the lock. He got a red light. He tried a second time and failed again. They exchanged a look, both of them listening for any sounds inside the room. Stepping forward, she tried her keycard, but it failed, too.

With a finger to his lips, he held up a second keycard.

She could only watch and wonder where he'd picked it up as he swiped it through the lock and the light turned green.

As she silently stepped into the room, nothing was out of place. Everything she could see looked precisely as they'd left it, even the shopping bag on the table and Jason's damaged sport coat on the chair. Still, something was off.

She sensed the attack, but didn't have time to brace for it as the room door slammed into her.

Gin let the impact carry her into the wall and then stumbled back into Jason when the intruder kept pushing. She lurched forward, ready and able to handle this,

but Jason caught her and pushed her back into the hallway. She bristled, but they would deal with the implied
insult later.

Jason drove through the door with his shoulder,
pinning whoever was on the other side behind it. She
watched the door shift as they struggled, then Jason
pulled the door closer and quickly shoved it back against
the intruder. As Jason reached around and pulled out a
man dressed in a hotel uniform she gaped.

Hands and elbows became a blur in the tight space,
but Jason worked him deeper into the suite. She blocked
the door, understanding he wanted to prevent an escape.
They needed answers.

"You?" The intruder swore and gawked at her and
Jason took advantage, landing a solid uppercut, but the
intruder recovered. Jason warded off the next hurried
advance with swift blocks and a knee strike. The intruder stumbled over the coffee table and it broke with
a loud crash, but he rolled away from Jason's next advance.

Gin could see they were evenly matched. Though
Jason had muscle mass over the guy, the other man
was absorbing the blows and dealing plenty of his own.

Suddenly Jason reared back and she swore when
sunlight glinted off the blade of a knife. The intruder
feinted toward Jason, who dropped and swung out his
leg to trip the other man. The intruder went down and
Gin tried to scoot by and get to the weapons in the bedroom safe.

But the intruder jumped up faster than she expected
and he caught her. She went still as he jerked her back

against him, the cold, sharp edge of his knife pressed against her throat.

Instantly, her training kicked in. Her emotions drew deep inside with the blast of adrenaline, leaving her feeling as cold and hard as the blade of the knife.

Jason took a step and the intruder warned him off.

"Don't even think it," he warned.

"Let her go."

"Not just yet."

"What do you want?" Jason demanded. "Money?"

"Just the woman."

Gin silently commended Jason on the rambling effort and the big worried eyes, but everyone in the room knew this was no simple robbery attempt. Using her eyes, she tried to warn Jason of her intent as the intruder dragged her back toward the door.

"Wait," Jason shouted. "Let me open the safe. We have cash."

He sounded so desperate she almost believed he was worried.

Timing it, she drove her elbow into the intruder's side and twisted her hips, pinning him to the counter. The coffeepot crashed as he waved, tried to regain his balance. With the element of surprise she got her hand up and disarmed him. The knife clattered away and Gin thought it made the odds fair again, but that wasn't giving Jason enough credit.

Jason tackled the intruder and the men fumbled backward, the intruder caught between Jason's advance and the flat-panel television. He pushed Jason off him and they tumbled to the floor, scrapping and rolling for the advantage. This time she made it to the bedroom and, with shaking hands, she punched in the combination to open the small safe. She heard the two trading punches and crashing into things in the other room as she grabbed her revolver.

"Find something to tie him up," Jason called.

With the gun in one hand, she grabbed the roll of duct tape from her suitcase and rushed back out of the bedroom to see the intruder in a heap amid the mess of the broken coffee table and with Jason's knee in his back.

"Nice work," she said, handing him the roll of tape.

"Same goes for you. Where'd you find this?" he asked, accepting her preferred method of bondage.

"I never travel without it."

He shot her a look. "You can be a little scary." He bound the intruder's wrists and feet. "You'll have to show me that move you pulled."

"Anytime."

Jason flipped over the intruder and checked his pockets. "He's not carrying anything but the employee keycard."

"No ID?" She studied the face, the wiry build, but nothing was familiar to her.

"Only the bogus name tag. But I know this guy. His name is Rick Wallace, he works with Gabriel Frost, an assassin I had the misfortune of running into in Europe. He's an independent contractor. He's good and he takes work from the highest bidder. I'd say based on the angle of the shot at the pool, they accessed a room in this tower to take that shot at you." He made a sound that was part grunt, part hum. "I wonder how they managed the uniform and master key."

"Maybe the same way you did?"

His unrepentant grin flashed and she had to admit to herself at least, she found it charming.

"I lifted mine off the housekeeping cart down the hall," he confessed.

"Good hands."

"All the girls say so," he teased with a wicked wink. "This guy probably got his in a kit that accompanied the orders and the down payment. Go ahead and call security."

"Are you sure?"

"I'm not taking the blame for all this damage. Besides, what else are we going to do with him?"

She had a few ideas, none of them legal. "Fine," she said picking up the hotel phone and pressing the key for security. Letting her voice shake, she asked for assistance. "They're on the way," she said when she hung up the phone.

"He looked pretty surprised to see you," Jason said. "You must have been the intended target if he was willing to try to take you at knife point."

"I'd have to agree." She ran her fingertips over the scrape at her throat as she stared out of the window. "But he broke into the room registered in your name." She spun on her heel and glared at the unconscious man. "Wake him up so we can talk to him."

"Not a good idea," he said. "He already knows too much. Let security handle it."

"They won't ask the right questions."

"That might be for the best under the circumstances."

Jason's voice was calm and quiet. He stood beside her but was evidently wise enough not to touch her. His stable presence should have soothed her, but her stomach knotted more. She felt twitchy all over, as if she'd been rolling around in poison ivy instead of lounging poolside. But then again, the poolside fun had ended when someone took that shot at her, so maybe the poison ivy would have been better.

She had to be logical here. Someone had managed to identify them both, even though they hadn't been connected at all before last night. Gin pulled him away from the suite door. "Why are you in town?"

He frowned at her. "I told you—to recover an agent."

"An unnamed agent who has yet to show up." She ran her hands through her hair. "This makes me edgy." She didn't do edgy. "Something else is going on. What was he—" she gestured to the guy on the floor "—doing in here?"

"You got me. Is anything missing?"

"Nothing obvious, but I haven't taken a good look."

"Let's do that."

Swiftly, they searched the room and realized everything was accounted for. Both laptops, her tablet and the small stack of poker chips she'd left on the dresser in the bedroom. She returned her gun to the safe and was checking the status of the virus tracking signal when Jason swore.

"What did you find?"

He lifted the mattress and pointed to a small plastic envelope of ammunition.

"That wasn't here last night," she said.

"Glad we both know that," he said with more than a little irritation. "What are the odds this was left by the previous occupant?"

"Zero." She sighed. "Setting you up for the incident at the pool?"

"It's the wrong ammunition for that shot, but yeah, that's my gut reaction."

She crossed her arms and rubbed at the chill on her skin. "You said you ran into the man, Frost, when you were in Europe. What was your mission?"

"I'll explain while we pack." He snatched the ammunition and zipped it into a concealed compartment in his suitcase. "We have to get out of here."

"Security is on the way," she hissed. "And my op is *here*."

"I understand that," he replied from the closet safe. He pulled weapons, chips and a jewelry box out of the safe and dumped everything into his suitcase.

"We can change rooms," she said, gathering their belongings from the bathroom and tossing his toiletry kit on top of his clothes. "But it's too late to get out of the hotel unnoticed."

"We stand out more if we stay." He pulled on a gray T-shirt that did little to tone down his bright board shorts. With the flip-flops he looked like a surfer in need of a good wave. If only the hair were longer.

"I disagree." She shook her head. "We should go ahead with the report and convince the security team to help us out with surveillance."

"Right, because people in the hospitality industry love hosting sniper bait."

"We have to report the break-in." She stood her ground. This was where she needed to be.

"No," he argued. "Let them find the mess in the course of their investigation. I'm more concerned about who ordered a hit on you and getting you out of range."

"Spoken like a doting husband."

"When in Rome," he muttered.

She laughed, more than a little surprised that she could under the circumstances. This had to be the work of Isely. He was on to her. She should have admitted that when he followed her to the bar last night. Her cover was blown. No two ways about it.

"Seriously," she persisted, "we have to file the report. This room is booked under your name. As victims of attempted robbery we'll have their sympathy."

"They'll know I'm here for a security conference," he finished for her. "Even my cover story has a military history. The police and security will see the path of the bullet and put us at the scene quickly enough. If they haven't already."

"The hotel video record will clear you."

"Maybe. It depends on the angle. Brown hair, average height—anyone could be me in that pool."

"Running away definitely won't help your case."

He took a deep breath and pushed a hand through his wet hair. "You were booked here under an alias?"

"Of course."

He frowned. "You put Ginger Olin on the marriage license."

She nodded, ignoring the little shiver that skated down her spine as he spoke her name. So he knew her real name. Big deal. She should be pleased that her efforts in Colorado irritated him enough to dig deeper. Why did she keep underestimating him?

"And too many staff know our faces thanks to your little newlywed game."

"That's not so bad. We change rooms, of course, but we stay and use the temporary fame to our advantage."

"Fine," he said with a heavy sigh, looking around at the mess. "Are you going to claim anything was stolen?"

"No," she gave a nod to his zipped suitcase. "You?"

He shook his head. "Who wants you dead?"

"Any number of people, I suppose, considering my rate of mission success. My intel says none of them are in town." Except Isely.

"But any of them could hire a sniper to deal with you."

She ignored that. "What do we say about this guy?" She nudged the unconscious intruder with her foot.

"Do we have to say anything? We walked in and subdued him. The less we share about him the better our odds if we stay."

"If? Are you going back to the change hotels idea?"

"No. Do you still have the keycard for the room you booked with your alias?"

"Yes. Why?"

"We should go see if anything's wrong there."

"Agreed. But there's nothing to find. I moved all of my things here last night."

Further discussion had to wait as the security team

arrived with the hotel manager and a Las Vegas police officer. When they took in the scene, the hotel security team radioed for help to remove the intruder and refrained from detailed questions until he was out of the way.

She and Jason went through the standard background questions and gave the contact information that matched up with their cover stories. They both applied the right amount of bewildered distress mixed with the temper and shock of the pool shooting and room invasion.

No, none of their valuables were missing. Yes, they'd combined business with pleasure on this trip. No, they didn't have any idea who would want to harm them. Yes, they'd gotten married last night. No, they didn't have any connection to the intruder. And the duct tape was something they'd gotten for their honeymoon. That was the last question on that subject.

"Why did you leave the pool area?" the police officer asked.

Gin opened her mouth, but once more Jason leaped in to answer first.

"That was my fault. I know we should have stayed and given a statement. My wife tried to assist the lifeguard," he said, rubbing her hand where it rested on his thigh. "But I wasn't in the mood to be widowed on our honeymoon. I just wanted her out of there."

"Completely understandable," the hotel manager said with a smile, preempting whatever the officer would have said. "We are so terribly sorry and we'd like to do everything possible to salvage the situation."

Good luck, Gin thought. "Is the lifeguard okay?

There seemed to be a lot of blood." She let Jason pull her closer, offering comfort. If this mission fell apart, she would always remember how well he played his role.

After his act here, a real husband might be a bit of a letdown. She pushed the errant thought out of her head. This wasn't the right time to lose focus.

"The lifeguard was stable when the paramedics transported her." The head of security answered that one. "I'm sure she'll make a full recovery."

"That's good news," Gin replied.

"I'll see that your statement is added to the official report about the shooting," the police officer assured. "There may be some follow-up required if it turns out the incident at the pool is related to other recent crimes in the area."

"Other crimes? Plural?" Gin had only heard about one possible strike, and a quick glance at Jason proved he hadn't heard anything before he'd been drugged last night. "What do you mean? What's been going on?"

"I'm not able to elaborate at this time," he explained. "But there is an ongoing investigation related to other shootings."

"Sorry." Gin smiled. "Force of habit."

"She started her career as a police beat reporter. That's how we met," Jason explained. "I was a security consultant for a business that had been targeted by a drug ring."

She watched that sink in to all four faces and gave Jason bonus points for improvisation. She kept her mouth shut, but she would be digging into the details at the earliest opportunity. The ammunition in the bed had her wondering if any of the other shootings were better suited to the particular caliber Wallace had planted.

"Maybe we should just fly home early," Jason suggested.

"No cause for alarm," the manager intervened. "Here at the Palace we've doubled our security presence and coordinated with the Las Vegas police until this is resolved. You'll be safer here than anywhere else on the strip."

"I don't know," she hedged.

"As I said, follow-up may be necessary." The police officer got to his feet. "I think it's best if you stay in town at least through the weekend."

"So let us pamper you." The manager was all smiles. "I've got a penthouse with your name on it and a team of massage therapists standing by."

"Seriously?" Gin squeezed Jason's hand. "That's tempting."

"That's Vegas," the hotel manager added.

"What do you think, honey?"

"I suppose if we have to stay in town anyway…" He hitched his shoulders. "We may as well take them up on the offer."

"It's settled then." The hotel manager reached for his radio, calling in help to move them to the penthouse.

JASON LET GIN handle the final exchange of information. Their luggage was whisked away ahead of them, and they were escorted by the manager himself all the way to their new door.

The elevator doors parted on a luxurious vestibule that was nearly as spacious as her original hotel room.

More than the guards standing at the fire exit and elevator, Jason noticed the penthouse was locked with a key.

"I've disabled the electronic lock for your room. Only the key will open it, and you and I have the only two keys." He handed the brass key to Jason. "I hope that goes some distance to restoring your confidence in us."

"Absolutely," Gin said.

Jason nodded, simultaneously impressed and concerned by the extra precautions.

"When your room needs service, just call housekeeping and they will send someone right up to clean it at your convenience."

He supposed that made sense, especially because the intruder had been dressed in a hotel uniform. Their original reservation would show them leaving in less that forty-eight hours.

"We'd rather not create any more trouble or drama for you and your staff," Gin said.

"Please, this is not your fault," the manager said, pushing open the door to the penthouse. "Crime is a part of the Vegas landscape, but I prefer to keep it out of my hotel. Please enjoy the rest of your stay."

Gin gasped and Jason could hardly blame her. His suite a few floors down had been luxurious enough, but he'd only seen a room of this caliber in movies. There were multiple sofas, a kitchen, a dining area, a wet bar and two massage therapists standing like statues near the window.

"We can have dinner delivered at your convenience."

Jason studied the manager instead of the room. "Why do I get the feeling you'd like us to stay tucked away up here for the rest of our stay?"

"Oh no, sir. That's not it at all. Whatever suits you is what we will provide. I was just about to mention your credit line at the casino."

"House money? Talk about above and beyond," Jason said. He drew the heavier curtains together over the sheers, blocking out the late afternoon view of the city. It was stunning as the sun faded and the lights took over, but standing in front of an open window wasn't his idea of a smart move, not even at this altitude.

"What my husband means is thank you." Gin guided the manager toward the door. "We're just a little overwhelmed by your generosity, but we appreciate it very much."

Jason let her smooth over his deliberate cynicism while he explored the rest of the penthouse. He couldn't imagine what this was costing the hotel. Two people could get lost in this place that was better suited to a celebrity traveling with an entourage than to a bride and groom.

Despite the ample space, the lavish décor and the hotel's commitment to anticipate their every need, he couldn't shake the feeling that they'd been neatly trapped. It was a luxurious cell, but it felt like a prison all the same. Being celebrity victims would only make it more of a challenge to do what they'd come here to do.

Well, what he'd come to do since his original recovery mission seemed to be a bust. He kicked that thought out of his head. There would be hell to pay when he got back to the office. Holt was pissed.

Jason decided he might as well make the most of the rest of the weekend. He wanted to enjoy the lush atmosphere, knew he'd probably never see another room like this on his own dime, yet he couldn't. Not when what had begun as a simple recovery was spiraling out of control. Gin might not be the agent he'd been sent to assist, but she didn't stand a chance with Gabriel Frost hunting her.

The irony of the situation was not lost on him.

Walking through the rooms, he didn't see the beauty or design; he saw the hiding places and firing solutions, the potential injuries that every vase, table or chair could inflict. He knew the adrenaline letdown after the pool attack and the following fight in the room a few floors down was driving him closer to paranoia. But bullets were flying faster than chips lately.

Gin joined him as he closed the curtains in the second bedroom. "What is wrong with you?"

"We're boxed in," he whispered, matching her quiet tone. "There are more eyes on us now. It will be impossible to get anything done."

"Just what do you want to do?" She stepped in close and wrapped her arms around his waist.

He had to remind himself it was an act for Sven and his twin masseuse waiting for them out in the main room. "You know what I mean. This is…" He shook his head. "Over the top."

"So let's adjust our priorities in light of the new circumstances. A massage is the perfect way to detox after what we've been through."

"I was thinking ice packs and a beer." He glared down at her but knew he couldn't hold out long against the mischievous sparkle in her emerald eyes.

"You want a massage." She caught his hands, laced her fingers with his. "You know you do."

"Not really." The last thing he wanted was to close his eyes. It seemed like every time he blinked he saw that terrible image of the bullet hole in the chair…the bullet that might just as easily have put a hole through her heart.

He pushed her hair back from her neck and examined the red scrape where Wallace had held the knife to her tender skin. Her life had been measured in millimeters today. It was a wonder she didn't need a sedative. "Are you sure you're okay?"

"I'm okay." Her smile looked genuine enough. "But I'd be better with a massage."

"You go ahead. I'll keep watch."

"But you need one, too." She brought her hands to his shoulders and made little circles with her fingertips. "You're all tense."

"Can you blame me?"

"It's complimentary," she sing-songed. "That doesn't happen every day. It's the smart move."

"Unless Sven and his twin are on the enemy's payroll," he whispered in her ear. "They could snap our necks and call it a day."

"Don't worry. I'll protect you." She tugged his head close and kissed his nose. "Just do your doting husband thing and we'll figure the rest of it out when they're gone."

"Gin," he pleaded. He didn't think it was possible for him to relax in the presence of strangers. "Reschedule for tomorrow."

"Jason," she mimicked his tone. "Our honeymoon's been interrupted by a terrible fright and a burglary." She touched her hand to her heart. "Come on, honey. This is the perfect way to reclaim our time. You know I'm right."

He rolled his eyes but kept his hand in hers as he followed her out to the main room.

Sven and his brother were actually named Paul and Terry and not related at all. For the next ninety minutes, Jason experienced more relaxation than he thought possible with another man's hands on him.

Gin kept up a light commentary for his benefit, and he decided to make it up to her later, assuming she would have preferred to simply sink into the experience rather than chatter for his comfort.

The massage therapists left them with advice to drink plenty of water, skip the alcohol and eat lightly tonight.

When they were finally alone, each of them slumped on the couch, he took a long pull on the bottle of water. "Eat lightly. That explains why the manager comped dinner. They're planning on serving us twigs and leaves."

Gin snorted. "Give it up, Mr. Cynical. The manager isn't winning on any part of this deal." She rolled to her back and the hotel robe slipped, revealing more of her creamy, toned thigh. "I bet a couple's massage is a bigger investment than any of the fine dining options."

"No bet. You're probably right."

"Trust me. I'm one hundred percent right on this."

"Such an authority on decadence. Guess that means I'm not your first?"

She slanted him that sly look he found so intriguing. "First what?"

"Forget it," he said, hiding the truth of his question behind a lazy smile.

No point explaining he'd meant first husband. That wouldn't matter with Gin. Married or not, this was all temporary. With the help of his friend at Interpol, after they'd met in Colorado, he'd done enough digging to know Olin was her real name and that her cases had never intersected his. The recognition he'd sensed in Colorado last month had stemmed entirely from a long-distance surveillance photo taken when she happened to walk by a café his friend had had under surveillance.

To get his mind off of her tempting gaze and even more enticing bare leg, he reached for his phone and pulled up the police reports for the past few days. "What do you think they meant about other shootings in the area?"

"You're going to make me think, aren't you?"

"The guys didn't specifically warn against it."

"Maybe they should have," she muttered, sitting up.

For a moment he regretted the change of subject if only for the loss of scenery, but then she came over and sat down beside him and the soft scent of her washed over him.

"Might be easier if I get my laptop."

"Nah, that's too much effort right now." She waved a finger at the phone. "What's bugging you?"

"The shot at the pool." He pulled up a website that posted local crimes according to police reports. "You were obviously the target."

"Not so obvious."

"What do you mean?"

"Well, I've had some time to think it through. I know luck happens, and me suddenly reaching for your phone would have been unexpected, but why didn't he just bury the second shot in my brain since he was all lined up and everything?"

Jason's stomach bottomed out. She hadn't said anything he hadn't thought himself, but the finality, the harsh nature of her statement was somehow a thousand times worse when spoken. It shouldn't be this difficult to regain his objectivity. He studied the sculpted ceiling, hoping it would be easier if he didn't look at her.

Any way he looked at it she was right. "Not taking the kill shot doesn't fit. When we caught Wallace in the room, he was shocked to see you."

"I swear I've never met him."

"I believe you." But believing it didn't change the fact that Wallace had apparently expected her to be dead and had planted the ammunition to frame Jason for the kill. After studying the bastard in Europe, Jason understood Frost and had learned a little about how he accepted contracts. "I'm wondering if the other shootings they mentioned are simply to divide the local investigation focus."

"To lump my potential assassination in with other random lives cut short?"

"Maybe. Look." He tipped the phone so she could see the screen. "There was a shooting death last night around 3:00 a.m."

"Hmm." She scanned the article. "Doesn't say sniper." She leaned back, turning the water bottle around. "If there was a sniper in Vegas, why didn't the news report it?"

"They might have. You have to work pretty hard to get real news once you're in a casino."

"True, but it can be done. Due to the nature of my case, I've made the effort." She sipped at the water. "Our respective offices know we're here. If there was a sniper in the area, they would have told us."

"Maybe."

Her leg rubbed against his as she sat forward once more. She reached out and gently turned his chin her way so he had to meet her gaze.

"Explain."

"You said you didn't drug me. What if the person who did wanted me indisposed so I wouldn't have an alibi for your death today or the guy last night?"

"You'll notice news of my death is highly exaggerated."

He picked up his phone and showed her the other reports he'd tagged. "Yes, I'm making assumptions, but the first event that might be related happened within eight hours of my arrival in Las Vegas."

"Did you have orders to shoot me?"

He patted her knee. "No. My orders were to wait here in Caesar's for the compromised agent to contact me."

She turned the water bottle around again. "Like I told you this morning, I'm supposed to follow the virus vial. No backup required. It's my personal challenge to spot the buyer. My assignment isn't that complicated."

There was a little furrow between her brows that he was starting to learn meant she wasn't telling him all of it. "But you were desperate enough to haul me out and marry me last night after shooting at someone tailing you."

"You can let that go anytime. I promised you a quick divorce."

"Gin, last month my director was set up."

She nodded. "Bad news travels fast."

"I received a note at the wedding reception that said, *You're next.*"

"Is that some kind of joke? A male version of the catching the bridal bouquet?"

"No." He shook his head. "I didn't tell anyone in Mission Recovery about it."

"Why not?"

He didn't want to get into all of his reasons, especially because she'd been one of them. "I questioned the waiter who delivered it, had it tested by a friend in the lab and got nowhere. Wasn't much point in sending it up the line."

"But you think the note is related to what happened to your director."

"Yeah. Whoever rigged the setup nearly succeeded." Mission Recovery had suspects but hadn't moved on them yet. Jason wasn't privy to all the details and had assumed it was due to a lack of evidence. Now he wondered if there was a bigger problem. "What if my office hasn't mentioned an active sniper in Las Vegas because they believe *I am* the shooter?"

She rubbed a hand along his arm. "Relax. Even if the local police decide to announce a sniper is active in town, you have airtight alibis for last night and today."

"Not if the woman who drugged me had succeeded. That's my point. Whoever is setting me up didn't expect me to have an alibi."

She tugged at the sleeve of his robe. "But she didn't and you're welcome."

"Thanks, but whoever hired Frost wouldn't have expected your intervention."

"Which means we're in more danger than before?"

"It's a possibility we should consider." And the list of suspects who knew who he was, what he could do with a rifle and his general location last night was ridiculously short. "Who knows about your mission here?"

"You know I can't answer that, Jason."

"Fine. Let's go back to the question of who wants you dead."

"A great many people, I suppose." She shifted, crossed her legs. "I told you, none of them are here."

"What about Isely?"

"He's never seen my face. He has no reason to connect me with anything he's done or plans to do."

"And still he followed you last night."

"So the man has instincts." She bolted to her feet, but he caught her hand before she could stalk away from him. "Explains his longevity in a treacherous career as a black-market weapons dealer."

"It scared the hell out of me." It wasn't at all what he meant to say, wasn't at all professional. He was about to cross a line good agents stayed well clear of. "The bullet hole in that chair. The knife at your throat."

Her gaze softened and her lips parted. It reminded him of last night for some reason. He needed a new memory, something full of life to burn through the haze left by the drugs and to break the icy grip of nearly losing her at the pool. A new memory he wouldn't forget no matter which direction their careers took them from here.

"Is that the doting husband talking?"

He shook his head and gently pulled her down into his lap. Her sultry chuckle faded to a sweet silence full of promise and potential. Her gaze lingered on his mouth. He pushed the vibrant red silk of her hair behind her ear, then cupped her nape and drew her mouth closer to his.

Close enough to kiss. The first touch of lips, sweet and gentle, turned needy from one beat of his pulse to the next. Her mouth was still cool from the water she'd been drinking as directed. But that didn't last long. She grew hotter and hotter with each swipe of their dueling tongues.

He lost himself in her soft sigh of pleasure and when she shifted, straddling him, he tugged her hips closer, let her feel how much his body wanted hers. How much he needed the connection she'd offered from the moment she walked into that bar.

Her hands parted his robe, pushed it away from his shoulders. Her touch created such a craving inside him, a craving his body knew only she could satisfy.

With a soft scrape of her teeth on his lower lip, she leaned back, her hands hot on his shoulders, her breath coming in little pants as she rested her forehead on his. "Wait," she whispered.

Looked like the ground rules had just been demolished.

She sat back a little more and he fisted his hands at his sides because he wanted to hang on to her, to keep her close and never let go. His every instinct screamed it was the wrong move. Excuses, bargains, everything but an apology wanted to come spilling out of his mouth, but he bit back all of the words.

Nothing he said would do any good.

If he understood anything about this particular woman it was her ruthless independence. His physical desire was obvious enough. And mutual, he surmised based on her passionate response to him. Beyond that, what could he offer that she might accept?

She touched her lips with her fingertips, but he didn't think she meant the move provocatively. Her eyes were dark as she studied him. He felt a precious opportunity slipping through his hands and there was nothing he could do.

Not yet.

"I'm going to take a shower and dress for dinner."

He nodded.

"We should choose a restaurant. Not, um, room service."

He nodded again.

She walked out of his line of sight, her feet padding softly across the thick carpet. Then she stopped.

"I need to keep an eye on that vial. And we have to get a line on whoever is setting you up."

Business. It was the right answer, the safe topic. He didn't say anything, didn't need to. He heard her feet once more, but he waited until the sound of water running in the shower reached him before he got up from the sofa.

His damn imagination gave him an all-too-clear picture of what she would look like, hair slicked back from her face and soapy lather slipping over her curves.

Clinging to his willpower, he grabbed his shaving kit and suitcase from the room and headed for the bedroom suite on the other side of the penthouse.

Chapter Eight

Mission Recovery headquarters

In the wind.

Holt stared at the message on his monitor, still not quite able to comprehend how Grant had avoided the perfectly crafted noose. The man always followed orders, always found a way to succeed whether the assignment was tedious or overwhelming.

He'd put him in Las Vegas and told him to wait. What the hell had happened to the scheduled pickup? Painting the miscommunication as a failure, he'd ordered Grant out of the area, and now he was practically a missing person. *In the wind.* He was certain the contact wasn't implying Grant had actually boarded a plane.

Why in God's name had one of their top Specialists chosen this particular moment to buck a career-long pattern of obedience?

Feeling like it was *his* neck caught in the noose Holt tugged on his tie and undid the button at his throat. He struggled for a deep breath and refused to give in to the hard knot in his chest.

Everything—*everything*—was riding on this. Grant

might have unknowingly botched the latest battle, but Holt could still win the war.

The only good news was that local law enforcement hadn't gone public with the sniper theory and therefore Grant didn't have clues to develop a theory of his own.

Leaning against the wide window, he stared out at the dark landscape, not caring to see the stars or the moon or anything else beyond the dark haze of his own frustration.

He should have shifted Grant's role in this. He should have been clever enough to find a different method. But it was too late now and all the should-have-dones weren't going to get this resolved.

Like all the Specialists in Mission Recovery, Holt believed in success above all else. Setbacks were temporary, and a Specialist embraced by added motivation often overcame the obstacles that discouraged others.

He looked around his office, reminded himself what was on the line. It was all the motivation he needed to take the next step.

He buttoned his collar and straightened his tie before he opened his office door. Nadine sat at her desk, doing whatever she did to keep him organized and connected to Specialists deployed on various assignments.

"Has Specialist Grant arrived?"

"No, sir. Were you expecting him?"

Yes, actually. But he could hardly say that to Nadine. "At this morning's check-in I ordered him back to D.C. Has he booked a flight?"

Her monitor flashed with different logos and windows as she started her search. "Nothing on his corporate credit card. I'm checking airline manifests now."

"Thank you. Check his personal accounts and any aliases you know about."

"Yes, sir."

Nadine would have some leads, but Holt knew Grant had others. Every Specialist had alternate identification or knew how to create it quickly. Holt leaned against the doorjamb while he waited, the only sounds the soft instrumentals of the classical music Nadine preferred and her fingers on the keyboard.

"Anything?"

"Not so far. I can have the analysts dig deeper if you like."

Holt sighed. "We can give him some time." His personal cell phone started ringing. "Let me know when you get something," he said as he picked up the call and headed back into his office.

"Holt."

"Are you trying to renege?"

Isely. Holt wasn't surprised, though he knew how to fake it for the right effect. "Why are you calling me here?"

"Answer the question."

"I'll deliver as discussed."

"Ah, that is good. Things so often get messy when we improvise."

What the hell did that mean? "Patience pays off," Holt reminded him. The game wouldn't be out of balance for long and he sure as hell wouldn't be the first one to blink. "Your patsy is still in town."

"True. And with a lovely new wife who is complicating matters."

Holt barely restrained his shock. Grant was married? How did Isely know that before anyone here at Mission Recovery? "It's nothing," he said.

"It is out of character and off script," Isely bit out, his cold voice a clear indicator of his brutal intentions. "Do not cross me, *Deputy*."

The call ended before Holt could reply. Damn the man and this whole twisted business. And damn Jason Grant for choosing the absolute worst time to mix romance with a mission.

Holt looked back at his screen. Who the hell had he managed to exchange vows with if the woman who should have him contained had missed him?

"Sir?" Nadine's voice followed the beep of the office intercom.

"Yes?"

"I have something you should see."

"Bring it in."

Ignoring the bad feeling in his gut, he clicked on the small icon that appeared on his monitor as Nadine walked into the office. It was a certificate of marriage from one of the many chapels in Las Vegas, signifying the union of Jason Grant with Ginger Olin. "What do we know about her?"

"I'm working on that now."

"Good. What else?"

Nadine swiped something on her tablet and another document popped up. "I'm not sure how to interpret this, but the marriage isn't legal. The marriage license application was completed, but the official license has not been issued."

Maybe Grant hadn't lost all of his faculties after all. "See what you can do to sort it out."

"Shall I contact Specialist Grant?"

"Absolutely not. It could blow his cover with whatever angle he's working on." Considering he hadn't returned as Holt demanded, it was only reasonable that Grant was on to something else. But what? He couldn't possibly know about Isely.

"Yes, sir."

"Keep me posted."

With a nod, she exited his office and left him alone to sort out a mess she couldn't fathom.

His hands clenched around the leather-covered arms of his executive chair. He'd been working this for so long, he'd started to believe the light at the end of the tunnel was freedom, not a head-on collision with a train. If Grant screwed this up with an ill-timed and fake marriage or some off the wall rescue, Holt might just let him take the rap for the crimes about to occur in Nevada.

There was nothing he could do...but ride it out.

Chapter Nine

Gin washed away the sunblock and massage oil, all the while wishing she had the courage to invite Jason to help her. The hot spray of the waterfall showerhead drenched her body, and she trailed a finger over her lips, unable to put that kiss out of her mind.

Oh, who was she kidding? She didn't *want* to forget it. This time not even thoughts of a catastrophic epidemic could completely silence the part of her that wanted to explore what was happening between them.

She twisted the handle to cold, telling herself it was only to put more shine in her hair. Ha! Stepping out of the cavern of a shower and looking to the vanity, she realized his personal things were gone from the countertop.

Sneaky. Smart, but sneaky.

It couldn't be called cowardly—that had been her, pulling back from that kiss and practically running away from the temptation of Jason.

She dried her hair and slipped into a black sheath that zipped up the side. Getting away from the seclusion of the penthouse had sounded like a good idea at the time, but now she realized the error. Dinner in public meant they would have to play the role as celebrity newlyweds, as Jason called it.

She paused, mascara wand halfway to her eye. They were just caught up in the moment, the atmosphere and the wild feel of the town. When he did that doting husband routine parts of her she didn't know existed just melted. But that wasn't a reflection of feelings as much as a commendation of his dedication to the job.

Except that kiss…

Her phone rang and Gin jumped. The number meant business, and she couldn't have been more grateful for the distraction. She set the mascara aside and picked up the phone.

"Yes."

"Our wiretap says the exchange happens tomorrow night."

"Understood."

She ended the call and resumed applying makeup, enormously settled by the thought of business. She swept her hair into a French twist and reached for the sexy black shoes.

Ready, she walked out of the bedroom, her strappy heels hanging from her finger and her clutch bag under her arm. She'd packed her lipstick, revolver and cell phone, which was set to vibrate. She wasn't worried about calls, but she needed to know if and when the virus was on the move.

It was a good thing the heels were in her hand because the sight of Jason made her knees buckle. He wore a navy suit with the crisp white shirt open at the throat. Freshly shaven, he looked so handsome and as sexy as hell. But it was the wedding band that made her wish this moment could be real...that he could be hers.

As much as she wanted to look at him as a tool, as simply a means to accomplishing her goal, she just couldn't do it. This was quickly becoming far too personal. She wasn't sure how to pull back to a professional distance.

It would have been easier if even the smallest part of her wanted to pull back.

"You look fantastic," she said with her brightest smile.

"Thanks, but I think I must only be a backdrop next to you."

She did a little turn for him and then leaned a hip against the sofa for balance as she slid into her heels. "According to the latest intel, the sale goes down tomorrow night."

"In the casino?"

"Maybe." She shrugged. "Could be anywhere in the resort."

"That leaves us plenty of options," he said. "Is there a time frame?"

"Not anything precise." She patted her clutch. "I've got the app open and working. We'll know when the virus moves, and we can follow it."

"Do you have orders to intervene?"

"Not necessarily, though I'd rather secure the vial than let it out into the world. Why?"

"Just debating how we ditch the protective detail if it comes to that."

She moistened her lips and wiggled her eyebrows. "We can always improvise."

"After we eat." He motioned her toward the door. "I called down to the restaurant and asked them to prepare a table."

"Great."

"Why make the sale here?"

She shrugged, looked up at him. "It wasn't my choice."

"I realize that, but I can't help wondering if this location has significance to the deal."

"That's doubtful. Probably just because it's a landmark with lots of tourists. An easy place to get lost."

"Sounds reasonable." With a flourish he opened the door and let her proceed.

But the question got her wondering. Maybe there was a clue to the buyer—or seller—that she'd overlooked.

Even expecting the security presence, it was a bit unnerving to step out into the vestibule and see the posted guard, but she recovered with a bright smile.

She cursed herself for choosing a sleeveless dress when Jason put his arm around her as they waited for the elevator. *For show,* she chanted in her head. The guards expected warm, familiar behavior from newlyweds and she had to play along.

The elevator arrived and another guard was waiting for them. It was a little much. Jason was right—the extra security would make her task more challenging. She'd worked in all kinds of conditions and under all sorts of security umbrellas, but having a private shadow hovering over them meant she'd have to get creative if she was going to catch this sale.

It was a relief to step out into the anonymous crowd and put some breathing room between them and the security detail.

"The Isely family was sidelined for five years when they tried to sell it last time," he murmured into her ear as they strolled toward the restaurant. "Seems a little brash to return to business here of all places."

She snorted, covering it with her clutch. "The initial deal for this product went sour, but they aren't the sort to let anything shy of the apocalypse stop them."

She shivered at her own words, recalling the fortuitous timing of seeing Jason at the bar when she needed to evade Isely. Unless. A terrible thought occurred to her. Maybe Isely had been tipped off about her and she'd been ushered toward Jason on purpose. Obviously someone knew Jason was here. That guy Wallace had planted incriminating evidence in his room. If that was the case, it was a newbie mistake to fall into a trap that resulted in more eyes on both of them. She couldn't have made that kind of mistake...could she?

Jason's warm breath brushed across the shell of her ear. "Smile, darling, or they'll think I'm useless in bed."

She complied immediately, feeling the heat of a blush on her face. The two kisses they'd shared were enough to convince her that the exact opposite would be true.

The maître d' escorted them to a table in the true Vegas paradox of implying privacy while managing to display their presence to anyone watching.

"Does the seller know you're here for the sale?"

"No. I've been in various disguises along the way. If they recognize me now—a highly doubtful scenario—our secret marriage and quick honeymoon are enough to chalk it up to coincidence."

He frowned at her. "You don't believe that?"

"Now who needs to smile?" She turned his hand over and stroked a slow path across his palm to his wrist. "We've seen each other around often enough to know it could happen. But, you're right. I'm having some second thoughts."

"That would be wise," he agreed. "Otherwise, why shoot at you?"

"Maybe I was wrong about that and it *was* you they were after in the bar last night."

"Anything is possible," he said with way too much innuendo.

"Possible but not likely." She couldn't believe neither of them had recognized such an obvious manipulation… if that's what it was. "You might not have noticed, being a slave to that newlywed glow, but I can get a little persistent and annoying at times."

He stared at her for a split second and then roared with laughter, causing heads to turn their way.

"Oh, stop." Was causing a scene part of his game? She leaned back, sipping her champagne and trying to catalog the faces aimed at them. "Stop it."

"I can't." He gulped in air. "Sorry. I just—just can't picture you a little bit of anything," he finished breathlessly.

"Should I be flattered?"

"Yes, please." He bobbed his head in the affirmative. "It was a compliment."

She gaped as the man actually wiped tears from his eyes. It didn't feel like a compliment. "Fine."

"Oh, no you don't." He reached across the table, lacing his fingers with hers. "We're not going to have our first argument in public."

"I see no reason to argue at all."

"So you're an anomaly?"

She frowned at him.

"I thought redheads liked drama." He scooted closer, nuzzling her neck. "And blondes are all about the fun."

Oh! It *was* a performance. He wouldn't have mentioned blondes without a reason. She tilted her head back, giving him better access and still managing to stay alert enough to scan the room. "I booked a facial for eleven o'clock," she said, indicating the direction she thought he meant.

"That's good. I'll use the time out on the driving range."

So they agreed about the woman waiting alone a few tables away. Playing it to the hilt, Gin used her phone to get a picture of their wedding rings, managing to get the blonde in the frame. She wasn't sure where or who could analyze it for them, but that was a problem for later.

They parted long enough to listen to the evening's specials and place their respective orders. And while every touch and little whisper through each course looked like a devoted couple lost in each other, they continued to exchange information and theories.

Unfortunately it kept her body running hot. If they'd

stayed in the room, she could have tried to reclaim the ground rules. Out here, being a couple in love—or at least enjoying the lust of a honeymoon—was eroding her ability to resist him.

Too bad staying in the room wouldn't get the primary job done. Well, she'd never been one to run from a challenge.

"We need to find out who she is," she murmured as she scraped off a tiny piece of the decadent chocolate torte they were sharing. "I don't like that neither of us knows her."

"You want to give her a chance to poison me again?"

"It's an option. I saved you once, and I can do it again."

"Hmm. Whatever helps you sleep at night," he said with a wink.

Her mind went back to last night, when they'd shared a bed, though not in the intimate way she'd staged it for him. It was an image guaranteed to keep her up tonight. And more than a few nights in the future.

She let another sliver of the rich cake dissolve on her tongue. "I was thinking we should go dancing, gamble a bit and see who is most surprised to see us."

"Other than Wallace?"

"He'd better be in custody," she grumbled. It had required a great deal of concealer to cover the scrape on her neck.

"Then maybe we can pay a visit to security and ask to review the tapes from the bar."

"I'm a tad overdressed for a visit to security. What happened to letting them handle it?"

"I don't know." He gazed at her cleavage then cleared his throat. "In that dress, we're likely to get everything they have on the pool and burglary investigations. A reporter and security expert would naturally be curious."

"Even a reporter would focus on her honeymoon. The hotel team said it was all in LVPD and FBI hands now."

"As if any man would resist you if you asked nicely. Besides, you must have connections."

She frowned at him. "Are you fishing? You know I don't have connections or any backup here aside from you." Reaching over, she brushed a crumb of chocolate cake from his lip. "What about you?"

"Not *here,* exactly."

She gasped when he caught her thumb with a nip of his teeth and soothed it with his tongue. Could the man be any sexier?

"I was thinking of—"

"Lucas Camp," she finished for him as the only possible answer dawned on her. Camp connected them both—loosely—due to his former position as the deputy director of Mission Recovery and his own alliances within covert agencies like her own CIA.

"There you go reading my mind."

"If we called him, what would you expect him to do?"

"The man has friends everywhere. He practically introduced us."

"True." And he was inherently trustworthy. Jason seemed to be reluctant to trust his own team.

"Maybe he has insight we're missing."

It was possible. She knew Jason hadn't told her everything about his reasons for keeping the note a secret. Now that she doubted her own anonymity where Isely was concerned, they probably needed someone on the outside they could trust.

She hadn't seen Isely so far tonight, but that didn't mean much. Since his father had died five years ago, he had become militant about his personal security and those he let in on his plans to rebuild the family business. Micromanaging a deal like the virus transaction didn't fit the original profile she'd assembled on him, but people did strange things under duress.

Like get married.

Thoughts like that had to go—and quickly. She pulled out her phone.

"Is the virus moving?"

"Not yet. I'm just sending an email." She held the phone so Jason could read over her shoulder as she drafted a note, attached the photo of the blonde and sent it to the email address Mr. Camp had used to contact her last month.

"Thank you."

The sincerity in Jason's voice startled her. The urge to comfort him was automatic and she patted his knee. "We'll figure this out."

Though they had a better chance if he'd tell her everything he knew. But then that would mean she would have to tell all she knew.

Eventually, she supposed.

Chapter Ten

When they finally called it quits on that amazing chocolate cake, Jason signed the check and they headed into
the casino. He did his best to relax and blend in, but
without Gin by his side he would have stormed out after
only a few minutes. No matter how posh, how clean or
how many years had passed, when he entered a casino
he smelled stale booze, cigarette smoke and the unmistakable stench of losing. His father's gambling addiction
had destroyed his family and nearly broken his mom's
spirit in the process.

He wondered—again—if Holt had sent him here on
some wild-goose chase as a test of his willpower and
ability to overcome the ghosts of his past. If so, despite
the supposedly failed recovery, he intended to pass the
test and restore his reputation.

Winding through the craps room they settled in to
watch a gambler on a hot streak. Jason recognized the
men in the shadows who kept a loose perimeter around
every move he and Gin made. Having such an attentive
audience went against his most ingrained instincts, but
he couldn't argue with the precaution. Anything that
kept her safe was fine with him.

He knew the manufactured background provided by Mission Recovery would hold up under scrutiny and Gin's rash move to marry only bolstered his reasons for being in Las Vegas, but he couldn't shake the feeling that everything was about to come crashing down.

No fewer than six pairs of eyes were on them at any given time. More, if you counted the electronic surveillance he knew watched from behind the discreet black bubbles dotting the ceilings.

It wasn't worth thinking about the cameras he couldn't see.

"Do you need a drink?" Her hand linked with his, she leaned in close. He was starting to like the habit. "You're twitchy."

He smiled down at her. "Blame the extra security."

"Aw. Got a case of performance anxiety?"

"Not even close." He kissed the smirk off her face. "But it is our honeymoon. Shouldn't we be upstairs, doing..." He didn't finish the thought, too pleased by the soft pink color staining her cheeks.

Maybe he wasn't the only one affected by this happy couple role-playing gig. When they were tucked into that booth, the floral scent of her perfume had been more enticing than the perfectly prepared steak. It wasn't the smartest idea, but he was more than ready to toss the ground rules out the nearest window.

"You know I have a job to do."

"Any messages?"

She peered into her clutch. From his vantage point he could see the little tracking icon. The virus remained stationary. "Nope."

At least one of them had info that made sense because the deal was slated for tomorrow.

He leaned close to her ear as bets were placed on the next throw of the dice. "What do you think of making a side bet?"

She peered up at him from under her lashes. "Such as?"

He reeled in the request he wanted to make and opted for something less likely to scare her off. "A hard eight and we blow this pop stand and go dancing."

"Pop stand?" she chuckled.

"Bet or no?" He called as the dealer said much the same to the gamblers surrounding the table.

"Says the man who doesn't gamble."

"You're stalling."

Her wicked smirk lit up her face. "You're on."

He grinned back. To the rest of the world he was amused by the player milking the moment for all it was worth before he sent the dice flying down the table. In reality, it was the anticipation of holding Gin close that put him in a good mood.

"Looks like I'm a lucky loser," she said when the dice stopped and the dealer raked away the two chips she'd placed on the table.

"Let's hope you still feel that way when we're dancing."

They made their way to the club, slipping through the crowd, the security team surrounding them but never crowding them.

"What do you think they'd do if we were attacked?" Gin asked.

"More than necessary considering what the two of us are capable of. If something does happen, we should probably let them take the lead."

"It would be the polite thing to do because it's their house."

"Well said."

Jason realized someone must have called ahead as they neared the club and a hostess appeared to escort them inside. "I could get used to this," he admitted.

Gin nodded her agreement, but conversation halted as he swept her out onto the dance floor.

Thanks to a required cotillion class as a kid, he was probably better equipped for the structure of a tango or waltz, but he could hold his own with the steady beat that currently had the dance floor jammed to capacity.

Gin moved well to the music, and for a few minutes it was a relief to just be a couple out on a date. He couldn't recall the last time that had happened.

He didn't resent his career or the hard choices he'd made along the way. The various challenges were what got him fired up until the mission was complete. He just didn't realize how long it had been since he'd had a different kind of fun.

When she fanned her face with her clutch and gestured to the bar, he nodded, ready for a cold beer. With his hand at her back they slipped through the crowd and when they reached the bar, he double-checked with her and ordered bottled beer for each of them. The bartender didn't bat an eye when Jason requested the bottles be opened in front of them.

Gin elbowed him. "Paranoid?"

He smiled. It was becoming a habit when she was around. "Doesn't mean they're not out to get us." He tapped his bottle to hers. "To paranoia."

"Cheers." She took a long drink, then patted the bottle like an ice pack along her low neckline and up over the place where Wallace had held the knife. "I haven't danced like that in years."

"Me either."

"Why do you hate casinos?"

"That's not an accurate statement."

"Bull."

He debated how much to share, knew it was better not to share anything that could be used against him later. The urge to tell her everything surprised him.

"Come on," she prodded. "I'm your wife."

He shook his head, still adjusting to the concept of wedded bliss. "My dad was a gambler. Always looking for the big score."

"So you had to be Mr. Dependable in the family?"

"Something like that."

She leaned forward, her hands on his knees, and he struggled not to stare at the sexy display of her breasts. Was that black lace under the dress?

"You're not making this easy, sweetheart."

"Well, you're distracting me." He dropped his gaze, just for a second, to her full breasts, then jerked his eyes back up to meet hers. He nudged her shoulders until she was sitting upright.

"Look, my past is over and done."

"But it made you who you are."

"*I* made me." He smiled to soften the contradiction.

"With more than a little help from the U.S. Army." The music changed to the slower pace of a love song and he seized the opportunity. Standing, he held out his hand. "May I have this dance?"

She tilted her head, blatantly studying him, and the little furrow appeared between her auburn eyebrows.

"I'd love to," she replied, putting her hand in his.

When they were swaying to the music, he wasn't sure he'd ever felt anything more right than having Ginger in his arms. "Is this our first dance as husband and wife?"

She nodded and one corner of her mouth kicked up into half of her usual grin. "I'm sorry—"

"Shh." He didn't want to hear an apology right now. This marriage might not be destined to last, but he wanted to pretend, at least for tonight. "Then that makes this our song."

"Oh, that's not playing fair."

"Isn't it?"

"Not even close." But she laid her head on his shoulder.

Mesmerized by the play of light on her hair, he found the various colors from deep gold to auburn that gave her hair such a rich glossy hue.

He pressed his lips to her hair with all the affection he would show if they were meant to stay together. If he'd thought about it, he would have called it sappy. Then again, they were in public and that had been the game plan.

"Do you really have a facial tomorrow?"

She looked up at him. "With our access, I can book

one easily enough. Are you implying I need some work done?"

"No." He ran his finger down the loose curl by her ear. "Do you golf?"

"Yes. Though it's been a long time." She gave a little sigh.

"Let's go play tomorrow. We could use the fresh air and sunshine."

She looked up at him, and he knew she saw more than he wanted her to see. "We can do that. The sale is an evening thing."

He dropped a kiss on her lips. "Thank you."

"Thank me later." She glanced around at the dance floor. "I wish I could just spot the buyer already."

A movement near the bar caught his eye. One of their tall, dark and stoic entourage was on the radio.

"We may have trouble," he murmured, turning as they danced so she could get a look.

"How do you want to play it?"

"I'd rather not aggravate the locals. We need to get access to the security videos."

"We can be casual. But it does look like something is up."

Definitely. Their protection approached the dance floor and signaled them toward the bar. Keeping her tucked to his side, they left as the song faded.

He exchanged a look with Gin as they followed the team behind the bar and through the kitchen.

"Hang on," Gin said, bringing the whole group to a stop. "What's going on?"

"Details are sketchy," the team leader said. "But someone just tried to break into the penthouse."

"That's ridiculous." Gin shook her head. "There's a guard posted in plain sight by the elevator."

"He's been drugged. The guard posted inside the door caught the burglar before any damage could be done."

"Inside?" Jason questioned.

"Just inside the vestibule, sir."

Jason waved it off. "I'm not trying to challenge your methods." He was more worried they'd see he'd taken up residence in the second bedroom and question the newlywed story. "Can we talk with him?" It had to be Frost trying to track down Gin. He reached for the inner pocket of his jacket, where he'd stashed the identification he'd brought along tonight.

"You're welcome to watch on a monitor, but I can't let you in the room with her."

"Her?" Jason and Gin said in unison.

The team leader shrugged a beefy shoulder. "Female burglars are more common than you think. Her method's a little different, but she's not nearly as bizarre as some we get around here."

"I bet," Gin muttered.

"Can you think of any reason you've been targeted?"

Gin looked up at him and gave an almost imperceptible shake of her head.

"No," Jason replied for them both. "We came here for a convention and got married." He put on his best besotted groom smile. "It's that simple and shouldn't matter to anyone but us."

"Well, come on then. But you're only invited as a professional courtesy."

"Thanks," Jason said. One step at a time. If they proved they could maintain their composure and just watch, maybe they could press the advantage and get a look at the security cameras.

They followed the team through the extensive network of halls and facilities that made everything run so smoothly for the guests and patrons of the hotel and casino.

There were plenty of cameras back here, too. Beside him, Jason knew Gin was also memorizing the route and prepared for the situation to change at any moment.

Mr. Latimore, chief of hotel security, met them at the door with a friendly introduction and ushered them into his office. The space looked more like a large living room with all the expected creature comforts than an office.

"I thought you'd be more comfortable watching from here." Latimore raised a remote toward the flat-panel monitor on the wall. "Have a seat. Would you like a drink?"

They declined the drink but sat together on the leather sofa, hands linked and balanced on his thigh. Just two normal people who'd inexplicably found themselves targets. If they got any better at this marriage and partnership thing, Jason might have to find a better-looking ring than the simple gold band she wore now.

He waited for the cold fear that should accompany such a thought, but it didn't come. Strange, but the thought of forever with this woman felt right. He'd have to figure it out later because he could see on the monitor that a blond-haired woman had entered the other room, a hotel security guard behind her.

Jason narrowed his gaze. It was the same woman they'd seen earlier in the restaurant, the one who'd tried to poison him in the bar last night.

"That's who tried to break in?" he asked.

"Yes, sir," Latimore replied.

She was seated at a small table, and the security officer across from her started his questioning.

Gin didn't twitch and her breathing didn't change, but somehow Jason knew something was wrong. They listened to the standard series of questions, but no one in either the interrogation room or here in the office was buying the answers.

"It was a dare. I just went up to look around." The blonde leaned forward. "Which celebrity is it? Come on," she wheedled. "I can't go back to my friends empty-handed."

"Discretion is part of our service."

"You're no fun."

The interrogator ignored that. "You aren't registered in our hotel."

"Does that mean you're about to be indiscreet with me?"

Jason recognized the dumb blonde routine, figured she'd ride it all the way to a misdemeanor charge—and a hefty fine—except for the poison thing.

"Do you know what she used on the guard?"

"Nothing lethal, just enough to knock him out. Probably a derivative of ketamine, based on his reactions.

The guard inside heard voices near the elevator and assumed it was the other guard's girlfriend, but when he looked out, it was this woman."

"So she really didn't get past the vestibule?" Gin asked.

"No, ma'am."

She squeezed his hand, and when he met her gaze he saw tears welling in her eyes. He knew the tears were for show, but something had spooked her.

"Jason," she whispered. "This is ridiculous." She cleared her throat and turned to Latimore. "We appreciate all you've done, but maybe we should change hotels," Gin said.

"I'm not sure that would make any difference, honey," Jason argued gently. "Someone is determined to ruin our honeymoon."

"Our staff doesn't intend to let that happen. Our teams can keep you safe."

Jason knew it wasn't true. The woman was likely nothing more than a pawn in the bigger game. She probably didn't even know who really hired her to give them grief. "Does this woman have any ties to the person who opened fire at the pool?"

"Not that we've been able to connect, but we've just started investigating. I have teams going through all of the footage over the past several days, tracking her movements through our property."

"That doesn't eliminate the idea that she met with someone elsewhere."

"That's true." Latimore shook his head. "All of the casinos share information about this sort of risk." He turned down the volume on the monitor as the woman started weeping loudly.

Jason leaned forward, balancing his elbows on his knees. "This woman sent me a drugged drink at the bar last night."

"I haven't seen that report."

"We didn't file one."

Latimore leaned closer to his desk. "Would you like to?"

"No, thanks." Jason reached into his pocket for a business card. "We handled it. If you'd just keep us updated, please."

"I can do that. Standard procedure is to hand her over to LVPD. I can assure you she won't be allowed back on the premises."

"Thanks," Gin said. "That's the best news I've heard so far."

Now that Latimore had seen his business card, Jason ventured into deeper water. "What's the status of the incident at the pool?"

"The room he most likely used to stage the attack was clean. From what the police have told me, the shooter hasn't been caught, but he has not struck again."

"Thank you." To Gin, he said, "Shall we go?"

Gin nodded and they got to their feet.

"Please enjoy the rest of your evening. My team will make sure no one else can bother you." As they left, they were once more flanked by burly men in dark suits who escorted them back to the public areas of the hotel.

"Where to now?"

"The room," Gin replied. "I'm tired of these heels."

He didn't believe it. "We could rest your feet at a blackjack table for a bit. There's that line of credit with our name on it."

She shot him a look. "Maybe tomorrow."

"What about the sports betting room?" He couldn't risk being alone with her right now. That dance had him wanting something she wasn't offering. They were supposed to be platonic in private, but he wasn't sure he could manage that anymore. "A show maybe?"

She stopped short and went toe to toe with him. "What am I missing?"

Me, he thought but couldn't say it. "Have you spotted someone?"

"No." The defeat in her voice had him wanting to make all of this right for her.

The truth was, in a crowded place like this the only way to find anyone was to become an easier target. She might be tracking the virus, but he wasn't convinced Frost had vacated the premises, which meant she was still in danger for reasons neither of them comprehended.

"Let's go upstairs." She pressed her body closer to his, whispering in his ear. "We need to talk."

Talk. If that was her plan, he needed time to cool off. "Thirty minutes." He'd spotted Frost playing blackjack before. Maybe he'd show up again. "I want to look around."

"Fine. But we leave when you're five hundred down."

Chapter Eleven

Gin couldn't believe Jason was up two grand after an hour of play. Her feet had never really been the problem, but the champagne she was sipping was starting to take a toll. It was enough to give her a sweet buzz but not so much that she couldn't keep an eye out for Isely or anyone who might be connected to him.

She had no idea what Jason might be looking for beyond the next card, the next bet. For a man who didn't care for casinos, he sure knew how to play with house money.

"That's it for me," he said, gathering his chips and pushing back from the table at last.

His hand was warm across her back, his palm resting lightly at her waist. Oh, she needed to find something else to think about. Casting her gaze over the faces in the crowded casino, she prayed for some sign of the seller or Isely to distract her from Jason's touch.

The second glass of champagne was clearly a mistake, making her all too eager to forget the thrill of the mission in favor of the sensual promise of the man at her side.

Upstairs he was supposed to stop touching her. That

was good, though she was having a difficult time re-membering why right now. If he kept touching her, she could keep touching him and she wouldn't have to tell him she recognized the blonde in the interrogation room. It should have been obvious last night, and she felt like a fool for not seeing it, not putting the pieces together.

"Can we take a turn through the shops, please?"

He gave her a dubious look. "I thought your feet hurt."

"They're rested." She needed a bit of time for the champagne to wear off before she was alone with him. The ground rules might have been her idea, but she'd broken them once with that kiss before dinner. And with this buzz, she'd lost her professional detachment where Jason was concerned.

He turned down the promenade, the security detail shifting along with them.

"Mrs. Grant?" One of them stepped closer.

"Yes?"

"This was just delivered for you."

She stared for a long moment at the note he tried to hand her, finally accepting it and tucking it into her purse. "Thank you."

"You aren't going to open it?" Jason asked.

"Hadn't planned to."

"I think you should."

"It can wait until we're in the room."

He shook his head. "We're a team at this point. Se-crets will only get us hurt. Open it."

Sexy and logical. She liked the combination a little too much.

"Fine." He led her to a bench and they sat down. She withdrew the note and opened it.

You can't protect him.

The letters were clipped from a glossy magazine and glued into the hotel stationery like a retro-style ransom note. It sent a chill down her spine and instantly cleared the champagne haze from her brain.

"We have to review the video from the front desk."

"Why?" He smiled at her like the note contained a sweet gift rather than a bold threat. "It won't do any good."

He was probably right, but she wasn't ready to give up. "It must be from the woman who's been bothering us."

"You know her?"

"I've been thinking about her the past few hours. I don't know her directly. She worked at a restaurant Isely favored in Germany. I saw her around. She was a brunette then."

"Now we just have to figure out why Isely wanted me out of commission."

"How can you be so calm?"

"A lesson I learned from you, perhaps? After all, you were the one being shot at poolside."

She glared at him.

"All right." He leaned back, spread his arms wide and all she could think was that he was inviting whoever was behind this to take their best shot. "This means we're making progress."

She exhaled, long and slow. "Maybe."

"Definitely. We just have to figure out in which direction."

"Yours apparently," she grumbled. "All is holding steady on my end."

"Except for the would-be burglars." His fingers teased her nape. "I was sent here to back up a human asset. No need to shoot at me or break into my rooms for that."

"No. But the sniper targeting me doesn't fit either. And they planted evidence in *your* room."

"Are you implying we're outmatched? Let's go upstairs and see if I can track down any news on other shootings or preliminary evidence on the ones that have already taken place."

As they started back toward the bank of elevators that served their penthouse, Gin had to know. "Are you telling me you're a hacker, too?"

"Not even close." He pressed the button for the elevator. "I'm just good at tracking down information." He scowled. "But I do have limitations."

Further discussion had to wait for privacy as two men from the security team boarded the elevator with them. The car surged up toward the penthouse level, but Gin's instincts prickled with warning. Jason sensed something, too; she could tell from the quick tap of his fingers against her lower back.

The guard to her left punched the button for the floor just below the penthouse then turned around, brandishing a knife. "Cooperate and no one gets hurt," he ordered.

Gin shifted closer to Jason. "I guess the manager doesn't know his staff as well as he thinks."

"Guess not," Jason agreed.

"I'm sure you have your orders," she said to the guard, "but please, we've been through enough. Can you put that away?"

"Shut up," the second guard barked, his deep voice resonating in the small space.

"Rude," Gin observed, offended and pretending this wasn't a life or death situation.

Feeling Jason tense beside her as the elevator slowed, she glanced at him. He winked and she understood he had a plan. He gave her a little nudge and she ducked. Jason spun, knocking away the knife.

With a bellow, guard two rushed them. Gin kicked and he went down with a shriek as his knee buckled in a way nature never intended. She then landed a blow to his larynx, cutting short his pained cries. She slammed the stop button on the elevator, hoping no one would override it and change the odds before they could wrap this up.

Behind her Jason exchanged blows with the other guard. He was holding his own, dodging and swerving, barely escaping a rib-crushing punch by sliding closer to the bigger man.

She wasn't counting on any help. If these two had been bought off by the enemy, chances were good they'd paid someone in the security room to look the other way during this attack.

The guard she'd dropped was struggling to get back in the mix, using the corners of the car to help get back on his feet. Gin laced her fingers for more power and took a swing like a batter hitting for the fence. The blow snapped the man's head back and he dropped to the floor, out cold.

"Best sedative I've found," she said, dusting off her hands while Jason pounded his opponent into a puddle on the floor.

"Nice work," she said. "Again." She reached around and put the elevator into motion for the penthouse.

"Same goes for you. *Again*." He rubbed his jaw and cracked his neck, then smiled. "Have you checked for IDs?"

"Go ahead," she shrugged. "It can't matter. They're obviously hired help."

"They might know which one of us is the target."

"However it started, I'm pretty sure we both are now. Whoever hired these two obviously knows who we are and that we're working together."

The elevator chimed and the doors parted. Jason peered out first. "Looks clear."

"No surprise," Gin muttered. "They were probably told we didn't need them anymore." She grabbed the ankle of the man nearest her. "Help a girl out?"

Jason grabbed the other ankle and together they dragged him into the penthouse. "You get the other one. I'll get the old reliable duct tape."

Jason had the traitorous guards in a heap by the wet bar when she returned. They taped each of the men's wrists and ankles together, then taped them to the pipe under the small sink.

"That should buy us a few minutes."

Jason agreed. "I've got their phones. That might give us something. And I sent the elevator back down so no one would come looking for it."

"Then we'd better hurry."

For the second time in hardly forty-eight hours, they packed in a rush. This time she knew they had to leave the hotel. Whoever was behind the problems plaguing them had enough money or leverage to get the cooperation they needed. Gin was done playing the game with a stacked deck.

She paused at the door to the penthouse. "Goodbye, best room ever." Couldn't blame a girl for enjoying a penthouse suite…even for just a little while.

"It was nice."

"*Nice?* That's the best you say about that glorious space?" She started for the stairs, but Jason led her in the other direction.

"Service access is safer."

"Hello? It was service guys who just tried to kill us."

"No, they were extras, hired on just to deal with us."

She didn't bother asking him how he knew this for certain. They started down the stairs, Jason carrying both suitcases while she had the computer bag. After half a flight, she slipped out of her heels. "Are we going the whole way like this?"

"I hope not. Do you still have your old room key?"

"Yeah."

"Which tower?"

"This one."

"Good."

"You can't be serious about staying here. Talk about

long odds." Funny, last time he was the one who wanted to leave this hotel. A few more attempts on their lives were required to get her there, but she was squarely there now.

"We have to stay. All the players are here."

Duh. "And they know us now."

"Exactly."

"Jason." She stopped and forced him to do the same. "That doesn't make sense. Safety, regrouping—that makes sense."

"Only if you want to keep playing defense."

He winked at her and she sputtered, unable to think how to contradict him.

"How many more flights?" She was already getting dizzy from the fast pace. The man had a keen sense of balance as he somehow managed this with a suitcase in each hand. She, however, was likely dehydrated from the two glasses of champagne. And she was frustrated and flustered. She *never* got flustered. He did this to her. She was certain of it!

"Two more, then we'll try for an elevator."

"You know security is probably wondering what we're doing."

"They see plenty of weird stuff. By the time they catch up with us—if they even bother—we'll have a story together."

She hoped he was right. The etched treads of the cement steps bit into her feet, but as long as she wasn't leaving a trail of blood—she looked back to confirm—she would make it.

"Behind-the-scenes Vegas isn't so posh," she decided, suddenly feeling utterly disillusioned.

"It's a service stairwell, Gin. What did you expect?"

"I expected to stay on the pretty side of the hotel," she admitted.

"You've worked in grittier places."

"True." Which was only one more reason she appreciated the luxurious jobs.

She stopped when he did and held her breath while he opened and peered beyond the door. He listened for a few seconds then looked around the corner to see if the way was clear. Easing the door closed, he took a deep breath.

"We'll move out and to the left to the guest elevator. Take that to your floor."

She nodded.

He opened the door and she followed him, grateful for the reprieve of the soft carpet under her feet. He pulled out both suitcase handles and rolled them along, like any other guests in search of their room.

"Keep your head down," he muttered when they reached the elevator.

She leaned against his shoulder, doing her best weary wife impersonation. He kissed her on the top of her head. How many times was that now? He was so good at this married thing, she wondered if he'd ever done it for real. What she'd dug up on him said no, but there had to be a serious relationship somewhere in his past. In her experience men didn't nurture women the way Jason had been doing it without prior on the job training.

She cultivated lust in her male targets because it

blurred logic and served her better in the field. But there was an inherent kindness in Jason that had her longing for something different. Something more...personal. And no cultivation had been required with him. The lust came naturally.

For a moment she tried to imagine sharing so much with other men she'd used or targeted, and she couldn't see it happening. Neither could she see it working out with men she'd worked with inside the agency.

Only Jason.

Must be the kisses, she thought, pressing the number for the floor where her alternate identity was still checked in. When they reached her room, they'd review the ground rules again. She was a big girl and didn't need more tenderness from him. As for whatever that moment was in the penthouse before dinner, well... probably best if they avoided an encore performance of that, too.

"Do you have your keycard?"

"Hmm?" She looked up at him. "Oh, yes." She fished it out of her clutch. Because he was in front, she handed it to him to slide through the lock.

The do-not-disturb sign was still on the door and she hoped it meant no one had connected this room to Ginger Olin, CIA.

He pushed the door open and they stepped into the room. Nothing had been tossed or damaged. Everything was just as she'd left it.

"Wait here."

She stood by the door, humored by his gallant effort to clear the room of any threat. Hadn't she just proved she could be an asset in a conflict? For that matter, hadn't saving his reputation, if not his life, last night proved as much?

Of course he didn't remember that clearly, but she felt they needed to get a handle on it soon. She couldn't let her rash decision to drag him into her case prevent her from accomplishing her task.

"Satisfied?"

"Almost." He turned on the television and tuned it to a music channel. Leaving the suitcases by the bed, he came back to join her at the door. His warm hands glided over her shoulders and down her back until he cupped her bottom and pulled her close to him. Oh, my, she thought, suddenly all too eager to toss out the ground rules. But when she met his gaze, she saw his eyes weren't full of desire but rather sharp and focused. He was in business mode.

"The room might be bugged," he whispered against her ear.

Why didn't she think of that? Because it was all she could do not to melt into his touch. "Okay," she murmured, nipping lightly at his earlobe. "Got any protection?"

"Always," he teased.

She gave a throaty laugh, though it was tough to tell where the game stopped and her real hunger for him began. "How should we proceed?"

"Careful and thorough or fast and hot." He trailed kisses down her neck. "Your choice."

"Mmm." She ran her bare foot up and down over his

calf. "I like thorough." Reaching back, she threw the dead bolt then twisted to push the swing lock into place.

"Me, too." He pulled a signal jammer from his pocket and turned it on.

Together they searched the room for listening devices and cameras. Even though finding a camera might alert the party on the other end, no way was she going to let anyone watch what probably wouldn't happen anyway.

Probably? Tempting as he was, taking this fake marriage to the next level of intimacy would be the worst possible thing to do.

Cases in the past had required the use of her every feminine skill. During some cases she'd met someone along the way and enjoyed a brief passionate affair. As much as her hormones shouted *do it,* her instincts declared he was a danger to her ability to focus and getting in deeper would change everything.

Done checking the vent near the bed, she hopped down to the floor and gave a soft cry at the hot bolt of pain shooting from her left foot to her knee.

"What is it?" Jason rushed to her side.

"Nothing. I bruised my foot in the fight and it's mad at me."

"I'll go for ice," he said.

She was going to protest, except she noticed the swelling along his cheekbone. "Good idea. I think we could both use some. I'll find the aspirin."

"Deal."

Alone in the room, she looked around. What had seemed so fabulous when she checked in looked almost dingy compared to the penthouse they'd just escaped.

Maybe they should have locked themselves in up there and made a stand. Except they didn't have a clear lead on his enemy and she could hardly follow the virus vial if she was locked in a room.

The more she played it through her head, the more convinced she became that the personal attacks were about him. There might be a few international guests in town who would rather she were permanently out of their lives, but none of them knew her well enough to target her.

She changed the television station to the news network, but she turned the volume down. They didn't need all the local downers typical of news programs, but they did need to know if the local police had announced they were hunting a sniper.

Her foot was aching more as the adrenaline faded from her system. Adrenaline was more than a small factor in her attraction to Jason. Yes, he was gorgeous, and each time he was kind to her, every little touch that set her nerves reeling made it that much harder to remember this was temporary.

He returned with the full ice bucket topped with the liner bag full of more ice.

"It's not champagne, but it might feel as good."

"Probably better." She remembered the heady sensation as she'd watched him at the blackjack table. "I've had enough alcohol for now anyway." Vegas did enough to reduce the few inhibitions she still had.

He prepped an ice bag for both of them and smiled as she traded him two aspirin for one ice bag. He raised his bag in a toast. "To ease what ails you."

She chuckled and tapped her ice to his. "Hear, hear," she said, sinking onto the love seat while he took the chair.

JASON RELAXED AS the news anchor's voice droned quietly in the background and they sat in a comfortable silence. It was strange to be so at ease with a woman he barely knew. Maybe it was as simple as being with someone who understood the unique challenges of covert operations. When you had a chance to rest, you took it. It was a rare thing to meet a woman who knew how to live in the moment as well as he did.

A face popped up in the corner of the screen and Jason sat up, the idea of rest momentarily forgotten along with the throbbing in his cheek. He reached for the remote and dialed up the volume to listen to the report.

Bullet points appeared on the screen, giving a brief overview of the known facts. The body of James Redding, retired military expert who was in town for a security conference, had been found under the convention center monorail station early this morning. "Redding told friends he felt poorly and planned to go to his room to rest, according to a conference spokesperson. The apparent victim of a shooting, his body was found by monorail personnel early this morning. If you have any information relevant to this investigation, please call…"

Jason muted the volume but couldn't stop staring at the picture of Redding's face as he carefully leaned his cheek against the ice bag again.

"Jason?"

"Hmm."

"Did you know him?"

Jason nodded.

"Did you know he was here?"

"No."

"But isn't that conference your cover?"

"Yes, but I haven't bothered to do more than check in and occasionally walk by the vendor booths."

"Instead you've been waiting here to be contacted."

"Yes." He knew she was starting to draw the same conclusions about this being a setup. But only Holt knew he was here. Only Holt knew his orders and cover. The logical conclusion—that Holt was behind this—made him sick to his stomach.

She continued softly, "That shooting was supposed to look like your work." Her gaze locked on the television screen, where shots of the area where the body was found flashed in sequence.

"Agreed." Wasn't much point in arguing it and definitely not with the only person who knew he was innocent.

"Drugged, you wouldn't have had an alibi for that."

"Are you fishing for more gratitude? Because I have plenty, believe me." Jason rubbed the ice pack over his bruised knuckles, but it was Gin who shivered. "Were you trying to make a point?"

"Whoever wanted to pin that on you must know the blonde failed to contain you."

"You're saying all our recent fun is about killing me instead of framing me? The pool incident sure looked like it was all about you." Calling it a shooting rather than a mere "incident" made it too real.

"If Frost is as good as you say—"

"He is."

"—then you have to consider he missed me on purpose. Think about it. There were too many variables. You're the expert in the field—could any innocent bystander have moved into the shot?"

"Not from that angle," Jason argued.

"Exactly! He had no idea where we would sit, what we would do. But he had elevation and angle on his side."

"That's why he works with Wallace. To keep him informed, to stage the scene to misdirect the investigation."

"Wallace tailed me? Us? I don't think so. I would have noticed," she rebutted.

"Or not," Jason said with a shrug. "Makes sense. Whatever you're working on, someone wants to stop you."

"Then why not just kill me?" She gave an exasperated sigh. "Going way out on a theoretical limb here, even if he really was after me, he still missed me on purpose. It was either a scare tactic or part of a setup. Maybe both."

"Tell it to the lifeguard," he grumbled. He shifted the ice pack to his cheekbone, irritated he hadn't dodged the elbow strike more efficiently.

"She'll be back on the job in two to four weeks," Gin said dismissively.

"You can't really be that cold." In fact, he knew she

wasn't that cold. She put on the master spy, cold, hard mask but underneath she was warm and soft…. *Stop, Jason.*

"I can be when we should be focused on who's out to get *you*."

He wasn't ready to go there just yet. "How's your foot?"

"Fine." She moved the melting ice bag back over the bruise, which was turning the side of her foot red and deep purple. "Don't try to distract me. I think you have a working theory about the sniper."

"Contrary to popular belief, snipers don't always stay in one place for days waiting for the shot." He shook his head, his mind in the past. During his stint with Interpol, he'd been ordered to line up a shot on a woman who'd ordered the assassination of a British spy. She enjoyed sunbathing topless on the French Riviera. He had the clear shot and his finger on the trigger when he'd been called off. He'd packed up his gun and spent the rest of the day flirting with a lovely brunette farther down the beach.

He could count on one hand the people who knew about his involvement with that operation and numerous others. The logical conclusion was about as illogical as anything could be. Holt hadn't reached his current position without being thoroughly vetted by more than one agency and undergoing extensive background checks and psych evaluations.

There had to be another answer. A mole in a nearby department somewhere. An undetected bug in Holt's office. There had to be an explanation that didn't involve his direct superior's plans to put the blame on him for murders in Las Vegas. "How many covert operations do you think go down in Vegas on an annual basis?"

"Not enough of mine," she groused.

"You like it here?"

"What's not to like? The food is fabulous, you can dress up or down, there's always something going on, and you can hide in plain sight."

"Or get married, if all else fails."

"I told you I was saving your butt. You'd remember that if your brain had been working properly." She limped over and perched on the side of his chair, pushed his hair back from his forehead. "Worried I'll take half of your assets in the divorce?"

"Nothing to take," he lied. "Government salary, government car."

"I don't believe you." She pulled the ice bag away from his cheek and brushed the spot with her lips. "Your ops are so black, there's no way they'd risk a typical government fleet contract. You shouldn't lie to your wife."

"Pot." He pointed to her, then to himself. "Kettle." He put the ice pack back on his cheek just to take away the heat that lingered from her touch. "Tell me more about your case. Any chance you're the operative I'm supposed to escort out of this town?"

"I answered that yesterday." She stood up and started to pace before her bruised foot stopped her. "CIA has no other assets here that I know of."

"Technically you shouldn't be working here."

She turned, her grin positively impish. It shouldn't

amuse him, but it did. "Technically I'm not." Her grin faded. "Months ago, I was tasked with following the virus. I've found two of the four known vials, but the biologist who created it is still out there somewhere."

"Or dead."

"That tends to happen when people cross the Isely family." She slumped onto the couch.

He walked over and picked up her feet, propping them up with pillows to ease the potential swelling. Her level of pain made him worry she was nursing a hairline fracture. It was a common enough injury from the way she'd made the strike against the thug's knee.

"If the biologist is dead, that makes the product more valuable."

"Not necessarily," she countered. "Only the whole-saler needs to know about the supplier or manufacturer. They can spread whatever lies work to their advantage to boost the market value of a product."

"So what is the wholesaler saying about the virus you're tracking?"

She frowned. "Nothing."

"Why not?" He returned to his chair, needing the distance to keep his hands off her.

"Well, until you started asking questions I assumed it was because the stuff is so new and relatively un-proven."

"Relatively?"

Her eyebrows climbed toward her hairline, and he realized he didn't want to hear the answer. "Do you know the seller on sight?" he asked.

"Yes. But he isn't really my goal. I've been tracking GPS tags on the vials themselves."

"Can the seller identify you?"

"Highly unlikely." She sat up and tossed a small pillow at him. "Hey. You got me off topic. We were discussing the shooting and who's behind it. Talk to me. I'm a great listener."

"Except I don't need a great listener. I'm used to working alone." Irritated, he stood up and walked toward the bathroom, dumping the melting ice out of the bag and into the bathtub.

Talking about this wouldn't help. He needed some quiet to review the facts and crack the phones he'd taken off the thugs. Wouldn't it be ideal if he could get a look at the bullet that had ended Redding's life? How much could the cover story work to his advantage? A security conference offered a variety of suspects for this incident. Thanks to the media, most people liked to assume those in private security frequently went off the deep end. Whoever caught this case at the local level should know better, but stereotypes were hard to overcome.

His cover story closely mirrored his real story, including his military background, but not his sniper expertise. It was only a matter of time before the local law enforcement realized he had a potential connection to Redding. Along with his presence as a witness to the incident at the pool, this setup might catch him yet.

Without Gin—and her timely intervention at the bar—he might already be a person of interest in this case. He couldn't see any way that his involvement and possible detention benefitted Holt, but no one else knew he was here. There had to be another answer, or he had to accept a terrible truth about betrayal.

"Jason?"

She was right behind him. He'd felt her before she'd said a word. He met her gaze in the reflection of the mirror. "Yeah?"

"What can I do?"

He shook his head. He wasn't a fan of her tactics, but there was no doubt getting married offered him an incontrovertible alibi.

"Keep the marriage certificate close, I guess," he suggested.

"That's hardly a real answer."

True. He couldn't give her an answer while his mind wrestled with the best way to get a look at the crime scene and maybe the evidence in last night's murder. What the hell was going on here?

"Right." She slid down the zipper hidden in the side seam of her dress.

He'd wondered how she'd poured herself into the snug, black sheath.

She started peeling the dress from her body and he caught sight of sheer black lace against the pure ivory of her skin. He stilled her hand before he saw more than she intended to show. Married on paper didn't give him the right to ogle her. No matter what happened last night, no matter that he couldn't remember it, he'd been indisposed. He was in full control now and he refused to take advantage of her.

"What are you doing?" he asked.

"Changing clothes. You want to go out to the crime scene."

"Did I say that out loud?"

She smiled, and it was warm and kind without an ounce of smirk in her expression. She reached up but stopped short of touching him. Her hand fell away. "You didn't have to."

He stared as she pulled jeans and a sweater out of her suitcase then rooted around until she found socks and tennis shoes.

The woman had packed duct tape, so he shouldn't be surprised that she was prepped for any occasion.

"Are you going like that? Crime scenes usually aren't formal events." She kept herself covered with her dress, but it was clear that wouldn't last much longer.

He lurched into motion and headed for his own suit-case. "No." He couldn't figure out his sudden modesty. That had flown out the window this morning when she'd put him in the shower. But it was different now when he was completely aware of her and completely aware of his reactions to her. He swapped dress slacks for his own jeans and traded the shirt and tie for a polo shirt.

Before he could pull it over his head, he felt her staring at him.

He swiveled around. "What is it?"

"Admiring your tattoo. What does it symbolize?"

"A night of drunken stupidity." He pulled his shirt over his head and turned around before she could blink away the flash of pain in her eyes.

"Why are you pushing me away again?"

He bit back the truth. Letting her in only meant a bigger ache when this was over. They could hardly stay married, considering their divergent careers. "I'm not. I'm just thinking."

"So give me the short version."

"We were working a case in Dublin during my Interpol days. O'Marron convinced me a Celtic warrior dragon was the right choice."

"I'd agree." She looked at him. "It suits you." She tied her shoe with a bit too much enthusiasm, wincing when the laces cinched tightly across her injured foot.

"You could wait here."

"Not a chance." Her emerald eyes were snapping with ire and he regretted putting it there. "Whether or not you want to admit it, you need me. Especially at the crime scene."

"Okay." He wouldn't argue, afraid of revealing more emotion than she might be ready to take from him. He clipped his holster onto his belt and slid his sport coat over it. Tucking the wallet with his badge into the inner pocket, he looked at her. "How do you suggest we proceed?"

"Did you rent a car?"

"Yes."

"Great. Let's drive on out to the scene and then you can let me do the talking."

He found the key to the rental and confirmed she had a key for the room, and together they cautiously made their way out of the hotel to the valet stand.

Caution was the word of the day. They'd been lucky so far. Another run-in with trouble and their luck might just run out.

Chapter Twelve

When the valet returned with the car, a bright yellow Corvette, Gin had more cause to re-evaluate Mission Recovery's golden boy.

It would be easier if he'd open up to her, but he wasn't big on sharing. She could hardly fault him for that, but after what they'd recently survived she'd expected him to be more forthcoming.

Common sense and a basic understanding of investigative curiosity was enough to convince her he needed to visit the scene. Something about either the victim or the method of the shooting had tripped up Jason. Which meant there was no way she was letting him do this alone.

She recognized a setup and knew he did, too, and if he wouldn't share his theories, she'd develop her own.

The big engine purred as he pulled out on the Strip, and she couldn't help but admire the glitz of all the lights and stunning casino facades. "When you were with Interpol, did you ever run across Isely or his family?"

"No."

"You're sure?"

"Yes. And you're fishing."

Like she had any choice but to fish for information when he was doing the strong, silent routine. At this rate he was as useful to her as one of the marble statues planted around Caesar's.

"Just trying to determine if my connection to you puts my own case at risk."

"Is that your way of asking for a divorce?"

"No." The question automatically drew her eye to the lights bouncing off his wedding band as he used his left hand to steer while his right rested lightly on the gear shift. Within reach if she chose to make personal contact.

Too bad he wasn't giving off any signal that said he'd be receptive to her touch right now. She might have teased him more when he'd reacted to the glimpse of her lacy bra, but when they did make love—and she decided they would—she wanted his undivided attention.

As they turned off Las Vegas Boulevard toward the crime scene at the monorail station, he cleared his throat. "Since you're doing the talking, why don't you give me a general idea of your approach?"

"I tend to wing it. Just play along."

"Great."

"It will be." She pulled a camera out of her tote. "And memorable. You can be my cameraman."

He turned toward her, one eyebrow arched. "We're still talking about the case, right?" He pulled to a stop behind a line of police cars and other official vehicles.

She handed him the camera. "Of course we are." She

was out of the car, game face on, purpose in her stride as she sought out the lead investigator on the scene.

The news trucks were gone but the scene was plenty busy. Crime scene techs in their well-known jackets with cameras and evidence bags crawled over every inch of the site where Redding's body had been found.

Gin knew she probably should have pushed Jason for a few details about how he knew the man. Then again, winging it hadn't failed her yet.

"Wait," Jason stopped her with a hand on her arm. "Don't do this."

"You need a look at the scene and the evidence." She smiled at him. "Trust me."

She felt him at her back as she walked up to the yellow tape barrier and stepped into character. The one she chose was a familiar British role. "I need a minute with the lead investigator."

The police officer stared at her. "He's not available. I can give him a message."

"Thanks, but that doesn't always work out so well." She handed him a business card that showed her as a reporter from London. "I'm working a story and I have information that might help with his case."

"Really?" he asked, clearly unconvinced.

"Really." She grinned at him, turned on the charm, as she caught movement from the corner of her eye. Jason was moving toward the techs. "Would you give me a quote?"

"Can't do that."

"Not even off the record? We believe there's a vigilante on a world tour picking off criminals. And, personally, I believe it's the local cops on the ground like you who'll make all the difference." She made a face and shook her head. "Not the feds or Interpol."

She had the cop's interest now and she tweaked his curiosity. "Interpol says the bloke can make a long distance shot as cleanly as a small-caliber double-tap execution. But that's hardly relevant if this was a close-range sort of thing."

The cop leaned forward, his attention completely with Gin. "It wasn't." He glanced side to side and lowered his voice. "You can't quote me, but we're thinking sniper here, too."

"One shot?"

The cop shook his head. "Two."

She waited, leaned in just a smidge more.

"Head and heart. I heard one of the other guys say the bastard—pardon my French, ma'am—was showing off with the second shot."

She nodded as if this was familiar news. In reality, it scared the hell out of her.

"That's not all."

She gave him a wide-eyed, tell-me-more look. "We think this victim is related to a fatality on the highway a couple days ago."

"The big pileup I heard about?"

The cop nodded.

"But I thought that was just an accident."

"We don't want to cause panic, but between you and me, it was a bullet in the tire of the first car that started the whole thing."

More likely, the local team didn't want to have the

FBI breathing down their necks and stealing the investigation. Which would happen if word got out they were dealing with a U.S. Army–trained sniper.

Jason's cover was just too close to the truth on this.

"Have they found where the shot came from?"

"That's the real mystery in this incident. We found the nest for the highway shooting but not this one yet."

"Hmm." She looked around, as if she could see anything useful in the dark. "Please, please give my card to the lead detective on this. What we've gathered from other incidents might be helpful."

"Have you had any incidents in the past week?"

Gin winked at him. "There's a reason I'm here and not in the UK."

"Well, Vegas is a great place for a vacation."

Wasn't he well-trained to toe the tourism line even at a crime scene? Of course, she wasn't the typical tourist. "Quite true. I've found a wealth of diversions since my arrival." She wanted to glance at Jason but didn't want to break the spell she held over the cop.

He tapped her card against his palm. "If you need a guide, I could show you around when I'm off shift."

"That could be lovely." She used her left hand to smooth her hair back, flashing her wedding band. "Go ahead and make a note of my number there." Jason was striding her way, grim determination clear in the set of his jaw. "Thank you for your time," she said extending her hand to shake his. "We'll just get out of your way."

Back in the car Jason glared for a long moment before he put the key into the ignition.

"Problem, dear?"

"A flirty reporter? That was your big idea?"

"Flirty, British reporter," she corrected. "I left my shiny fake badge in my other purse," she added.

"Right."

"What's the problem? I got useful information out of him."

"The poor sap thinks he's going to get something more than useful out of you."

"Are you jealous?"

"Of a Las Vegas rookie cop ogling my wife? No."

She watched the way he shielded his face as they rolled slowly by the personnel at the scene. "If not jealousy, what's crawled up your rear?"

"Do you even know you do that?"

"What?"

"Resort to a more colorful dialect when you're irritated."

She'd never been accused of doing it before. "I don't believe you," she said in a flat Midwestern accent. No way she'd admit the amount of concentration it took to pull it off.

"You're saying it's my influence, then?"

"No."

"My proximity?" He reached over and patted her leg, then left his big palm warm on her thigh.

With deliberate motions, like she was disposing of something unpleasant, she removed his hand from her leg and dropped it back on the gear shift between them. "Stop teasing me and just say what's on your mind."

"Now you're all business."

"I'm always all business." But she was watching his

hands as he negotiated a turn and clicked the headlights to bright. "Where are we going?"

"To check out the nest for this hit."

"You figured that out?"

"We'll know in a few minutes."

"The cop said the pileup on the interstate started with a bullet to the left front tire rather than an accidental blowout."

"Sounds about right."

"Right for what?" She wanted to shake him. Why wouldn't he share the theory he was working on? She'd been open with him. More open than she'd ever been with anyone else—including her fellow agents within the CIA. Gin wasn't sure she wanted to evaluate that development any time soon. No matter what she did or thought, her emotions were fully engaged with this man. Whoever was after him shouldn't be her concern, but she couldn't maintain her professional distance. As much as she wanted to chalk it up to the close call at the pool, or Wallace's knife at her throat, lying to herself would only make it worse.

Her heart had skipped at the sight of Jason in that bar and it wanted to keep on skipping the longer they stayed together. An agent falling like this was never a pretty sight. She was in deep here.

Not just because she knew he'd help her; she had a variety of skills to coerce any red-blooded male into providing assistance when she needed it. It hadn't just been about seeing a friendly face, either. His initial greeting had been less than encouraging.

It had been him. No more, no less than the simple

truth. Jason Grant had managed to ignite a spark of hope or happiness inside her she'd decided wasn't within her capacity to feel.

Good Lord, she wished the man would talk so she could stop thinking!

He pulled the car into a parking garage and drove up the ramps. "Let's just see if we find the nest."

"Okay." If he wouldn't share, she'd just have to figure it out. "The cop said the man was shot twice."

"Show off." Jason stopped on the top level and got out of the car, walking forward in the wash from the headlights.

"The local officials agree with you," she said, catching up to him. "The sniper put a bullet through his brain and then the heart as he went down just to prove he could."

Jason shook his head.

"Have you ever done that?"

"Only on a training dummy. I was the only one who could pull it off perfectly. Straight through the center of the heart before the victim—dummy, of course— slumped too far from the head shot that had already killed him."

"Something else in your closed file?"

He nodded.

A chill slid down her spine as potential connections bumped around in her mind. "So whoever is behind the rifle is trying to get your attention?"

"More likely he's trying to get me blamed. He just has to blow apart my cover story about why I'm in Vegas."

She patted him on the back. "No worries. I can arrange an exit strategy for you, Specialist Grant."

"Funny."

She was trying to lighten the mood, if only to prevent the unprecedented worry from choking her. Getting emotional was way, way out of character and entirely dangerous for all involved.

Jason stopped, stepping carefully using the glow of the headlights. "Here we are." He knelt down and used a flashlight to poke around the trash that had been blown against the low wall.

Gin looked down toward the crime scene to the big lights set up around the area. It appeared more than possible to her that a sniper had made the shots from here. "Why aren't the police up here?"

"Probably because the body was shifted so they would be looking at a different trajectory."

"Something else you learned in training?"

"No, that's something I heard about in the field."

When he didn't explain, she sighed. "Jason, darling, you simply must learn to keep some information to yourself. The way you go on and on it's a wonder you qualified for a security clearance."

"Unlike your new admirer down there, I know better than to talk with cute reporters."

"Cute?" She snorted. "No one's accused me of cute since I wore pigtails in grammar school."

"Ladies and gentlemen, may I present our Irish lass, Ginger Olin." He shot her a wink.

"You're a mixed-up sort of Yank," she said in her best Irish lilt. She punched him in the shoulder and set her voice to match the locals. "Keep it up and I'll have no choice but to seek revenge."

He looked up at her, his face an odd blend of humor and regret. "Let's hope you get the chance."

"What does that mean?" She dropped to her knees beside him, peering at an object he'd picked up. "Is that shell casing related to this case?"

"I believe so. There's another right over there."

"Sloppy to leave them lying around."

"Not if you want to get caught. Or rather, get *me* caught."

"No way." She frowned at the brass casing on the end of his pen. "Have you ever left a shell casing behind?"

"No."

"I didn't think so. I bet that detail is even a notation in your service record. Jason, you can't believe I'll let them so much as question you. I'm your alibi. Rock solid with a marriage certificate to prove it."

He stood and she followed suit, gazing up at his troubled face.

"Thanks. But doing that could blow your own mission here. You might be better off to hurry up with the divorce."

"Despite our whirlwind courtship, I'm not eager for the dubious honor of shortest marriage on record."

He laughed, just as she'd hoped, though it was painfully brief. "How do you want to deal with this?" He held the brass casing up between them.

"I say we leave them here." She planted her hands on her hips. "If we do the police work for them, it only raises more questions about how we knew where to look."

"How *I* knew where to look," he said.

"We. For better or worse, remember?"

His smile didn't reach his eyes. "No. I don't remember to be honest. But this is definitely one for the worse column."

She pushed his hand down until the brass shell slid off the pen and landed at their feet. He looked so desperately alone, she couldn't bear it. Taking his hand, she led him back to the car and opened the passenger door for him.

He slid in without protest—which worried her more. Before she could close the door, the window shattered, spilling safety glass across her shoes.

"Keys!" She scrambled around the back of the car, staying low even as she opened the door and adjusted the driver's seat.

Jason shoved the key in the ignition and she started the car and put it into reverse. They flew backward down the parking garage ramps, both cars. Keeping low in the seats as bullets peppered the windshield she prayed they wouldn't encounter a vehicle coming up.

"What the hell is this?" She wrestled with the steering wheel.

"A trap," he replied. "Small caliber. Go faster."

Judging the space wide enough, she executed an impressively fast three-point turn and worked the high-performance engine until they were out of the garage and flying toward a main road. She heard the engine behind them closing in, swore when another bullet clipped her sideview mirror.

"Where's a cop when you need one?" she muttered.

Jason's hearty belly laugh made her jump. "At the crime scene with your new admirer."

"Funny." Grumbling, she turned away from the direction of the crime scene and headed south, determined to get back toward the famous glow of the Las Vegas strip. They needed a crowd and cops. Cops cruised the Strip 24/7. "Can you see anything back there?"

"Just headlights." He jerked and raised his hands to shield himself when the passenger-side mirror blew apart. "Head for the interstate."

She adjusted her course. "We'll be lucky to avoid a ticket for safety violations."

"That'll be the least of our worries if you can't lose them."

"The task would have been far easier if you'd rented a normal car."

"A normal car wouldn't have this engine."

"Mixed blessings," she allowed. Working through the gears, she edged away from their pursuers.

"Why didn't they shoot us while we were looking at the casing?"

"Guess they don't want us dead."

"Then it would be best to stop shooting in our general direction."

"Agreed. It's small-caliber fire." He dug a bullet out of the seat area near his shoulder.

She could tell he was mulling over this weird development, but discussion would have to wait as she navigated the increasing traffic.

"Slow down."

"You just told me to lose them."

"I know." He drew his own weapon, a semi-automatic nine millimeter. "Humor me."

She eased off the accelerator and downshifted, her palms damp on the leather-covered steering wheel as the other car closed the gap. "What's your plan?"

"I'm just going to wing it."

"Assuming we survive," Gin vowed, "I'm plotting a prolonged revenge at the earliest opportunity."

"That's just proof I'm the luckiest husband in Vegas," Jason said. He reclined the back of the seat, then tugged at the seat belt as he shifted and twisted around to get a better position.

"You shoot left-handed?"

"Only when I have to."

She was cruising now, exactly at the posted speed limit.

"If he's smart, he'll go for the tires," she muttered, mostly to herself. As if on cue, she caught the muzzle flash in her rearview mirror, and she braced to work with the spinout. Avoiding collateral damage out here was her first priority.

The first shot hit the car, and she heard the deep pop of Jason's gun as he returned fire.

Another flash and the left rear of the car lurched as the tire came apart.

Sparks of the wheel against the roadway reflected in the remaining shards of her side mirror. Gin didn't have time to appreciate the artistry of it as she struggled to maintain control of the Corvette. Steering into the spin, she said a prayer when the interstate median stopped the momentum with a sickening crunch as the front end crumpled.

Jason gave a victory whoop. When her stomach settled and the airbag deflated, she understood why.

The other car was stalled in the left lane, a few yards in front of them, the hood popped and smoke and steam pluming.

"You tagged the radiator?"

"Took me two tries."

"In the middle of a spin?"

"No, before that." He leaned over and planted a hard kiss on her mouth. "Listen."

She could only stare at him as the sounds of emergency sirens drew closer.

"Come on. Let's go make a citizen's arrest."

Jason bolted out of the car as the driver who'd been chasing them started limping away from the scene. She watched him go as she inventoried her situation. Her foot was more unhappy than ever and her lip was swelling from the airbag.

"The man is insane." This she knew with complete certainty.

Climbing out of the car became a problem. Her foot was caught between the clutch pedal and the crushed left front quarter panel. The painful bruise from the earlier fight would no longer be ignored. She could only watch as Jason ran down the other driver, tackling him to the pavement.

"Yay team," she muttered, leaning her head back against the headrest. Hopefully this would be the lead Jason was looking for. If she was really lucky, it would be the catalyst to get him talking about whatever he really thought was going on.

Wishing he'd come back to help her out of the car, she opened her eyes and screamed. Flames were licking at the hood and closing in on her. She scrabbled against the seat and pulled at her foot, but it wouldn't budge.

She refused to panic, told herself she'd been in worse situations and swore that later she'd laugh at the overwhelming urge to panic. Now, she had to think.

There was always a way out.

"Cover your head!"

She looked up into Jason's face at her window.

"Do it, Gin!"

She met his gaze and choked back the panicked scream. Flames at his back, he showed her a crowbar. She had no idea what he meant to do, only that any moment he could be in as much danger as she was.

"Get away! I'm stuck."

"Cover your head."

He didn't wait, and she turned her head as he smashed the window. What he might do against the crumpled door, she had no idea. Emergency crews were racing toward them. Over the sound of the fire and traffic, she heard Jason barking orders, and she saw shadows through the smoke and blue flashes of police lights.

Her thoughts disjointed and muddled by the swirling smoke, she vaguely wondered if she'd get ticketed for speeding.

Beneath her the car rocked and metal and fiberglass crunched with whatever they were doing. Then suddenly the pressure on her foot released and she scrambled back as white foam covered the car and doused the flames.

She wasn't ashamed to cling to Jason, was too relieved they were both alive as he carried her to the waiting paramedics.

"I'm fine," she began, but her protest was cut off by a fit of coughing. An oxygen mask landed on her face and she was urged to lie back and relax. An order that became more challenging when they pushed Jason out of reach and out of her sight.

Someone packed her foot in ice and propped it up, then covered her with a blanket while they measured her pulse and blood pressure. No surprise that both were slightly elevated.

They asked her several questions, which she remembered to answer as the British reporter. Hopefully Jason had grabbed her purse from the wrecked car. Aside from being a bit groggy and sore, she wasn't in terrible condition.

Another police officer stepped up beside her. Despite the oxygen mask she tried to smile when she recognized him from the murder scene.

"We should thank you."

She raised her eyebrows, her throat too raw and tender to speak much.

"You and your photographer found the sniper's nest for the Redding shooting. We were looking in a different area."

She nodded.

A warm hand landed on her shoulder, and she recognized Jason's touch. "Feeling better?"

She nodded again.

"They want to transport you for X-rays on that foot."

She shook her head. "Not broken," she rasped.

"You should make sure."

"I am," she said with a pointed look. Certainly he'd realize she had plenty of experience diagnosing and managing physical injuries. Her head clearing and her lungs feeling better, she nudged the oxygen mask out of the way. "Are you hurt?"

"Just a scratch."

He pointed to his head. It looked more like a gash to her, with four butterfly closures holding it together.

He smoothed a hand over her hair. "Neither of us is concussed and if you're sure about the foot, we're free to go."

Gin sat up, more than ready to get out of here. They needed to discuss this situation with the sniper and put a lid on it before it got any more out of control. Maybe her smoke-roughened throat was a good thing if it meant Jason had to do more of the talking.

What the hell were they going to do? That gorgeous car was destroyed. More important, where would they go? Sure they had a room, but returning to the hotel in this condition would raise eyebrows and suspicions.

Jason smiled down at her, smoothing her hair from her face. He couldn't seem to stop touching her, and she soaked up the comfort he offered.

"What now?"

"I'm not without resources. Trust me?"

She did, she realized, more than she'd ever trusted anyone else. "Lead on."

Chapter Thirteen

Holt's phone rang, interrupting his workout. He answered it when he saw the number from the Mission Recovery analyst department.

"Sir, our contact in Nevada wants to confirm a new requisition."

Holt stifled his first response. "Who is asking for what?"

"Specialist Grant requested a car, among other things."

Grant should have been out of the way by now, and "other things" covered a lot of gray area. "Approve it all and make sure I have a list on my desk in the morning."

He disconnected the call and dialed back his frustration. Intelligent, capable people were a boon when they were working with you. Having so many variables in play, so many people who could turn his plans inside out was a pain in the ass.

He threw a series of uppercuts into the heavy bag he'd been punching when Nadine had interrupted. As far as he could tell the woman never slept. Not that he could say anything. He rarely did himself.

What didn't kill him made him stronger. It would appear the same held true for Grant. Holt tried to be objective and find a way to turn this to his advantage.

The arrangements had been clear and specific; he didn't conduct business of this nature in any other fashion. He jabbed twice and came around with a left hook.

As his body worked out the combination, his mind flipped through the potential pitfalls like a slide show. Move one way, get result A. Move the other, result B.

His counterpart had dropped the ball, giving Holt a new opening. He just had to decide how to use it.

He drove his fists into the heavy bag then slumped against it, catching his breath. He checked the clock on the wall and knew he should get some of that sleep he more often than not denied himself.

Instead, he turned on the television in the corner and drained a bottle of water while he cruised the news stations.

Only a few more weeks. He could sleep for a month on a warm beach in a nonextradition country when this was over. Or he was dead. At this point he wasn't sure which outcome he preferred.

As long as it was done.

Chapter Fourteen

Jason watched Gin's face as she tried to figure out what resources he might have called on, but now wasn't the time to explain it all. Right now he was just relieved she was alive. When the car had stopped spinning and the airbags deflated, he'd had one goal: catch the attacker and squeeze him for information before the cops pulled him out of reach.

Except Gin hadn't been beside him as he'd expected. He'd turned around just in time to see the fire catch, and his heart just stopped.

Looking at her now, he wondered when she had become so important to him. It couldn't be because of a piece of paper. Not when he couldn't even remember the wedding. He wanted to chalk it up to proximity and the camaraderie of working together, but he knew it went deeper than that.

She was gorgeous and he was thoroughly attracted, but there was more. Even knowing it would make her mad, he wanted to comfort and coddle. She could take care of herself and the paramedics had cleared her, but he couldn't shut down the instinct to protect her. To treasure her.

There probably wasn't an accurate term to define his degree of foolishness when her smoke-damaged voice only made her more appealing.

He could just imagine her laughter if she knew.

"Come on. Your new pal is giving us a lift to a truck stop."

She shot him a skeptical look.

"You said you'd trust me."

She smiled and when she put her hand in his, he felt like he'd won the jackpot at the Palace. In that habit she had, she rested her head on his shoulder and rubbed his arm with her free hand as she limped along to the patrol car.

He knew he was reading too much into it—they were in public after all—but something in her touch felt more sincere this time. A survivor's euphoria and definitely an adrenaline rush were going on here with both of them. Maintaining logic was critical to sorting out their respective missions and keeping their emotions in perspective.

They rode together in the back of the police car because he didn't want her out of reach.

"I'm okay," she whispered, but she kept her body pressed along his side for the duration of the twenty-minute ride.

"If you need anything, just give us a call," the officer said when they reached The King Truck Stop.

"Bet they try to call us first," Gin said as he pulled away, a tired smile on her lips.

Jason bent down and kissed her. "Probably. We should make the most of our time before that happens."

Those green eyes lit with a determined fire. He appreciated her enthusiasm, could only hope it lasted after she understood his theory and how he wanted to deal with it.

"Is your contact inside?"

"Should be." Jason nodded. "Lean on me," he offered when she started to limp. "If he's running late, we can ice that foot again."

"It's fine," she insisted.

"I could just carry you."

"In your dreams," she said, but the bravado wasn't as effective when she bit her lip with the exertion of the next step.

"Come on." He knelt in front of her. "Hop on."

"That's ridiculous."

He looked over his shoulder. "It'll be fun. You probably haven't had a piggyback ride since your *cute* days."

"Fine." She looped her bag across her body, then wrapped her arms around his neck and leaned onto his back. He reached around and, holding on to her thighs, stood up. He could have sworn she giggled, but she said, "You are impossible."

"Just what every husband wants to hear."

"Men are so easy," she whispered at his ear.

A trucker exiting the diner held the door open for them as they entered. Jason carried her to the counter and let her slide down onto one of the tall stools.

"I must look terrible." She pulled the barrette out of her hair and tried to smooth all the wayward strands back into place.

He shook his head. "Not as bad as you think."

"That doesn't make me feel one bit better." She pulled a face and rooted through her bag, holding up a small compact like a trophy. She took one look at her reflection and the color drained from her face. "I can't believe people aren't running away in terror."

Jason knew better than to protest while she tried to minimize the damage. "I can buy us a couple of T-shirts."

"Don't bother," she said, wiping mascara from under her eyes. "Who are we here to meet?"

Jason liked that *we* more than he should. "Just a contact." He didn't see anyone in the diner who fit the description in the Mission Recovery files. "He'll be here any minute. Are you hungry?"

"I could eat."

When they'd placed orders for bacon cheeseburgers, fries and milkshakes, she reached over and patted him on the knee. "You *are* going to talk to me."

He smiled, understanding it wasn't a question. "Not here."

"That's fair."

Her expression was ample warning that she wouldn't be distracted this time. Jason was surprised that didn't bother him. He clearly needed an ally—even though until this mission he'd preferred to work alone. He leaned close to her, his fingers tracing the fine bones of her hand. "Tell me something about you while we wait."

She sipped her water, and remembering her scorched throat, he felt like a jerk for making her talk.

"I was recruited at university," she said.

Of all the things she might have said, that one startled him, but he didn't show it. The timing of the recruiting wasn't the shock, but her accent and phrasing raised more questions. She had an enviable range of authentic-sounding accents.

"By whom?" She shook her head, her gaze locked on their joined hands. He reached over and gently tipped up her chin. "Tell me."

"IRA."

The Irish Republican Army was no easy group to get into. Or out of. It was hard to imagine the idealistic girl she must have been getting mixed up in the dangers of that world. He had a vivid image of her as a young girl in a school uniform jumper, red braids down her back and that pixie smile on her face. During his time with Interpol, he'd seen still photos of similar girls before and after the bombing they'd investigated.

"You weren't in deep." It wasn't a question. If she had been, she wouldn't be here now.

She shrugged. "Family connection."

That kind of background and hard-knock training would explain her indomitable spirit and headstrong methods in the field. She must have been turned into an informant for American interests somewhere along the way.

He wanted the whole story but not at the price of her pained voice. Whether physical or emotional, he could tell this conversation was taking a toll.

Rubbing her shoulder, he grinned at the waitress when their food arrived. "Dig in," he said trying to send her the signal that nothing in her past mattered to him. Definitely not tonight, when they should be celebrating being alive and generally uninjured. "Want to prop up your foot?"

She shook her head, her mouth full of burger.

He had just poured the last of his chocolate milkshake from the stainless cup into the tall classic serving glass when his contact finally walked in.

He slid onto the stool next to Jason, ordered coffee and a slice of cherry pie, and then placed a car key on the counter. "You're all set, man. I even gave her a fresh coat of wax."

"Thanks." Jason reached for the key and saw the man's eyes go wide when he spotted the shiny gold wedding band.

He leaned forward and gave Gin a long, appreciative look.

"Nicely done, man."

Jason cut him a sideways glance. "Keep your distance." The last thing he wanted was this guy sending details up the line to Mission Recovery before Jason had a chance to sort things out for himself. He'd never had to put an unplanned marriage on a mission report. He supposed he should be grateful she was CIA. At least their security clearances would match up.

"Dude." The guy shrugged a shoulder. "Whatever."

Gin elbowed Jason. "An introduction?"

Jason shook his head. "Not today." He pocketed the

key and placed a couple of bills on the counter. "You ready?"

"I am." She showed off her to-go cup to prove it.

"Want a lift?" He patted his shoulder.

She shook her head. "I'll risk it this way."

He gave her as much support as she'd accept as they went out to the parking lot. The sedan gleamed in the glow of neon from the signs fronting the truck stop. Jason resisted the urge to check the merchandise before he got in. This was a trusted Mission Recovery asset. The rifle, ammunition, infrared scope and binoculars, along with another sidearm and ammunition, would be hidden in the trunk and back seat. It was a risk, but one he had to take. If he was right about the sniper, time was running out.

"Where's the virus?" he asked as they approached the Strip.

She checked her phone. "Not in the Palace anymore. It's moving north." She pounded a fist into her knee. "Damn it. I've missed the deal."

He hit the accelerator. "Thought that was tomorrow night."

"That's what they told me."

"Maybe the seller got spooked. Or the buyer changed it up. Let's go see."

"Hurry."

He couldn't do much about the congestion. "You think someone has eyes on us and moved when you were out of range?"

She sneered at the screen in her palm. "Has to be it."

Who knew them both and had the resources to pull

it off? Someone on the inside. Betrayal prickled along his skin like the pressure of a sharp knife between his shoulder blades. He shifted in the seat, trying to shake it off.

"What now?" Gin whispered into the silence.

"The car is clean. We talk." And try to find the point where her virus and his past intersected.

"We?"

"Well, you can listen."

She gestured for him to continue.

"You might be right about the miss at the pool. This guy seems to be re-creating some of my hits."

"You killed a woman at a pool?"

"No." He flexed his hands on the steering wheel. "I was called off killing a woman on a beach."

"Not the same."

"Close enough." It bothered him that his past had put her in danger and he struggled to push that back and stay focused on the primary issue.

He slowed down as they hit the thicker congestion of cars cruising up and down the glaring canyon of the strip. It wasn't fun, but it was relatively effective cover—for the moment.

"Movement?"

"No." She frowned. "Still holding north and east of Caesar's."

"I'm going to make a tour around the area, and let you confirm."

"Thanks." She kept her screen in her lap. "Continue."

She'd been serious about not being distracted this time. "My cover of being here for the security conference should hold up. Unless someone tips the local police department about who I am."

"What's your real-life connection to Redding?"

He nodded. "Way back he was one of my instructors."

She sipped at her milkshake. "Which makes you think your cover is about to blow wide open."

"Ironic, isn't it? Considering what I was sent to do."

"What you *thought* you were sent to do."

"Right." Although he appreciated her quick understanding, affirming his theory of betrayal didn't make it any more comfortable. And with every twist the inevitable conclusion loomed nearer. With Director Casey on his honeymoon and Holt the possible problem, Jason's back was against the wall and he didn't know which way to turn.

He could wave goodbye to his career and any hopes of moving up if he became a suspect in any of these events.

"Did you ever take anyone out by causing a traffic accident?"

"Other than tonight?"

"You didn't kill anyone tonight."

"Not for lack of trying." He hitched a shoulder. "You're thinking of that accident that happened on the interstate two days ago."

"Hours after you arrived, you said."

"Uh-huh."

"My cop buddy said the tire was shot out."

Jason cringed. "Yeah. I had a mission like that once."

"Hold that thought. The vial is moving again," Gin

said. "I want eyes on this. We need to know if this is the buyer."

There was that *we* again. "Which direction?" He looked around, knowing he wouldn't be able to do much about it immediately. "We could walk faster than this."

"One of us could," she grumbled.

"True. Sorry."

"It's okay. Same side of the street." She pointed, her eyes still on the screen. "Are these places connected?"

He looked through the windshield. At the snail's pace, he had plenty of time to read the signs advertising various slots. "There are all kinds of marketing and security secrets in Las Vegas."

She snorted. "I've heard."

"Think either your seller or buyer likes slots?"

"Huh?" She glanced up and followed his gaze. "That would be lucky. Let's get in there."

"Thought our stench couldn't blend." They both looked pretty much like hell.

"It's slots. No one cares."

"If you say so."

"Which ID do you have with you?"

"Only the FBI one."

"We won't use it unless we have to."

"Planning to wing it again?" he asked, trying not to sound jealous. The way men reacted to her made him crazy.

"No. Let's check in as the reporter and her strapping husband."

He shot her a look. She winked. "It's true enough.

Then you can put me on a slot machine and herd the virus my way. Just for a visual."

"And checking in?"

"Gives us free parking."

"Is the CIA pinching pennies now?"

She nodded, then smacked his shoulder when he laughed. "Be thankful your division is under the budget radar."

"Duly noted." He maneuvered toward the next valet stand.

"Wait," she tapped his leg. "Do you have anything in here that could, umm…"

"Not that they can find."

"Good."

"What about our lack of luggage?"

"We'll worry about that after we find the virus."

"Got it." In other words she really was winging it again. Not that he could blame her—they were running out of options.

He pulled up to the valet stand of the Flamingo and handed over the key, then helped Gin inside to the registration desk. "We had a little mishap on the way from the airport," she said to the clerk. "We lost our luggage and had to wait for a replacement rental car."

"We can send fresh items to your room, if you'd like," the clerk offered.

Gin glanced up at him and he nodded, adding a tired shrug. "That would be wonderful."

He liked her British reporter accent a little too much, and reminding himself to focus on business, he scanned the lobby.

Gin provided a list of needed items to the clerk, accepted the keys and handed him one. Checking her phone, she looked him up and down and brushed at his jacket. "We're as good as it's going to get right now. Let's do this." She hobbled toward the end of a long row of slots.

He set her up with a stack of tokens and she handed him the phone, the tracking signal flashing like a beacon.

He wandered around the slot machines, flanking the signal until he spotted the likely candidate. No one he recognized. Checking faces in the vicinity, and relieved to come up empty, he started the process of herding the target in Gin's direction.

He hovered right behind the guy giving off the signal and pretended to talk on his phone. The guy looked to be in his early twenties and the poster child for nervous. His suit was black, and his skin looked as pale as the white shirt he wore. He moved to a different machine. A moment later Jason followed, pacing up and down the row, pausing at the end to drink a coffee a waitress brought him.

Looking annoyed and a little nervous, the guy sporting the signal moved toward Gin's row. For a second Jason thought he wouldn't have to show the badge or gun. Then his next visual sweep landed on the blonde who had drugged him at the bar and had tried to break into the penthouse. Who was bankrolling this woman to be the common denominator between Gin's walkabout virus and the sniper imitating him? And who was she informing about their actions?

He bent down, pretending to find a token on the floor, and hurried after the beacon on Gin's tracking app.

He tapped the shoulder of the guy giving off the signal and made a clumsy offer of the token that revealed the gold shield at his waist. "You dropped this," he said, holding it out.

"Not mine," his target grumbled.

"I saw it fall." Jason was earnest and sincere as he subtly nudged the guy back toward the row where Gin was waiting.

"You can keep it."

"No, I can't." Jason leaned close and confided the truth. "I'm an officer of the court. Just here on a tip."

The ploy worked. The guy, who was basically a rookie kid, blanched and stutter-stepped backward. "I don't want to be involved with anything."

Jason caught Gin's sly expression over his shoulder as she trapped him.

"Oh, but you already are," she said with no discernible dialect.

"No." The kid looked around. "No. I'm just on vacation. I swear it."

Gin met his gaze and shook her head. "It takes all kinds. Come over here with us for a minute."

"I—I can't. I have to get out of here. You should get out of here."

His eyes were wide with panic now, and his gaze was darting all over the place.

"In just a few minutes," Jason amended. "We think

you might know who we're looking for. We can do this here or at the bar."

"Here," Gin corrected with a glare.

The guy looked ready to burst into tears as she pushed him down onto the nearest stool and helped him play.

Gin fed the tokens and asked questions while Jason kept an eye out for the blonde or anyone with too much interest in the three of them.

"Are you the buyer?"

He shook his head.

"A courier for the buyer?"

"Look happy," Jason ordered as the machine paid out.

The resulting smile on the kid's face was closer to a grimace, but it was an admirable attempt.

"Keep playing. And relax," Jason suggested.

"How'd you get the package?"

"Look, I'm just a bellhop at the Palace. A woman gave it to me. Told me to carry this thing—"

"What thing?"

"In my pocket."

Jason pulled it out, showed it to Gin and replaced it when she nodded.

"I was just supposed to carry it around for a few hours. Work my way down the Strip."

"And if you didn't agree?"

"If I don't make it to The Sahara by five o'clock this morning, they won't pay me. I need the money to get clear with my bookie."

Jason met Gin's gaze and knew they were thinking

the same thing again. This had been another test to see how they'd respond. He was tired of getting jerked around by Isely and his crew.

Jason patted the guy on the shoulder. "Who's meeting you at five?"

"The woman who gave it to me said she'd be there."

"And she's been following you?"

"I think so."

"Stalking men—her favorite hobby," Gin said.

"When it's time to move on I'll get a text."

"Give my friend the package," Gin ordered.

Jason handed Gin the small case, which resembled an EpiPen a person might use for an allergic reaction, and then sent her a questioning look over the kid's shoulder. She ignored him.

"You just keep doing as she says."

"What about when I have to give it back?"

"Give her this."

Jason couldn't see what Gin dropped into the guy's pocket. He wasn't sure he wanted to know.

"Now go on and do your thing. When she pays you, settle your debt and then take a couple days off work."

All three of them played in silence for a few minutes before they told the kid to move on. Jason shifted to take the machine next to Gin's. "What did you give him?"

"A benign duplicate of the vial he is supposed to be carrying. No way to tell the difference until they go to use it. Or check the tracking tag."

"Why? Don't you want the buyer?"

"Not really. Other agencies can handle that. I just

needed to know where it is. Now the virus is with me and off the market."

"So you're done?" The realization landed like a sucker punch across his jaw. His ears were actually ringing and not just with the random bells and slot machine sound effects.

"Are you okay?"

"Yeah, sure." He stood up. "Just tired. It's been a hell of a day."

"You're right." But she fed another token into the machine and watched it play. It didn't win. She repeated the process.

"Do you want help up to your room?"

"My room? Not *our* room?"

Her expression was inscrutable. Any attempt to interpret it would only be skewed by his desire for her and what might have been if they were normal people.

The last thing he wanted was to leave her, yet...the best thing for her safety was for him to walk away. They'd been in more trouble together than either of them had been alone. Well, aside from the woman who'd drugged him. If he knew Gin was safely in her room, he could tail the woman and find out who hired her to get him out of the way.

"You want to go after her without me." Gin wasn't asking.

"No."

She drilled a finger into his chest. "Yes you do. I can see it all over your brooding face."

He trapped her hand against his chest. "You can't

walk and you've got what you came for. Your best bet is to rest up and then get out of town."

"No one tells me what I can and can't do. I am perfectly capable of seeing this through."

Exasperated, he rolled his eyes. "Gin, you just said you were done."

"Assuming my precautions work, and they will, Isely can't track his product anymore. I am done." Her eyes flashed. "Which means I've got all kinds of time to help you with your problem."

"Not tonight, dear," he said through gritted teeth. He jerked his chin, trying to make her see the people staring at them.

"But we know where she'll be and when," Gin countered. "Her repeated involvement means something."

He shook his head. "Another hired hand."

"Come on. I'm just getting my second wind."

"Go to the room now or I'll toss you over my shoulder and tuck you into bed myself."

"Promises, promises." Her eyes locked with his, she deliberately dropped another token in the machine.

He wasn't sure what possessed him to do it, but he couldn't let the dare in her eyes ride. Even as the payout began pouring from the machine, he scooped her into his arms.

"Wait! We won!"

"Looks that way."

"Just let me collect."

"Nope. Let someone else enjoy it. We have other things to do." She kicked her feet and squirmed, apparently all deals about how they'd behave in public forgotten. "Just married," he said with a wink for the closest group of people gawking at the scene they were making.

"Stop," he muttered close to her ear. "Or I'll drop you and you can't outrun me on that foot, which means when I catch you, you'll go over my shoulder."

She glared at him but went still, even wrapping an arm around his neck as he headed for the bank of elevators. It made carrying her easier, but he didn't think she was done fighting.

Not a problem. He wasn't ready to quit, either.

"Put me down," she said when they were alone in the elevator.

"No." He didn't trust her not to take a cheap shot.

"That scowl of yours doesn't scare me."

He kept his gaze on the screen showing the elevator's upward progress. "Maybe it should." He didn't know what he meant to do—only that he wanted her out of the casino, out of danger. It had been nothing but one problem on top of another since they started this married farce this morning and second wind or not, she needed rest.

It wasn't over. She wasn't walking away from this until he said so.

Chapter Fifteen

Gin tried to stay mad, but it was becoming more of a challenge with each passing second. Not even thinking of the coins she had left pouring from the slot machine squashed the excitement kicking through her bloodstream. The sexual energy was rolling off him like a cloud of steam. Her body was only too happy to respond in kind.

"This Neanderthal routine is not cute."

"No one's ever accused me of cute," he said without looking at her.

His refusal to make eye contact frustrated her. She wanted those rich brown eyes—and much, much more—on her. What started as a purely feminine appreciation when she'd undressed him last night had grown into a serious craving. The elevator rushed closer to their floor and her pulse rushed along with it. This close to him, the smooth, warm scent she recognized as all Jason teased her nose under the lingering bits of fire and hotel soap.

The doors parted and she nearly whimpered aloud when she felt the strength of his arms and abs flexing as he carried her to the room.

"Key."

She fished it out of his jacket pocket and pushed it into the lock. At the green light, she turned the handle and he kicked the door wide to carry her inside.

"That's becoming a habit," she teased when he set her gently on her feet.

"What do you mean?"

His confusion showed on his face and gave his frustration a target other than her. She should have been grateful for the reprieve. Should have been immune to the urge to soothe him. Nurture wasn't her strong suit.

"You insisted on doing the same thing last night after the wedding. Not all the way from the chapel—just when we reached the room," she explained. "You carried me over the threshold."

"I don't remember that."

"It was fun. *You* were fun."

"Fun." He grunted.

She nodded. She'd told some big fat lies in her career, but this one had to be the worst. Last night he'd been so loopy she worried he wouldn't pull out of his drug-induced haze.

"Have I wounded your pride?" She licked her lips, eager to see what he'd do about it.

He shoved his hands in his jacket pockets. "You should rest."

"That's why you brought me up here. To rest."

He jerked his chin affirmatively, but he refused to look at her, studying a spot just over her head.

"I told you I'm not tired."

"No. It's obvious you're wired from your success. You should sleep it off."

"We both know that's unlikely." She tugged on the zipper of his open jacket, running it up and back down again, the back of her hand brushing against his shirt. "If you won't let me help you track down the woman, you'll have to let me help with something else."

He twitched, not quite a flinch, when she tugged his shirt from his jeans and ran her fingertips along his warm skin just above his waistband. She wanted tonight to be something to take with her when this was over. She'd wanted it since spotting him last night at the bar.

Or maybe she'd wanted it since she ran into him in Colorado last month.

"We both could use a shower."

She shrugged out of her denim jacket and let it fall to the floor. His eyes tracked her movements as she unbuttoned her jeans and pushed the zipper down. Grateful for the smaller room, she hid the pain of her aching foot behind a smile as she walked backward toward the shower.

"Come on, Jason." *Why wouldn't he make a move?* She reached in and turned on the shower, then peeled off her sweater. "Come have some fun with your wife."

At the last word, his dark eyes flared and he advanced, stripping away his jacket and shirt as he rushed toward her.

She reached back to unhook her bra, but he caught her in that awkward position, arched her back a little more and bent his head to her breasts. His mouth, warm and wet, worked her nipple into stiff, needy peaks through the sheer fabric of her bra. She twisted a hand free and pushed her fingers through his thick sable hair, desperate for more.

He'd been tempting enough when he was incapacitated; she could hardly stand it now that he seemed ready to do all the things he thought they'd done last night.

She moaned a little as he shifted his attention to her other breast and she gripped his strong shoulders in an effort to keep her balance. Caught between the steam of the hot shower and the wall of heat Jason provided, her desire spiked to unprecedented levels. She pushed her jeans down over her hips then struggled to step out of them with her sore foot.

Jason knelt down and carefully resolved the problem, taking time to feather kisses over her midriff and thighs as he did. He slid a finger between her skin and the sheer fabric of her panties then slowly pulled them down and away.

Naked in front of him, she'd never felt more exposed or a more delicious anticipation. She experienced a sensory overload as he stood up, his rough jeans against her legs, his big hands trailing little fires over her skin.

His mouth closed over hers and she opened to him fully, her hands fumbling with his jeans. He nudged her back just so he could tug them off, then he nabbed a condom from his wallet. Watching him put it on was one of the sexiest things she'd ever watched.

He lifted her against his chest and stepped into the shower, the hot water cascading over their bodies.

He boosted her up and she wrapped her legs around

his waist. He reached down and stroked her until she was rocking against his hand and using the last of her abused voice to beg him for more.

"Look at me," he said, his voice as hoarse as hers.

She pushed her hair back and met his hungry gaze as he entered her slowly. She flexed her hips, so damned impatient for what she knew he could give her.

He obliged, thrusting inside her, and she rocked against him as he set the pace. She watched the water bead against his skin and she leaned forward, licking it away.

He nipped at her ear and whispered words she couldn't make out over the rush of water and the pounding of her blood through her veins. Her climax rolled through her and over him and she clung as he stroked into her twice more and then joined her in that place of pure sensation.

His breath sawing in and out of his lungs teased her breasts as his chest pressed against her. She sighed when he parted from her and lowered her legs to the shower floor, making sure she was steady.

Her knees were weak and her pulse didn't want to stop racing. She nudged him under the spray of the shower and indulged herself with washing his body. When they swapped places she discovered it was equally exciting to be on the receiving end of such tender treatment.

She never expected these feelings, never experienced this level of a connection with a lover. With a glance at the ring circling her finger, she wondered if the slim gold band was playing tricks on her mind. Tricks her heart was only too happy to fall for.

"Hey, where'd you go?" He traced the curve of her shoulder. "You'll give a guy a complex."

"Not you."

"You tired?"

She walked her fingers up his biceps. "Not even close."

"There's some good news." He grinned and kissed her as he reached around to shut off the faucet. She let him wrap her in one of the thick towels and was about to tease him when he kissed her so thoroughly she would have been hard pressed to remember her real name.

It was a heady sensation, to be swept away by the moment and the man guiding her through it. He lowered her to the bed without letting loose of the contact of their mouths.

"Jason."

"Hmm?"

She didn't know what to say, couldn't remember why speaking was important. She explored his stunning body as he touched hers, slowly stoking her passion and leading her up to another climax. Her entire world zeroed down to him. The concerns of the case—hers and his—fell away to a hazy place in the back of her mind and she forgot whatever she'd intended to say.

That had never happened to her, no matter the personal involvement or isolation during an assignment. But right here, they were two normal people sharing something extraordinary.

When their bodies joined again, it was with a steady

rhythm, less frantic, but just as intense and passionate. And when at last they parted, she curled next to his side, his heart beating strong under her hand as she let sleep claim her.

JASON, MORE THAN a little overwhelmed by what they'd just shared, let her sleep. Intoxicating didn't begin to describe her. He wanted to tell himself he should have resisted, but it would have been a waste of energy.

He was no stranger to temptation, but she'd been utterly irresistible. Already, his mind turned over the immediate and long-term options. They might be married, but would she want to stay that way?

It wasn't just the physical connection. Smoothing her hair back from her cheek, he kissed her, smiling as she snuggled closer. Had last night been this way for her? He wished like hell he could remember.

He also loved the way her mind worked, loved her dedication to the job.

Oh, Lord, it hit him like a fist to the gut. He loved *her*. Was there any way to actually make a marriage between them work?

Chapter Sixteen

Saturday, November 22, 9:30 a.m.

Gin awoke with a delicious contentment. She couldn't remember feeling quite this good. Ever. Warm and relaxed, with Jason's masculine scent surrounding her, she reached out. She wanted to indulge herself, to touch him when he wouldn't be awake enough to know how he fascinated her.

Her hand found only air and soft bedding. She sat up, confirmed the bed was empty, then grabbed the bedside clock. Half past nine already?

She pushed her hair behind her ears and, drawing the sheet up to cover herself, leaned against the headboard. He must have gone out to watch the blonde take back the vial.

A thousand dark thoughts and theories raced for dominance in her mind. The thought that wouldn't go away wasn't about the case at all, but rather about Jason.

The man had fooled her completely. Seducing her, lulling her into a deep sleep with his talented hands, then sneaking out to interfere with her case. Damn it!

"You would have done the same," she whispered to the empty room. She had, in fact, been considering it as a viable plan of action. Until somewhere along the way she'd gotten lost and let the fantasy become the reality. She buried her nose in the sheet, inhaling his lingering scent and remembering falling asleep in the perfect security of his embrace.

She swore. If she never saw the man again—and why would she—the past few hours had been worth it. Pragmatist that she was, it no longer mattered which of them was seducer and which one was fool because they'd both managed to win along the way.

Too late to go after him, she headed back to the shower to clean up. Her superiors would want that virus locked up in the lab as soon as possible so no one else could make a play for it.

She stopped, let the sheet fall as she rushed to the chair where she'd dropped her purse last night. It wasn't there. He couldn't have done it. Could he? Her breath stalled in her lungs and her hands fisted in her hair as she tried to think it through.

He wouldn't have done this—had no reason to do this. But he obviously had. She looked everywhere in the room, but her purse—and the virus—were gone. He was a spy, like her, and sides were never as clear-cut as the lines of white picket fences of happily-ever-afters that had danced through her sappy love-blind dreams last night.

Choice words for Jason Grant rolled through her mind and were nearly out of her mouth when she heard the soft click of the electronic lock on the door.

Caught, she brazened it out, irrationally hoping it was Jason and her raw physical state would divert attention from her raw emotional state.

She enjoyed a fast, grim vision of attacking him for his sneaky betrayal, but it fizzled when he quietly backed into the room towing a hotel luggage cart loaded with everything they'd left behind at the Palace. As he turned to unload the cart, he saw her and almost dropped the white bag in his free hand.

"You're awake." He quickly closed the door behind him.

"I am." She'd gone from angry to shy to needy in such a short span she couldn't keep up with herself. Her head was spinning and her heart was pounding.

Feeling ridiculous modesty under his heated stare, considering all the things they'd done a few hours ago, she couldn't think. "Is that breakfast?" She forced herself to move forward, to smile, as she took the bag and set it on the table. "Smells good."

"I thought you might be hungry."

"In a minute. I was just about to hit the shower."

NOT WITHOUT ME, Jason thought, but he didn't say it. Faced with the stunning beauty of her body, it took him a little longer to process what he'd walked in on. His gut twisted at the reality of what the scene told him. "You thought I left."

She paused, tossed him a look over her shoulder, then turned to face him again. "You weren't here."

He wasn't buying the casual routine she was trying to

sell. Trust didn't come easily to either one of them—for good reason. "Your purse is in the room safe."

Her face colored, along with the delectable column of her throat. "Thanks."

"I wanted to put as many layers as possible between that tag and any other tracking device. Especially since you were alone and asleep."

"I appreciate that." She turned on her heel and continued toward the bathroom, where she closed and locked the door.

Jason smiled to himself, more than a little pleased he'd surprised her. She shouldn't be stuck expecting the worst from everyone she met—especially not from him.

He unloaded the luggage cart and pushed it back into the hallway, relieved beyond measure he'd told the bellhop he could manage on his own. He didn't want anyone else enjoying the view of Gin's amazing body. At least not while she was his wife.

"Fool," he muttered.

Maybe he should have left her a note, but he'd thought it would be a quick trip. As smoothly as the casinos managed people and details, he'd learned the hard way the streets were crowded no matter the hour. Getting sidetracked at the jewelry store hadn't helped his timing. The rings in his pocket would probably get returned when this was over, but he'd bought them anyway. Just in case what they'd shared felt as real to her as it did to him. Sure, the sex had been incredible and he'd be forever grateful for the memory if she did walk away. But the more time he spent with her, the more he realized he wanted whatever they'd started as part of her mission to go beyond that. Infinity might be enough time.

He'd recognized the calculating look in her green eyes when he'd returned. She most likely believed he'd stolen the virus and gone after the blonde.

To be fair, he'd thought about it for all of two seconds. The virus thing was her case, and he didn't need to interfere beyond the point the blonde intersected with his situation.

He carried Gin's suitcase to the bed and then returned to the table to start up his laptop. Getting into the protected systems of the hotel security offices might be a challenge, but he knew he could hack the email of at least one of the reporters covering the shootings.

He heard the bathroom door open and close, but he didn't turn around, didn't want to push her.

"Did you check me out?"

With a laugh, he shook his head, eyes still on the laptop. "Is that a trick question?"

She walked up behind him and gave his shoulders a rub. "I meant did you check me out of the other hotel room at Caesar's."

"No. I thought you might want access."

She bent down and kissed his ear. "You're a smart man."

"I try."

"What's this?" She peered over his shoulder at the screen.

"Grab a coffee and I'll tell you."

"*Mmm.* Okay."

Wrapped in the hotel robe, she pulled a chair around and propped her feet in his lap. He couldn't help but study the purplish bruise on her foot. He didn't touch it though. "Does it hurt?"

"It's not happy, but it'll be fine."

"Do you want ice?"

Her eyes twinkled with a smile over the rim of her coffee cup. "I want to hear what you've been up to."

God, he was starting to like that sly expression. Especially now that it felt like they were on the same side.

"I've been digging through the email accounts of local reporters on the police beat."

She arched an auburn eyebrow.

"Easier than hacking the hotel security feeds."

"If you say so."

"With Redding dead it's past time we find where Frost is hiding."

"And who's giving him the orders and targets."

"We'll get there." Jason nodded. "One step at a time."

She sipped her coffee. "How do the reporter emails help you?"

He sat back and ran a hand up and down her healthy foot as he explained. "I usually use a police scanner app when I'm working, just to get a pulse on the area. This time it was to keep an ear out for trouble that might involve the agent I was sent to assist."

"Not me."

"I think we both agree I've been sent on a wild-goose chase. By reviewing the incidents that caught my attention on the scanner app against the emails, I'm trying to sort out which events might be Frost."

"And..." she prompted.

He turned the laptop so she could see the incidents he'd highlighted. "Three so far."

"Including Redding, who you knew personally."

"Yes."

"There's more?"

"These three incidents loosely mirror my career strikes when I was with Interpol." The words seemed to drag at him. The memory of who he'd once been weighed heavy on his conscience—even if he'd been one of the good guys, so to speak.

She gasped and he was sure she'd recoil, but she only rubbed his arm in a soothing pattern. "You can't blame yourself for a job well done. You have a skill and you applied that skill to the service of your country and the world at large."

He smiled, but the weight of those lives he'd ended was heavier than it had ever been. "I used to think so."

"I know so. Trust me. You can't second-guess missions long over. Water under the bridge, right?"

"Clichés, Gin?"

"If they fit." She held his face close to hers, held his gaze. "We do what must be done, what others can't do. Believe that above all else, Jason, my love."

He knew those last two words weren't the thing to focus on, but he couldn't help it. It took a long moment for him to regain his composure. "With my service record, the Mission Recovery office should have notified me and asked me to look into it. The local media is talking *sniper* this morning. I heard the unofficial reports on several stations on the way back over here."

"If they haven't asked you to look into the rumors by now," she said, her voice somber, "they want you to take the fall."

He nodded, unable to say those words out loud himself. The betrayal stung too much. Of all he'd seen and survived through the military, Interpol and in Mission Recovery, this felt like the worst way to go out.

He shrugged. "I can disappear for a while."

"You can't believe your own office is picking off innocent people to get rid of you."

"I don't want to believe it, but not many people can access my full service record. Re-creating the beach strike at the pool..." He hated revisiting that scene because it filled him with irrational fear for Gin. He rubbed her foot. She was alive and well and they would get through this. "I think you should leave town now that your mission's accomplished."

She froze, her eyes wide. "Where is my phone?" She looked around.

"Must be in your purse. Why?"

She scrambled to her feet, sloshing coffee across the hotel robe in her rush to reach the safe. He was about to tell her the code when she typed in his birthday and the door swung open.

Too bad this wasn't the time to point out how in tune they were. "What's wrong?" he asked, coming up beside her.

"I haven't checked my email. But you're right. Those incidents would get attention, and any assets nearby would be called in to investigate. They'd never let local law enforcement try to handle you, I mean Frost, alone."

She pulled her purse from the safe and sat down right there in the closet doorway. "I don't have any new emails about a sniper or you in particular. Now that's weird. If the rumors of a sniper are making the media rounds, *they* have to know."

"What does that mean?"

"Only one thing I can think of," she said. "They must know we're together."

"But who would know that? Who told them?" He looked at her and they said it at the same time.

"The blonde."

"She dressed like me that night, and I don't think it was coincidence. We have to track her down and find out who hired her."

"She's a pawn." Jason shook his head. "I'm more concerned about who hired Frost and how they dug up my career history. If I'm right about mimicking the pattern, the next hit will take place somewhere at the Paris."

"What?"

"A club strike in Paris was my next mission after the Riviera."

"Same woman?"

"Still classified."

"My clearance is up-to-date and higher than yours, I bet."

"I'm not taking the bait."

"Then at least take my help."

"I don't want you to get hurt."

"Jason." She glared at him. "Having sex doesn't turn me into something fragile."

"I know that." He pushed a hand through his hair. "It's just—"

"Whatever it is, get over it. I'm not leaving you to deal with this alone. Call it jealousy if you like, but I'm not letting that bimbo get her claws into you."

He chuckled. "Jealous?"

She opened her mouth and quickly snapped it shut. He could almost see the tirade ready to trip off her tongue.

He reached for her, but she dodged him. "Oh, no you don't." He faked one way and caught her when she fell for it. Bringing her up against his body ignited his senses. "You accused me of the same last night."

"And I believe you denied it."

"My mistake." Slowly he lowered his mouth to hers for a lingering kiss. Reluctantly, he eased back, pleased to see his own emotions reflected in the dazed green pools of hers. "No one but you is invited to get their claws in me." He wrapped her hair around his finger.

She swallowed. "Glad to hear it." She slipped her arms around his waist, linking her hands at his back. "Now, will you accept my assistance graciously, or will I be forced to coerce you?"

His curiosity piqued. "What methods of coercion are you considering?"

"That's for me to know and you to find out." She

winked at him then stepped back. Her hands went to the tie of her robe and when he followed the movement, she laughed. "Get your mind back on the case, Specialist Grant. I'm going to dress while you tell me about Paris."

"Right." He would be sure to get even for that little bit of teasing later. "It was a night strike outside of a busy club. Night was the only thing that made it possible."

"The target?"

He returned to his computer. It was the only sane move. Watching her dress was far too distracting.

"Mid-level arms dealer."

He knew she'd stopped moving, knew she was thinking the same thing he'd thought at the time. The mid-level guys usually gave up their bosses for the right incentives.

"Can I borrow your computer?"

He nudged his laptop toward the chair she returned to. "Checking the local registry for arms dealers who like to gamble?"

"Close." Her fingertips flew across the keyboard. "You're not the only one with access to databases." She finished and leaned back in the chair. "So if you were tasked with replicating Jason Grant's biggest hits, how would you do that here?"

"If I'm not after anyone specific…" His voice trailed off as he put his hands on the keyboard. "I could ask the analyst at the office to check the registry at the resorts closest to monorail stops. There might be a bigger fish than Isely taking a holiday, and Frost would have to stay close in order to get in and out."

"True." She stopped him with a gentle touch on his arm. "But let's hold off on that for a few minutes. Follow the nonspecific solution. What would you do in Frost's place?"

"Okay." He sighed, closed his eyes and put himself back in that world. "I'd perch on a rooftop at least a block away and take out the target while he was waiting in line. Chaotic, crowded, instant panic means I get away clean."

"So we can go clubbing at the Paris tonight."

He slanted her a look that warned he wasn't so sure that was such a good idea.

"Don't argue. I'll get dressed and then we can go over and poke around, study the skyline, do the tourist thing."

"You're forgetting I have a tee time at eleven and you were going to have a facial."

"So we cancel both. You might get lucky and stop Frost before he can get set up."

Jason checked the time. "We can walk through, but I have to get some fresh air and sunshine before I lose my mind."

"That's fine, sweetheart. We'll just pick up some golf clothes."

He eyed her suitcase.

"Don't judge me. I can hardly go out in that bikini you bought or any of the cocktail dresses I packed."

"That sparks a few interesting images. The club would have a fit." He held up his hands in surrender.

"I get it." The image of her playing golf in that bikini danced through his head, making him smile. "The Paris has stores."

"You better believe it."

And, oddly enough, he was looking forward to spoiling her. While they searched for Frost's nest, of course.

Chapter Seventeen

Gin wasn't sure what was an act and what was real anymore. Especially since Jason had walked through that door with her luggage and breakfast and been kind enough not to alter her original reservation at the Palace.

Well, he was turning into a man her mother referred to as a keeper. Until Jason, she'd given up on the idea that men like him even existed anymore.

But here he was in the flesh, doting on his *wife* with the best of everything from golf gloves to shoes. The lingering glances and breathtaking kisses made the sales clerks swoon with envy.

She could get used to this.

Yesterday she might have thought it was all an act. Today she was all too aware of how real she wanted it to be.

Oh, she kept an eye out for Isely, the blonde woman or other faces she might recognize from either the criminal world or the spies who tried to counter their moves. Beside her, she knew he did the same.

Once they finished shopping, they strolled hand in hand through the resort, cruising by the inside entrance of the club. "He could set up in here just as easily," she observed, looking up at the elaborate architecture.

"I see that," he replied. "Let's go be tourists," he whispered at her ear.

"Right." She should be used to the tiny shivers created by his touch. With sunglasses on, they left the climate-controlled casino for the bright Nevada sunshine. "Wow," her eyes watered. "I either need more coffee or more sleep."

He squeezed her hand. "I vote for more coffee."

"You're greedy."

"For you, always."

The words shouldn't matter so much to her, but they did. She jerked her attention back to business. "Look." She turned their joined hands toward the club entrance.

"Yeah, I noticed." He raised his camera and took snapshots of the most famous rooflines and facades in the heart of the Strip.

She could tell by his tone it didn't make him happy. "There are a dozen places he could hide and reach anyone waiting in that line tonight."

"Uh-huh." Their reconnaissance complete, he guided her back to their hotel to pick up the car and head out to the golf course.

"But you're thinking."

"Only about you, sweetheart."

"Not buying it," she said, leaning into him.

"I'm thinking about the course. It's a tough nine we're about to play." He handed over the valet ticket, and the young man went racing off to find their car.

"I'll probably double bogey everything." She knew

he wanted to wait until they were in the car and couldn't be overheard. They chattered on about golf until they were safely in their vehicle and could speak freely.

"Weren't you nervous standing around outside? He might already be in his chosen nest."

Jason shook his head, and this time she didn't have to prompt him into talking. It was progress. "Frost has a routine. He'll be sleeping or gambling while he waits for nightfall."

"Where do you think he'll set up the nest?"

"Outside."

She snorted. "Obviously."

Jason turned off the Strip toward the golf club where he'd booked the tee time. "I'm thinking we find a way to close that inside access for the evening."

"You said the club strike was an outside deal."

"Yes, out of necessity." He patted her knee. "The real Paris isn't self-contained like the Paris"

"Low blow," she grumbled. "I'm quite familiar with the real Paris," she said in flawless French.

"Impressive."

"About time you noticed. Why, if Frost is mimicking you, would he take the shot inside?"

"This whole business feels rushed to me. Things are accelerating and none of it adds up. I understand who might win if I'm labeled a loose cannon, but who gained from the hit on Redding?"

"No one has to gain anything—the connection strengthens the case against you."

"Only if you don't know me."

She twisted in her seat. "Are you planning to shut me out again?"

"No." He scowled at the road ahead, clearly lost in thought. "There's nothing in my record that would indicate I'd go off the deep end this way."

"Except the stigma of being a successful sniper."

"Touché."

"Redding was at the convention for a reason. Last I heard he was with a defense contractor working on new technology."

"So?"

"So who loses if new tech helps the good guys?"

"In case you haven't noticed, the bad guys usually adapt faster than the good guys."

"Exactly."

"Jason, I'm not following your logic, if there is any here. Before we realized the pattern, you suggested Frost was here for me."

"That would be nice."

"What?"

"Relax." He reached across the seat and caught her hand. "I only meant that kind of mission would be cut and dried."

"Less than forty-eight hours and my husband already wants me dead."

"You know that's not what I meant."

She chuckled. "I do. But—wedded bliss aside— having been acquainted for such a short time, I'd think being framed for several sniper shots would put you on the offensive."

"This marriage thing rocks." He turned into the long

drive leading to the low stone building of the golf club. "You know me far better than whoever is behind this. If the woman at the bar succeeded and the sniper succeeded, and my real name and history came up through the course of the investigation and I didn't have an alibi for Redding's death, I'd disappear, reverse engineer the shooting and call in a few favors to prove my innocence."

"Assuming the woman at the bar hadn't just killed you."

"Well, true. Then all of this speculation is moot. But if they wanted me dead, Frost had the shot at the pool. They want me alive to take the blame."

She nodded. It bothered her when she thought of that moment—not just the near miss for herself, but that the shooter might have simply put the bullet through Jason's head rather than through the deck chair.

Clearing her throat, she tried to keep it professional. "Aside from you being charged with crimes you didn't commit, who is the big loser in that scenario?"

"Mission Recovery." He pulled into a parking space a couple of rows back from the entrance. "After the rumors last month about the director, a rogue Specialist shooting up Las Vegas would be enough to shut us down."

Neither of them moved to get out of the car. "That opens the suspect pool again. Your department must have hundreds of enemies."

"But not all of them have access to my file."

"What are you thinking?"

"Worst case scenario?" He took a deep breath, poking at the key fob and watching it swing from the ignition. "This is an inside job. Someone in Mission Recovery is pulling the strings."

"Finally."

"Finally?"

She shook her head. "I thought you were never going to say it out loud, that you were going to give me some line about old enemies."

"You knew?"

"Not officially, and I was trying not to leap to conclusions. There might be an old enemy in your past."

"No, I don't have those. My missions were long distance, practically hands-off. All of them are still classified. Whoever is behind this has full access to my record. There's no other explanation for the replicated strikes." He slammed his fist against the steering wheel. "We shouldn't be golfing. We should be turning this over to the authorities."

"Later. First you have to stop Frost. You're the only one who can find him."

"That would be easier if we weren't in Las Vegas, land of a gazillion hotels and nearly guaranteed anonymity."

"Come on." She opened her door. "Let's see if some fresh air and sunshine help you sort this out before nightfall."

"All right. It's not like we have a lot of other options." He twisted around and flipped up the back seat, withdrawing a pistol. "Let's go."

She grabbed the shopping bag. "All set. When was the last time you picked up a golf club?"

"Beginning of last month," he replied, taking her hand as they crossed the parking lot. "You?"

"Let's just say I'm probably better at shopping." As she'd hoped, her answer had them both smiling when they walked into the cool lobby of the club.

It was easy to be with Jason, and now that he was opening up and trusting her, being partners of a sort seemed like a natural progression. The whole situation made her long for something more permanent.

She was starting to think sentimental was going to be a way of life from here on out. Watching people was part of her job, one she enjoyed and excelled at. She imagined the same was true for Jason.

Is that why he was so good at playing the doting husband? According to that theory, she should be good at portraying an enamored wife. She knew better. Years ago, she'd nearly botched a married cover story because she was too stiff with the agent assigned to be her husband.

But this time, with Jason, they had everyone they encountered convinced of their mutual devotion. Which, she knew, meant she was becoming seriously attached to him.

Not such a bad thing…as long as she wasn't in this attachment thing alone.

Chapter Eighteen

Desert Ridge Golf Club,
1:05 p.m.

Jason stopped the cart at the ninth tee, reluctant to move because it meant letting go of her hand. There were fewer people to judge the newlyweds out here, but by now they both knew he liked touching her.

If all went well tonight, they had a date with a divorce drive-through and he might never see her again. He didn't like way his stomach clutched at the thought.

"I should tell you something." She squeezed his hand. "Promise you won't interrupt?"

"Promise."

She took a deep breath. "There's two things. First, the morning after I saved you, I got an alert about a sniper in Vegas."

Jason kept his mouth shut—he'd promised to listen—but he pulled his hand from hers. He could tell he wasn't going to like whatever she was about to say.

"The police hadn't yet announced anything official about Redding and you were right there with me, so I knew it wasn't you."

He stepped out of the cart and walked back to get their drivers.

"Jason?"

"I'm listening." Except he wasn't. She'd done a fine job pretending she hadn't known anything about the sniper in Vegas. Acting was part of the job description for covert agents, but suddenly he didn't know if anything they'd shared had any meaning. She might as well have punched him in the gut.

How many ways could he screw up on this assignment? First he let a stranger drug him, then he let Elvis marry him, and now he'd let Gin put her life on the line.

She accepted the club he handed her. "Did you know he was in town?"

He stared at her. "Are you asking if I was tasked with removing him?"

"Is that what you call it?"

He sneered. "In polite company." He bent down to put his tee in the ground. "Why does it matter? We both know I didn't shoot him. You went through my belongings. Did you find a dossier or ammunition?"

"Lower your voice," she snapped in a whisper, glancing around. "You know I didn't."

The fact that she didn't deny performing the search made it worse somehow. As if being dragged to the altar while he was out of his mind on a drug wasn't enough of a problem.

He battled against the anger building inside him. Not because she'd lied—that was a frequent necessity—or even that she'd married him—apparently that was her best option at the time. No, he was furious because knowing there was a sniper in the area, she'd put herself in danger.

To protect him.

"You interfered—"

"They were setting you up!"

"—and willfully made yourself a target," he said over her justification.

She took a practice cut with the driver, then let the club swing from her hand. Her sunglasses hid her eyes, but it was a safe bet she was considering the appeal of bashing him over the head with it.

He couldn't blame her. Not for that anyway.

"Don't pretend it was about me." He told himself to shut up, but he just kept talking. "You like the rush of cheating death. Crave it."

"That's what you think of me?"

He jerked his chin in the affirmative. It wasn't even close. Professionally, operatives with that attitude didn't survive, and personally...he couldn't risk thinking personally right now.

She pursed her lips. "I see." She waved a hand toward the fairway. "Carry on or we'll soon be holding up the group behind us."

Though he heard the faint lilt in her voice that revealed how hard she was working to hold onto calm, Jason couldn't seem to stop himself. "What else are you keeping from me?"

"Oh, that's more than enough." She slammed her club to the ground. "I don't have to tolerate this." She started marching away toward the clubhouse.

He let her go. She had the right idea. They both

needed to cool off, and some distance would give him a chance to get a grip on the irrational distraction about what would happen when they were done here.

So much for the happy couple cover, he thought as she stalked up the small rise. What was *wrong* with him? They couldn't afford to split up—not before he stopped Frost and they turned in the virus.

"Gin! Wait!"

She broke into a run.

Swearing a blue streak at his stupidity, he jumped into the golf cart and raced after her.

But the battery was fading and with a head start fueled by temper, she was getting away even with an injured foot.

Hopping out of the useless cart, he chased after her. In the back of his mind he wondered if the casino had a couple's therapist on call. They had everything else.

He'd almost reached her when the turf flew up in front of him and just to her left. Bullet. Had to be. The breeze had carried it just wide of her.

"Down," he barked.

But she stood there, frozen in place, a perfect target even an average shooter could pick off. He didn't need to see her face to know it was blank with shock. A second bullet sent gravel spraying out of the landscaping to their left.

He couldn't be sure which of them was the real target, but it hardly mattered. They were out here with zilch for cover and he couldn't live on the hope that the next shot would miss. Whoever was behind the trigger was either impatient or new to the job. On his worst day, Frost would have tagged them both by now.

Of all the gambles in his career, all the hunches, everything that mattered was riding on this one. If they could make it to the clubhouse, or at least the deep sand trap, they had a chance.

Jason surged up behind Gin and forced her toward the sand trap and what he hoped was the better safety of the clubhouse beyond.

The sniper squeezed off two more shots before Jason shoved Gin deep into the bunker. It was a guess, based on the angle, but pressed against the carved-out edge, he thought they were out of harm's way.

For the moment.

He fumbled for his phone and dialed 911, reporting a shooting at the golf course as if he'd been a witness and not the potential target.

"Thank you," Gin said, tucked between him and the sand. "I can't believe I froze."

He looked down into her clear green gaze, grateful her sunglasses had been lost in the scramble. He kissed her lightly. "It happens."

"But it's not the first time I've been shot at. Not even this week."

"I'm aware of that," he said through gritted teeth.

She pulled him down for a more thorough kiss. "I am not an adrenaline junkie."

"I know. I was just so mad thinking you put yourself at risk for me on purpose."

"Don't flatter yourself."

"Hey. You married me."

"Well, sort of anyway."

"What's that mean?"

"I'll tell you later."

"Now is good."

She rolled her eyes and shoved at his shoulder, but when he raised himself up and off of her, she yanked him back down. "No. He might try again."

Jason smiled, understanding the depth of her concern completely. "Does that mean you don't want to be a widow?"

"Not today." Her smile was soft and full of an emotion he wasn't sure he wanted to decipher. "How do you think Frost got back on task so fast?" she asked.

"This wasn't him. He never works alone." He told her about his interpretation of the misses being impatience and poor timing. "Frost wouldn't make that mistake. Whoever just fired at us didn't allow for wind," he added. "And as far as I can tell, he doesn't care which one of us dies."

"That's new."

"Agreed." Sirens wailed in the distance. He wanted to get up and snag one of the bullets for closer inspection before the crime scene techs stashed them into evidence bags. "Maybe we're a two-for-one special because we're married." Hearing shouts from the clubhouse, he decided they were safe enough. "Come on."

"Jason." Her voice cracked on his name.

"What's wrong?" He reached down to help her up, but she held up bloodstained fingers.

"You're hit." Fear roared through him.

She shook her head. "No, it's you."

He felt fine, but she rolled to her feet and ripped open his shirt. "This kind of thing should wait until we're back in our room," he said.

She batted his hands away, clearly not amused, when she spotted the injury.

He shushed her when she gave a panicked shout for help. "It's just a scratch, Gin. I can't even feel it."

"Sit down."

"I'm not going to pass out." He walked out of the sand trap, buttoning his shirt as he went. "It's nothing." Now that she pointed it out, it had started to sting, but it wasn't a big deal. "We need a look at one of the rounds."

"Now who's the adrenaline junkie?"

"I would still vote for you," he said with a warm smile. He knelt by one of the furrows in the turf and used the pencil to dig the bullet out so he could look at it. "That's what I thought."

She crouched beside him. "Different ammo?"

"Definitely. This isn't the .338 Frost would use for a shot like this. I'm probably the only person other than Frost or Wallace who knows that. And Frost never works alone, remember? Last I checked no one had posted Wallace's bond on the burglary charge."

"Which means?"

"Whoever hired Frost has taken matters into his own hands."

"That implies a certain desperation. Why take the risk?"

"That's the million-dollar question, isn't it?"

He could tell from the look on her face that they were thinking the same thing. Only two men knew his past well enough to create such a viable and elaborate setup. One of them was on his honeymoon. The other had ordered him to sit in a Vegas casino and wait for a contact.

A contact that might have led to his incarceration, or even his death, if not for Gin's timely arrival at the bar.

Could Emmett Holt really be in league with Isely? Jason didn't want to believe it and refused to say it aloud. It would make it too real. Still, he had to get this information to the director. The way Washington politics operated, even in agencies that didn't officially exist, the rumor alone would be enough to crush Mission Recovery.

Why would Holt want to do that?

"Killing both of us expedites something we're not seeing. But we survived, which means Frost has to go through with the club strike tonight in order to finish the setup on me."

"Shh." She gave him a little shake. "The authorities are here. Let's give a bystander statement and get back to the room," she said, rubbing her hand over his shoulder. "I can clean you up as well as any paramedic."

"Sure." He pressed a hand to the wound. "One favor?"

"Anything."

"Update Camp about the inside job theory."

"Are you sure?"

Jason nodded. "Do it now. He'll tell Director Casey. And he's the only person I can trust right now."

"I'll take care of it," she promised.

They answered the questions for the police, and Jason relented when the paramedics insisted on treating him. He refused any painkillers or to be transported to the hospital. He just wanted to get back to the room and figure out which angle Frost would take for tonight's strike. That would require a clear head.

Chapter Nineteen

Flamingo resort,
8:52 p.m.

Jason and Gin had talked it through, analyzed the best intelligence offered from his friend in Interpol and her support team and developed a plan. Jason didn't like that she'd be in the mix—alone—her life as likely as any other for Frost to end, but it had to be done.

When he walked out of their room in a few minutes they might not meet again until the divorce. If he succeeded tonight—and he had to succeed—he'd be spending the night with the local police offering up evidence.

If she followed her standard procedure, she'd leave town to track the last of the virus vials and Isely. His new goal was to change her plan.

"So if I understand you," Jason said as he dressed for a night leaping rooftops, "sort of married means we've been living in sin these past few days?"

"Well, it is Sin City." Dressed for a night of clubbing, Gin sat back on the bed and he watched her twist the wedding band on her finger. Her foot was still a little swollen but she insisted on dressing the part. "Would it have been so bad if it was real?"

It would be the best thing that ever happened to him, Jason thought, but he didn't say the words. Studying her, he saw the price of asking was clear in her eyes. Nothing they'd faced in the past two days had put that vulnerability in her eyes. Only the possibility of his rejection.

Here was a woman he admired for her calm under fire and quick mind. A woman he trusted despite her tricks and the shadowy elements inherent to their line of work. Here was the woman he loved above all else.

For a man trained to work alone, it was a big change to admit he needed her. More than that, he wanted her. Now. Always.

He stepped close and reached out to trail a finger across her collarbone. He wanted to press a kiss to the spot he knew would raise goose bumps across her body, but he restrained himself. They had a lifetime ahead of them.

"Is that a proposal? It's not very romantic." He shrugged. "Just saying."

She cocked an eyebrow, clearly annoyed, and he almost cheered that he knew her every expression—or lack thereof—so well.

"Traditionally, proposing is the man's job."

"It's a little late for tradition in our case, don't you think?"

"Maybe," she admitted, the brief flare of bravado flickering back to vulnerable.

He almost relented and dropped to one knee, but she'd jerked him around so much at the start of all of this, he was due a little fun of his own.

If she was ready to make this official, he knew just what he had to do as soon as they captured Frost. He had tickets for an Alaskan cruise on hold along with an engagement ring and wedding bands engraved with Celtic warrior knots. He couldn't wait to see her face when he slipped it on her finger. He'd arranged to have them married by the ship's captain, but if she had something else in mind, he'd happily adjust his plan.

"Are you going to answer me?"

"Just as soon as you ask me the only question that matters."

Her tempestuous emerald gaze might well have killed him if such a thing were possible. He rocked back on his heels, smothering a laugh.

"Fine."

That one word, bearing a faint trace of her Irish blood, told him how much this meant to her. It was all he could do to keep from blurting out the question himself.

She took his left hand in both of hers and ran her thumb over the plain gold of the wedding band he already wore. When she looked up, her heart was shining in her eyes.

"Jason Grant, if you'll be my husband, meet me at this address tomorrow afternoon." She pressed a card into his palm, then a soft kiss to his lips, preventing him from answering. "Now let's go get this bastard."

Las Vegas Strip, 9:24 p.m.

IT SURPRISED HER to be nervous now, standing here in the club line as sniper bait, when she hadn't been nervous before in too many situations just like this to list. Not to mention she hadn't really been nervous when she'd proposed.

Oh God, she had.

Gin took a deep breath and reminded herself to focus. Jason was up there somewhere, ready to spring their trap on Frost. She trusted him completely to manage that before the notoriously accurate sniper ended her life for real this time. She had to believe Jason would prevail, couldn't bear the idea that she'd fallen in love only to die in the line of duty before she had a chance to enjoy it.

She had to believe she'd see him tomorrow.

Scanning the crowded line for a glimpse of Wallace, or whomever Frost might have been forced to help him misdirect the investigators who would be saddled with this crime, she was as surprised as everyone else when a neon sign across the street burst into a showy display of sparks.

People stared upward, but Gin sheltered her eyes and watched for anything out of place around her. She spotted the blond woman scurrying to catch a taxi across the street and smothered a shocked cry when she fell to the ground.

Had Jason taken that shot? *No.* He was a professional. But Gin knew the plan, knew Jason was on one of the rooftops on her side of the Strip taking aim at Frost—if he'd located him—who would be eyeing the crowd around her.

Police cars and emergency vehicles screamed to a stop in front of the Palace and fanned out. A helicopter lit up the rooftops on her side of the Strip with a roving spotlight until it found its target and held steady.

She sighed, moving with the crowd and squinting up at the lights and drama going on overhead. Of course, she realized it now. Jason had tricked her, and he'd done it so smoothly that she could only give him bonus points.

His assignment after the Riviera must not have been Paris after all. By putting her here, he'd effectively put her out of Frost's reach while he'd gone hunting on his own. She didn't like it, but she had to admit he'd been damn clever about it.

A voice barked orders from the helicopter, but here on the ground with the clamoring crowd, the words were impossible to make out. She could only imagine what was going on up there on the rooftop.

Suddenly the spotlight went dark, thanks to a bullet from Frost no doubt, but she caught the two muzzle flashes from the rooftop of the casino just up the block from the Palace. Gin held her breath. Had Jason just put Frost out of commission? Likely with the same ammunition Wallace had tried to plant as evidence against him.

When nothing moved and no other shots were fired, she relaxed. Jason had done it. Wrapped his case with an elegant symmetry she appreciated despite her strong objection to his overprotective methods.

It was a detail they would have to work out. If he had the guts to show up and marry her tomorrow, it would prove his dedication and courage. He had to know that after pulling this stunt, she'd be hard pressed not to rough him up a little before the ceremony. The man had to learn to respect her ability to watch out for herself and handle things on her own.

"Your new husband's handiwork?"

Recognizing Isely's cultured voice, she turned to face him. She'd been so distracted, it wasn't a shock that he'd managed to sneak up on her. She ordered her heart rate to slow and slipped into operation mode. "I'm not married." *Yet.* She slid her clutch over her left hand. "What do *you* want?"

"Merely to say hello. You are a hard woman to track," he said his appreciative gaze sweeping her from head to toe. "I believe I prefer you as a blonde."

"Too bad."

"It is." The crowd shifted again as people tried to get a better look at the commotion across the street.

"Thanks for making my Vegas vacation so exciting," she said, daring to challenge him even as her nerves jangled.

"It was a pleasure. You have played a good game, my dear, but now I would like my product."

She laughed. "Sorry. It's long gone."

He gazed at her purse then leaned in close. "My intel suggests it's right here."

She muttered under her breath and Isely had the audacity to scold her for her foul language. "Fine. Here. You win." She shoved her glittery clutch into his chest. "It goes better with your tux anyway."

When the crowd shifted again, she slipped along with it, ignoring the persistent ache in her foot. Putting distance between her and Isely and the vial of hair gel she'd changed out for the real virus was essential. He might have back-tracked the tag, but she'd had one trick left.

She grinned. Just for him.

As much as she wanted to stay and take the guy down personally, it was better to let the casino authorities get the credit. "That man," she pointed in Isely's direction. "He stole my purse!"

And wouldn't they be thrilled by the card-counting app on the phone she'd dropped in his pocket. She watched a moment as security closed in on her nemesis, then she disappeared into the crowd and immediately turned her attention to more important, personal concerns.

Would Jason show up tomorrow or not?

Chapter Twenty

Holt settled into his first-class seat and watched the flight attendant open the small bottle of whiskey and pour it into the glass. "Thank you," he said with a curt nod.

A drink was his best hope of dulling the sharp pain behind his eyes and silencing the little voice in his head berating him for his mistakes. He'd flown in last night only to see the reports of a sniper in custody, but not the one he expected.

Hard to believe Jason Grant had not only slipped through an intricate web relatively unscathed, but come out the other side with a new bride. He checked his watch. They'd be toasting the happy union in just a few more hours.

He recognized the bulk of his irritation stemmed from the failed trip to Vegas. Oh, sure, Mission Recovery had captured a sniper and, with another vial of that dreaded virus off of the black market, the director would count it a victory—personally and professionally.

Any other time Holt would join the celebration, but not this time. He wanted Isely. He'd put every available resource into this operation, and leaving Vegas without a face-to-face meeting put him in the frustrating position of the underdog.

He knew his own team suspected him, was looking over his shoulder and waiting for him to slip up. He'd think less of them if they didn't, but he berated himself for letting things get to such a delicate impasse.

Having to evade both friends and foes made it hard to see which of the dwindling options was best as he moved forward.

"Looks like you dropped your phone, sir."

He frowned as another flight attendant handed him the device. It was a logical assumption because he was the only person in first class so far and the other passengers were boarding through a door behind him. "I would have missed this," he said with a self-deprecating smile. He waited until she walked away before checking the inner pocket of his suit coat where he'd stowed his phone after clearing security. His phone was right there, so what was this?

It vibrated in his hand and the screen showed an envelope indicating a new text message, but the sender's number was blocked. Holt opened it.

We had a deal.

Furious, Holt started to reply when another message came in.

Last chance.

As if he didn't already know time was running out. Holt kept his cool, though he was tempted to stand up and search the plane until he found the sender. As much as he wanted to believe it was Isely, he knew better. Isely was cocky and determined, but he wasn't dumb enough to lock himself on a plane with Holt for four long hours.

He refused to reply and was about to take the phone apart when another message arrived. This time it was one word, *Beware,* with a picture of Cecelia Manning, Director Thomas Casey's sister.

Holt set the phone carefully on the armrest between the seats and sipped his drink. Whoever Isely sent to watch him would be disappointed. He refused to offer up any kind of reaction.

If Isely was still in the game, he'd soon discover Holt was more than eager to finish it.

He wasn't worried about Cecelia Manning or anyone else.

A smile stretched across his face. "To next time." He toasted the prospect of winning.

He hadn't lost...yet.

Chapter Twenty-One

Gin stood calmly in the waiting room of Happily Ever After wedding chapel, which was just outside the door to the chapel itself, keeping her eyes anywhere but on the front door. She would not be caught pining for him.

Why were the only clocks in Vegas in hotel rooms and wedding chapels? She didn't need a fancy one on the wall, with the hours marked by rosebuds, to know how many minutes had passed.

He was late.

She'd apparently been a fool to think this could work out. She'd compounded that foolishness with this dress and flowers.

Whatever she and Jason had shared over the past days, deception had been a big part of it on both sides. That was no foundation for a marriage, not even a marriage between spies. For a woman who knew how to control her nerves in all circumstances, a woman who'd cheated death a few times over these past days, she couldn't believe she was losing it over a wedding.

Her heart pounded harder with each passing tick of the clock. Her palms were damp and she knew no amount of training would compensate.

Love was the greatest joy and the worst pain she'd ever experienced. She peeked at the clock. Five minutes late. It might as well be a day.

He wasn't coming.

Chin high, she told herself to march over to the desk, take her name off the list and leave. *Just do it and don't think twice. Don't look back.* But her feet, in the shimmery heels she'd picked up last night stayed rooted to the small square of carpet she occupied.

Silly feet. He wasn't coming. He was getting even.

"Miss Olin?"

Oh. Her heart clutched. It was their turn and she had to either tell someone to go ahead of them or she had to just leave. Ridiculous emotions became tears, blurring her vision. She blinked rapidly. She would not leave this place with pathetic smears of mascara trailing down her face.

"Yes?" She managed to get the word past the lump in her throat.

"There's a call for you."

She forced her feet to move closer to the desk, knew it would take her by the wide front window. The jerk she loved probably arranged this so he could watch her misery through a sniper scope.

Deciding she'd use the time off she'd allotted for their honeymoon to track down Jason and make him pay, she accepted the call. "Yes?"

"You look stunning."

She spun toward the window, but her glare faded when she saw him on the other side of the glass. Right there on the sidewalk. Her heart, full of hope, pitched to her stomach in another moment of fear.

"Y-you are coming in?"

His cell phone to his ear, a smile spread slowly across his face and she realized her only foolish thoughts had been her doubts.

"Bet on it. I wouldn't miss this for anything. I was just afraid you'd given up on me and left."

He knew her so well. Her eyes on him, she didn't see the people in his wake until the small lobby was bursting with enthusiastic congratulations for both the mission and the wedding.

"We needed witnesses, right?" Jason introduced her to Director Thomas and his new wife, Jo, and then she smiled as she recognized Lucas Camp and his wife, Victoria Colby-Camp.

When Jason leaned over the flowers she held in her shaking hands and kissed her, the chapel receptionist scolded him for doing things out of order.

Laughter filled the air as they entered the chapel for the ceremony. They exchanged vows, grinning as each said 'I do' and slid rings onto trembling fingers, all under the caring watch of friends. Gin had never felt more loved.

She truly was Mrs. Grant now. And she'd not only gained a husband, she'd also gained a big family with the Specialists and the Colbys.

* * * * *

MISSING

CAST OF CHARACTERS

Jonathan Foley—As one of the new Equalizers, Jonathan must help Melissa find her missing niece—but can he do it without losing his wounded heart?

Melissa Shepherd—As a nurse, Melissa attends to the sick and injured every day of her life. But she can't seem to heal her own heart...the one Jonathan Foley shattered three years ago. No matter that it might cost her more than she can bear to pay, she needs him to help find her niece.

Polly Shepherd—This little girl is missing. Who will find her and bring her home safely?

William Shepherd—His child is missing. But did he have anything to do with it? Did he pull this disappearing act to punish his cheating wife?

Harry Shepherd—William and Melissa's uncle. He will do anything to keep William home and away from serving as a soldier in Afghanistan.

Presley Shepherd—She swears she was at home when her daughter was abducted in the middle of the night, but is she telling the truth?

Reed Talbot—He is the chief of police. It's his job to find this missing child, not some hotshot's from out of town...but can he stick by his guns when the bodies start to pile up?

Carol Talbot—She lost her only child. Can she survive watching her husband investigate this too similar tragedy?

Johnny Ray Bruce—He is in competition with William for Presley. He intends to win...even if he has to do it with the nastiest kind of blackmail.

Stevie Price—He went missing the same day as the child. Is he a harmless mentally challenged man or something far more sinister?

Floyd Harper—He is the only witness to Stevie's alibi.

Scott Rayburn—He's the town's rich boy lawyer. He knows everyone's secrets. He's about to reveal the biggest secret of all.

Slade Keaton—Slade isn't his real name, but he now owns the Equalizers. But his primary agenda isn't about the Equalizers at all...he has plans for the Colby Agency.

Victoria Colby-Camp—Has no idea that her world is about to be turned upside down.

Lucas Camp—Will do anything to protect his family.

This story is dedicated to the real Melissa and Jonathan. As you take each other's hand in marriage, I wish you the most wonderful storybook ending of all!

Chapter One

Chicago
Thursday, May 27th, 10:30 pm

There were better ways to die.

But never a good time.

Jonathan Foley wouldn't have chosen to die in a vacant warehouse with the river lapping at its crumbling foundation. Definitely not while shackled to a cast-off swivel chair beneath the glare of a single bare bulb.

But life stunk that way sometimes.

"Amp it up another notch," the punk gripping the defibrillator paddles ordered. Then he smiled at his prisoner. "Last chance, tough guy."

Evidently the trigger-happy lackey was through playing. Foley braced for the electrical charge that would throttle through his chest the instant the paddles touched his naked skin. Nope, there was never a good time to die. But then he had accomplished his mission. This was likely as good a time as any. He lifted his gaze to the nimrod currently holding the power. "We both know I'm not going to talk."

The jerk laughed, his pale blue eyes glittering with anticipation. "I was hoping you'd say that."

The one manning the controls gave the appropriate knob a violent twist then checked the readout. "Ready," he announced.

Jonathan's jaw clenched and his fingers tightened on the arms of the chair, but he refused to close his eyes. He stared straight at the SOB with the paddles. Refused to allow even a glimmer of fear or defeat. This waste of DNA might kill him but he couldn't make him cooperate. Better men had tried.

"Stand down."

The sharply issued order echoed in the stale air of the long-abandoned warehouse, wiped the smile right off the paddle punk's face.

Foley should have relaxed. After all, he was just a few volts from dead. This unexpected interruption provided a momentary reprieve. He shifted his attention in the direction of the footsteps coming nearer. Not that he needed visual confirmation. He knew the voice.

Victor Lennox.

Tall, distinguished, with just enough gray at the temples to lend an air of wisdom. Even at a time like this—in a place like this—the man sported a three-thousand-dollar black silk suit. No doubt the leather shoes he wore were handcrafted. Nothing was too good for a Lennox. A similarly dressed underling, briefcase in hand, rushed after him.

Well, well, Foley mused. Would wonders never cease? He'd thought Lennox was long gone by now. Yet, here he was, in the flesh, assistant in tow.

"Sir," the underling urged, "the Learjet is waiting. There's no time."

Lennox held up a hand, cutting off his much younger colleague. "Before you die," Lennox said to Foley, his gaze narrowed with disdain and fury, "I have one question."

Foley licked his cracked lips, noted the taste of blood and sweat. "For the past two hours I've been beaten—" his ribs ached with each indrawn breath "—shocked with ever increasing amperage and—" he jerked his head toward the punk with the paddles "—I still didn't talk. What makes you think I have anything to say to you?"

"Let me give it another go," paddle punk pleaded. "He'll talk." He smirked at Foley. "They always do."

Lennox shook his head firmly from side to side. "Not this one."

"Sir." The assistant dared to intrude into the exchange yet again. "You must hurry."

Lennox ignored him. "I did my research, Foley. I know all about you." He made a disparaging sound deep in his throat. "And you're right, you won't talk." He crossed his arms over his chest then reached up and tapped his chin with a finger as if mulling over the situation. "I have friends in places you can't even fathom. I'm aware of your military career, *Major* Foley."

One corner of Foley's mouth twitched with the ghost of a smile. "Then you know it was over a long time ago." Bits and pieces of images flickered through his brain. He banished the memories.

"You endured days of torture," Lennox went on as if

recalling documents he'd only just recently read. "Never uttered a single word while every member of your reconnaissance team was executed right in front of you." A hint of respect flashed in the man's eyes. "Still you remained strong. Loyal to the bitter end. Didn't let your country down." He gave another shake of that distinguished head. "No, no. You didn't talk then. You won't talk now."

"Then what's your point?" Foley looked him dead in the eye. He would have a point. A man who'd just been nailed for treason wasn't going to hang around for anything without a compelling reason.

"After a few years of doing nothing significant, you joined a firm called the Equalizers," Lennox explained, as if he had all night and wasn't the slightest bit worried about the feds who no doubt had already turned Chicago upside down to find him. "Your most recent assignment was to do what no one else had been able to do."

"That's right." Foley had gotten Lennox. Gotten him good. No one else had been able to penetrate the perfect shield he'd built around himself. No one had had a clue that it was the esteemed Victor Lennox who was selling out his own company, his own country. Now his crimes were bared to all. He could run, but he would never again possess the power he had flaunted. Checkmate.

Lennox leaned down, stuck his face in Foley's. "Who sent you?"

"The head of the Equalizers."

Rage tightened the features of the man's face better than the Botox he likely used on a regular basis. "Three people were involved in that aspect of my business," Lennox hissed. "Only three. Not one of them sold me out."

Foley shrugged. "I guess you'll never know for sure."

"Oh, I already know. You see, every man has his breaking point. Each of the three broke eventually. Like you, they remained loyal until the end. Though I suspect they were motivated by fear rather than anything else. You," he accused, "already knew coming in what you were after. All you had to do was find concrete evidence."

Foley stared at him. He wasn't denying or confirming that assertion.

"It's not necessary for you to corroborate the statement," Lennox assured him. "I know."

"Mr. Lennox," the well-dressed assistant interrupted again, "we must go. *Now.*"

Continuing to discount the warning, Lennox demanded, "Tell me who sent you."

That ghost of a smile materialized fully on Foley's lips. "I told you. My employer—the head of the Equalizers."

"A name, Foley," Lennox pressed. "I want a name."

Foley could tell him that he didn't know, because he didn't. No one did. The man behind the Equalizers was a complete unknown. So Foley did what he did best. He said nothing.

"You've won," Lennox fairly shouted. "I've been exposed. I'm on the run. Even I know that it's only a matter of time before they catch up with me. What difference does it make now? I simply want to know the identity of the man who discovered what no one else could."

Foley wondered if Lennox had any idea just how much satisfaction his sheer desperation prompted.

"Cut him loose," Lennox ordered.

"What?" the paddle punk demanded.

"Sir!" the assistant declared, his panic clearly mounting.

"He's going with us," Lennox announced. "I will know who sent him." He stared directly at Foley once more. "Every man has his breaking point. All I need is time to find yours."

While the assistant argued with Lennox, the punk tossed aside the paddles and reached for the knife lying on the cart next to the controls. He grumbled curses under his breath but followed the order. His cohort passed a handgun to Lennox.

Lennox waved the weapon toward the rear door through which he'd entered. "Let's go."

Foley pushed to his feet, the pain radiating through his muscles and settling deep into his bones.

Lennox nudged him in the side with the weapon. "Move," he commanded.

Foley had taken two steps when a cell phone blasted a familiar tune. He glanced over his shoulder at the phone lying on the table next to the portable defibrillator. *His* phone. He'd been relieved of his weapon, his wallet and his phone hours ago.

"Check the screen," Lennox directed.

Foley resisted the urge to roll his eyes. Wouldn't matter if it was his employer, the name and number would reveal nothing. A trace on the call would divulge the same.

"No name," paddle punk reported as he scrutinized the screen. "Out of area call."

A frown attempted to stretch across Foley's brow but he schooled the expression. His employer's number usually showed up as a local call. A different number every time.

"Accept the call," Lennox instructed his torture technician, "and put it on speaker." He glanced around the room. "Not a word from anyone."

The creep holding Foley's cell punched the necessary buttons.

Another waste of time. Foley's employer wouldn't leave a voice mail or speak into dead air. Maybe if Lennox wasted enough time, the feds would be waiting for him at whatever airfield where his Learjet waited on standby.

"Hello, Jonathan…"

Emotion exploded in Foley's chest. Three years… three long years of sleepless nights and pent-up frustration leached into his blood. Haunting snippets of whispered words, the brushing of lips and the hot, smooth feel of bare skin against bare skin rushed into his brain.

It couldn't be…

"I hope this is your voice mail…" A shaky release of breath sighed across the silence. "Call me, please." She stumbled through a number. "I…I need your help. *Please*. It's a matter of life and death."

Silence reigned for three beats, then Lennox smiled.

"Ah. Perhaps we've found the missing piece we need."
Certainty glinted in his eyes.

Foley's mind churned with emotions. Why would
she call him now?

Didn't matter. He knew her inside and out.

Something was very wrong.

Lennox nudged Foley in the spleen with the weapon.
"That sounded exactly like the sort of leverage I need
to obtain the answer to my question."

Ice formed in Foley's gut. No way was he letting this
ruthless monster learn her identity and use her.

"Bring me that cell phone," Lennox ordered his
underling. He reached out in anticipation of having it
placed in his palm.

Foley whipped around and in one second had Lennox in a chokehold, the weapon he still gripped aimed
at his proud brow. "Don't ever let yourself be distracted
when you've got a gun to a man's back."

Paddle punk's cohort dared to reach for his weapon.

"Nobody moves," Foley warned. He bored the barrel
of the nine millimeter into Lennox's temple.

Both men inched forward, testing the line Foley had
drawn.

"Do as he says!" Lennox squeaked around the pressure on his throat.

Smart man. "You," Foley said to the underling who'd
followed Lennox into the warehouse, "call 911 and give
our location. Then give me my cell."

Weapons clattered to the floor as the two thugs who'd
tortured Foley raised their hands in surrender. "You
got what you want," the one who'd brandished the pad-

dles said. "You don't need us." The two started backing away, most likely toward an exit somewhere beyond the scope of the single bare bulb's illumination.

"You're right." Foley studied the two men. "But you're walking away from your best chance at cutting a deal," he warned. "Your prints are all over the place." He nodded to the tools of the torture trade. "Chances are the police will find you eventually."

Paddle punk's eyes narrowed. "What kind of deal?"

Now that was loyalty. "I'm sure the DA will be very interested in any details the two of you can give regarding his—" he tightened his hold on Lennox "—activities. Your cooperation could earn you a very sweet deal."

Lennox attempted to blubber his own warning. Foley clamped his arm tighter around the bastard's throat and shot a look at the man who'd trailed in here after him like a puppy. "Make the call," Foley repeated.

While the assistant in the expensive suit entered the necessary digits, the two thugs dropped to their knees then went facedown on the concrete floor.

"You might think you've won," Lennox screeched, "but you and your employer will suffer the consequences."

"Maybe." Foley nodded to the guy who'd made the 911 call. "Bring my cell to me," he ordered a second time, "then join your pals on the floor."

The younger man glanced at the filthy floor then swallowed hard.

"Now," Foley prompted.

The man inched close enough to give Foley the

phone, then side-stepped in those same small incre-
ments back toward his partners in crime. It was almost
worth the torture Foley had endured to watch that silk
suit kiss the dirt and, during the short minutes before
the cops arrived, to listen to Lennox's offers of exces-
sive amounts of cash for his freedom.

But Foley had one thing on his mind. *Her.* She'd
called. Unbelievable. He hadn't seen her, hadn't heard
her voice in three years.

I need your help.

Worry throbbed in his skull, flexed in his jaw.

She wouldn't call him…unless it truly was a matter
of life and death.

Fear trickled into his veins.

He had to get to her.

When the cops arrived, Foley gave one of the of-
ficers his business card and walked away. He ignored
the warning that he wasn't supposed to leave until the
detective in charge of the case arrived.

There wasn't a force on earth that could prevent him
from going.

The cell in his pocket sang its annoying tune.

Foley withdrew it, checked the display in case it was
her calling again.

It wasn't. It was his employer.

Not at all surprised his employer already knew Lennox was down—he seemed hotwired into everywhere
with everyone—Foley hit the answer button even as he
quickened his pace. "Foley."

"Outstanding job," the voice on the other end praised.
"I knew you were the right man for this one. File your

final report and relax. I'll contact the office with your next assignment."

What kind of man could position a player to bring down a man like Lennox? A god in the murky and political world of government contractors.

"Who are you?" Foley had been hired as an Equalizer more than five months ago. He'd heard this voice a dozen times, but he had no idea who the guy was or even what he looked like. Foley and the other two Equalizers currently on staff had done their research, gone to all sorts of lengths to find that answer.

And there was nothing. It was as if the man behind the voice didn't exist.

"One day you'll know," the voice promised. "For now, your payment will be deposited into your bank account today."

The connection severed.

Foley stalled, stared at the phone a moment. One day he would know? What did that mean? Then he shook off the questions and broke into a sprint.

She needed him.

He shouldn't care.

Stepping back into her life would be a mistake…for both of them.

But he couldn't ignore the call.

Not even if he tried.

Chapter Two

Bay Minette, Alabama
Friday, May 28th, 9:15 a.m.

Calling *him* had been a last resort.

Melissa Shepherd hugged her arms around her middle and stared through the window over the kitchen sink at the drizzling rain. She was desperate.

Or crazy.

She shuddered. Jonathan Foley had disappeared from her life three years ago. The ache, though dull, still swelled deep inside her whenever he came to mind. She shouldn't have called him. Bay Minette's entire police force, aided by numerous volunteers from surrounding towns and counties, hadn't been able to find her niece, so why in the world would she believe he could?

Misery washed over Melissa. Polly had been missing for five days. Five endless days and nights.

Melissa's brother was scheduled to ship back to Afghanistan on Tuesday, the day after Memorial Day. She shook her head. How could he leave with his three-year-old daughter missing? The military didn't seem to care.

Closing her eyes, Melissa blew out a heavy breath.

That wasn't fair. It wasn't that they didn't care. Her brother, William, was trained in a highly critical MOS—military occupational skill. It was a miracle he'd even gotten this too-short, two-week leave in the first place.

That was the real reason Melissa had called Jonathan. He didn't like talking about his past career in the military but, from what she'd gathered, during that time he had been connected to extremely high-level people—important people. He could call someone. She was certain of it.

She'd asked him to do that when he'd returned her call in the middle of the night last night. He'd promised to call her back this morning.

So far she hadn't heard a word.

Melissa opened her eyes and searched the backyard of her childhood home, her heart automatically hoping her gaze would land on sweet little Polly playing there. But the yard was empty. The old rope and wood swing her father had built for her as a child hung empty from the big old pecan tree's massive branch.

She'd tried. For days Melissa and the rest of the family, along with friends and neighbors, had searched. And nothing. It was as if Polly had vanished into thin air, leaving no trace of the reason for, or the person behind, her disappearance.

Other than the fact that Stevie was missing, too. Melissa shook her head. She couldn't believe that Stevie would ever harm Polly. He loved her. Stevie Price had suffered immense cruelty and severe trauma as an infant. The physical trauma had resulted in brain damage, leaving him mentally challenged. By the time he was four his self-centered mother had abandoned him. His father had tried to take care of him, but he'd had problems of his own. When Stevie was nineteen his father had died. He'd lived off the kindness of folks in the community ever since. And though he was thirty now, his mind was like a child's. The children in the community loved Stevie.

Melissa had played with him as a kid.

He wouldn't do this.

Someone else was responsible for this horror.

Hadn't the Shepherd family suffered enough tragedy? First her father had been killed by serving his country while she and William were just kids. Melissa was convinced that was the reason William insisted on joining the military in the first place—to somehow feel closer to his father. Then, as if that hadn't been a kick in the teeth, their mother had died four years ago. Melissa hadn't been anywhere near ready to lose her mother. But Polly had come along and she'd brought new light to that dark, empty place.

Now she was missing. After five days Melissa feared the worst.

A lump rose, tightening her throat. *Please, God, don't let that sweet baby be hurt.*

As if her agony had summoned him, William came up beside her. "The chief sent me home."

Melissa turned to her brother. He looked beyond exhausted. She knew full well the agony she felt was nothing compared to what he suffered. Polly was his first and only child. He loved her more than life itself. He'd done everything in his power to give her a good life—in spite of the difficulties he and his wife had in their marriage.

The whole town despised Presley. Whispered ugly things behind William's back when he'd announced that he and Presley were to be married. Melissa wasn't blind or stupid. She knew full well the stories, some all too true, that traveled the gossip circuit on a regular basis about her sister-in-law. But Melissa chose to give Presley the benefit of the doubt. Everyone deserved a second chance and Presley'd had a rough go of it as a kid. William loved her. That was enough for Melissa.

"Presley was sleeping," William said, his voice weak with fatigue and fierce worry. "I didn't want to bother her so I came here."

Melissa's chest tightened. Whatever anyone thought of Presley, she worshipped Polly. As much of a nightmare as this was for her, Melissa couldn't begin to fathom how Presley felt. "You need sleep, too." She brushed the back of her hand across his shadowed jaw. He felt cold despite the unseasonably warm weather. "You can't help Polly if you're too worn out to think straight."

William shook his head. "I can't bear to sleep." Emotion glistened in his bloodshot eyes. "Who would do this?" His lips trembled. "Who would take my baby?" He dropped his head.

The sheer agony in his voice tore at Melissa's heart. Just looking at him brought images of Polly to mind. The little girl had her daddy's blond hair and blue eyes. She was a little duplicate of him and she'd brought so much joy to their lives.

The loud chime of the doorbell echoed through the too-quiet house.

Melissa's and William's gazes locked.

What if they'd found Polly or…Melissa swallowed tightly…her body?

Dear God, no, no, no. Don't let that be.

Melissa pulled her bravado up off the floor and wrapped it around her. "They would've called," she said aloud. That was right. She let the air seep back into her lungs. "If they'd found her, they would've called." The courage she'd dredged up and the words she'd spoken for her brother's benefit did nothing to slow the thundering in her chest.

William nodded. "Guess so."

The chime echoed a second time. "Stay here." Melissa squeezed his arm. "I'll see who it is."

She turned from her brother, her heart somehow rising into her throat while it continued to pound frantically, and started toward the living room. The dishes she'd intended to wash when she'd come into the kitchen still waited, but she didn't care. It was difficult to keep her mind on anything except Polly.

Chief Talbot, the town's chief of police since Melissa was a kid, had ordered Melissa back home this morning, too. He didn't want her or William out there. Maybe because of what he feared finding or maybe just because they both looked like death warmed over.

At least the chief had allowed their Uncle Harry to continue helping with the search. Harry would call the instant he knew anything. He was practically a second father to her and William. He'd stepped in when their father was killed, taking over for the younger brother he'd adored. Melissa felt certain that was why he'd never married and had a family of his own. He'd been too busy taking care of his younger brother's.

Holding her breath, Melissa opened the front door.

She'd braced for the appearance of one of Bay Minette's finest or a family friend bearing bad news.

But not this. She wasn't prepared for this.

Jonathan Foley.

The breath she'd been holding whispered past her lips, his name forming there without conscious thought. "Jonathan."

"Melissa."

The sound of his voice echoed through her being, made her soul ache with the need to reach out to him. He looked exactly the same. Tall with shoulders that filled the doorway. Thick black hair still military short. Chiseled jaw that gave the impression of unyielding stone. But it was the eyes that made her already pounding heart stumble drunkenly.

They were ice blue, so pale they were almost gray. She'd always been certain that he could see right through her. That he could read her every thought.

"I've been waiting for you to call." She managed to keep her voice steady, which was an outright miracle.

"May I come in?"

Shaking off the shock and confusion, Melissa stepped back. "Of course." *Get your head together, girl.*

Jonathan Foley stepped across the threshold and into her family home. Melissa's breath deserted her once more. He was here. After nearly three years without a word, he was here.

He waited patiently, his eyes searching hers.

She summoned the courage that had apparently run for parts unknown. "I'm glad you came." It was the truth. She'd expected nothing more than a phone call but she was damned glad he was here. The urge to fall into his arms consumed her again.

"Has there been any word on your niece?"

Melissa moved her head side to side. The movement felt stiff and jerky with the tension ruthlessly gripping her neck.

Silence pressed against her, filled the room for half a dozen beats of her aching heart.

She gave herself a mental kick. "Please sit." She gestured to the sofa and chairs. Wherever he lived now, whatever his job or personal status, he'd come to Alabama to help her family. For that she felt immensely grateful.

He waited for her to take a seat first, then he settled in the chair directly across from her position on the sofa. Old, well-worn, the sofa had been around since she was a kid. The upholstery had changed a couple of times, ending up a wild mix of pink and red flowers against a green and white background. Her mother had picked it out and Melissa didn't have the heart to change it.

Jonathan considered her a moment, his posture straight and rigid as if he expected a general to enter the room at any moment and he might have to jump to his feet and salute. His forearms rested along the length of the chair arms, his hands palms down, his long fingers extended as if that were the only part of him fully relaxed. Then he finally spoke. "She's been missing for five days?"

"Yes." That sinking feeling that bottomed out in her stomach each time Melissa thought about sweet little Polly out there alone or worse dropped like a stone deep into her belly now. "They're continuing to search for her." She shook her head. "But they haven't found anything yet."

His gaze narrowed so very slightly that she might have missed the change if she hadn't been staring so intently at him. "No suspects? No evidence discovered?"

"Nothing at all." She clenched her fingers together and pressed her fists into her lap to prevent them from shaking.

"Has the FBI been called in to assist?"

Melissa had to really concentrate to pull the answer from the mass of painful and confusing information she'd attempted to process the past few days. "There was talk of someone coming from Montgomery." What had the chief said? Her mind was a total blank! What was wrong with her? Taking a deep breath, she finally pieced it together. "I think a consult was done by phone."

She waited for a response, physical or verbal, but he said nothing. Sat utterly still. Analyzing her answer, she supposed.

Memories flooded her brain. Moments shared with this man that she had shared with no other human being. Secrets…feelings. *Stop.* She ordered herself back to the matter of importance. "Is that normal procedure?"

she asked when he continued to sit stone still without saying a word.

"Sometimes." He paused a moment as if to be sure of his words. "The Bureau's involvement is strictly on a case by case basis. If they're not on the scene they feel there is nothing their presence could add at this point."

Did that mean the FBI felt Polly's case was hopeless? Before Melissa could ask as much, he said, "Walk me through exactly what happened."

Where was William? Melissa glanced at the door that separated the kitchen and dining room from the living room. Forcing him to relive that night would only add to his misery. "It was late. William and his wife had a fight." Melissa took a moment to tamp down the renewed rush of emotion. "You know how young couples can be. A little too much passion and not quite enough common sense. William didn't want Polly to be awakened by the arguing so he left and came here for the night." Melissa's throat attempted to close again. "The next morning when he went home Polly was gone and Presley was sleeping off the vodka she'd used to drown her frustrations."

More than one well-meaning neighbor had commented that no decent mother would drink herself unconscious with her child in the next room. But that was the main emotional outlet Presley had been exposed to growing up. It was what she knew. Melissa wanted to shake her every time she thought about it, but that wouldn't change a thing.

Even more troubling, the house had been unlocked when William arrived home that awful morning. William insisted he had locked up when he left. Presley claimed he clearly had not since the back door had been wide open with no indication of forced entry. Melissa wanted to believe William, but he'd been damned upset that night. He was only human.

Sweet Jesus, how could this have happened?

"He called the police," Jonathan prompted.

"Yes." Melissa chewed at her bottom lip. Her throat was so dry she could scarcely breathe much less swallow. "The chief and one of his deputies arrived within minutes. William and Presley were arguing." Melissa shook her head. "It was terrible...just terrible."

Another long moment of tension-filled silence passed, with Jonathan watching her, assessing her. What was he thinking? Had he already formed some sort of conclusion? How was that possible? He didn't know her family. Certainly she'd mentioned her brother and niece, and her uncle, but Jonathan hadn't bothered to stick around long enough to meet any of them. Melissa had been living and working in Birmingham at the time. Still would be if her mother hadn't gotten sick and then if her brother hadn't deployed to the Middle East.

William had begged Melissa to come home and keep an eye on Polly. And Presley. Determined to help, Melissa had come home and still this unthinkable tragedy had occurred.

"The investigation has uncovered nothing?" her visitor asked again.

"Nothing." It was disheartening, awful even, but it was the truth. "No one saw anything or heard anything," she explained, hoping to make herself perfectly clear this time. "Whoever took Polly left no evidence. Nothing."

"I spoke to my contact at the Pentagon."

A little hitch disrupted her respiration. "And?" This was what she'd called him about, what she'd needed from him. Not this interrogation. His questions felt exactly like that. As if he was interrogating her. Stay calm, she ordered herself. He was trying to help. Her fingernails pinched into her palms.

"Your brother's orders have been put on hold indefinitely."

Relief flooded Melissa with such force her shoulders trembled. "Thank you."

"But…"

Fear and something resembling anger swirled fast and furiously in Melissa's stomach. "But?" This was going to be something she wouldn't like. She could feel it. Jonathan's hesitation spoke volumes.

"If your brother was somehow involved," Jonathan warned, "there will be serious consequences."

Melissa blinked. At first his words just sort of bounced off the wad of emotions swaddling her brain. Then the realization filtered through. He was suggesting William was somehow involved with Polly's disappearance. "What?" She couldn't have heard him right. There had to be a mistake. The very idea was ludicrous.

Jonathan didn't look away. His gaze held hers with the same ferocity as when she'd first found him standing outside the door. "It happens, Melissa."

The way he said her name, with that same thick

huskiness as when they'd made love, ripped open the wounds she'd thought long healed and forgotten.

"More often than you know," he went on while she scrambled to regain her equilibrium. "These soldiers experience things…see things that change them from the inside out. Sometimes they can't accept the idea of going back. They'll do anything to ensure that doesn't happen. The suicide rate is incredibly high."

She couldn't move, couldn't respond. Melissa knew her brother. No matter what he'd experienced, he would never, ever put his daughter in harm's way. Never. Anyone who suggested such a thing either didn't know him or was a fool.

"Most of the families feel that way, even after the worst has happened."

His answer told her she'd stated her thoughts aloud. Looking down, she unclenched her fingers and swiped her palms against her jean-clad thighs before clenching her fingers into fists once more. Meeting his gaze would take some regrouping. He couldn't be right. No way. William would never do that. He'd been questioned along those very lines the same day he'd discovered Polly was missing. He wouldn't, couldn't do it.

"You're wrong." Her gaze locked with Jonathan's once more. "William would sacrifice himself in a heartbeat for his child. No way would he do this."

"War changes people. Some more than others, but no one is exempt. Whether it's visible or not, the change is there." Jonathan took a deep breath, the rise and fall of his chest the first indication that he had even that essential human need. "The only person who can be certain of William now is William himself."

Melissa opened her mouth to defend her brother but never got the chance.

"He's right."

She twisted around to look at William. The idea that he might have overheard all that had been said in the last few minutes wrenched her heart.

"Sergeant Shepherd," Jonathan acknowledged.

"Major Foley." William stepped past Melissa and settled into the chair next to hers.

"It's just Foley now," Jonathan corrected.

William made a sound in his throat, not quite a laugh. "Are you sure?"

Melissa watched the interaction between the two men, her pulse thumping in her ears. The connection between the two was instantaneous and palpable. They'd never met, yet the military connection somehow made them familiar.

One corner of Jonathan's mouth quirked with an almost smile. "You've got me there. But today we're not soldiers so let's keep things informal."

William gave an agreeable nod. "My daughter is my heart," he said, his tone flat. His emotions had run so high for the past few days that his mind and body could no longer maintain the necessary energy for emotional nuances. "I would gladly die right now if it would bring her back here."

"I have no doubt," Jonathan concurred. "However, even the best of us have moments when we snap. Maybe do something we didn't intend to do." Before William could counter, he added, "Then denial kicks in and we genuinely don't believe ourselves capable of such an act. The mind is a powerful thing. It sometimes protects us from that which we cannot bear."

Unlike Jonathan, William's shoulders were slumped, his usually handsome face lined with fatigue. He turned his hands, palms up. "Believe what you choose, Foley. I had nothing to do with my baby's disappearance." His voice cracked with the last. "My only guilt is in not being there like I should have been."

Melissa took his hand in hers. His felt limp and cold. "You don't have to convince anyone," she soothed. "He just doesn't know you, that's all." She glared at the man she'd called to help. "Thank you for making that call." She squared her shoulders. "Right now William and I should get down to the command post and see what we can do to help." Melissa didn't care what the chief said, she wasn't going to sit here and do nothing.

She absolutely was not going to put William through another interrogation.

Jonathan stood. "I'm glad I could help."

Every fiber of her being screamed at her to say something, to stop him from leaving. But she wanted him to go, didn't she? He'd made the call. William didn't have to leave until Polly was found. Melissa didn't need anything else from Jonathan. He should go.

William pushed to his feet, letting go of Melissa's hand and reaching for Jonathan's. "Sir, you don't know how much I appreciate what you've done." He shook Jonathan's hand with a firmness that Melissa would have thought him too weary to generate at this point.

"I have no qualms about serving my country." His hand fell back to his side. "I just couldn't go…yet."

Jonathan nodded. "When this is resolved, let me know and I'll make the necessary calls."

"Yes, sir."

Jonathan strode toward the door.

Melissa's feet remained glued to the floor all the way up until the moment he opened the door.

She was across the room and calling after him before her brain caught up with her actions. "Jonathan." What the hell was she doing? She should let him go!

He stopped, nearly to the steps, and turned, that ice blue gaze colliding with hers.

"We're scared." She pressed her lips together a moment and fought to hold back the tears. "We…we've never been in a situation like this. We don't know if the police are doing everything they can do." She shrugged, tried to hold back some of the truth spilling out of her, but that wasn't happening. "We ask questions and get answers we don't understand. We try to help but they…"

Jonathan was coming back toward her, one steady step at a time, his gaze never leaving hers, not even to blink.

"They don't know anything…" A sob halted her words. "They can't tell us anything except to be patient and to pray." Frankly, she was beginning to doubt her link to the Almighty. She'd about prayed herself out, about lost hope.

Jonathan stopped toe-to-toe with her. "It's possible that what the police are telling you is all there is to tell." He shook his head slowly, somberly. "These cases can go unsolved for years." A shadow moved across his face. "I have to tell you, after five days, if there's been no ransom demand, the chances of the child being found alive are slim to none."

"Polly." The name trembled on Melissa's lips.

A frown line formed between his eyebrows.

"That's her name," Melissa said. "She's three years old and the most precious child." She smiled even as a hot tear slid down her cheek. "She has to be alive. I'm not willing to accept anything else. If—" Another of those halting sobs caught her words. "If you can help us, it would mean a great deal to me if you would stay."

The morning breeze whispered across her skin, sending goose bumps scattering up her arms. She waited for his answer, prayed some more in spite of herself. Maybe he couldn't help, but somehow, deep in her heart, she knew that his presence would make a difference. She had denied that knowledge, had told herself she'd called him just for the military connection, but that had been a lie.

She needed him right now. Melissa didn't want to admit any such thing, but it was true.

Damn it, it was true.

"Make no mistake," he said quietly, "I can't promise you anything."

She shook her head adamantly. "You don't have to promise anything. It's enough that you try." Her lungs dragged in a deep, much needed breath.

Their gazes held for one, two, three beats. "All right then. I'll try."

Chapter Three

11:05 a.m.

Jonathan stayed on the front porch of William Shepherd's modest home while he and Melissa argued with his apparently uncooperative wife. The windows were raised, allowing the breeze to drift inside and also permitting the raised voices to carry right out to where Jonathan waited on the ancient wooden swing.

Presley's argument was simple. She'd been interviewed by the police twice, the family half a dozen times and she had no desire to answer questions from some friend of Melissa's. The way she said her sister-in-law's name suggested a serious dislike. In sharp contrast, Melissa patiently and gently urged Presley to reconsider.

Melissa.

Jonathan drew in a breath, the heaviness in his chest fighting the effort. What the hell was he doing here? He'd made the call. That was all she'd asked him to do when they'd spoken on the phone. Her brother now had whatever time he needed to resolve this terrible state of affairs. The local police seemed competent; the FBI had been consulted. There was little else Jonathan could do other than retrace already taken steps. He nudged the porch floorboards with the toe of his boot, setting the swing in motion.

And yet he had agreed to stay when she'd asked.

Because he had to.

Jonathan closed his eyes and let the memories he'd dammed years ago flood his mind. Their meeting had been nothing more than a chance encounter. He'd been on the final plummet of a serious downhill slide. Walking away from his military career under the circumstances at the time of his official exodus had plunged him into a thirty-month descent of self-pity and denial. Denial of who he was and what he'd done.

Until a midnight brawl in a bar in Birmingham had landed him under arrest and with a nasty gash as a souvenir. He rubbed at his forehead where the scar still ached whenever he thought of his former stupidity.

Registered Nurse Melissa Shepherd had been on duty at the ER that night. She'd patched him up and, after he'd made bail, she'd said yes to his offer of dinner as a way of showing his gratitude for her extraordinary patience with a less than amiable patient.

The ability to draw in a deep breath deserted him once more as the memories poured through him. No one had ever pulled him in so deeply. He hadn't been able to get enough of touching her, of looking at her. He would have done anything for her—except put the past behind him and make a real commitment. The dreams—no, the nightmares—he'd suffered since that last military mission had prevented any possibility of moving on with his life. Jonathan Foley existed in the moment.

Even Melissa's unconditional love hadn't been enough at the time to help him move beyond the past. The facts listed in his official military jacket that explained the decisions—decisions he had made that protected the mission but ultimately cost the lives of good men. The same facts that still allowed him to call up a top-ranking official at the Pentagon and make things happen.

Jonathan surveyed the small yard that flanked the little house Melissa's brother called home. The picket fence needed a fresh coat of paint. The house could use one, too, but it was a home. Maybe not such a happy home, but a home where a man and woman had made a commitment to give life together a shot. A home where a child played. The colorful sandbox beneath the oak tree, along with the big plastic, equally colorful building blocks made for climbing marked this as a home where a child lived.

Except that child was missing. Probably deceased.

Regret twisted in Jonathan's gut.

Melissa didn't want to consider that possibility but the chances the child was deceased were far greater than the likelihood that she would be found alive.

Melissa and her family didn't deserve this horrific pain. Unfortunately Jonathan doubted he would be able to make it right. He would try. He owed Melissa that. She had given everything she'd had to give and he'd walked away.

He'd let her down just as he had his team two years prior to that.

His work as an Equalizer now allowed him to do what he couldn't do over five years ago for his team, what he couldn't do for Melissa three years back. Make a wrong right.

Maybe if he could in some way make this tragic wrong right, he could forgive himself for hurting Melissa with such nonchalance.

He had to try.

The screen door opened and Melissa leaned out. "You can come in now."

Jonathan pressed the soles of his boots against the porch floor, stopping the swing and simultaneously pushing himself up.

"Just one thing." Melissa looked embarrassed. "Presley has a serious hangover. She's a little cranky so tread lightly."

"Yeah." Jonathan forced something as close to a smile as he could produce. "I got that part."

He immediately regretted the words. Melissa's look of weary exasperation had him rethinking his lack of tact. When she turned and went inside, he followed.

The interior of the house was as humble as the exterior, and equally in need of attention. Toys lay scattered about, but the glaring theme was disorderliness. Under the circumstances it was expected, but Jonathan sensed the house had always been untidy. Clearly, living up to "Suzy Homemaker" standards was not on Presley's agenda.

Presley Shepherd, twenty-three according to her

DMV record, currently had auburn hair. Her DMV photo showed her as a blonde with a brazen blue streak down one side. She was dangerously thin and quite happy to show off as much of her slight frame as possible. The shorts and tank top were two sizes too small even for her.

"Presley," Melissa said, "this is my friend Jonathan."

The missing child's mother peered up from her perch on the sofa, her gaunt cheeks making her eyes appear inordinately large. "Let's just get this over with. I have stuff to do."

William indicated the end of the sectional sofa farthest away from where his wife lounged. "Please, have a seat, sir."

Jonathan waited for Melissa to settle first, then lowered onto the upholstered sofa beside her. The brush of his arm against hers made him flinch. Thankfully she didn't seem to notice.

"What do you wanna know?" Presley demanded. She combed her fingers through her hair and looked him up and down as if she'd only just realized he was male.

"Why don't you walk me through the night Polly went missing," Jonathan suggested.

Presley rolled her eyes.

"I know this is hard," Melissa said softly, "but we have to try every avenue."

Jonathan was amazed by her patience. He wasn't so sure Presley deserved so much slack. He didn't need a shrink to analyze this woman. Her indifference and self-absorption were glaringly evident and, based on what he'd read of her background when he'd looked into the characters related to this drama, likely related to her neglected childhood.

"William and I had a big fight." Presley glanced at her husband, who looked as miserable as he no doubt felt. "Polly was asleep. I didn't want her waking up with us fighting again so he went to his folks' house for the night. No big mystery." She threw her hands up. "Same old, same old." She made eye contact with Jonathan only once and only briefly as she spoke.

"Again?" he asked.

Her pale face scrunched into a frown. "What?"

"You said," Jonathan clarified, "that you didn't want Polly to wake up with you fighting 'again.' Have you been fighting frequently?" He glanced from Presley to William and back. "Since he returned home on leave?"

Her thin, pointy shoulders hunched. "I don't know. Yeah, I guess. We always fight." She looked to her husband. "It's just the way we are."

William said nothing.

Jonathan moved in a different direction. "According to the police report, there was no sign of forced entry. Did you ensure the door was locked after he left?"

She twirled the fingers of her right hand in her hair. "Course. I'd be stupid not to."

William cut a look at her but quickly glanced away.

Jonathan let several seconds lapse before broaching the next question. He wanted both of them to squirm a moment. William's posture and outward expression never changed. Presley's, on the other hand, became more agitated. She changed positions on the sofa twice and tugged at her skimpy blouse.

"Besides yourself and William who has a key to your house?"

William looked to Melissa. "You have one."

Melissa nodded. "I keep it in the key box at home." To Jonathan she added, "It's on the wall by the back door. That's where we hang the keys."

"No one else." William turned to Presley. "Right?"

"You'd know better than me," she said, incensed. "You got the locks changed the last time you were home."

Jonathan considered her statement a moment as she and her husband discussed the issue of keys. "Why did you have the locks changed?" he asked, the question directed to William.

"Presley was being harassed by this jerk," William said, "and I was about to be deployed for six months." He shrugged. "I was trying to protect my family."

"Worked out real good, didn't it?" Presley snapped.

A new layer of agony settled deep into William's features.

"Blaming William or yourself won't help right now," Melissa said in that same gentle tone. "Is there any possibility someone else had a key? One of your friends maybe?"

Presley shot up from the sofa. "I knew this was the way it would be." She planted her hands on her narrow hips. "I've been through this crap with the cops already. I don't need to go through it with you. Everybody knows that retard Stevie took Polly." She glared at Melissa. "He probably got the key from your house.

You let him hang around all the time like he's family or something."

Melissa flinched. "The key is right where it has always been. And you know Stevie wouldn't do that. He's family. We're the only family he has."

Presley's eyebrows reared up in skepticism. "You sure about that, Miss Goodie Two-shoes? They won't let him play with the kids at the day care center no more cause of what he did. Maybe you'd better get your facts straight."

Jonathan exchanged a look with Melissa. Had he missed something?

Melissa shook her head, weariness and worry heavy in her eyes. "That was a misunderstanding. Stevie was a volunteer. The kids loved him. That one little girl was new. She didn't understand Stevie was only playing. Chief Talbot cleared Stevie of any wrongdoing. He doesn't go back to the center because it puts *him* at risk. Not the children."

"Whatever." Presley slinked out of the room.

William heaved a weary sigh. "I'm sorry." He glanced in the direction his wife had disappeared. "She's not herself."

"A missing child is the sort of nightmare no parent ever wants to go through," Jonathan said, acknowledging the difficulty of the situation. "We all show our pain in different ways."

As if he'd said the words about their situation Melissa turned to him, her gaze searching his.

An old familiar pang ached through Jonathan. He banished the ache and focused on the questions he needed to ask. "The windows are open," he said to William. "Were they open that night?"

William shook his head. "That night it was cold for May. One of those dogwood winters the old timers talk about."

"May I see her room?" Jonathan couldn't name what he was looking for but he needed to get a feel for the family life. He'd formed a pretty strong opinion already and it wasn't good. With William away serving his country most of the time, it didn't appear that anyone was watching after the child in any significant and consistent manner. He felt confident that Melissa did all she could, but he doubted that Presley allowed her interference often.

With visible effort, William nodded and pushed to his feet. "It's, uh, this way."

Jonathan waited for Melissa to go ahead of him but she hesitated. "She knows something." Melissa checked to ensure her brother was well out of hearing. "Something she's afraid to tell."

He didn't have to ask whom she meant. Her sister-in-law. The pain on Melissa's face even as she voiced what Jonathan himself sensed with little doubt made his gut clench. "I agree."

Melissa turned to lead the way to the child's bedroom without saying more, but the relief Jonathan had noted on her face at his agreement made him wonder just how bad a mother Presley had been. Maybe not that bad, he amended. Melissa would never overlook abuse or neglect.

The small house had two bedrooms separated by a

bathroom down a short hall from the main living area. The child's room was a little tidier than the rest of the house he'd seen so far. The bed was unmade, stuffed animals lined shelves and themed curtains dressed the windows. The signs of a forensic tech's work remained visible. The room had been dusted for prints and the bed linens had been removed for collection of trace evidence. That last part surprised Jonathan. The official report had shown no indication that sexual abuse was suspected.

Jonathan checked the window. It was closed and locked, presumably the way it was the night the child went missing. The pink paint around the window looked clean and undamaged. The curtains showed no tears.

There was nothing about the room that appeared out of place to an outside observer. Jonathan turned to William. "Does Presley work outside the home?"

"Sometimes she helps out at the diner downtown."

"Who takes care of Polly when her mother works?"

"She goes to the day care center at the First Baptist Church." William's gaze stayed on the child's pillow as he spoke. "It's kind of a mother's day out program. Polly likes going there."

Jonathan wanted to ask about the guy who had harassed Presley, but he would get that information from Melissa later. "Are there any other places Polly goes regularly? Any friends she plays with who live nearby? Any neighbors who were home the night she went missing?" The street was lined on both sides with small homes. Not more than a dozen feet separated them. The police had interviewed neighbors and those who had regular access to the child. He'd read those interviews, as well. Jonathan's strategy would duplicate a lot of that ground. But sometimes the same question asked twice reaped different answers.

"She goes to church with me on Sundays," Melissa said before William could. "The same church where she goes to mother's day out."

Melissa had gone to church when they were together, Jonathan recalled. He wasn't surprised that she did still. "Any children she plays with regularly? Other parents who are friends of yours, or Presley's?" he asked William.

"The kids next door once in a while," William said, "but not really anyone else outside the kids in the church program."

"Was anyone home that night at the neighbors' on either side?" According to the police report the neighbors had been home, but no one heard or saw anything.

William nodded. "Most were already in bed. The police canvassed the entire street. No one remembered hearing anything that night."

"Do you remember what time you left?" The time stated in the report was midnight, which provided a reasonable explanation for no one having been in a position to see or hear any comings and goings.

"A little after midnight." He scrubbed a hand over his face. "It was late. I tried to reason with her, but she insisted I leave."

Not midnight. *After* midnight. "You're sure about the time?"

"Maybe. I guess. I was too angry to really notice. But it was around twelve-thirty when I got home."

"By home," Jonathan clarified, "you mean the house where you and Melissa grew up?" Where Melissa lived now.

William nodded.

Melissa walked to the window and peered out. This was hard for her, too. She wanted to protect William and Presley, but who was going to protect her?

Who had protected her when he'd walked out on her?

Clearing the past from his head yet again, he asked, "Has Polly ever gotten out of the house or unlocked the door for anyone?" Jonathan couldn't see that being the case at such a late hour, but it wasn't impossible.

William shook his head. "Polly doesn't take to strangers. She'd never leave the house alone or open the door for anyone."

"Never," Melissa confirmed, turning back to the conversation. "She's a sweet child and plays well with the other kids, but she's a little shy around adults that she doesn't know."

Under the circumstances, Jonathan felt there could be little doubt that the child's disappearance was foul play. The only questions were how the person got in and why no one, the mother in particular, heard anything. At least one door had to have been left unlocked.

"Presley didn't unlock the door for any reason after you left?" Jonathan pressed. "And no one was allowed in the house?"

William stared at the floor. "She says she went straight to bed and no one called or came over."

That he didn't meet Jonathan's gaze as he spoke greatly discredited his words and concurrently alluded to what he wasn't saying.

"Does Presley have a habit of hosting company at late hours or leaving the house while Polly is sleeping?"

William met his gaze then. "I can't say for sure. She swears not, but—" he shook his head "—she's lied to me before."

"We think she may have left the house that night," Melissa said, visibly struggling with the fact. "After William was already gone. But it couldn't have been for long. She loves Polly too much to take chances like that."

It was wrong and crazy as hell. But Jonathan knew it happened. "She won't admit as much?" He knew the answer before he asked but he needed confirmation.

William shook his head again. "She's sticking to her story that she went to bed and didn't wake up until I came in the next morning."

Pounding echoed through the house, waylaying Jonathan's next question.

"I should get that…" William gestured toward the door. "I'm pretty sure Presley doesn't want to talk to anyone else right now."

"We have other aspects of the case to look into," Jonathan offered. "We'll get out of your way for now."

William nodded and went to answer the door.

Jonathan hung back, letting the others go before him. He took one last lingering look at the child's room. Afraid of strangers. Possibly left at home alone. No signs of forced entry or struggle.

Polly was taken by someone she knew. Or she remained asleep during the abduction.

Jonathan's money was on the former.

By the time he reached the living room, William had opened the door to an older man.

"William, what's going on here?" The man looked past William to Jonathan. "Who is this?"

Melissa stepped forward. "Chief, this is Jonathan Foley, a friend of mine."

Jonathan knew all about Chief Reed Talbot, having read a lengthy profile on the man. The chief glared at Melissa, then at Jonathan. "Presley called all upset about some stranger interrogating her about Polly's disappearance."

Jonathan thrust out his hand. "Jonathan Foley. I apologize for not making your office my first stop, but I wasn't sure you'd be available under the circumstances."

Talbot's gaze narrowed with suspicion. "I've been heading the search for Polly. That's where I should be now." He tossed this statement, chock-full of accusation, at Melissa.

"I don't want to get in your way, Chief," Jonathan insisted. "I'm just here to provide any support I can to a friend."

"Then I'm sure you'll want to hear the news I've come to pass along."

Melissa's breath caught. William's eyes widened with hope.

"We've learned Stevie Price's whereabouts," the chief announced in a rather flat tone.

"Is Polly with him?" Melissa asked, her voice scarcely a whisper.

The chief shook his head. "No, but at least this latest break clears up that question. An eyewitness saw Stevie board a bus for Nashville that left early in the evening. Well before the child went missing."

Jonathan recalled reading that a local had gone missing the same day as the child. A local who not only knew Polly but who played with her frequently.

The confirmation that the child wasn't with that missing local opened up the possibility that she was with a stranger. But Jonathan's instincts still leaned toward an intimate—someone the child knew well.

If she was still alive.

Chapter Four

11:20 a.m.

"I may have gone too far." Harry Shepherd dropped his face into his hands. His heart ached with agony. "What have I done?"

Carol Talbot got down on her knees in front of him. "Harry." She took his face in her hands and drew his gaze to hers. "You did the only thing you could."

He wanted to believe she was right. Her eyes shone with the same pain he felt, but also a hope he couldn't quite feel. They were in this together. She'd made a pact with him to do whatever needed to be done…and no looking back. Dear God. He pulled her into his arms. He'd needed someone for so long.

So very long.

This necessary horror had brought them even closer.

"You're right." He kissed her cheek. "It was the only way." As painful as it was, in the end his actions would make everything all right again. The ends justified the means.

He'd worried himself sick for all these months. When William had gotten orders to deploy to Afghanistan,

Harry had almost lost his mind. He couldn't watch this happen again. Once in a lifetime was more than enough. He'd had to come up with a plan.

Carol pulled far enough away to look into his eyes once more. She caressed his jaw with the pad of her thumb. "You don't have to worry. Stevie will protect her with his life." The promise of a smile tugged at the corners of her mouth. "This will all be over soon. William will be safe and, if he ever learns the truth, he'll be thankful for the intervention once the initial shock has passed."

Harry wasn't so sure about that, but what the boy didn't know wouldn't hurt him. Keeping the awful details secret would be the best way. Harry closed his eyes. He couldn't love that boy more if he were his own son. *Should have been his son.* Harry shook off the heart-wrenching feelings. That had been a long time ago.

Another lifetime ago.

"As long as it keeps him away from that terrible place," Harry agreed, "that's all that matters." He reminded himself of that fact every hour of every day. Without this intervention William might have perished just as his father had.

Carol moved up to sit on Harry's knee. He smiled in spite of the misery twisting his soul…in spite of the terrible reality of what he'd done. Doubt nudged his determination once more. *Dear God, please let this be the right decision.*

"Having that no good bum recall seeing Stevie get on that bus was a stroke of genius." She hugged Harry tightly. "You're so smart. Reed didn't suspect a thing.

He swallowed the story as easily as he does that home-made cherry pie of mine."

Something else Harry wasn't so sure of. "I would've thought the chief would assume Stevie had taken the bus when the salesclerk came forward to say that Stevie had bought a bus ticket to Nashville." Harry had planned this out very carefully. He'd instructed Stevie to buy that ticket two days in advance of setting this strategy in motion. But Reed Talbot had kept digging until Harry had had to come up with a way to provide confirmation.

Stevie Price had been fascinated with Nashville and country music since he was a kid. Playing guitar was his passion, and he was pretty damned good at it. No one ever believed the mentally challenged man would actually attempt following that dream. It had made complete sense to Harry to go with that idea. Most of the folks in the community didn't care one way or the other about Stevie. Plenty of them were glad he was gone, for whatever reason.

Harry hadn't expected the chief of police to push for finding a witness who'd actually seen Stevie get on the bus. The driver had insisted he couldn't recall any specific passengers. Too many faces, he'd said. Harry had had to step in and pay that drunken fool Floyd Harper to say he'd seen Stevie get on the bus after begging him for a few dollars to buy a bottle of the rot-gut he preferred. Considering Harper's reputation, Harry hadn't been sure the sham would work. Evidently adding the part about his begging for the booze money did the trick.

Apparently it had. The chief had called Harry not

twenty minutes ago to confirm that Stevie was in the clear for now. The Nashville police had been notified to keep an eye out for him, but the search for Polly couldn't wait for confirmation of Stevie's whereabouts. The investigation had to move forward under the assumption that Stevie wasn't actually missing in a criminal or legal sense and obviously wasn't involved in Polly's disappearance. That was the chief's position unless Nashville PD called with conflicting information.

After the call, Harry had felt as if a massive boulder had been lifted from his chest. Yet he still couldn't draw a deep enough breath. No matter that the little ruse had worked, this nightmare was far from over.

"What about that man?" Carol asked, worry showing through the courageous face she'd no doubt kept in place just for Harry. "Jonathan Foley? Will he be trouble, you think?"

Harry wished he knew. "Melissa has never said much about him. She'd seemed pretty broken up when their relationship ended a few years back. It's hard to say." Harry exhaled a heavy breath. "What I do know is that Foley's got far-reaching connections in the military, which Melissa believes will help Will." Harry's niece had done the one thing she felt she could to help her brother. But Harry's gut had tied in knots this morning when she'd told him about the step she'd taken.

He was trying hard to give the idea the benefit of the doubt and not to borrow trouble.

This Jonathan Foley could be a godsend.

As long as he didn't sniff around and get a whiff of the truth.

That would destroy the family. And Harry couldn't bear that.

Mercy, what had he done?

Sinners!

Scott Rayburn gritted his teeth as the disgust roiled in his belly. Harry Shepherd and Carol Talbot stood on her porch and hugged.

Scott shook his head. Did they have no shame? What if the chief arrived to find another man on his porch, hugging his wife?

Something was going on between these two. Scott had suspected as much for months now. Bay Minette was a small town. Folks had keenly honed eyes and ears and wagging tongues. He wasn't the only one who'd noticed the looks these two shared whenever they bumped into each other in town.

"Adulterers," he muttered. Scott wished the chief would come home right now. That he would put Harry Shepherd in his place. The man had lorded over his family all these years as if no one in Bay Minette was good enough to get close to a Shepherd.

Fury simmered in Scott's veins. They weren't even Harry's family. But he'd sure as hell stepped in like they were as soon as his little brother was shipped home in a box by the military.

All these years, old Harry had remained unmarried and completely devoted to his dead brother's wife and children. Then she had died and Harry had turned his attention to another man's wife—only the chief wasn't dead. The missing child had evidently given these two the nerve to flaunt their illicit affair a little more flagrantly.

Scott rolled his eyes. Either that or they were up to something more than tawdry behavior. He wouldn't put this whole charade past the two of them to distract folks from their adulterous affair. Could be Harry's attempt to rescue his nephew from going back to that godforsaken place the military had sent him.

No. That couldn't possibly be right. Old Harry worshiped William and his sister, but he loved that little girl even more. He wouldn't dare risk her safety in an outlandish plot such as this.

As boring as the concept was, Scott felt confident the child's disappearance was about her no-good momma. That Presley was a worthless slut. Knowing her, she'd taken the kid off into the woods and left her, hoping she'd never find her way home. God knew Presley showed no real motherly feelings toward the child, much less wifely feelings for her fine husband.

Scott's teeth set hard enough to crack the high-priced enamel of the crowns he'd lavished his daddy's money on. William deserved a whole lot better than that worthless woman. But some men were stupid like that. Let a woman use and abuse them. For what? An heir?

Adoption was far less painful.

Carol Talbot, the chief's cheating wife, patted her lover on the back. Scott's lips curled in disgust. Sickening.

The chief had better get on the stick with his retirement. If he kept hanging around Bay Minette he was going to end up retiring alone. He would be rambling around in that big luxury cabin he'd built in Gatlinburg all by himself. What retired couple needed such an enormous home? But nothing would do for his cheating wife but to have the very finest. Far away from the sweltering heat of southern Alabama.

Actually, Scott was in no hurry to see the chief go. The deputy slated to step into his position was about as worthless as a hung jury. With the older generation like Reed Talbot retiring, those Scott's age were stepping into positions of power.

Anticipation trickled into his veins. He couldn't wait for old Judge Baker to retire…or die. Scott was the top attorney in town. Between his stellar reputation and his daddy's money, he was a shoe-in for the judgeship.

Scott slid down in his seat as Harry Shepherd drove past. Scott had parked at the corner of the block just beyond the Talbot home, but he wasn't taking any chances. Harry might be crazier than Scott knew.

When the coast was clear, Scott started his car and eased out onto the cross street. He had a client coming. A wife who'd worked up the nerve to divorce her husband. Poor slob. He had no idea.

As an attorney, Scott knew all about trickery and surprise attacks. But if dear old Uncle Harry was pulling a fast one on William, Scott intended to find out. William deserved the truth.

The chief of police had better get this investigation moving. The longer it took to find the child, the more William would suffer.

Scott considered the outsider Melissa had called in. Maybe this Jonathan Foley would prove more useful than the chief, who was clearly blind. Scott pursed his lips. Somehow he had to ensure that this Mr. Foley had all the facts. No one else would tell him the whole truth the way Scott would. He would have to make that happen, as soon as possible.

That child had to be found.

It was the only way to make William happy again.

And Scott would do anything to see him happy.

He couldn't just sit around here and wait for the chief to get the job done. Every minute that William agonized was one that Scott suffered, as well.

Whether he slept or ate or kept all his appointments or not, Scott intended to ensure the job was done.

Then William would know that there was no one he could count on the way he could count on Scott.

Scott would be a hero.

Chapter Five

1:00 p.m.

William refused to talk to Melissa now. She shouldn't have pushed the issue of Jonathan questioning Presley right away. They hadn't learned anything new and now Presley was even more upset—which made William all the more miserable. Jonathan had kept quiet while Melissa and William argued about Presley's story. She was leaving something out. Something she was too afraid to tell. Melissa wished she could make her understand that if whatever she was holding back helped find Polly, then nothing else mattered. But Presley hadn't been raised in a safe, nurturing home environment. More like a dog eat dog world where only the most cunning survived.

Melissa shifted in the seat of her car and studied Jonathan's profile. What was he thinking? That her family was a little messed up? Probably. Melissa rested her head back against the seat.

"Arguing with your brother isn't going to make his wife confess to whatever wrongdoing she's committed."

Melissa turned to the driver once more. She wasn't surprised that he'd read her mind. It didn't take ESP to know exactly what she'd been thinking. She shifted her attention back to the street in front of them. "Whatever happened that night was a mistake. Presley would never hurt Polly. She's scared and William is terrified. It's easier not to know, even if it's a mistake."

"I wouldn't misread William's long-suffering attitude for blissful ignorance."

The statement hit a nerve. "I know my brother isn't ignorant," she snapped. "I didn't say that." Why was she biting Jonathan's head off? Good grief, she had to get a grip here. "Sorry. I'm just tired." She was. Totally exhausted, and worried sick. Part of her wanted to shake the hell out of both Presley and William. But more than anything she wanted to protect them…and find Polly.

Jonathan braked at an intersection. "Which way now?"

Melissa sat up straighter. "Sorry. Left. Then right on Blossom Street." Jonathan had offered to drive considering the way her hands had been shaking when they'd left William's. Now she had to focus. Of course Jonathan didn't know which way to go. He'd never been to Bay Minette.

Not once during the six months they were together had he visited or even met her family. Obviously he hadn't cared enough for her. More of that agitation churned inside her. It didn't matter now. Their relationship had been over for three years.

Finding Polly was all that mattered now.

"This Johnny Ray," Jonathan began as he made the turn, "is he going to be cooperative?"

"Depends upon his mood," she answered. "Johnny

Ray thinks he's God's gift to women. He can be charming when he wants and a total jerk other times. Honestly, I doubt he'll be any help." But they had to try. She doubted that the chief had pushed him for information. Johnny Ray Bruce had been getting away with just about everything in the book—except murder—since he was born.

Johnny Ray was the same age as William, twenty-five. The two had gone to school together. Had even been friends, sort of, at one time. But Johnny Ray preferred breaking hearts to settling down. As a teenager he'd had a knack for trouble—particularly because the chief of police was his uncle and he wasn't worried about the consequences. Accountability had not been one of his strong suits. Thankfully he'd grown out of that part of his bad boy reputation.

Johnny Ray and Presley had a long, volatile history. One that hadn't completely ended with Presley's marriage to William.

Jonathan parked in front of the small house Johnny Ray's parents had left to him. Neither was dead, just moved down to coastal Florida to retire.

"I guess we'll see," Jonathan said before getting out of the car.

Melissa stared at the small white house. A shiny red sports car sat in the drive out front. Johnny Ray worked as a certified nursing assistant at the same hospital where Melissa worked as a registered nurse. Johnny Ray was a kind and charming caregiver at work. It was only his sexual appetite when off duty that he didn't appear to be able to control. Unfortunately his craving for Presley hadn't lessened with age.

Melissa's car door opened, startling her. Jonathan held it open, waiting for her to climb out. "Thank you." When her mind began drifting off into disturbing memories, she stopped it. Focusing on the here and now was absolutely essential.

The air was thick with humidity, the sort they didn't typically endure until late July or August. The idea that Polly might be trapped out in this heat made Melissa shudder despite the sweltering temperature. The child wasn't old enough to understand that staying out of the direct sun was essential in temperatures this extreme. Dehydration was a major concern. Some had speculated that Polly had gotten up in the middle of the night and wandered off. Every neighborhood in town had been searched. The woods, the parks, no place had been overlooked. She hadn't been found.

Or someone had taken her to a place far enough away that she wouldn't be found.

Tracking dogs had failed to pick up on her scent no matter that local hunters had shown up with their hounds mere hours after word got out that a child was missing. Two days of rain after that had rendered any trace of her scent undetectable.

As much as Melissa didn't want to believe anyone could have taken that sweet child, defeat was crushing in on her now.

The high-pitched whine of the screen door being opened brought Melissa out of her reverie. She heard Jonathan rap on the faded green door, once, twice.

Melissa swiped at the sweat on her brow with the back of her hand. Johnny Ray had to be here. He worked eight to five most days, but today he was not scheduled. She'd called one of her friends and checked.

Jonathan glanced at her, then pounded on the door a third time.

While they waited he surveyed the yard. Melissa started to ask what he was thinking, but the door flew open sharply enough to have shaken loose some of the flaking green paint.

"What?" Johnny Ray demanded, his eyes slitted against the sun's bright light. He stood in the open doorway, his jeans not even fastened and his muscled chest bare, looking from Jonathan to Melissa and back with blatant irritation. That was another thing Johnny Ray Bruce spent most of his spare time on, pumping iron.

"Johnny Ray, I hate to bother you on your day off," Melissa said. Damn it! Why did her voice have to sound shaky? "But it's urgent." She gestured to the man beside her. "This is my friend Jonathan Foley. We need to speak with you."

Jonathan extended his hand; Johnny Ray hesitated, but then gave it a shake. "Johnny Ray Bruce." He smirked. "Guess you already knew that."

"You work at the hospital with Melissa," Jonathan said. The way he said her name made her chest ache with an old, far too familiar tenderness.

Johnny Ray nodded. "That's right." In Melissa's direction he flashed a smile that didn't reach his eyes. "'Course, unlike me, she makes the big bucks."

Ignoring his jab, she got to the point. "Jonathan's

here to help with the investigation into Polly's disappearance."

Johnny Ray's cocky expression softened a fraction. "They haven't found her yet?"

Melissa shook her head. "We're hoping we can count on your help."

He took another look at Jonathan then shrugged. "Sure. Come on in."

Melissa followed him inside, with Jonathan close behind her. The place smelled of stale cigarette smoke. Beer cans cluttered the coffee table and both end tables.

Johnny Ray cleared off a spot on the couch and took a seat. "Make yourself at home." He gestured to the other available chairs but didn't bother to clear the mess.

Melissa moved a stack of magazines. Her cheeks burned when she noted that they were the sort that featured unclothed females in lewd positions. Jonathan took the seat beside her.

Johnny Ray lit a cigarette. "What can I do to help?"

He sounded surprisingly amiable. Melissa looked to Jonathan. She knew what she wanted to ask Johnny Ray but getting emotional wouldn't keep him cooperative. Better to leave this to Jonathan.

"Polly's mother, Presley," Jonathan began, "insists that on the night her daughter went missing, she turned in shortly after midnight and her daughter was in her room asleep. She claims she had no company that evening after her husband left."

Johnny Ray flicked ashes onto the wood floor and shrugged. "Those two fight all the time. If I was a betting man, I'd wager Presley drank herself to sleep after Will left. That's her M.O." He turned to Melissa. "Wouldn't you say, Mel?"

Melissa didn't like when he called her that. No one called her that except him. "I imagine we've all done that at one time or another." Presley had more than her share of issues, but she was Melissa's sister-in-law.

"I'm sensing," Jonathan went on, "that Presley isn't being totally up-front about what happened after her husband left. You're wired in to the local grapevine, from what I hear," he added with something that sounded like respect. "Have you heard any rumors to that effect?"

Melissa held her breath. She felt guilty for sitting by while Jonathan talked behind Presley's back, but if it helped find Polly, she would allow it.

And no one was more connected to the rumor mill than Johnny Ray. That was the reason she and Jonathan were here.

Johnny Ray's expression went from relaxed to guarded despite Jonathan's careful wording of the question. He poked his cigarette into a beer can. "I can't say that I'm wired in to anything." He shot Melissa an accusing look. "But I do know that Presley's marriage has been less than the happily-ever-after she'd expected. Will just can't seem to make her happy." Johnny Ray shrugged. "Sometimes wives seek out that missing happiness in other places."

Rage blasted Melissa. As if he'd felt the detonation, Jonathan put a hand on her arm.

"Are you implying that Presley is having an affair?" Jonathan ventured.

Melissa wanted to be equally angry with Jonathan for voicing the question, but time was slipping away. Painful questions had to be asked. Johnny Ray was the person to ask. He and Presley had carried on a love-hate relationship since she was fourteen. If she had gone that far, chances were the man who'd filled the room with unpleasant secondhand smoke would know.

Johnny Ray executed another of those careless shrugs. "I didn't say that, but I couldn't blame her if she went that route."

This time Melissa couldn't hold back a rebuttal. "William loves Presley. Yes, they have their problems but no marriage is perfect."

Johnny Ray laughed as he lit up another smoke. "I can't argue with that last part."

Melissa bit her lips together. Arguing would be a waste of time, and it might hinder full disclosure. The cockier Johnny Ray felt, the more he'd run off at the mouth.

"So in your opinion her husband hasn't showered her with the attention she deserves. Is that the case?" Jonathan wanted to know.

Melissa glared at him before she could school her expression. How dare he suggest such a thing? William had been deployed for the past six months. That kind of separation strained the best of marriages.

"That's right." Johnny Ray leaned forward and braced his elbows on his knees. "Fact is, she didn't want to have a baby, but Will wouldn't have it any other way. He forced her into going through with the pregnancy and she's been miserable ever since."

No way could Melissa sit here and listen to this. She lunged to her feet. "I need some air."

"Come on, Mel," Johnny Ray said, "you know it's true. She wanted to get rid of the kid and your brother threatened to get a court order to stop her."

Melissa pointed every ounce of rage she felt at the arrogant man. "William had every right to want to save his child. Presley was young and confused—"

"Maybe she couldn't take it anymore," Jonathan said, cutting Melissa off, "and did what she'd wanted to do all along."

The room filled with silence.

Johnny Ray didn't even blink beneath the weight of Jonathan's stare.

The utter emptiness left by the silence held Melissa in a chokehold.

Presley loved Polly. Melissa would not even entertain such a notion. The idea was unconscionable, downright crazy.

"I'm not saying she did or didn't," Johnny Ray announced, shattering the silence first. "I'm just pointing out that everyone has their limits. Maybe Presley reached hers and made a mistake."

Defeat sucked the anger and certainty right out of Melissa, left her swaying on her feet.

He was right.

Damn it. Johnny Ray knew Presley better than her own husband did, and the point he'd made was frighteningly correct. She hadn't wanted a child. But that was before they'd all fallen in love with Polly, Presley included.

"Johnny Ray, if you know something—"

He held up his hands. "I'm just speculating here, Mel. Laying out some of the facts that some folks don't want to remember."

Jonathan stood, leaned across the cluttered coffee table and offered his hand once more to Johnny Ray. "I hope you'll let us know if you hear anything that might help find that little girl."

Johnny Ray pushed to his feet, gave the outstretched hand a shake. "Sure thing, man. I'll keep my ears open. No problem."

Melissa swallowed back the crush of emotions swelling her throat. "Thank you." Then she walked out. She couldn't look at him anymore. Not with the ugly truth of his words ringing in her ears.

She didn't stop moving until she was in the car with her seat belt fastened. Her gaze frozen on the street ahead, she couldn't speak as Jonathan started the car and drove away from Johnny Ray's house.

"Is there any possibility he might be right about Presley?" Jonathan asked.

Melissa blinked back the sting of angry tears. Jonathan didn't know her family. His questions were logical and reasonable. She wanted to shake him and make him see that for all her past mistakes and unwise decisions, Presley would never, ever hurt Polly. There were a lot of things about Presley that bothered Melissa. The way she treated William. Her immaturity. But she would not hurt her child. "No." The single syllable echoed in the quiet of the car, the certainty in her tone reaffirming her resolve.

"We need to talk."

"Isn't that what we're doing?" she said, rather than the barrage of excuses on her family's behalf she wanted to offer. She dropped back against the seat, hauled in a deep breath and slowly released it, reminding herself that Jonathan was here to help. She needed to let him.

Jonathan took the next right.

Melissa frowned. "Where're we going?"

"I noticed a cemetery on the way to Bruce's house." Jonathan pulled the car under a massive shade tree that held court over the small parking area that flanked the oldest cemetery in town. "We should have some privacy here."

"Can we walk?" Anxiety and fear were crushing in on her. She didn't wait for his answer. She got out of the car and dragged in a chest full of air. Polly was missing. Possibly dead. Emotion burned Melissa's eyes. It wasn't fair, damn it! She and William had lost their father and their mother. She shot a look at Jonathan as he came around to her side of the car. He'd broken her heart. And now the biggest bright spot in her life was gone. It just wasn't fair!

"I know this is difficult," Jonathan said, his voice soft and understanding.

She didn't want to hear that softness. She wanted him to be strong and do what no one else had—find Polly.

He moved closer and Melissa wanted to back away. She couldn't trust herself with him, not even after all this time. But his eyes—those pale blue eyes she'd dreamed of for so damned long—held her still.

"The police have found nothing. No one is talking."

As he spoke his fingers curled around her arms, making her shiver in spite of her determination not to let him see how he affected her. He pressed her with that penetrating gaze. "But I know, just as you do, that someone knows the truth. If we rattle the right cages, that someone will get nervous and make a mistake."

She wanted to fall against him, have those strong arms hold her and those inviting lips promise her that this would be okay. That Polly would be okay. "It can't be Presley. She wouldn't…"

"It's hard. Putting that harsh glare of suspicion on the people you love." He moved closer still, so close she could smell his skin. "But this is the fastest way to get a reaction. There's no time to waste. Too much time has passed as it is."

He was right. A moan rose in Melissa's throat. She had seen the glances exchanged between the policemen working the search. She knew what they thought. Hope was fading.

Melissa couldn't help herself. She fell against Jonathan's chest. His arms went around her and she shuddered with the overwhelming emotions.

"We'll find her," he promised, his lips whispering against her ear. "I won't stop until I do."

Melissa didn't know how he could make such a promise, but somehow she trusted him to be true to his word.

Though she had every reason not to, Melissa believed in Jonathan and the promise he'd just made. He might not be able to commit to a relationship, but she knew enough about his past and his work to know that he would find a way to get the job done. That was the one thing he never failed to do—his job.

She tried to pull herself together, telling herself that as a nurse she faced sickness and death every day at the hospital.

She braced her hands against his chest, resisted the urge to curl her fingers into his shirt and pushed away. She drew in a breath and met his gaze. "What do we do next?" Polly was counting on her. William and Presley were counting on her. Melissa had to be stronger than she'd ever been before. For them.

"The one other person who hasn't been in his or her place since Polly's disappearance is Stevie Price." Jonathan dropped his hands to his sides. "We're going to find out where he really is and what he's up to."

"The chief said he went to Nashville." In truth, she would be the first one to say that she wouldn't have thought Stevie brave enough to attempt to follow that distant dream he'd carried around with him for as long as she could remember. Stevie was only a year older than her. They'd played together as kids, and her family had pretty much taken him in after his folks were gone. He had a good heart, but he just didn't have the mental capacity to pull this off.

Still, she recognized that it wasn't completely impossible.

"The chief could be right," Jonathan acknowledged. "That's what we're going to determine."

She nodded. "Okay. I know Stevie better than most. Where do we start?"

The crunch of tires on gravel drew Melissa's gaze

to the entrance of the cemetery. Will's truck came to a
screeching halt next to her car.

Her heart rammed hard against her sternum. Was
there news?

Will got out, slammed the truck door hard then
stormed in their direction.

The grief she would have seen in his face if there was
bad news was absent. Instead, what emanated from his
expression and his stiff movements was white-hot fury.

William was mad as hell and ready to fight.

Chapter Six

"She's off-limits."

Jonathan kept quiet as Melissa and her brother argued. The pain on her face made Jonathan want to step in and defend her position, but it wasn't his place.

Not anymore.

This was a family matter and he hadn't been anything to Melissa except a bad memory in a very long time.

"I'm not accusing Presley," Melissa repeated, her exasperation showing at this point. She reached out to her brother, but he avoided her touch. The hurt his move generated played out on her face. "You have to see that there's something about that night she's not telling."

William leaned in closer to Melissa, a new blast of fury darkening his face. Jonathan stepped forward. "This isn't going to help us find your daughter."

William glared at Jonathan, his mouth twisted with rage. "You…" He dragged in a shaky breath. "I appreciate what you did for me, Major, but *this* is none of your business. Upsetting Presley was bad enough, but going to Johnny Ray was crossing the line. How do you think that made her feel? She can't take much more."

Jonathan couldn't deny that charge. "You're running on empty, Shepherd." He kept his tone calm and even despite the impatience charging through him. "Fear and frustration are preventing you from seeing the logic in Melissa's words." William started to argue, but Jonathan stopped him with a shake of his head. "Trust me, I know exactly where you are. It's a bad place to be. But alienating the people who care about you because you don't want to see what's right in front of your face is the wrong route to take."

Fury still simmered in William's eyes but he kept his mouth shut.

"I'm sorry, Will." Melissa folded her arms over her chest and lowered her eyes. "I'm not trying to make this any harder. But I'm scared to death that Presley is hiding something that she doesn't realize might help." She lifted her gaze back to her brother's. "Something that might help us find Polly before it's too late."

William swayed back a step. He scrubbed his face with his hands as if he could erase the misery, the confusion. "Presley didn't do anything wrong. It was me. I'm the one who left. I should have been there. But I wasn't and somebody took my little girl."

Melissa pressed her fingers to her trembling lips. She was barely hanging on to her composure. "You couldn't have known." She wrapped her arms around her brother and held him close. "We just have to find the truth and that means asking the hard questions Chief Talbot seems to be avoiding."

Melissa's brother pulled free of her embrace. "Why did you talk to Johnny Ray?" The anger resurrected in

Shepherd's eyes. "What does that bastard have to do with anything?"

Melissa glanced at Jonathan. Not for moral support, he suspected. He held up his hands. "I'll take a walk." The two clearly needed some space.

"Johnny Ray keeps up with everybody's business, Presley's in particular. I think maybe he's still stinging that you got the girl he always thought would be his," Melissa was explaining as Jonathan walked away.

Keeping the two in sight, Jonathan moved along the path that skirted the garden of headstones. He needed to clear his head and analyze the meeting with Johnny Ray. The guy had come off as nonchalant. Not quite indifferent but definitely detached. Could be that he could care less about Presley or her child. But based on what Melissa had said about the man's long-running relationship with Presley, his attitude seemed a little too detached.

Jonathan's first thought was that the two had rendezvoused while the child slept—after William Shepherd had departed the home. But there was no evidence of that scenario. Jonathan doubted that either one would admit to having left the child unattended.

There was no reason at this time to consider that Johnny Ray Bruce had anything to do with the child's disappearance. If Polly was the only reason Presley stayed married to Shepherd that could, of course, be considered motive. Yet there was no obvious evidence to that end.

Jonathan stalled. Unless the goal was to do away with the child and then to blame the father. That would get him—as well as the child—out of the picture permanently.

An icy sensation slithered up Jonathan's spine. He hoped like hell that wasn't the case. But there was a ring of clarity to it that unsettled him greatly.

Still, Melissa staunchly stood by the idea that Presley loved her daughter. Was that only what Melissa wanted to see?

"Mr. Foley," a voice whispered from behind Jonathan.

Jonathan shifted to his right, away from Melissa and Shepherd. His muscles tightened in preparation for battle.

"I need to speak to you in private, Mr. Foley."

A man, thirty or so maybe, hovered in the trees that bordered the cemetery on three sides. He leaned to the right and peeked at the couple still debating the subject of Johnny Ray Bruce.

"What about?" It was difficult to dredge up any wariness for a man who crept around in the woods and made contact in such a manner. Particularly one who wore big glasses and a bow tie. But even more surprising was that he'd gotten so close without Jonathan noticing. Definitely not of the norm.

The man nodded toward Melissa and her brother. "Them."

"Who are you?" The guy looked harmless enough. The glasses he wore had inordinately thick lenses. The shirt and bow tie along with the crisply creased trousers didn't really fit with his sneaking around in the woods like this.

The man looked again to see that Melissa and Shepherd were distracted. "My name is Scott Rayburn." He straightened, as if just saying his name out loud called for additional posturing and preening. "There's something you need to know."

Ensuring that Melissa and Shepherd appeared to be discussing their differences calmly, Jonathan moved toward Rayburn. "What is it you have to say?"

"You're not from around here," Rayburn said, seeming nervous with Jonathan's approach. "You don't know these people."

"I know Melissa." Images of her nude body entwined with his made Jonathan flinch.

Rayburn shrugged. "She's blind to what goes on around her."

Jonathan glanced at her, certain this man was incorrect. "I'm reasonably sure she's not as blind as one might think." Just caring. Forgiving. Loving. Passionate. More of those haunting memories whispered through his thoughts, making him weak. He couldn't be weak right now. His jaw clenched. There was never a good time to be weak.

"Perhaps so," Rayburn admitted. "But she's standing by while the rest of her family continues to commit egregious atrocities."

Jonathan's gaze narrowed. What was this guy up to? "Such as?"

"Her uncle is carrying on with the chief's wife while supposedly distraught over William's child."

"Chief Talbot's wife?" Interesting but not necessarily relevant.

Rayburn nodded. "That tawdry affair has been going on for several years now." His head moved from up and down to side to side in a maneuver that made Jonathan think of a bobblehead doll. "The chief's as blind as Melissa."

"Does this have anything to do with Polly's disappearance?" Didn't sound that way to Jonathan, but information, however seemingly irrelevant, couldn't be cast aside out of turn.

Rayburn twisted up his courage, or appeared to. "I'm just warning you that you should look into this illicit affair. There's more going on, I believe, than meets the eye."

Jonathan considered the warning. "How can you be certain the chief isn't aware of his wife's extracurricular activities?"

Rayburn covered a grin with one hand. "You really aren't from around here. The chief is completely oblivious to his wife's immorality, just as he is blind to that sorry nephew of his."

Jonathan inclined his head. "Nephew?"

"Johnny Ray Bruce," Rayburn explained. "Presley's lover."

Now they were getting somewhere. "Do you have proof that Presley is still involved with Johnny Ray?" That the man was the chief's nephew might explain why he wasn't under closer scrutiny as a part of the investigation—or at least didn't appear to be. Jonathan had obtained copies of the police reports as well as the witness reports before he'd flown down. Johnny Ray Bruce hadn't been mentioned in any capacity.

"They've never stopped being involved," Rayburn informed him with haughty condescension. "She only married poor Will because his family has a little something and he's likely to make something of himself. Johnny Ray is as lazy as a summer day is long. He's never going to be anything but a worthless bloodsucker."

"Have you spoken to any of the authorities investigating this case? There are others you could tell besides the chief."

Rayburn harrumphed. "The chief is too well known in this area. No one's going to stand up to him, much less tell him his wife is having an affair with the man who used to be his best friend."

Another interesting detail. "Harry Shepherd was once the chief's best friend?"

"That's right." Rayburn preened, attempting to appear nonchalant as he boasted his great insights. "Played high school football together right here in Bay Minette. Went off to college together. Where you saw one, you saw the other."

"What went wrong?" Again, Jonathan didn't actually see the relevance, but the more information he commanded, the better his ability to analyze.

"Harry's brother, William senior, wanted to serve his country. Harry objected. The chief argued that William senior had a right to follow his own calling. The two have scarcely spoken since."

Melissa had told Jonathan that her father was killed in a military conflict and that her uncle had stepped in to fill his shoes. If this guy's conclusions were correct,

Shepherd held the chief's encouragement of his brother against him. Not exactly rational but a reasonable reaction, Jonathan supposed.

"I have to go." Rayburn backed deeper into the tree line. "The police aren't going to look into this," he warned. "Someone needs to."

"What about Stevie Price?" Jonathan asked before Rayburn could creep away. "The chief said he'd taken off to Nashville. Any theories on that one?" Jonathan suspected that Price's disappearance the same night as Polly's was no coincidence.

"Stevie is a mentally handicapped grown man," Rayburn said with glaring disdain. "Folks around here allow him to play with their children as if he's one of them. But he's not." Rayburn pressed Jonathan with an accusation in his gaze. "I say good riddance."

"Do you have proof that Price isn't as harmless as most seem to think?" An uneasiness settled in Jonathan's gut. This guy Price was an unknown variable.

Rayburn snorted. "Ask Mrs. Syler at the day care center. She'll tell you she almost had to get a restraining order to keep him off the playground. He used to go there and play with the kids sometimes." He shook his head. "But not anymore."

The chief hadn't mentioned that in his reports, and Melissa had insisted the incident was a mistake. That Stevie's work as a volunteer was sanctioned by the day care owner. They were going to have to dig a little deeper. Melissa seemed protective of Stevie; then again, she tried to protect all those she cared about. But finding the child trumped all else.

"I have to go now."

Jonathan glanced toward Melissa and Shepherd. As Shepherd climbed into his truck and started the engine, Melissa watched, her arms folded over her chest.

Before Jonathan could ask any more questions, Rayburn disappeared into the woods.

Strange character. Jonathan walked back to where Melissa waited, watching her brother drive away.

"You okay?" Dumb question under the circumstances.

She quickly wiped her eyes. "I guess so. He wants me to back off where Presley is concerned and—" she released a heavy breath "—I can't. She's afraid of something. We have to know what that is."

Understandable. Presley was the last person to see Polly before she disappeared and was supposedly in the house when she went missing. That made her the primary person of interest if not the prime suspect.

"Has Chief Talbot voiced any concerns about Presley?"

Melissa shrugged. "Not really. Until now he's been solely focused on Stevie."

That was the problem when bad things happened in small towns. Everyone knew everyone else. Made objectivity next to impossible.

"What about your uncle?" Jonathan asked as he ushered her toward the car. "Is there anything going on with him that we haven't talked about?" He figured he might as well explore Rayburn's allegations.

Melissa stopped and turned back to him, confusion cluttering her face. "What do you mean?"

This line of questioning would be more than a little

sensitive. "Your uncle has never married. Is there a particular reason?" That was about the only way Jonathan could think to ask about his social life without asking outright about the rumor he'd just heard.

"I don't know. He's taken care of William and me since we were kids back in elementary school. I guess he never had time to focus on his own life." Her confusion turned to suspicion. "Why would you ask that?"

He could dance around the question or he could just ask. "Are you aware that there is a rumor that he's carried on a long-term affair with the chief's wife?"

The suspicion morphed into dismay. "Who would say such a hurtful thing?"

"Scott Rayburn." Jonathan wasn't going to hide anything from Melissa. He'd done enough of that in the past. Finding her niece was too important to play games on any level.

"Scott?" Renewed confusion chased away the rest of the emotions playing out in her eyes. "Why on earth would he say something like that? We went to school together. He's come to picnics and family get-togethers at our house for as long as I can remember. He helped Will through physics in high school." She reached into the pocket of her jeans and pulled out her cell phone. "I want him to say that to me."

"Wait." Jonathan put his hand over hers. The contact made his breath catch. She stared up at him as if she'd experienced the same jolt. When he'd recovered, he offered, "It's important that we consider all the possibilities, even the ones that turn out to be rumors. Tell me about Rayburn."

She relaxed a fraction. "He's a little older than me and kind of different from most guys around here."

"Define different," Jonathan suggested.

She shrugged. "This is Alabama. Football is a religion and hunting is a male rite of passage. Scott preferred reading and *socializing*. He was always more like one of the girls. He went to law school and has his own boutique law firm downtown. Never married. He loves his work too much."

"Do you know of any reason why he would dislike your uncle? Does he have a grudge against your family? Any reason at all that he would spread these kinds of rumors?"

Melissa shook her head. "That's the part that doesn't make sense. My mother always said that actions speak louder than words. Scott has always acted as if he loves us." She rubbed her eyes. "Folks used to insist he had his eye on me, but I never noticed."

When he didn't respond, Melissa glanced around and said, "I guess we should get going."

An intense sensation jabbed Jonathan. He stood very still, denied the feeling, as she walked toward her car.

Jealousy.

He gave himself a swift mental kick. He had no right to be jealous where Melissa was concerned.

A few hours in Melissa's presence and already he was losing his hold on control.

The cell in Jonathan's pocket vibrated. He checked the screen and saw it was an Out of Area number. *The boss.*

"Foley," he announced in greeting.

"Thought I'd let you know that Victor Lennox has agreed to flip on his connections."

Not really news to Jonathan. He'd expected as much. "I suppose that's a good thing." To Jonathan it meant that the man would get off with a slap on the wrists for his crimes.

"Don't worry," his employer said knowingly, "he's not going to get off as easy as you think. Lennox isn't the sort they let walk away."

Jonathan sure hoped not.

"How are things in Alabama?"

The question surprised Jonathan. His employer rarely delved into personal territory on any level. "The child is still missing and the investigation is moving at about the speed of molasses."

"Let me know if you need anything in the way of backup. I stand behind my people on and off the job. You don't need to tread water there or anywhere else."

"Thank you, sir. I'll keep that in mind."

The connection severed.

Jonathan slid the phone back into his pocket. Strange. He'd never worked for an employer whose name he didn't know much less whose face he'd never seen.

Nonetheless, he trusted his instincts and not a single warning had gone off where the man was concerned. He operated this new Equalizers agency with utter discretion and immense compassion.

A man like that couldn't be all bad.

Jonathan joined Melissa in the car. She'd settled into the passenger seat. Driving wouldn't be in her best interest or anyone else's just now.

For a moment they sat in silence. He didn't want to prod her for answers. She was tired and worried. Jonathan could understand each of those reactions.

"I'm scared, Jonathan."

He turned to her, his chest tight at the sound of her voice. "I know."

"If someone has hurt that baby…" She closed her eyes and held back the emotions making her lips tremble.

He wanted to tell her not to worry, but the truth was, at this point, the possibility that Polly was a victim of some unspeakable violence was extremely high.

"We'll find her," he promised. "And then we'll deal with whatever we have to deal with."

A tear slid down Melissa's cheek. "I've spent my entire adult life taking care of people as a nurse. Helping those who can't care for themselves." She moved her head side to side. "But I swear, if someone hurt that child, I want to hurt them." She compressed her lips and visibly fought for composure. "If she's…" she swallowed with difficulty "…dead…I want whoever is responsible to…" she drew in a jerky breath "…I want them to pay."

Chapter Seven

Chicago, 4:00 p.m.

He sat at a table inside Maggie's Coffee House. The one closest to the window that provided the most direct view of the building across the street.

The Colby Agency.

Maggie James swiped at the counter, her attention not on business as it should be. Her entire being was focused on *him*.

Every day he came into her shop and sat from three until six or seven, depending upon when the staff at the Colby Agency left for the day. He stayed, staring like that, until the lights on the fourth floor across the street went out.

Her chest ached as she drew in a ragged breath. She wanted to order him out of her life. For months now she had known this thing between them would come to no good, but she couldn't bring herself to let go. He was an addiction to her. She couldn't sleep if he didn't come by the shop every day. Couldn't breathe if he didn't make love to her almost as often.

Night after night he came to her bed and made love

to her as no other man ever had. Then he disappeared into the night, like the fog after a long, hard rain. He'd told her his name was Slade Keaton. That he was thirty. A full two years younger than her. She had no idea where he'd come from or what he'd done before. He was here now, and that was what mattered. That was his stock answer.

A big mistake, Maggie.

She forced her attention back to cleaning up after the last of the lunch stragglers. She had worked hard to make something of herself, to make this coffee shop the place to stop for a relaxing break on the Magnificent Mile. Why screw it up now by getting involved with trouble?

She had been asking herself that question for well over six months now. Somehow she never seemed able to dredge up the proper answer. The answer that would put her back on track and out of this crazy spin cycle.

Broad, square hands flattened on the counter she'd just scrubbed. Maggie's breath caught as her gaze lifted and collided with steel-gray eyes. She laughed tightly. "You startled me."

That smile that swept away every fiber of her resistance spread across his handsome face. "I'll be back around seven-thirty."

She covertly glanced at the fourth floor of the building across the street. He was leaving before the lights went out? "Seven-thirty?" she asked. It wasn't exactly a clever response, but it was all she had.

"We're going to dinner."

She perked up. "Dinner?" Jeez, she sounded like a

canary, repeating everything he said. He so rarely did anything spontaneous, the announcement had anticipation zinging through her.

"That's right." He winked. "Wear that little green dress I like so much."

Her head moved up and down and her lips smiled. She recognized both these things but her heart wouldn't slow down enough for her to respond any other way.

He squeezed her hand.

Then he was gone.

She watched him stride down the sidewalk until he was out of view, then her gaze drifted to the fourth floor across the way.

As if he possessed some sixth sense or ESP or whatever, the lights went out.

The folks at the Colby Agency were going home.

8:00 p.m.

VICTORIA COLBY-CAMP placed the linen napkin in her lap as her husband took his seat across from her. He looked more handsome than ever in his navy suit. She loved that color on him.

Incredibly, Lucas Camp had, indeed, retired from his government consulting work. He spent several days per week working alongside her at the Colby Agency. Victoria could not be happier. Having both her husband and her son at the agency with her was a dream come true. Contentment settled deep inside her.

She had waited a long, long time for this level of happiness.

"Wine?" Lucas asked as the waiter approached their table.

"Absolutely."

Lucas ordered the finest house wine. She loved that he knew her so very well. This was her favorite restaurant, and he'd ordered her favorite wine.

When the waiter had moved on, Lucas settled his gaze on her. "Victoria, I have a proposition for you."

She lifted her eyebrows in question. "Sounds intriguing."

"We haven't taken a vacation since our honeymoon." He deftly draped a napkin in his lap. "I'm thinking white sands and sparkling blue waters."

"Ah, Grand Cayman." She'd mentioned never having been there. Once again, her dear husband wanted to please her. But she also knew a place he treasured very much. "How about Puerto Vallarta?"

His knowing gaze narrowed. "Shall we toss a coin?"

"We took a cruise last time," she reminded him.

He nodded. "We'll look into reservations for Mexico then."

The waiter arrived and poured their wine. Lucas thanked him. "Speaking of reservations," he said when they were alone again—if one could be alone in a popular restaurant during the dinner hour. "I presume you have no reservations regarding Jim's ability to handle the agency if we're gone a week or two."

"I do not." Her son had done a spectacular job. The merger between his staff of former Equalizers and her investigators at the agency was now seamless. The final result was a phenomenal team.

"Jim doesn't appear to miss running his own shop," Lucas commented.

"I agree." Jim had sold the brownstone as well as the Equalizers business several months ago. "He's home now, in every respect." Lucas knew how much that meant to her. "I am so grateful."

Lucas reached across the table and patted her hand. "As am I." He inclined his head and looked past Victoria. "Isn't that Maggie?"

Victoria turned to see who'd entered the dining room. The hostess led a handsome couple through the maze of elegantly dressed tables. "Yes, it is Maggie." Maggie James owned and operated the coffee house across the street from the agency. She noticed Victoria and smiled, then waved.

Maggie touched her dinner companion's arm and gestured to Victoria and Lucas's table. The man with Maggie said something to the hostess, then the two of them made their way over.

"He's quite handsome," Victoria said in an aside to Lucas.

"I'll take your word for that," he murmured back, then stood. "Maggie." Lucas gave her a peck on the cheek.

Maggie literally beamed. "What a coincidence."

"Vinelli's is my favorite restaurant," Victoria said. "If you haven't been here before, you're going to love it."

"Oh." Maggie pressed a hand to her chest. "Forgive me. This is Slade Keaton." She turned to the tall, silent man at her side. "Slade, this is Victoria Colby-Camp and her husband, Lucas."

Slade nodded to Victoria. "It's a pleasure to meet you, Mrs. Colby-Camp."

Lucas extended his hand. "Keaton."

"Mr. Camp."

Maybe it was Victoria's imagination but Maggie's friend seemed slow to take Lucas's hand. Once he did, however, they shook firmly. Maybe she was just tired. They'd had a long week at the agency. Closing up shop a couple of hours early had been the least she could do for her staff.

Victoria studied the man, Slade Keaton, while Maggie and Lucas made small talk. Lucas, she knew, had a soft spot for the hardworking lady. Maggie was utterly charming and quite lovely, with fiery red hair and vibrant green eyes. She and her companion made quite a handsome couple.

Keaton watched Lucas closely as he spoke. Was it a protective instinct toward his lady? Perhaps, Victoria thought. But something about him didn't feel quite right to her.

Keaton suddenly turned his face ever so slightly and smiled at Victoria, as if he'd heard the thought.

Don't be foolish. Victoria blamed her suspicions on her state of fatigue. Besides, how was a man supposed to act when introduced to total strangers in the middle of a restaurant when he had obviously come to be seated and served?

"The hostess is waiting," he said to Maggie. To Lucas and Victoria, he said, "Enjoy your meal."

When the two had moved on to their table, Lucas

leaned forward. "I think this is the first time I've seen Maggie on a date."

"She works so hard," Victoria agreed. "I'm glad she's taking some time for herself."

Lucas made an agreeable sound, but his attention remained on the couple being seated a few tables away.

Victoria started to ask Lucas if he'd sensed anything odd about the man but decided against it.

Tonight was about relaxing, not dissecting the social life of someone as kind as Maggie James.

Victoria glanced at the man accompanying Maggie once more. He looked directly at her as if he'd felt her gaze on him. A second, then two and three passed before he looked away.

Odd.

Victoria banished the idea…but the one thing she had always trusted, besides her husband, of course, was her instincts.

Funny how they were humming just now.

Perhaps it would be in Maggie's best interest if Victoria did a little looking into this Slade Keaton. It wouldn't hurt and Maggie never had to know.

"I know what you're thinking," Lucas said, summoning her from the scheming thoughts.

"I'm certain you don't." Victoria reached for her wine.

"You're thinking," Lucas said, picking up his own glass, "that you might check out Mr. Keaton, just to make sure Maggie isn't getting herself into any trouble."

Victoria tried to keep the guilt out of her expression.

It didn't work. *I knew it* flashed in Lucas's eyes. "She's likely quite lonely. A lonely woman is easy prey."

Lucas held up his glass for a toast. "To the most caring and compassionate woman I know."

Victoria blushed and clinked her glass against his. "And one who can be somewhat nosy from time to time."

"Don't worry about Maggie," Lucas assured her. "I'll look into Keaton myself."

"Now who's being nosy?" Victoria laughed. It felt good after the busy week they'd had.

"What can I say?" Lucas enjoyed a long swallow of his wine. "I cut my investigative teeth on the CIA. I can't help myself."

Victoria stole a look at the couple in question. "Well, I hope Mr. Keaton is on the up and up." If he wasn't, he wouldn't be hiding anything for long. No one could hide a single fact from Lucas Camp when he chose to find the whole story.

"We'll soon know."

Victoria relaxed. Maggie was in good hands with Lucas providing backup.

The world needed more men like Lucas Camp.

Chapter Eight

Where was Harry? Melissa needed him here. He always made the most confusing or troubling situations better.

Melissa paced the length of the living room again. She'd been doing that for hours now. Jonathan had tried to calm her but his reassuring words had not helped.

Floyd Harper was dead. He'd fallen off the overpass on Main Street. It appeared to be an accident, but the chief wouldn't make an official announcement until the forensics work was completed.

That Harper was the only witness to Stevie having left town made his sudden death suspicious.

Chief Talbot had called with word on that awful development an hour ago. He hadn't wanted Melissa to see it on the news or hear it any other way. Already folks were tying it to Polly's disappearance. Calling it murder.

Melissa hugged her middle. Mr. Harper was an alcoholic, that was all too true. But, to her knowledge, he had never hurt a flea. He lived in an old run-down house trailer on the edge of town and spent most of his days liquored up on whatever he could afford. Yet, he never got into trouble. Never bothered anyone. The only time he'd ever spent a night in jail was the time he'd passed out on a park bench and the chief had insisted he sleep it off in a cell so Harper would remember never to do anything like that again.

How could he have anything to do with Polly's disappearance? The only connection was that Harper had been the one to confirm Stevie had gotten on that bus to Nashville.

Melissa raked her fingers through her hair, massaged her skull in an effort to ease the tension there. This just didn't make sense. Stevie would never hurt Polly. Certainly Mr. Harper wouldn't. How on earth could this be happening?

"Tell me again what happened to Price's family."

She turned to Jonathan when he spoke. He sat on the sofa surrounded by old high school yearbooks and family photos that included Stevie. "His mother abandoned him when he was just a kid and his father passed on years later. His father was another Floyd Harper. He couldn't stay sober, much less take care of a child. Folks around town, my family in particular, picked up his slack. Stevie's parents weren't bad people, they just had a lot of bad breaks."

Jonathan studied several photos that he'd spread on the coffee table in front of him. "He seems very happy with your family."

Exhausted, Melissa sat down on the sofa next to him. Her pulse sped up with the brush of their shoulders. She'd been reacting that way all day. It was ridiculous but she couldn't suppress her body's reactions. "Stevie

has been like a part of the family since he was a kid."
The theory that he might have taken Polly didn't make
sense. None at all. It was about as far-fetched as the
idea that Uncle Harry was having an affair with Carol
Talbot. Ridiculous.

Yet, deep down Melissa understood that Harry had
been very lonely since her mother had passed away and
she and William had grown up. But Harry just wasn't
the sort of man to do such a thing.

"Tell me about the chief's wife," Jonathan said, as if
he'd picked up on Melissa's last thought. He'd always
been able to do that. When they were together, she'd accused him of reading her mind too many times to count.

"They've lived here for as long as I can remember.
The chief is preparing for retirement. They bought a
place in Gatlinburg, Tennessee. They were supposed
to leave already but he doesn't want to go until this…"
she swallowed hard "…is resolved. His wife has never
worked outside the home despite having a degree in
education."

That Jonathan wasn't letting go the idea that Harry
and Carol were having an affair raised Melissa's hack-
les. He was right, she realized on an intellectual level,
to consider every possibility. Even though this possibility was a waste of time.

"She planned to teach," Melissa explained, "but
they wanted children first." She replayed the com-
ments she could recall that her mother had made over
the years about the chief and his wife. Most of the ladies in town considered Carol Talbot a bit uppity, but
Melissa's mother had always spoken kindly of her. "I

think there were several miscarriages before Carol had a successful pregnancy."

Jonathan looked surprised to hear this. "I was under the impression they didn't have children."

"They did," Melissa explained. "Just one. A little girl. She was born when I was about four." Dragging up those awful memories sent another stab of misery deep into her chest. "A beautiful little girl. Like her mother." Carol Talbot was a gorgeous woman. "When she was four she drowned. It was really awful." Melissa shivered, hugged herself again. "I don't know how a person gets over something like that." And she didn't want to know.

"I don't think they do."

Melissa searched Jonathan's face, his eyes. There had always been something he held back from her. That had been part of the problem, she suspected. "You lost someone?" He wouldn't tell her. She'd asked that question before, but he'd never elaborated on the shadow that hung over his past. They talked about his history to a point, but there was always that place he avoided.

"You could say that."

And that was as far into his past as Jonathan Foley ever allowed her. It shouldn't bother her all these years later, but somehow it did.

Jonathan turned his attention back to the photos again. "That's why the chief isn't retiring as planned."

"Yes. He won't leave without finding Polly." The chief wouldn't leave this investigation up to anyone else. He knew every citizen in this town, some since birth. He wasn't going anywhere until this was done. Melissa appreciated his loyalty. Calling Jonathan for help was no reflection on the chief's determination to solve the case. He had gone above and beyond. And he'd found nothing. Chief Talbot could use all the help he could get, whether he wanted it or not.

In truth, it was that close-knit relationship between the chief and the citizens he protected that worried Melissa. She couldn't imagine anyone in town being responsible for Polly's disappearance. Would the chief's training and years of experience help him to see beyond what he thought he knew to be true?

"Sometimes," Jonathan began, "in their grief, people go to extremes they wouldn't have gone to before to assuage the pain."

"Like having affairs." Melissa knew where he was going with this. "I just can't see Carol or Harry doing something like that. He and the chief have been friends for most of their lives. They played football together in high school. Harry was the chief's best man at his and Carol's wedding." Melissa hadn't been born yet, but she'd heard all the stories, seen the photos.

"Rayburn suggested your uncle and the chief haven't spoken in years."

A frown furrowed across Melissa's brow. What was Scott up to? He loved stirring trouble, thrived on drama. He never hurt anyone, just kept small-town life interesting. But this was a missing child. Polly, for God's sake. Setting her frustration aside, she weighed the comment he'd made to Jonathan. "Uncle Harry was always too busy taking care of us to have much of a social life."

Melissa tried to think of a time when she'd seen

him and the chief together—in any setting—carrying on a conversation. Surely she had. Yet, strangely, she couldn't recall even one. Scott could very well be putting one and two together and coming up with four. Just because the chief and Harry were busy didn't mean they weren't friends anymore. And just because Carol had suffered an agonizing loss didn't make her an adulteress.

Still, Melissa recognized that Jonathan had a point. "Carol Talbot shops." Those same ladies in town who didn't care for Carol whispered behind their hands about her outrageous shopping sprees. "She goes on big shopping trips, sometimes all the way to New York. She wears only the best. Her home is decorated equally beautifully." Melissa shrugged. "I guess buying things became her distraction."

"Sometimes a distraction works for a while," Jonathan put forward, "then that person needs something more. Like a drug addiction. When the same old drug doesn't do the trick anymore, it takes something new and stronger, more daring than the last."

He was preaching to the choir. As a nurse, Melissa understood the human psyche. She shook her head. "Maybe. But not with my uncle. He's not that kind of man. He'd never do that to the chief." Harry had been like a father to her and to William. He'd sacrificed any thoughts of having his own family to take care of his younger brother's. A man like that didn't get involved with another man's wife. He wouldn't be that selfish. Melissa refused to believe that for a moment.

"According to Rayburn," Jonathan said, despite her

wish that he would forget about Scott, "Stevie's fascination with the children in the community is trouble waiting to happen. Is there any possibility that he has inappropriate feelings for any of the children? Have you watched his interactions closely enough to truly judge that aspect? I'd like you to put your feelings for the man aside. Is it possible?"

Melissa rose and started pacing again. She didn't want to think of Stevie in that way. He wasn't really a man, in that sense. He was a child. Why did someone always have to make every little thing bad? She hated that. "I played with him myself growing up." She shook her head adamantly. "Stevie doesn't think that way. I'm as sure of it as I am of anything."

"But you were both kids then," Jonathan reminded her. "What about now? Physically, Stevie's a man. Think, Melissa." He pressed her with that deep, deep, penetrating gaze that still haunted her dreams. "Are you absolutely certain Rayburn is wrong?"

Hesitation and confusion muddied her thinking process. "I don't know." She turned away from him and walked to the window. It was dark outside. Nothing to stare at but the moon. "I guess it's not completely impossible." She looked over her shoulder at Jonathan. "But I've never witnessed anything untoward in Stevie's behavior in any setting with anyone." That was the truth. She would stand by that until solid evidence proved otherwise.

And if she was wrong...

Don't let him have started with Polly.

Not Polly.

Jonathan joined her at the window. "You don't want to consider this line of thinking," he said quietly. "But Harper was the one witness who could place Stevie on that bus and now he's dead. Stevie has deep affection for Polly and the two went missing the same day. That can't be coincidence, Melissa. No matter how you look at it—no matter what you think you know—the facts speak for themselves."

She closed her eyes, held back the emotions that threatened. He was right. She couldn't deny his words any longer. After all her family had done for Stevie, surely he wouldn't have hurt Polly. Yet, on an intellectual level, she knew those very things happened.

Not to her family...they'd suffered enough already.

"Tomorrow," Jonathan said gently, "we'll confront Rayburn together. I'm certain there is more he didn't tell me. He seems like the type who won't want to be one-upped. If you refute his claims, he may spill more than he intends in order to prove you wrong. Any information we gain from him could prove useful."

She nodded. "I can do that." Scott loved being right. And most of the time he was. Just not this time.

Headlights flashed across the window, then extinguished. Melissa peered through the darkness to determine who had arrived. Her heart rate kicked into a faster rhythm. Harry.

"It's my uncle." She turned to Jonathan. "Maybe I should talk to him alone." Harry hadn't seemed as enthusiastic about her call to Jonathan as she'd hoped he would be. If she intended to ask him any sensitive questions, he would be most unhappy if she did so in front of Jonathan.

"I have some calls to make." Jonathan stepped away from the window. "I'll be out back if you need me."

Melissa resisted the urge to launch into his arms and go with him. She didn't want to think about these questions, much less ask them. And she was tired. So very tired. She closed her eyes and banished the images of sweet little Polly out there somewhere, alone in the dark.

Or worse.

Melissa shuddered. She had to keep herself strong. Polly needed her.

The front door opened and Harry stepped inside. He didn't live here but he might as well have. He'd been a part of this family in every sense of the word for Melissa's entire life.

Their gazes collided. "Hey." She couldn't manage a respectable smile for him, but she tried to infuse hope into her expression. The grim set of his made her heart pound harder. Surely there wasn't more bad news.

"I need to talk to you, Melissa."

Fear skittered through her veins. "Is there news?" *Please, please don't let it be bad.*

Harry trudged over to a chair and dropped into it. He was showing every day of his fifty-eight years tonight. They were all showing signs of sheer exhaustion and overwhelming misery.

She sat down on the sofa and clasped her hands in her lap to prevent them from shaking. "What's wrong?"

"William is beside himself." Harry swiped a hand over his face. "He's torn up over the idea that you and your friend believe Presley had something to do with Polly's disappearance."

Melissa hated that Harry and William were hurt by Jonathan's questions, but they had to be asked. She had come to terms with that painful fact. Presley was hiding something. There was no doubt in Melissa's mind.

"I know Presley would never purposely do anything to hurt Polly," Melissa explained. "But William's got to see that something's wrong with her story. She's hiding something. Whatever she's leaving out might be relevant in a way she doesn't understand."

"I can't deny that likelihood." Harry slumped back into the chair. "But, good God, girl, she's William's wife. You can't expect him not to be hurt by those kinds of allegations."

Melissa's guilt for hurting her brother or Presley gave way to frustration. "I'm sorry as I can be that either of them is hurt by this, Uncle Harry, but Polly is missing." Melissa lifted her hands, turned her palms upward in question. "She's been gone almost six days. We can't afford to take the chance that there's some aspect of the circumstances of that night that isn't being considered. Those of us closest to Polly have to double the scrutiny on every step we made before her disappearance."

Harry lowered his head and gave it a shake. "You're right, of course." He heaved a burdened breath and met Melissa's gaze once more. "But it's so hard to watch him suffer like this."

Melissa got up and walked over to kneel down in front of her weary uncle. "I know." She reached her arms around his neck and hugged him close. "We'll get through this. Momma always said the Shepherds were made of strong stock. We can do what has to be done."

Harry hugged her close. "We will. I promise you that. We will *all* get through this."

Melissa closed her eyes and inhaled deeply, drawing in the familiar, comforting scent of the man who had been more father than uncle to her. He patted her back, murmured reassuring words.

She stilled as she sniffed another scent on his collar. A cloying smell that overpowered his usual herb-scented aftershave. Melissa analyzed the sweet fragrance. Perfume. She vaguely recognized the expensive designer brand.

Where had she smelled that perfume before?

Carol Talbot.

The air exited her lungs in a whoosh.

All the reasons why that scent might be clinging to her uncle's shirt filtered through her, ramming against the logic that could not be denied. He may have bumped into Carol that evening. She might have hugged him in deference to this nightmare in which the whole family was trapped. He might have...

Don't be stupid, Melissa.

There had to be a reasonable explanation for the dose of Carol's perfume that permeated her uncle's shirt. A good, long hug under current circumstances wasn't outside the realm of possibility. And just because Carol was the only woman Melissa knew who wore that particular perfume didn't mean there weren't others. Maybe.

Melissa drew back, propped a smile in place. "You're

right. We'll find Polly safe and sound and everything will be all right."

"No question." Emotion shimmered in his eyes. "You have my word on that. The whole family will be all right. I promise."

She nodded, couldn't bring herself to speak. He was so sure. He'd always taken such good care of Melissa and her brother. His confidence now heartened her, despite Scott Rayburn's accusation echoing in her brain.

"I know your friend is trying to help," Harry said. "Nothing I could say or do would ever be thanks enough for what he did for William, getting those orders delayed. Maybe if he could just go a little easy on William and Presley it would be better."

"I'll talk to him." Melissa got to her feet and backed away a step. Carol Talbot's preferred scent haunted her senses. There had to be an explanation. *There just had to be.*

Harry stood. "Get some rest. I'm going back out on the search tomorrow morning."

Melissa nodded. "I'll be there, too."

She walked her uncle to the door and said goodnight, her head reeling with questions.

Could she really have been that blind all these years? Harry Shepherd had always been a hero to her, the man she could call upon for anything at any time. The idea of him having an affair with his best friend's wife... well, it just didn't make sense.

Melissa took a deep breath, pushed that worry away and went in search of Jonathan. She wasn't ready to admit Scott Rayburn might be right—not until she had more solid proof. If Harry was having an affair with Carol, it had nothing to do with the search for Polly.

Jonathan leaned against a porch post, staring out into the night. The big moths flying around the glow of the overhead light sent fluttering shadows over his tall frame.

"My uncle's gone now."

Jonathan turned to her. "Is there news?"

Melissa shook her head. She folded her arms over her chest and moved up beside Jonathan. "He's worried about William. He asked if you could go a little easier on Presley next time you speak to her."

Jonathan resumed staring out into the darkness. "Even if doing so stonewalls finding the child?"

Melissa's belly cramped with agony. "He didn't mean that. He's just worried about William. And Polly," she added to ensure Jonathan got it. She thought of all the times she and William had depended on Harry and he'd never let them down. "He's certain we'll find her and that everything will be all right again." That part bothered her a little for some reason. He was so sure. Maybe he just wanted to give Melissa more confidence. That would be just like him. He'd done the same thing when she'd tried out for the girls' volleyball team in high school. He'd sworn she would make the team. And she had. To this day she wondered if he'd put a bug in the coach's ear.

Jonathan turned to stare at her, his doubt set in grim lines on his face. "I heard that part."

Melissa's jaw dropped in surprise. "You were listening to our conversation?"

Jonathan held her gaze, his expression unflinching. "He's very confident considering this investigation has gone nowhere and the child has been missing for nearly a week." He turned to face her fully. "There's something you need to understand."

She braced for the words to come. Judging by the unyielding look in his eyes, whatever he had to say was going to hurt.

"There's no evidence. No ransom demand. Nothing."

Each word was like a spear sliding through her chest.

"The chances of finding that child alive after almost a week are slim to none."

She opened her mouth to rail at him but he stopped her with a raised hand. "Unless," he qualified, "the person who abducted her is someone she knows. Someone who has an ulterior motive for keeping her hidden away. And safe. If the motive for taking her is not for money or some perverted pleasure, there has to be another reason."

Melissa's eyes widened with the disbelief pounding against her sternum. "You're accusing William or Harry, aren't you?"

He shrugged. "Maybe Presley."

"That's crazy." Melissa wasn't buying that. She twisted away from his hard gaze, refused to be swayed by the conviction on his face, in his tone.

"Four people have something to gain by William's deployment orders being changed," Jonathan went on, the truth in his words like salt in her aching wounds. "William, Harry, Presley and you."

Melissa whirled toward him once more. "Now you're accusing me?"

"I'm merely pointing out that the four of you have motive. That is what the chief should have looked at first. Considering the lack of a ransom demand, who had the most to gain by her going missing? It's a hard question, Melissa, but it needs to be asked. If Talbot isn't asking, he's making a mistake. No matter how well he knows you and your family."

She lifted her chin and glared at him. "I'm not discussing these ridiculous accusations with you another moment."

"I'm not suggesting," he offered with a calmness that infuriated her all the more, "that your uncle or your brother or his wife did any harm to the child—"

"Polly," Melissa corrected. No way was he getting away with making her a case statistic or mere victim. She was Polly. Pain sheared through Melissa again. "Her name is Polly."

"Polly," he acknowledged. "I don't believe harm to Polly was intended. But what I do believe is that one or all three knows far more than they're telling. Until we know all the facts, we're wasting our time."

Melissa had had enough of this. "Fine. Tomorrow morning we'll have a family meeting. You can present your suspicions and no one will leave the room until you're convinced that we're all innocent. I'll lock the doors." Fury squeezed out the pain radiating inside her. She wasn't afraid to put any member of her family on the spot. Not one of them would do this. The idea was ludicrous.

"Melissa."

That she melted a little at the way he said her name made her all the angrier. "Don't."

He cupped her cheek with his hand, stroked her skin with the pad of his thumb. "I need you to trust me. This is hard. I understand that more than you know. But emotions won't find Polly. We have to operate on the facts, on logic and motive. There's no room for anything else."

Tears welled up in her eyes. She wanted to shout at him that he was wrong, but the ache in her throat held back the words.

"If no one close to Polly is involved," he said softly, "then we have to assume that the person who did this had other motives. Motives that will in all likelihood ensure a bad outcome."

A sob ripped from her throat. Melissa tried to hold it back but the agony would not be contained.

Jonathan pulled her into his arms. She'd missed having him hold her this way.

"The chances that this was a stranger are minimal. If not a family member, it's definitely someone you know. Maybe well."

Melissa closed her eyes and burrowed her face in his shirt. His scent filled her and made her want to stay in his arms until this horror had passed. *Dear God, who would do this?*

"We'll get to the truth," he promised. "But it won't be easy and no one is going to like the route we have to take to get there."

He'd said that before and on some level she understood that he was all too right. Melissa lifted her face to his. "The chief interviewed all of us. Anyone who had any contact with Polly whatsoever." Surely a man with as much law enforcement experience as the chief would have picked up on any discrepancies.

"Unfortunately, he's too close to the people in this town. Like you, he's not going to believe anyone here is capable of this sort of evil. With Floyd Harper's sudden death, the chief seems to be convinced Stevie Price is the culprit. Narrowing his suspect pool that way defeats his efforts before he even starts."

Jonathan's assessment made sense. She knew this. "I'm so tired." She leaned her cheek against his chest and tried to borrow his strength to chase away all the horrible thoughts and images in her mind.

"You rest." He caressed her hair. "I'm not going anywhere until we figure this out."

She'd wondered so many times during the past three years if he'd moved on to someone new. If he'd gotten married. But she didn't see a ring. The urge to ask him was suddenly overwhelming. She understood that need for what it was, a necessary distraction. Her mind and body were beyond exhausted. She was empty, empty and desperate to be filled with something other than the agony that swelled each time she thought of Polly.

Melissa lifted her face to his. "Will you stay here?" The look on his face told her she needed to explain. "There's plenty of room. It's just me rambling around in this old house." Heat flushed her cheeks. Could she not have worded her explanation a little differently?

"If that's what you want."

What she wanted was for him to take her to bed and help her forget the misery for just one night.

But that would be a mistake. Her heart couldn't take losing him again.

"Good." That she managed the one word without her voice shaking was a miracle. "I'll show you to William's old room."

When she would have turned away, he pulled her back to face him. "There's just one thing I need to get out of the way first," he said, his voice thick, his gaze intent on her mouth.

And then he kissed her.

Not a soft peck on the cheek or lips, but a hungry, raging, mouth to mouth kiss. Her arms went around his neck and he pulled her body against his. The feel of him had desire burning through her. He kissed her harder, deeper, and she lost herself in the incredible sensations.

When the need for air would no longer be ignored, he pulled his mouth from hers, but kept her forehead pressed to his. "I won't cross that line again," he vowed. "I just needed to get that out of the way."

"Okay." She couldn't catch her breath anymore than he could.

"I'll get my bag from the rental car."

And just like that he walked away, leaving her standing there, even hungrier and needier than before.

Melissa recognized one absolute certainty. Jonathan Foley was a man of his word. If he said he wouldn't cross that line again, he wouldn't.

Unless she dragged him over it.

Chapter Nine

10:00 p.m.

Scott parked his car alongside the dirt road and sat in the dark for several minutes.

He'd followed Harry Shepherd here just before dark. The narrow deserted road made tailing him damned hard considering there was no traffic in which to blend. Old Harry obviously had had other things on his mind. Otherwise he'd surely have noticed Scott in his rearview mirror.

Scott had stayed way, way back, mind you. But even at dusk and with his headlights off, the man should have noticed a vehicle following him. All the more reason to be suspicious.

Harry was up to no good.

Now, well after dark, Scott had returned. He would soon know what Harry had been up to.

Fumbling for his flashlight, Scott wrapped the fingers of one hand around his granddaddy's shotgun and snatched up the flashlight with the other. His granddaddy had used the shotgun to keep the riffraff run off his place. When he'd died he'd left it to Scott. Scott had done a mental eye roll at the time. Like he would ever shoot a gun for any reason.

But he'd matured since then. He now knew that there was a time when a man had to do things he didn't like to do. Like carry a gun. He wasn't about to go into those woods without something to defend himself. His grand-daddy's shotgun would do just fine. Luther Stubble-field at the hardware store had suggested buckshot since Scott wasn't an accomplished marksman. All he had to do was get close enough, and the buckshot would spread out in a wide pattern when fired, making it pretty difficult to miss a target.

The remark had offended Scott. So he'd opted for the kind of ammo that would take down an elephant. Besides, Scott had no fear of missing if anyone got in his face. In particular, he was not afraid of Harry Shepherd. Whatever he was hiding in that old dilapidated shack in the woods, Scott intended to have a look.

If it was that child, Polly, he also intended to see that Harry Shepherd paid for his evil, conniving ways. He and that harlot Carol Talbot.

Climbing out of his car, Scott couldn't help seeing the irony in the moment. This pathetic shack was on the old Talbot place. The farm hadn't been lived on or tended in decades. The woods had taken over the clearing where the chief's great-great-grandfather had homesteaded way back when. Nobody ever came out here. Not since the chief and his wife had abandoned the place after their daughter's death. Why should they come anyway? There was nothing here. It was places like this that affirmed Scott's certainty that he did not belong in Alabama. A judgeship would make his life here more tolerable, but that wasn't likely to happen for a few years yet.

As for the missing child, Scott felt confident the chief's men had given the place a cursory search when she first went missing. No doubt that move had been anticipated and she'd been moved here after the search.

Assuming she was here at all.

Scott grinned. He had a feeling. He'd spent most of his adult life watching the folks of Bay Minette. He knew everyone of them like the back of his hand. Better maybe. He had a mental file on all the sneaky ones, the cheaters, the thieves, the ones who roughed up their wives. Not a single citizen was completely innocent or without secrets.

No. They all had their secrets.

And Scott was about to blow this one wide open.

The temperature had dropped considerably since nightfall, making it a little chilly. He didn't care. Adrenaline and anticipation kept him warm enough. He would be the hero of the town when he brought that little girl home.

Finally, perhaps, William would look at Scott the way he looked at William.

Was that so much to ask?

The old shack was dark. Scott hesitated a moment. What if he were wrong? It was possible that Harry and his harlot used this place for rendezvous when the chief was less occupied with his work. Harry might have come by to retrieve something he or she had left the last time they were here.

Didn't matter. Scott was about to find out.

The weeds were hip-deep as he neared the shack. There wasn't a sound, just the nocturnal insects buzzing and humming.

He stepped up onto the rickety porch. Boards creaked and moaned beneath his weight. He roamed the beam of his flashlight over the door and the boarded up windows. Still as quiet as a tomb in there.

The second thoughts he'd experienced a few moments ago were back, a little stronger this time. He reached for the rusty old knob on the door when a creak rent the air.

Scott's heart practically stalled.

He hadn't moved, and the sound hadn't come from behind him.

The door flew open, and something rushed him, toppling him to the ground.

Scott grappled to get a proper hold on the shotgun, despite the strong hands that manacled his arms. Male. Big. Strong. Filthy smelling. The two rolled on the ground, grunting and heaving.

Finally a blast exploded in the air, nearly shattering his eardrums.

The man's weight slumped atop Scott.

He lay perfectly still, waiting, afraid to even breathe.

The man still didn't move.

Scott shoved him off. Shaking all over, he tossed the shotgun aside and scrambled to his feet. Had he fired the shotgun? He wiped his hands on his trousers.

What the hell had just happened?

He nudged the heap on the ground with his foot. The man didn't move.

Scott swallowed hard. Where was his flashlight? He felt around on the ground, working his way back toward the porch. His fingers finally wrapped around the hard plastic cylinder. He clicked it on and swept the beam over the ground until it landed on the heap.

The big man lay facedown on the ground. Blood seeped from beneath him. Scott looked down at himself, turned the flashlight on his torso.

His breath caught when he saw blood.

Was he hurt?

He felt around on his chest, his abdomen. He was okay. Must be the other man's blood.

Easing closer, he tried to identify the man on the ground. He couldn't see his face. Holding his breath, Scott leaned and rolled the man over.

The squeak that echoed in the air came from Scott.

The man was Stevie Price.

Why had Stevie attacked him?

Scott stared at the gun on the ground. Because he'd sneaked up on him at night with a shotgun in his hand.

"Dear God." He'd killed a man. A mentally challenged man.

There would be no plea bargaining his way out of this. His daddy's money wouldn't buy him a get-out-of-jail-free card—

Had he heard that? A whimpering sound that brushed against his senses. His ears perked up, and this time he was certain. It was a soft, sad sound.

Scott whipped around and shone the light on the shack.

"Who's there?"

Faint cries whispered on the night air.

He moved cautiously forward, inching closer and closer to the shack.

"Hello?"

The crying didn't let up. Soft sobbing.

The porch creaked when he stepped onto it again. Scott braced for another attack that never came. He stepped gingerly through the open door. The place smelled bad, almost as bad as Stevie. Poor, stupid misfit. Scott put his hand over his mouth and shone the light around the room. In the beam of light he saw a sleeping bag. Bottled water. Food remains. And something in the corner. Something pink.

A dress.

Scott's heart almost stilled again.

In the corner, curled in a little ball, was a blond-haired child.

He swallowed back a lump of emotion. "Polly?"

Big tear-filled eyes looked up at him.

It was her. William's child.

A howl shattered the silence, and Scott whirled to face the sound. Before he could wonder where his shotgun was, something hit him in the stomach, knocking him to the floor.

The flashlight spun across the room.

Scott blinked as a fire lit in his belly. He touched himself and felt the warm, sticky wetness. He held his hand in front of his face. The meager glow from the flashlight on the other side of the room highlighted something dark on his fingers. Blood. His blood.

Agony swelled in his midsection.

He'd been shot.

Before he could cry out, the barrel of a shotgun appeared between his eyes. His gaze traced the long black barrel and settled upon the face staring down at him.

He opened his mouth and tried to speak but he couldn't seem to form the words. What was wrong with him? Finally he squeaked out one word, *"You."*

This was wrong. He had to do something.

When the shotgun disappeared from his view, he tried to turn his head but couldn't.

The room started to move… No, he was moving. His body was being dragged toward the door.

He opened his mouth again to scream but the blackness swallowed him.

11:15 p.m.

JOHNNY RAY BRUCE sucked on the cigarette dangling from his lips. She was late. Probably couldn't get away from her old man.

Fool.

He'd told her a long time ago that she would never belong to anyone but him. Too bad she'd been too stupid to listen. Now things were way too complicated.

Headlights appeared in the distance.

Johnny Ray threw the cigarette to the ground and stamped it out. "'Bout time."

The lights flashed on the park bench next to where

he'd parked his car. They didn't have to worry about being seen in the park. Folks around here went to bed with the chickens. Rolled the damned streets up at dark.

Johnny Ray hated this town. He'd have been gone long ago if it hadn't been for her.

Presley slammed the door of her car and sauntered over to him. "Gimme a smoke."

As he removed a cigarette from the pack, Johnny Ray let his eyes skim her body. Short shorts, halter top and bare feet. Man, it was a sin for a woman to look that good. He wanted her. Right now. Right here. But she was ticked off. She didn't have to say so. He knew her well enough to read her body language like an open book.

He flipped out his lighter and watched as she drew on the cigarette. His gut tightened. She was something, all right.

She exhaled a big puff of smoke. "We got trouble."

"Oh yeah?" He lit himself another smoke. "That soldier boy of yours finally grow a brain and figure out how to make you happy?"

She rolled her eyes and took another long drag from the cigarette. "He's suspicious about that night."

"It doesn't matter how suspicious he is," Johnny Ray shot back. "He doesn't have any evidence. My uncle said there's no evidence of anything."

Presley turned away.

"Hey, baby." He put his arm around her and pulled her close. "I know this is hard, but you gotta be strong. Falling apart now won't change anything."

She jerked away from him. "My baby is missing. You don't know how that feels."

Johnny Ray shrugged. "Maybe I don't. But I don't like it when you mope around like this."

She lifted her chin haughtily. "He says I can't talk to you anymore."

Rage roared through Johnny Ray. He charged up toe-to-toe with her. "So what? He's said that before. His threats have never changed anything."

"He says he'll get a divorce."

"Hey!" Johnny Ray threw up his arms. "That's great. He should've come up with that plan years ago."

She glared at him. "I don't want a divorce. That would leave me with no insurance. No money. Nothing. I'm not living that way again. And…"

"And what?" he snarled.

"Maybe I don't want to lose him."

Another rush of fury stormed Johnny Ray. "What're you saying?"

"That I can't see you anymore." She shook with her own anger and no small measure of fear.

She was actually serious.

Johnny Ray laughed. Long and loud. She glared at him. "Well, darling, I'm afraid that doesn't work for me."

She tossed the cigarette away. "Well," she mocked him, "I guess you'll just have to deal with it."

Johnny Ray stuck his face in hers. "I don't think so. You'll do whatever I tell you to."

"I'm through letting you run me. I deserve better and Will wants me to be happy."

"Sounds like your sister-in-law's been filling your head with fairy tales again."

"Melissa's been better to me than my own momma ever was. The Shepherds are my family." She folded her arms over her chest and shook her head. "I'm not cheating on Will anymore." Her chin quivered but she held it high. "We're done, Johnny Ray."

Shaking his head, he chuckled. "Well," he said cruelly, "you should've thought of that before you killed his kid."

Behind her, tires squealed.

Johnny Ray looked past Presley to see William's truck skid to a stop next to her car. The soldier boy jumped out, leaving the door open.

"Johnny Ray," William snarled, "you're a dead man."

"Call my uncle," Johnny Ray said to Presley as he walked past her. To William he taunted, "Bring it on, soldier boy. Let's see if the military made a man out of you after all."

Saturday, May 29th, 1:02 a.m.

MELISSA SHOOK LOOSE from the dream. It was the same one she had whenever Jonathan was on her mind. They were still together. He hadn't left, and they had children of their own.

A howl shattered the final remnants of sleep.

Melissa sat up. A curse hissed through the air.

Jonathan.

She threw back the covers and jumped up. When she reached the door to William's room her brain had only just conjured up the idea that she shouldn't go to Jonathan like this. It was too late.

He sat on the side of the bed, his hands braced on either side of him.

"You okay?" she asked him.

"Yes."

That was his stock answer. She crossed the room, using the moonlight filtering in between the curtains to avoid the clothing littering the floor, and sat down beside him.

"The same old nightmares?"

He nodded.

"I don't suppose you want to talk about it." He never had. Three years apart likely hadn't changed his mind about sharing with her.

"I led my team behind enemy lines."

Shock radiated through Melissa. He was going to tell her? Now? Fear of shattering the moment kept her from speaking.

"We were captured. As soon as I was identified, the interrogation started. They knew I had information that would help their cause."

She wanted to touch him, to put her arms around him and hold him close but she didn't dare move. The pain in his voice tore at her heart.

"When I wouldn't break, they moved on to another technique."

The ability to breathe eluded her.

"They tortured and killed my men, one at a time, in an attempt to make me talk."

Dear God. How could anyone hope to recover from that kind of trauma?

"I didn't break. I couldn't let my country down."

He fell silent for so long Melissa thought he'd finished. She reached out to him, but he flinched.

"They all died for nothing. The mission was aborted after our capture. But I didn't know." He shook his head. "I didn't know."

Melissa put her arms around him. He tried to draw away but she held on tight. "I'm sorry," she whispered. "You did your duty. That's all you could do."

He pressed his cheek to hers. "They died for nothing."

The agony in his voice had tears welling in her eyes. "They died for their country," she murmured. "It was all any of you could do." Though she didn't understand exactly what had happened, she knew full well if his men had been anything like Jonathan, any one of them would have done the same thing he had.

He turned his mouth around to hers. "I swore I wouldn't do this again."

"You don't have to," she whispered, her lips brushing his. "I'll do it."

A ringing sound made her hesitate. The phone.

For a moment she couldn't move. She could only breathe the same air as him.

The phone rang again.

"I have to get that." She forced her body to draw away from his and stood, then she practically ran. All the way back to her room. She snatched the phone from the nightstand. "Hello."

"Melissa."

"What's wrong, Uncle Harry? Have they found Polly?" Fear lodged in her throat. The sweet sensual heat Jonathan had stirred vanished in a heartbeat.

The overhead light came on and Jonathan stood in her doorway.

"It's William," Harry said, his voice haunted.

Melissa looked around for her clothes. "Is he okay?"

"He and Johnny Ray had a fight. Johnny Ray's beat up pretty bad. The chief's holding William until we come pick him up."

Melissa closed her eyes and scrubbed at them. Why in God's name didn't Johnny Ray admit defeat? Presley had chosen William. "I'll be right there."

"I'm on my way to city hall to pick up William. You stay put. I'll bring him back to the house and we'll try to talk some sense into him."

"Okay. Be careful." It was the middle of the night and Harry wasn't so young anymore. Melissa hung up the phone and met Jonathan's questioning gaze. "William and Johnny Ray got into a fight. Johnny Ray's in the hospital. Uncle Harry's going to pick up William from city hall."

"Has he been charged?"

Melissa sighed. "I don't know." She combed her fingers through her hair. How could any of them do this with Polly missing? It was insane.

"Where's his wife?"

Melissa shook her head. "I didn't think to ask."

For the first time since he walked in, she noticed Jonathan was staring at her. Heat rushed into her cheeks as she realized the state of her dress.

"Sorry." She wrapped her arms around her middle, covering her breasts. The nightgown was thin and from the look in Jonathan's eyes, he saw right through the fabric.

Jonathan took a step into the room. "I've seen every inch of you, Melissa."

The heat that had infused her cheeks started anew deep in her belly. "I know, but that was before." She pulled in a much needed breath. "I didn't mean to come into your room like that." What had she been thinking? If that phone hadn't rung, God knows what would have happened.

"I'm glad you did."

Their gazes collided and held. He'd dragged on his jeans but hadn't taken the time to fasten them. He was as lean and strong as she remembered and the need to touch him, every part of him, made her knees weak. But she couldn't go there, not and survive. Losing him had been too hard. That he'd shared his nightmare with her only made being together more difficult. Bruises, maybe a few days old, were scattered on his torso. She frowned. She hadn't asked what kind of work he did now.

As if he sensed the war going on inside her and the questions the bruises raised, he nodded. "I'll be waiting in the living room."

Melissa held her breath until he'd walked away.

By the time she'd gotten dressed and pulled herself together, Uncle Harry had arrived with William and

Presley in tow. William had a black eye, a swollen lip
and a few scratches. Johnny Ray on the other hand had
a mild concussion and two cracked ribs.

"The chief isn't pressing charges considering," Harry
explained.

"Considering what?" Jonathan asked.

William, she noticed, didn't say a word. Neither did
Presley. She sat on the sofa next to her husband, her legs
crossed and her foot tapping a hundred miles an hour.

Taking a breath, Melissa sat down next to Presley.
"You okay?"

Presley wouldn't meet her gaze, just shook her head.

"You want me to tell them?"

Melissa looked up at her uncle who'd asked the question. Harry starred at William who sat there, unblink-
ing.

"William?" Melissa said softly. "We can talk later,
if you'd prefer." She turned to Harry. "They're both exhausted. This has been—"

"She wasn't home when Polly disappeared," William said abruptly.

Melissa's heart bumped hard against her sternum.

"She was with him."

Presley stared at the floor where her foot tapped
faster and faster.

"Dear God," Harry groaned. "How could you do that
to William?" Harry demanded. "He deserves better."

The silence that held the room captive for the next
few seconds weighed several tons.

Presley nodded. "He made me."

"Who made you?" Jonathan prompted. Melissa greatly appreciated the sympathy in his voice.

"Johnny Ray."

William's face tightened. Melissa wished she could protect him from this.

"How so?" Jonathan nudged.

Harry stood. "I can't listen to any more of this." He gestured to the door. "I'll be on the porch."

Presley glanced at Melissa, then at Jonathan. "He blackmailed me. He said if I didn't meet him whenever he asked, he'd tell Will my secret."

Before Melissa could launch into a rant about what she'd like to do to Johnny Ray, Jonathan asked in that same gentle voice, "Can you share that secret with us now?"

Presley nodded. She stole a look at William. "After Will deployed to Afghanistan, I found out I was pregnant again." She made a keening sound and her lips trembled. "You know I couldn't handle another kid." This she said to Melissa. "I can barely take care of Polly."

"Dear God." Melissa knew where this was going.

"So I got Johnny Ray to take me to Birmingham and I had an abortion."

William lunged to his feet and walked out onto the porch with Harry.

Presley broke down, dropped her face into her hands. "I should've been home that night. But he made me meet him. I wasn't gone long. I thought Polly was in her room when I got back but I was really drunk."

Melissa wanted to hate her for what she'd done, but

she couldn't. She set aside the fact that Presley had just admitted terminating a baby she had conceived with Will. Presley had been abused her whole life. She wasn't equipped to deal with snakes like Johnny Ray.

Melissa pulled the younger woman into her arms. "You should've told me. I would've made sure he never bothered you again." Will had trusted Melissa to watch over Polly and Presley. But she couldn't do that if Presley wasn't honest with her.

Presley sobbed harder. "I didn't want you to hate me. Now look what I've done."

It no longer mattered that Melissa was right—Presley had been holding something back. But her revelation changed nothing.

Polly was still missing.

Chapter Ten

Jonathan followed the chief and his deputies around the perimeter that had been cordoned off as a crime scene.

Stevie Price's body had been discovered early that morning by two teenagers. The young men had insisted they'd come to the shack for a weekend of fishing in the nearby river. Judging by what the police had found in their vehicle, fishing hadn't been on the agenda. More like partying. Lots of beer and chips, and no sign of any fishing gear.

Stevie Price had been shot in the chest once. The coroner had concluded that Price had died within seconds of being hit. An autopsy would likely show the round had ripped through his heart.

Inside the shack, considerable evidence indicated that Polly Shepherd had been held there. But there was no sign of the child now.

More frightening was the blood trail that led from the floor of the shack, across the porch and deep into the woods. The blood had run out but the evidence that a body had been dragged had not.

Chief Talbot lifted his hand. "Hold up."

Jonathan studied the ground in front of the chief. A broken clump of small tree limbs indicated that perhaps whoever had been dragged wasn't quite dead at that point.

Talbot crouched down and inspected the ragged brush. "Those forensics techs here yet?"

"Ten minutes out, Chief," one of the deputies reported.

Talbot shook his head. "We need them now."

Jonathan scanned the woods in front of them. The hum of the river was louder now. They were close. His instincts warned that the body—whoever it belonged to—had been dumped in the river. Perhaps while the victim was still alive.

Jonathan crouched down near the chief. "This trail appears to be too large for a child's body. The perp would simply have carried the child." That was the only good thing about this day so far.

He glanced back toward the shack. Melissa and her uncle were being detained at the road. They didn't need to see any of this…not until they knew something conclusive about the victim.

"I'd say you're right." The chief pushed to his feet. "Looks like we're headed to the river."

The chief's face had paled. He took out a handkerchief and dabbed at his forehead.

The two deputies trailing their steps stared at the ground. Jonathan was clearly missing something here. As the chief moved forward, Jonathan hung back, falling into step with the deputies.

"Man, this sucks," the deputy to Jonathan's right mumbled.

"It does," Jonathan agreed.

The deputy shook his head. "More than you know."

The other deputy cleared his throat and exchanged a look with his colleague.

Jonathan slowed his step, hoping to slow the progress of the other two men. "What does that mean?" he asked when the chief was several meters ahead.

"This is the river where his daughter drowned." The one who'd spoken nodded toward the chief.

"He and his family used to come here in the summer and fish and swim," the other deputy said. He shook his head. "This place has been deserted since that little girl died."

Jonathan processed the information. Why would someone keep Polly Shepherd hidden away here of all places? The better question at the moment was who killed Stevie Price? And who else had been murdered in this place? Judging by the amount of blood the victim who'd been dragged had lost, it was unlikely he or she would've survived in or out of the water.

Why had Stevie bought a bus ticket for Nashville and then hidden away out here? From what Melissa had told him, Stevie lacked the mental capacity to formulate such a complex plan. Jonathan looked up and around at the thick canopy of trees that almost completely blocked the morning sun.

The tree line broke as the land disappeared into the murky water. Chief Talbot was moving faster now. Jonathan quickened his pace to catch up to him.

When they reached the water's edge, the chief staggered a bit. Jonathan moved up behind him, covertly steadying him. The chief glanced at him, a glimmer of gratitude amid the agony in his eyes.

The deputies scoured the shoreline. Jonathan studied the rocks protruding in the shallower sections of the water. "There." He pointed to a cluster of rocks down river. Barely visible was something light green or bluish.

Chief Talbot waded into the water.

"Chief, wait," one of the deputies called after him. "I can do that."

The chief kept going, trudging through the hip deep water toward what appeared to be a body trapped between two large boulders.

Jonathan was right behind him. He consoled himself with the fact that the body—if it was a body—was far too large to be Polly's.

The chief stumbled. Jonathan helped him up then plunged forward to reach what was indeed a body, facedown, caught between the rocks. He touched the carotid artery. Definitely dead.

"This one didn't make it, either," Jonathan said as the chief approached.

Talbot steadied himself and nodded to the body. "Turn it over," he said to his deputies. "Let's see who this is and get 'em out of this damned river."

The two deputies wrestled the bloated body free of the rocks and turned the man face up.

Scott Rayburn.

"Holy Moses," the chief muttered.

"We'll get him to the bank," one of the deputies said. He looked almost as pale as the chief.

Talbot motioned for the two to get on with it. He plowed through the water, stopped midway to the bank and surveyed the area.

Jonathan stayed close by. The man had the look of one about to keel over.

"This just doesn't make sense," the chief said more to himself than to Jonathan. "Why would Stevie and Rayburn do something like this?"

Jonathan didn't have to point out the obvious. A third party was involved. He understood what the chief meant. Why would either man be involved in abducting Polly Shepherd?

"I guess this explains why Harper is dead."

Chief Talbot shot Jonathan a look. "I'd say so."

Harper had lied, it would seem, about seeing Price get on the bus. Whoever had prompted him to do so had obviously gotten nervous and tied up that loose end. But why? What did Harper and Price have in common? And what did that have to do with Rayburn's accusations against Harry Shepherd, if anything? Was there bad blood between the elder Shepherd and Rayburn?

Not according to Melissa.

"Oh, Lord, have mercy."

The chief fell against Jonathan. "I've got you." As soon as the man was steadied, he lunged through the water. "Wait, Chief…"

Then Jonathan saw what had captured the chief's attention, what had taken him to his knees.

Amid the thick growth lining the shore a dozen or so meters away a small blond head bobbed in the water.

Jonathan bounded forward, the water pulling at his legs. His heart rocketed into his throat.

No. No. No. Don't let it end like this.

He reached the bushes before the chief. Jonathan reached through the limbs and closed his fingers around the…doll.

Jonathan's knees gave out under him. He sank into the water, its murkiness lapping at his neck. The chief practically fell on top of him.

"Let me see. For God's sake, let me see."

Jonathan held the doll up for his inspection.

A sob tore from the chief's throat.

It was a while before either of them could walk back to shore. By the time they reached Rayburn's body and the two deputies, the forensics techs had arrived.

Chief Talbot sat down on the ground and held his head in his hands.

The deputies worked with the techs to attempt recovering any trace evidence. At some point the coroner arrived to examine the body.

Jonathan watched, unable to speak or act. When he'd seen the blond head in the water all he'd been able to think about, besides the tragic loss of a child, was what this would do to Melissa, and to her family.

He closed his eyes and blocked the kind of pain he hadn't allowed in in years. Not since he'd watched his men, his squad, die one by one because he refused to talk. To sell out his country.

That was when he'd stopped allowing himself to feel.

Melissa had stirred the desire to feel again, but he'd blocked her out, too.

He'd stopped being human and he'd lost her because of it.

Jonathan opened his eyes. Fury tightened his jaw. Whoever had done this to her and her family, he would find them and he would make them pay.

Chief Talbot managed to pull himself together enough to finish the job he'd come here to do. He gave the order to drag the river.

If the doll was confirmed as belonging to Polly, and Jonathan felt certain it would be, the next step would be to search for her body.

He needed to break this news to Melissa before she heard it from the crowd that had in all inevitability gathered at the road. The news vultures would be monitoring the police band.

MELISSA WAS LOSING her mind.

Why didn't one of the deputies come back and tell them something? They'd been gone nearly an hour. She scanned the crowd that had gathered. Dozens of Bay Minette citizens stood alongside media crews, waiting for news.

William had been restrained when he'd attempted to breach the crime scene. Presley sat in the backseat of the patrol car with him. Both were out of their minds with grief and guilt.

A rumble in the crowd drew her attention back to the woods in time to see Jonathan appear. Melissa's heart thundered. Fear closed around her throat as he came near enough for her to see his grim face.

His clothes were wet.

Her knees began to buckle but she locked them, held on to her uncle's arm.

Jonathan crossed under the yellow tape and was immediately assaulted by reporters. He pushed through without a word. His right arm went around Melissa. "Let's get out of here."

"What happened?" Harry demanded.

"Not here," Jonathan warned.

Melissa's head spun. She and Harry clung to each other as Jonathan said something to the deputy at the car where Will and Presley waited. Then he ushered Melissa and her uncle to her car.

The reporters tried again to get some answers or at least a comment. Jonathan's lethal glare shut them up in an instant.

"What happened back there?" Melissa demanded when they were driving away from the persistent reporters. "Was it really Stevie?"

Jonathan put a hand over hers. "We'll talk when we get to your house."

When Melissa would have argued, he added, "We didn't find Polly."

Melissa wasn't sure whether to be relieved or more worried. For now, she chose the former. At least there was still hope that Polly was alive. When the call had come about Stevie… She closed her eyes. How could this be? Stevie had been like a part of her family.

The twenty minutes it took to reach her house felt

like a lifetime. The utter silence had been deafening and agonizing. She'd wanted to ask so many other questions but she'd been afraid of the answers. Harry had sat in the backseat, apparently suffering the same horrific fear.

Will and Presley arrived right behind them. When they were all inside, seated, braced for the worst, Jonathan finally broke his silence.

"Stevie was shot," he explained. "We're not sure by whom, but…"

Melissa couldn't imagine who would want to shoot Stevie. Maybe he'd discovered where Polly was being held and the person who'd taken her had shot him.

"Scott Rayburn's body was found, too. He'd been shot, as well."

"What?" Will demanded. "That's crazy."

Presley broke down into sobs.

Harry simply sat there. He said nothing and looked at no one. Melissa worried about him. He wasn't a young man anymore. As hard as this was on her, it was worse for him, on a physical level.

Jonathan shook his head. "There are no answers yet." He sat down on the sofa arm next to Melissa. "There was evidence that a child was being held in the shack."

"What kind of evidence?" Will was on his feet now instead of comforting his wife. "They should've let me in there."

"Toys. A couple of changes of clothes—girl's clothing."

Jonathan kept his voice steady and calm but his

words ripped Melissa's insides to shreds. "Was there anything else?" *Please don't let him say blood.*

"There was some blood inside," he explained, "but the preliminary estimation is that it belongs to Rayburn. It appears he was shot in the shack and then dragged to the river."

The idea that the chief's child had drowned in that river hit Melissa hard. What the man must have gone through. "But Polly wasn't there?" Melissa looked up at Jonathan. "This doesn't make sense. Two people are dead." She shook her head. "Three counting Floyd Harper. And Polly is still missing."

Jonathan scrubbed a hand over his face.

There was more. Melissa's heart sank. "What?" she demanded. It might have been three years, but she knew that look. "What aren't you telling us?"

"When we found Rayburn's body…" He struggled to find the right words, the battle playing out on his face. "In the water, there was a doll, too."

Presley sat up straight. "Pink dress?" she demanded. "Blond hair?" Her voice grew higher and tighter with every word.

Jonathan hesitated then said, "Yes."

Presley cried out in anguish. William collapsed onto the sofa next to her.

Melissa felt numb. She couldn't cry. She couldn't ask any more questions.

Jonathan exhaled a troubled breath. "The chief has ordered a team to drag the river."

Surely that river hadn't taken another child, Melissa thought. God wouldn't be that cruel.

"I have to go…" Harry stood. He looked around as if he were lost. "I need to help."

Melissa pushed to her feet, wobbled a little. "There's nothing you can do right now, Uncle Harry."

He shook his head. "I have to go."

Before Melissa could say more he rushed out the door.

Melissa looked from Jonathan to her brother and his wife.

They were all a mess. There was nothing they could do for Polly.

They had failed.

Pull yourself together. The inner voice reminded her of her resolve to be strong. She dragged in a broken breath. "I'm calling Dr. Ledford. He can call in something for Presley." Presley cried hysterically. The sound was devastating.

At the mention of his wife's name, Will met Melissa's gaze. "It would be better if Presley got some rest now," she told him. "Maybe you, too."

He shook his head. "I need to be out there." His voice was hollow, weak.

Melissa didn't argue with him. He was right. His daughter was missing. He needed to be out there. She nodded. "You go. I'll take care of Presley." Melissa walked to the window and checked the drive. "Uncle Harry's still out there. Ride with him," she said to William.

She worried about Harry. He'd rushed out of the house then just sat there in the car. He would need William with him. They needed each other.

When her brother had gone, Melissa made the call. Dr. Ledford's nurse, a friend of hers, promised to call the drugstore immediately and have someone deliver a sedative for Presley.

Melissa tucked Presley into the bed William had slept in growing up, then she wandered back into the living room. Jonathan was on the phone.

She stared out the kitchen window at the swing Polly loved to play on whenever she stayed over. Melissa could imagine the little girl swinging high, her blond hair flying behind her. She was the sweetest child.

Melissa refused to believe she was dead.

She was out there, waiting to be found.

And then everything would be all right. Just like her Uncle Harry said.

It had to be.

Jonathan ended his call and joined her at the window. "You need to eat."

Melissa shook her head. There was no way she could eat right now.

"There's not much else we can do until we hear from the chief," Jonathan offered. "I'll fix you one of my famous omelets and we'll review what we know so far. See what we can figure out."

What they knew was a lot of confusing details and not much else. But he was right. She needed to be strong. Part of being strong meant taking care of her basic needs. "Okay." Her lips lifted in a small smile that surprised her. "I remember your omelets. They were pretty darned awesome."

"Sit." He guided her to the table. "While I cook I want you to tell me more about Stevie Price and Polly."

Melissa felt sick to her stomach. Why would Stevie do this?

Jonathan pilfered through cabinets and the fridge until he'd gathered everything he needed. He prodded Melissa for answers as he worked.

She did the best she could, but that old, ugly fear kept vying for her attention.

Polly's doll had been in the river with Scott Rayburn's body. Images of Polly's favorite doll floating in that murky river kept flashing in Melissa's brain.

The hope Melissa had been holding on to slipped from her grasp…

Chapter Eleven

12:03 p.m.

"I did this."

Harry sat in his car, staring straight ahead at nothing.

Polly was gone.

Stevie was dead.

What in the world had Rayburn done? How had he found Stevie and Polly?

If they found that baby in the water... Harry's fingers squeezed into fists. There would be only one thing he could do.

He'd left William with the search team, but Harry had needed to talk to her. She was the only one who would understand.

"No," Carol argued. "You didn't do this. Something went wrong." She curled her arms around him, tried to comfort him. "It wasn't supposed to be like this."

Harry couldn't look at her. If he did, she would see the ugly truth in his eyes. He was a monster. One who had caused the death of his precious Polly. One who had destroyed his nephew. William would never forgive him. As well he shouldn't.

"Rayburn did this," Carol insisted. "He spent every waking moment attempting to stir trouble. To hurt someone." She pressed her forehead to Harry's arm. "Now he's done it. He's ruined everything."

"I was there," Harry said, his voice coming from a hollow place inside him. "Before dark last night. Stevie and Polly were fine. She…" He swallowed back the lump in his throat. "She was playing with that doll."

"Who else could have known?" Carol asked softly, the plea nearly more than he could bear.

Harry had no answer. No one had known. Only the two of them. Stevie hadn't understood. He'd thought he was babysitting for a few days. Floyd Harper hadn't known. He'd just done what Harry paid him to do. Until he'd decided he needed more money.

Dear God, Harry hadn't meant to kill him. It had been an accident. The old fool had tried to force Harry to give him more money—for an operation he'd claimed he needed. But that wasn't true. He'd have spent on liquor whatever Harry had given him. They'd argued and the crazy man had charged Harry. What else could he have done? He'd pushed the man off him. He hadn't realized they were standing so close to the edge of that bridge.

Now he was dead. And Stevie, as well.

Agony swelled inside Harry. Sweet, innocent little Polly was likely dead, too.

Dear God, this was all his doing.

He was a monster who didn't deserve to live.

"It's best that we don't see each other again." His empty words echoed in the confined space.

Carol stared at him. He didn't have to look at her to know. He could feel her gaze upon him. She was as devastated as he was. Except none of this was her fault.

"You can't mean that," she whispered.

"You'll only be hurt when the truth comes out." He closed his eyes to block the painful image of that doll floating in the water. The doll kept morphing into Polly. Lord, just strike him dead now.

"I don't care." She held more tightly on to him. "Reed will retire and move to Gatlinburg. I'll stay here with you. We'll get through this together."

Harry shook his head. "There won't be any getting through it." He turned to her. "Go with Reed, Carol. He's a good man. You deserve better than me."

Tears welled in her eyes. "You promised we would be together. Finally. After all this time."

"No one will ever know about us." He turned his attention back to the road. "That's the way it has to be. It's the only way to protect you. I've hurt too many people already."

"I won't let you do this," she cried. "I know what you're thinking."

She couldn't. She wasn't a monster like him. She couldn't possibly know.

"You believe everyone will be better off without you." She shook him. "That's wrong, Harry. You'll just hurt them all the more. You did what you thought was right—what would save Will. You had no idea this would happen. Rayburn messed everything up."

"No." Harry let go a weary breath. "I messed everything up. This is my doing."

"Will and Melissa will forgive you in time," she urged.

"They won't." They shouldn't. He didn't deserve forgiveness.

"Then they don't have to know." She reached up and caressed his jaw. "Why should any of them ever know? There is no evidence linking you to what happened. No one ever has to know."

If only it were that easy. "I'll know." And he couldn't live with it.

"I won't let you do this, Harry."

He patted her hand. Carol meant well, but she didn't understand. He had hurt the people he loved most. He had caused that sweet baby's death.

There was only one thing to do now.

Even if by some miracle Polly was found unharmed, he had caused three deaths. No matter who pulled the trigger, he was responsible.

He had to pay.

Chapter Twelve

The team dragging the river had found nothing so far.

William had just delivered the news, but he still refused to leave the scene. Harry, he told her, had left hours ago, but every time she called, he didn't answer his cell phone. Melissa was really worried about him. She wanted to go and find him, but William made her promise to stay with Presley. Finally giving in to the effects of the medication, she was sleeping soundly.

Jonathan had been back and forth. He called or came home every hour or so to check on her. He was the single reason she felt comfortable staying behind. She knew that Jonathan would do whatever needed to be done.

Melissa peeked in on Presley again. She was out. Most folks couldn't understand the patience and sympathy Melissa felt for Presley. They didn't comprehend how hard her life had been. Other than the Johnny Ray thing, Presley had come a long way. She tried hard. Some people just weren't strong enough to stand up to someone like Johnny Ray. Presley had been used and abused by him. Her childhood had deeply instilled in her that she didn't deserve any better. She'd once told Melissa that she didn't know why Will loved her. Johnny Ray had exploited that doubt.

Whatever pain he suffered as a result of the beating he'd taken from William, the bastard deserved.

Melissa picked up the phone and tried both Harry's cell and his house phone. Still no answer.

"Dammit." Where was he?

A soft rap at the front door snapped her from the troubling thought. Fear fired through her. Wouldn't Jonathan have called if there was news?

Not if it was bad.

Fear sucking at her composure, she trudged to the front door. She checked past the curtain.

Her heart battered her chest wall as she saw Jonathan. She opened the door. Her gaze collided with his and she wanted to ask—to demand—what he'd learned, but terror held her tongue.

"They're still searching," he explained, "but they haven't found her. That could be a good sign."

Relief made Melissa sway. "Thank God."

"The team leader said that with the lack of strength behind the current, even a small body wouldn't have been carried far. They're cautiously optimistic that she isn't in the water."

Melissa fell against him. She couldn't help herself. She needed his strong arms around her. And she cried. Her niece was still missing but at least she wasn't in that damned river.

Jonathan led her back into the living room after he

closed the door. "The thinking now is that she may have run. The chief's broadening the search grid in hopes of finding some trace of her in the woods."

"Then there's still hope." The weather wasn't a real issue. She'd been well fed, based on the evidence found at the shack, and clothed. There was reason to hold out hope. But searching the acres and acres of those woods could take too long.

"There's hope." He caressed her cheek and offered a smile. "The thrust of the investigation now is determining how Price and Rayburn were connected. There has to be a motive for their actions. If we learn the motive, we'll be far more likely to find her."

Melissa gave herself a shake. Jonathan looked exhausted. She hadn't considered that he'd scarcely had any sleep, either, much less anything to eat. "Would you like coffee? Or tea?" She really knew better than to ask about the tea. Jonathan didn't go for the Southern tradition of iced tea.

He shook his head. "I'm fine."

"Are you sure?" She searched his face, her pulse skipping at the memories of all they had shared. So many nights she had lain beside him and watched him sleep. She'd loved him so much…still did. But she would never admit that out loud.

"I need to talk to you about Rayburn and the accusations he made when he approached me."

The memory infuriated her all over again. "I hate to speak ill of the dead, but Scott Rayburn loved spreading rumors. Rumors," she reiterated. "That's what his accusations were about. I know my uncle Harry. He would never do anything like that." She blocked the memory of the perfume she'd smelled on his shirt. That didn't prove anything.

Jonathan guided her to the sofa. "Think about your uncle's reaction last night and this morning."

Now Jonathan was making her angry. "Last night he was exhausted and worried about William. This morning he was in a state of shock. We all were."

"Last night when Presley announced what she'd done," Jonathan recapped, "Harry said nothing about her leaving Polly alone. His anger was directed at the idea that she'd cheated on her husband."

"Jonathan." Melissa didn't know how to make him understand this. "All of us have already gone through a range of emotions that would put lesser folks down. Harry has been strong through all of it. But even the strongest breaks at some point. The idea that Presley was unfaithful was far less painful to latch on to." She'd witnessed it often enough as a nurse. She supposed Jonathan couldn't understand that because he was one of those rare people who had no breaking point. If she'd doubted that fact, what he'd shared with her last night about his military history confirmed her conclusion.

"Maybe so," Jonathan allowed. "I'm not so sure."

"Scott always liked being the center of attention," she said again.

"You trust your uncle that much?"

"I trust him with my life."

Jonathan's gaze held hers. "There was a time when you trusted me that much."

She had to look away. If he saw the feelings that still

simmered inside her… She couldn't let that happen. Last night she'd drifted far too close to breaking down. She couldn't risk doing it again. Unlike him, she did have a breaking point.

"I need you to trust me now," he murmured. "I'm not trying to hurt you or Harry. I'm only trying to find the truth."

His soft words kicked her defenses right out from under her. "I do trust you, Jonathan." She met his searching gaze, pushed aside all the frustration. "I wouldn't have called you otherwise."

He didn't respond, just stared at her eyes, and her lips.

She wished he would say something, anything, to break the tension building between them. But he didn't. Instead, he leaned forward and brushed his lips across hers.

Melissa warned herself not to cross that line—the very one he had drawn himself. But she just couldn't help it. She was so tired. So afraid. So desperate to feel his touch. No man had ever owned her heart, but him. No man had ever made her want to grow old with him, but him. No matter that he'd left her once already, broken her heart into a million pieces, she wanted his touch. Wanted his lips against hers—just like this—as long as it would last.

So much for standing firm. She was a lost cause when it came to this man.

He kissed her slowly, softly. Just a meshing of lips. A dance of wills to see who would give in first and open in invitation.

Melissa couldn't help herself. She parted her lips, invited him inside. His tongue slid over her lips, touched her own. Her hands glided up his chest and into his hair. She loved the feel of his thick hair. Soft and silky. Such a contrast to his hard, lean body.

He drew her to her feet, without breaking the contact of their mouths. Then he scooped her into his arms and carried her into the hall.

"The last door on the right," she murmured between kisses. She didn't know why she bothered; after all, he'd spent last night here. She wasn't thinking, only feeling.

This was going to a place it shouldn't, one that would bring immense pain. But, right now, she wanted to go to that forbidden place. As much as it would hurt when he left her again, this moment—his touch—would be worth the pain of losing him a second time.

Their lives were worlds apart, their desires for the future in completely different universes. But when they made love, that all vanished. There was only her and him, coming together in such a beautiful way that she couldn't possibly resist.

Taking his time, he unbuttoned her blouse, slid it over her shoulders and down her arms. She shivered when he reached for the waistband of her jeans, which landed on the floor next to her blouse in no time. He urged her hands to do the same to him.

Button after button, she opened his shirt. When her palms slid over his smooth, warm skin, she shivered in anticipation. Her fingers fumbled with the closure of his jeans. He tried to help, but she pushed his hands away. She could do this.

She pushed his jeans and boxers down his thighs. He fumbled with shoes, finally got them off, then tugged the jeans and boxers free of his muscled legs.

As unladylike as it was, she couldn't help staring at his body. She'd loved all that muscled terrain. Every single scar was dear to her. His time in the military had taken a physical and mental toll on him. But he'd survived. No man she'd ever met was as strong as Jonathan. Not nearly.

He lifted her into his arms and settled her on the bed. She gasped when he dragged her panties down her legs and off. He cuddled in close to her, allowing her to feel the desperation in his body. He wanted this just as much as she did.

As a nurse, she understood firsthand the importance of protection. But this was Jonathan. She didn't want anything between them. He was far too responsible to risk himself or anyone else to unprotected sex if there was any danger.

She trusted him. She'd never trusted anyone the way she trusted him. With her body, her heart…her soul.

He kissed his way down her body, pleasuring her breasts with his lips and teeth. She gasped again and again. It had been so long. Three years. She hadn't been with anyone else since they first met. He'd ruined her for anyone else.

His fingers traced her hips, slid between her thighs until they found that hot, damp place that throbbed with need for him and him alone.

As much as she wanted to revel in every sensation he elicited, she wanted him to feel those same wondrous sensations. She touched him everywhere. Kissed the scar on his forehead that had first brought them together. Then his broad, muscled shoulders. That strikingly taut abdomen. His tight buttocks. Lastly she wrapped her fingers around his large sex. She shivered, felt herself moving toward release before he'd even entered her.

It had been too long.

He nestled between her thighs, nudged his way inside, one thick inch at a time. She wrapped her legs around his, dug her fingers into his hot, smooth skin. By the time he'd filled her completely, she was too far gone to slow the spiraling sensations. Climax swirled and quaked through her. Before she'd caught her breath, he found a new way to take her back to that glittering edge of release.

His mouth, his fingers…all of him played her like a concert violinist touching those precious strings. He brought her to climax again and then again before succumbing to his own.

For long, long minutes after that, he lay beside her, holding her in his powerful arms.

He kissed her cheek, her earlobe. "You are so beautiful."

She blushed. "Not so much."

He smiled, his lips stretching against her skin, making her smile, too. "You should look in a mirror occasionally. I mean really look. You're very beautiful."

"And you're very handsome." It was true. More true than she'd wanted to admit these past three years. It had been easier to deny he'd been the man of her dreams than to own out loud the suffering she'd endured with the loss of him.

"We were good together."

The words vibrated against her ear, making her heart ache. "We were."

"I don't want to hurt you again."

She turned to him, studied those gorgeous eyes. An epiphany had dawned during their lovemaking. "You can't hurt me that way again, Jonathan. That's a once in a lifetime sort of pain. It'll be hard when you go this time, but it won't ever hurt like that again." Never.

The revelation appeared to startle him, but he didn't draw away. He held her close as if he feared she would take off and he might never see her again.

He tucked a wisp of hair behind her ear. "I couldn't be what you needed me to be. What you deserved," he explained. "I still can't. You deserve better than me. As much as I want you, it wouldn't be fair to you."

She laughed softly. "That's a cop-out, you know that, right?" Men always said that crap when they had commitment issues.

He smiled. "I guess it is." He nuzzled her neck with his nose. "You were as close as I've ever come to that place." He drew back, toyed with her hair. "As much as I hurt you by leaving, it would have been far worse for me to stay. I couldn't bear seeing you suffer."

She searched his face even as she looked for the truth in his words. "Do you still have the nightmares often?"

"Too often," he confessed.

She had nightmares, too, only they were about coming home from work to find him gone.

"I should be stronger," she admitted as long as they were confessing. "Giving in to *this* wasn't such a smart thing to do in the long run." Regret, she realized, had barged in, stealing the beauty of what they had just shared.

"You didn't exactly drag me into your bed," he reminded her. "I seem to recall carrying you into the room."

Melissa laughed. For the first time in nearly a week, she just wanted to laugh. It felt good, chased away the agony for a few moments. "What do you do now?" She skimmed her fingers over his bruised abdomen. "Seems like a tough job."

"It can be." He left a trail of kisses down her belly. She shivered. "Investigative work. Nothing interesting." Before she could ask any more questions he had her ready to climax yet again. She sank into the pleasure, drew him to that hot, fiery place right along with her. This time he couldn't hold out so long—maybe because he'd missed her just as much as she'd missed him.

But he would never say as much.

He was far too secretive. Far too unbreakable.

She lured him to the shower for a few minutes more of mindless pleasure. This escape was only temporary, she knew, but she needed it so badly.

Afterward, they dried their bodies and kissed some more. Then they ate. She hadn't been hungry in days. But she was definitely hungry now. She'd barely touched the omelet he'd gone to the trouble of preparing earlier. Anything sounded good at the moment. Cheese and crackers and the chocolate cake a neighbor had brought over. In times of crisis, Southern neighbors always brought over food. It was tradition.

For a little while, Melissa enjoyed a reprieve from the misery that had overtaken all their lives just six days ago.

There was no one else she would rather have enjoyed that time with. But as the heat of their passion receded, the glare of reality filtered in.

He would leave.

She would be hurt again. And this time there'd be no one to blame but herself.

The telephone rang. Melissa went to answer it, but someone banged on the door before she reached the phone. Confusion lining her brow, she moved to the door and checked the window.

Chief Talbot.

That old, ugly fear whipped through her, making her shake as she opened the door. "Chief." She wanted to ask if there was news, but the words wouldn't form on her tongue.

The news was bad. His face told the tale before he had an opportunity to say the words.

"Has there been a new development?" Jonathan asked, moving up beside her at the door.

The chief braced a hand against the door frame as if the news he had to pass was too heavy a burden to manage without support.

"It's Harry," he said, his voice uncharacteristically faint. "He's in the hospital."

A new kind of fear ignited inside Melissa. "Heart attack?" She'd worried about that. She'd known he was having trouble handling the building tension and worry. Dear God, she should have seen this coming and done something.

Chief Talbot shook his head. "I'm sorry, Melissa, but he…" A weary sigh escaped his lips "He apparently attempted to kill himself."

"What?" Not Harry. He would never do that. "That can't be right," she argued.

"I'm afraid so. He left a note saying he was sorry."

Her uncle had tried to commit suicide? He'd left a note? That was impossible. He wouldn't leave them this way.

"William is at the hospital with him now." The chief shook his head. "He's in grave condition, Melissa. The prognosis isn't good."

She didn't remember getting into the car. The next thing she knew she and Jonathan were on the way to the hospital. A neighbor had come to stay with Presley and to field any calls to the house.

Melissa closed her eyes. She couldn't take any more. The idea of losing Polly was horrendous enough, but not Harry, too.

This couldn't possibly get any worse.

Chapter Thirteen

Jonathan stood in the corridor of the Intensive Care Unit. Melissa had been allowed in Harry Shepherd's cubicle for ten minutes every three hours.

They'd been up all night.

Melissa refused to leave the hospital. William had rejoined the search for his daughter at daybreak this morning. Presley, his wife, was in the care of friends of the Shepherd family.

At this point, no one was considered safe from whatever was going on. Three men had been murdered, assuming Harper's death hadn't been an accident, and Harry Shepherd appeared to have attempted suicide.

Since the forensics wasn't back yet and despite the two word note he'd left, an official conclusion could not be reached. There was a chance someone had wanted his death to look like a suicide.

No matter that Jonathan's instincts leaned toward the idea that the man had wanted to take his own life, he wasn't taking any chances. He would not allow Melissa out of his sight. Leaving the hospital without her was out of the question.

The team dragging the river had called off the search at dark last night, but had resumed this morning for a final go over. Polly had not been found. Jonathan felt a massive sense of relief at that news. Melissa's family had just about reached their limit on bad news.

He closed his eyes and let the memory of last evening's lovemaking whisper through his mind. Most of his adult life had been spent focused on his career. Women came and went with the job and the location. No one had ever managed to keep a hunk of his heart.

The idea rattled him hard. He didn't try to push it away. It was the truth and that was the one ideal he'd always clung to. Truth, honor, courage, those words meant a great deal to him. Honestly, three years ago Melissa hadn't needed a man like him, nor did she now. Emotionally, he was a mess.

The military had done that for him. Not the military, really, but the powers that be. The ones who had made the final decisions, based more on political gain than on the greater good. All the while he'd watched his men die, the powers that be were finagling a new deal—one which negated the operation for which those men had given their lives.

Jonathan had sworn that he would never commit on an emotional level to anyone besides himself after that. He did his job, completed his assignments and went home—wherever home proved to be. There would be no attachments.

Then he'd met Melissa.

Bit by tiny bit, she'd taken a part of him. She'd given of herself completely, unconditionally and unrestrained. And he hadn't been able to cut it. He'd left her hanging by her heart.

He didn't deserve her forgiveness and he damned sure hadn't deserved her trust the way she'd given it last night. Hurting her again was the last thing he wanted to do. Maybe, just maybe, if he helped bring her niece back home safely, he would have earned all that Melissa had given him.

Finding Polly alive might just be impossible. But he had to try. For the child and for Melissa.

As if his thoughts had summoned her, Melissa appeared in the corridor. She looked tired and desperate for relief. Still she was so beautiful, Jonathan's chest ached. He'd never known anyone as beautiful, inside and out, as she was.

"How is he?" Only immediate family was allowed to see the patient or to be informed of his progress.

"He's still in a coma." Melissa brushed a wisp of hair from her cheek with the back of her hand. "The chances of him surviving without massive brain damage are…" her voice broke "…practically nonexistent."

Jonathan didn't hesitate. He pulled her into his arms and held her tight. "I wish there was something I could do."

She held on to him, making him ache all the more for his helplessness. "I don't understand why he did this." She drew back and shook her head. "He's not the sort of man to do such a thing. I know he's devastated by Polly's disappearance, but we all are."

She swiped at her damp cheeks. "I can't even begin to accurately gauge how William must feel. And Presley." She shrugged. "Uncle Harry has always been a rock. I don't understand."

Jonathan needed to get her out of here for a while. She was exhausted, but there were people he wanted to see, questions he needed to ask. "You need a break."

She looked back toward her uncle's room. "I don't know about leaving."

"They have your number, right?" He slowly ushered her toward the elevator.

A hesitant nod was her only response.

"They'll call if there's any change." Since there was little chance of Harry waking up, her vigil here wouldn't help him. But there were things they could be doing to help find Polly.

"I suppose you're right."

"Your uncle would want us working on finding Polly." Jonathan didn't know the man very well but he felt certain that was the case. "I've been thinking about a couple of scenarios the chief may have overlooked."

The elevator doors slid open and they stepped inside, thankfully alone.

"You have?"

She looked at him with such desperation, it clawed at his chest. He nodded, not sure of his own voice just now.

"Anything we can do is better than nothing," she murmured wearily.

Jonathan hated the idea of dragging her around to interview the new list of persons of interest he'd developed. But he wasn't about to leave her side. Not again. He'd taken that risk yesterday, but no more.

"Where are we going first?" she asked as the elevator lit on the lobby level.

"To see Johnny Ray Bruce." After the way he had blackmailed Presley, Bruce was capable of most anything.

Surprise flared in Melissa's eyes. "Isn't he still here, in the hospital?"

Jonathan shook his head. "He was released last night."

She appeared to mull over the idea as they made their way to her car. When he opened the passenger door she hesitated before climbing inside. "Why are we talking to Johnny Ray?"

"Good question." He gestured for her to get in. When she did, he closed her door and moved around to the driver's side. After settling behind the wheel and starting the engine, he explained, "Johnny Ray was with Presley that night. He must have picked her up and taken her home since her car remained at the house all night. That's why the chief bought her story about not leaving home the night Polly disappeared." One of Presley's neighbors had confirmed that Presley's vehicle was home that night.

"True." Melissa snapped her seat belt into place.

"Johnny Ray may have seen something that felt irrelevant at the time but could be far more significant than he realizes."

In actuality, Jonathan intended to push him for information. He had known the Shepherd family his whole life. Maybe if something was going on between Harry and the chief's wife, he would have heard about it. The guy struck Jonathan as the type to keep himself in the know about secrets—especially those people desperately wanted to hide. Considering the chief was his uncle, that knowledge could have proven particularly beneficial.

"I hadn't thought about that," Melissa confessed. "I'm sure the chief didn't question him since he was unaware that Presley left the house."

"We have a bit of an advantage," Jonathan acknowledged. Presley's coming clean may have given them the break they needed. His next stop after Johnny Ray's place was Scott Rayburn's office. "Did Rayburn have a secretary?"

"He did. Frances O'Linger."

"Good. We'll need to speak to her, as well."

Melissa turned to him. "You think she may know something?"

It was a stretch, but it was definitely possible. "She may not know anything specific but she may have overheard a conversation or read a note." Jonathan pulled out onto the deserted street. "Who knows, maybe Rayburn left a journal or notes on his delusions. We won't know for sure unless we ask."

Melissa nodded. "Good points."

THE DRIVE TO JOHNNY RAY's residence took less than ten minutes. His car sat in the driveway. If Jonathan was lucky the guy would be in a pain medication fog and considerably more cooperative.

A couple of knocks were required to get Johnny Ray to open the door. He looked every bit as woozy as Jonathan had hoped. His face showed the evidence of a serious butt-kicking.

Johnny Ray swayed forward and scanned the yard. He blinked, tried several times to focus on Melissa. "That brother of yours isn't with you, is he?"

"No," Melissa said with absolutely no sympathy. "He's out searching for his missing daughter."

"Oh." Johnny Ray swayed back on his heels.

"We need to speak with you in private," Jonathan informed him.

The man's eyebrows hiked up his forehead. "I don't know if I want you in my house." He shook his head, staggered back a step for his trouble. "Those Shepherds are nothing but trouble for me. My uncle has already threatened to haul me in if there's any more trouble."

Jonathan resisted the urge to tell him that he should have thought about that before he slept with another man's wife, repeatedly. "We'll only take a few minutes of your time. Your uncle isn't going to find out."

"Whatever." Johnny Ray turned around, braced against the wall for support and made his way to the nearest chair. "Have a seat."

His place was trashed. Not that it had been that organized or clean before, but this morning it appeared as if the man had had a party last night and the whole town had dropped off their dinner and drink remains in his living room.

"What do you wanna talk about?" he asked when

both Melissa and Jonathan were seated. "As if I didn't know," he added with a drunken eye roll.

"The night Polly went missing," Jonathan began, "you picked Presley up at the house, then dropped her off. Is that correct?"

Johnny Ray bobbed his head up and down. "Will wasn't home so she came right out the front door and went back in the same way." He picked up a pack of cigarettes, dropped it, then picked it up again.

"Approximately how long was she away from the house?" Jonathan felt Melissa fidgeting next to him. He hated for her to hear this, but he didn't want her out of his sight for any reason.

"An hour I guess. Maybe less." Johnny Ray lit the cigarette and blew out a plume of smoke. He leaned forward and picked up a beer and chugged a long swallow. "We spent most of that time fighting."

"About what?" Jonathan waited patiently for him to set the can of beer back on the table and make eye contact. "About what?" he repeated.

"The fact that she refused to tell Will the truth." He shifted his attention to Melissa. "She's been lying to him for years. I keep telling her to just do the right thing and end their farce of a marriage."

Fury tightened Melissa's features. "You would know all about doing the right thing."

Johnny Ray stared at her, blinked, then turned to Jonathan. "You see. Even if I try to do the right thing I don't get any respect."

Jonathan wasn't going down that path. He'd come here to get answers not to tick him off and walk away with nothing. "Why doesn't Presley want to do this thing you believe is right?" he asked. "Maybe she loves her husband."

"Yeah, right." Johnny Ray snorted. "That would be why she likes doing it—if you know what I mean—with me more than she does him. She says there's no passion between them," he sneered.

That Melissa didn't throw something at the guy was a miracle. "So," Jonathan ventured, "the two of you have continued to see each other the whole time Presley and Will have been married."

"Pretty much." This time when he reached for the beer he knocked it off the table. He swore a few times, then kicked the can across the room and turned his attention back to his cigarette.

"Did she say anything recently about wishing she'd never had Polly?"

Melissa stared at Jonathan. Though he didn't turn toward her he felt the heat of her glare on him. But the question was necessary.

"Nah." Johnny Ray put his feet on the coffee table. "She didn't really want to be a mother, but she loves the kid the best she knows how."

"No other vehicles were parked near the house when you picked her up or dropped her off that night? You saw no sign of anything out of the ordinary?" Jonathan doubted the man had paid any attention, but this was the only way to find out. He insisted Presley had exited and then reentered the front door, yet the back door was the one found unlocked and open the next morning.

Several tense moments elapsed with Johnny Ray

mulling over the question. "Nope, I can't say that I noticed anything. Most of the neighbors were probably in bed. I looked around for Will's truck but I didn't pay attention to anything else being out of place. I'd probably have noticed, though, since we were sneaking around, you know?"

"Yeah." Jonathan braced for an explosion from Melissa. She wasn't going to like this one. "Has Presley ever mentioned William regretting having a child?"

Surprisingly, Melissa sat stone still. Maybe she was in shock at his audacity.

Johnny Ray shook his head. "Will loves that kid more than he loves anything else—including Presley. She gets a little jealous about that sometimes."

Interesting. "Do you know of anyone else who would want to see William or Presley hurt?" If the missing child wasn't for ransom or trafficking, there had to be another motive. Hurting the family was at the top of the list in Jonathan's opinion.

"Well," Johnny Ray drawled, stretching out in his chair, "since you ask, I'd have to say Scott Rayburn."

"Scott Rayburn is dead," Jonathan reminded him.

"Yeah. Died at that old shack where the kid was being held, the way I heard it."

"That's correct."

"Melissa might not agree with me on this," Bruce continued, "but I always knew that Rayburn had a thing for Will." He gave Jonathan a knowing look. "You know the kind of thing I mean."

Jonathan nodded.

"But this is a small town. Folks don't go in for that,

especially his momma and daddy. Rayburn wasn't about to risk his inheritance." He shoved his cigarette butt in the nearest beer can. "Frankly, I'm not surprised he was involved with this somehow. He would've liked nothing better than for Will and Presley to split up. With the kid out of the picture I guess he figured he'd have a better shot at making his lifelong dream come true."

"That is the craziest thing I've ever heard," Melissa said, her voice tight.

Jonathan imagined the real meltdown would come later, when they were out of Bruce's house. She would let him have it then. "Are you speculating," Jonathan pushed, "or do you have proof of this accusation?"

"Let's just say I noticed the way Rayburn looked at William. He idolized the guy." Johnny Ray spat out another of those crude snorts. "Don't for the life of me see why, but I know what I saw. Back in school some of us used to rib Will about his secret admirer."

"Then you believe Rayburn was in on the abduction?" Jonathan pressed.

"Maybe, maybe not, but he damned sure knew about it. He couldn't have walked right up on the holding place."

"What about Price?" Jonathan asked. "Do you believe Rayburn was working with Price?"

"It's doubtful," Johnny Ray said with expanding self-importance. The drugs had obviously kicked in full gear. "Scott thought he was above working with what he considered lesser life-forms. To him Stevie was pretty much a worm or something."

Melissa didn't defend Price as she had before. Didn't

take a psychology degree to analyze her reason. Price had had something to do with Polly's abduction.

"Someone else was involved," Jonathan went on. "The shooter who killed Rayburn and Price. Any guesses on that one?"

"My uncle figures Rayburn shot Price, since the shotgun they found in the river belonged to him."

This was news to Jonathan. He wasn't aware the weapon had been retrieved.

Johnny Ray put his hand over his mouth. "I don't think I was supposed to tell that to anyone."

What else was the chief holding out on them? "The chief keeps me fully briefed," Jonathan lied. "You haven't shared anything I didn't know."

"Well then, you know that old Stevie had a piece of Rayburn's shirt clutched in his cold, dead hand. Them two most likely struggled before the gun fired."

More news. "That hasn't been confirmed," Jonathan said so as to sound knowledgeable of the details.

"Maybe not," Johnny Ray said, "but if my uncle said that's the way it went down, then that's the way it went down. He's been doing this a long time. He knows his stuff."

"You can't think of anyone else who might have wanted to hurt the Shepherd family?" Jonathan asked again.

Johnny Ray shook his head. "Not a soul. The whole town seems to look up to the Shepherds. Don't know why." He leered at Melissa. "They aren't that smart or that pretty."

Jonathan pushed to his feet. "I'll come back if I think of any more questions."

Now he was the one ready to go off. Kicking the butt of a man already injured shouldn't feel so appealing but Johnny Ray Bruce evidently could care less whom he angered. He likely assumed his uncle's position would continue to keep him out of trouble with the law. But one of these days his mouth was going to get him killed. His uncle wouldn't be able to get him out of that.

Melissa walked ahead of Jonathan toward the car, her movements stilted. Once they were inside, with the doors closed, she held up both hands. "If I'd had a weapon, I think I would have killed that egotistical SOB."

Backing out of the drive, Jonathan suggested, "That would be letting him off too easily." He didn't mention that he'd had the same passing thought himself.

"He's out of his mind."

"Perhaps. Pain meds do that sometimes."

Melissa glared at him. He got it. She would know. He hadn't needed to make that point.

"You're not buying his tale of unrequited love where Rayburn and Will are concerned?"

"Not really, but we can't rule it out, either."

Melissa made a sound that warned that he'd given the wrong answer.

Jonathan set a course for Rayburn's office. He'd already checked the address and determined the route. Knowing Melissa, he'd expected her to be angry with him, so he'd come prepared.

"Surely you don't believe him over me," Melissa demanded when Jonathan failed to retract his statement.

"In my experience," he said, hoping she wouldn't burn off any more of her pent up anger on him, "where there's smoke, there's fire. Rumors usually are seeded in some semblance of the truth."

She dropped her head back on the seat. "I don't believe it at all. I never saw or heard anything to that effect."

"Do you know Ms. O'Linger?"

"Yes." She sighed. "She was my English teacher in high school. She retired a few years ago and started working with Scott."

"Why don't you handle this one," Jonathan suggested.

"What am I supposed to ask?" Melissa didn't sound enthused by the offer. "I'm certainly not going to ask her if she thought Scott had a crush on Will."

"The answers you need will prompt the questions." That was Jonathan's method. There was no reason to ask a question unless the answer would serve a purpose. "I don't expect you to ask her about that part."

"Good. Because I won't."

Having Melissa ask the questions of a former teacher might garner more answers. If nothing else, the effort would make Melissa feel more useful, lessening the likelihood that she would work up another head of steam. She was already going to be angry enough when they moved on to the third name on his list.

Ms. O'Linger cried twice before Melissa and Jonathan were settled in Scott Rayburn's office. The woman was beside herself with grief. She couldn't imagine why anyone would want to hurt Scotty, as she called him. And he assuredly never had anything to do with Polly's disappearance. More likely he'd stumbled upon the truth and set out to investigate. Ms. O'Linger hadn't been able to bring herself to leave the office—even on Sunday—until she'd set everything to rights after the chief's search.

"Do you have reason to believe Scott was investigating Polly's disappearance?" Melissa asked.

Jonathan flashed a look of approval. He'd been correct when he'd said she would know the questions to ask. That he had faith in her ability to do the job made her feel a little better. Took her mind off poor Uncle Harry lying in that hospital bed.

Ms. O'Linger collapsed into the leather executive chair behind Scott's desk. "Mercy, let me think." She rubbed at her forehead. "I'm just so confused. I can hardly believe this has happened."

Melissa held her breath, hoping the woman could give them something, anything, that might help.

Ms. O'Linger pinched her lips together and glanced at Jonathan.

"Jonathan is here to help," Melissa assured the woman. "He's my friend." She'd introduced him that way, but evidently the message hadn't gotten through.

"I'm sure he's very nice," Ms. O'Linger agreed, "but the chief made me promise not to talk about this to anyone." She wrung her hands. "He went over Scotty's office and house. His momma and daddy were awfully upset as it was..." She shook her head. "But when the chief questioned me, he specifically said not to discuss what I knew with anyone. Not a soul."

Anticipation fired in Melissa's veins. "Ms. O'Linger, you've known me your whole life. I just want to find my niece. We're not planning to get in the chief's way. We want to help."

The old woman divided her attention between Melissa and Jonathan, her gaze sweeping back and forth repeatedly. "If he finds out I told you…"

"He won't find out," Melissa said quickly. "You have my word on that. You know I took care of Mr. O'Linger in the hospital. You know you can trust me." Ms. O'Linger had been most grateful for Melissa's help during those agonizing final days of her husband's life. That should account for something.

"Yes, you surely did and that's the only reason I'm having second thoughts on following the chief's orders." She shrugged her rounded shoulders. "Truth is, I don't think it's really about the case. The reason he doesn't want me to talk about it, I mean. I think it's just embarrassing to him."

Melissa sat up straighter. The allegations Scott had thrown at Jonathan sifted to the top of her worried mind. Could there be any truth to that rumor? Impossible! Harry would never—Melissa stopped herself. He'd proven her wrong already. At this point, she couldn't say what he or anyone else might be capable of doing.

Even herself. She'd made love with Jonathan when she'd sworn she would never make that mistake again.

"I didn't say anything to Scotty," his secretary admitted with a sheepish look. "I knew he wouldn't like me going through his briefcase. But he left it on his desk and papers were poking out. I only wanted to straighten up for him." She smiled at Melissa. "To me, you're all still just a bunch of kids who need a little extra mothering from time to time."

The urge to prompt her to get on with her story nearly drove Melissa to jump up and shake her. She didn't know how Jonathan stayed so calm when he questioned people.

"Anyway, I found a notepad where he'd scribbled several times and dates." She frowned. "I was curious because I wasn't aware that he'd taken any new cases that involved a divorce with a cheating spouse." She smiled proudly. "He liked following up on those personally."

Melissa sat on the edge of her seat, used her posture to urge the old woman to get on with it.

"But this was no divorce case," Ms. O'Linger said. "He'd been following Carol Talbot and Harry Shepherd around." She ducked her head toward one shoulder. "Of course I didn't question him about it, but it did appear obvious from his notes that he believed the two were carrying on an—" she looked around the room "—affair."

"Did you give that notepad to the chief?" Jonathan interjected.

Ms. O'Linger nodded. "Oh, yes. He insisted on having it. Scotty had locked it in his safe." She pointed to the floor. "He had that installed right after I came to work for him. He gave me the combination with strict instructions that I was never to open it unless it was an emergency."

"Was there anything else inside?" Melissa asked, her head spinning at the idea that her uncle might actually have been having an affair with his best friend's wife.

How could she have known these people her whole life and not suspected a thing?

"Nothing else," Ms. O'Linger assured her. "Just that notepad."

"Did you look at it before you gave it to the chief?" Jonathan prodded.

Ms. O'Linger's cheeks pinked. "Well, I didn't really mean to, but I guess curiosity got the better of me."

"Had he made any recent entries?" Melissa pressed.

"Yes." The older woman swiped at the desk. "He was going to that old shack again."

"The one next to the river?" Jonathan asked for clarification.

She nodded. "Yes."

"Did he note why he wanted to go there?" Melissa asked, her heart pounding so hard she could scarcely hear herself think.

Sad eyes settled on Melissa. "He was going back to see what was there. He'd followed your uncle to the shack earlier that evening."

The remainder of the conversation was lost on Melissa. Jonathan continued to chat with Ms. O'Linger, but Melissa zoned out completely.

Her uncle had gone to the shack *before* Scott Rayburn's murder.

Before Stevie's murder.

He'd gone to that rickety old shack. The one where the police had found evidence indicating that Polly had been held there for at least several days.

Harry Shepherd—the man who had been like a father to her—had taken Polly.

Chapter Fourteen

"This won't do any good."

Melissa ignored Jonathan's remark. She didn't care. She needed to do this.

As soon as the car was in Park, she wrenched open the door and hurried across the parking lot. This hospital was her home several days a week. No one was going to prevent her from getting in to see her uncle. Now. This minute. She had to talk to him. Whether he could answer her or not didn't matter.

In the lobby she didn't wait for the elevator. She took the stairs. Jonathan climbed right behind her.

"Melissa," he called out, "don't go in there like this."

He didn't understand. Polly wasn't his niece. Jonathan Foley had never connected on that level with anyone. He couldn't know.

As soon as the thought formed in her brain she felt guilty.

But that wasn't stopping her from doing this.

Nothing was.

"Melissa, wait!" head nurse Patty Wheeler cried as Melissa charged past the station on the ICU floor.

She ignored her, as well.

"Wait!" the nurse called again.

"Melissa, stop." Jonathan caught her by the arm.

She shook off his hold. "No. I have to do this."

Before the nurse could catch up to her, Melissa barged into the ICU cubicle—and stalled.

Her uncle's bed was empty. The sheets had been rolled into a ball.

Denial rammed into her with the same impact as butting a brick wall at a full run.

"Melissa, I'm sorry." The nurse, breathless from the rush, put her arm around her. "We tried to call your cell. Your uncle passed away twenty minutes ago."

The world tilted and bitter bile rushed up into Melissa's throat.

"I've got her."

Jonathan's arms were suddenly around her. Patty was asking Melissa questions but she couldn't answer.

Her uncle was gone.

As much as that hurt, what hurt even more was the idea that he may have taken Polly's whereabouts with him.

How would they ever find her now?

12:15 p.m.

JONATHAN HAD DONE SOME research while Melissa gathered her composure, curled up in an easy chair in her living room. If Harry Shepherd had been having an affair with Carol Talbot, what were the chances that she had suspected he was up to something?

If they were close, really close, had he shared his plans with her?

In Jonathan's estimation, the most likely motive was diverting William's orders. From all accounts, Harry had been beside himself when William joined the military. He'd basically come unglued when the orders for deployment had come down. Having his nephew survive six months was more than he'd hoped for, but having him go back was unthinkable.

How far would a man go to keep a loved one out of harm's way? Jonathan had never loved anyone like that. He glanced at Melissa, who was attempting to force down a glass of iced tea.

He couldn't love anyone like that. It wasn't in him.

He wanted to. He stole another glance at her. He surely wanted to. But she would be the one to pay for that indulgence. If he'd ever possessed the ability to love that deeply, he'd lost it during those endless hours as he'd watched his men die one by one.

Focus, Jonathan. This isn't about you.

The chief had called and royally chewed out Jonathan for what he called interfering with his investigation. His anger had nothing to do with the investigation. Chief Talbot was furious that Jonathan and Melissa had learned the truth about his wife's affair. He had warned them both to stay out of the investigation. Apparently he'd already warned most of Bay Minette's citizens not to talk to Jonathan or Melissa.

William wasn't even speaking to Melissa. He'd gone to the funeral home to make arrangements for his uncle and had outright refused to allow Melissa to accompany him.

Whatever the chief had told William, it had worked. For now.

Jonathan had no intention of allowing this case to go unsolved any more than he intended to allow Melissa to be treated like the bad guy. She had a right to know the truth. And if William weren't so riddled with grief over his daughter's disappearance and his uncle's suicide, he would see that.

"What do we do now?"

Jonathan met her gaze. Those big blue eyes held more pain than any one human should have to bear. "We move on to the one logical remaining person of interest."

Melissa nodded. "Carol Talbot."

"The chief's actions aren't completely consistent with those of a man who wants to protect his wife's reputation. He's certainly protecting her in every other way. But not on this count. He could easily refute the allegations by charging that Harry had been delusional and suggested these things to Rayburn as a result of those delusions. Harry isn't here to defend himself or to say otherwise. Neither is Rayburn."

"You think there's more."

Jonathan didn't want to give Melissa false hope, but she needed the truth right now. He couldn't ensure she got that from anyone else, but she was getting it from him. "My guess is he doesn't want her to become more collateral damage in this case. Four people are dead. Polly is still missing. And no one knows a damned thing, particularly the police who are investigating the case."

"That makes sense." Melissa shrugged. "Both he and Carol could deny the affair." She closed her eyes and exhaled a heavy breath. "I didn't have a clue. I doubt very many others did, either. Now the chief just wants to protect her from what? Accessory to murder? Conspiracy to commit kidnapping?"

"Exactly. Otherwise, why go to such lengths?" The more they discussed the theory, the more convinced Jonathan grew that the chief was covering for something his wife either knew or had done.

"There's no logical reason." The same realization that had dawned on him widened Melissa's eyes. "She knows something. Saw something." Melissa turned her hands up. "Something that could make her appear guilty."

"That's my thinking."

Fear abruptly froze in her eyes. "Oh, God. She may know…" Melissa hugged her arms around her middle. "She may have witnessed someone hurting Polly. May have had some part in it." Melissa looked ready to crumple emotionally. "He's definitely protecting her from any criminal charges."

Jonathan went to her. He knelt in front of her and took her shoulders in his hands, gave her a gentle shake. "We don't know that. All we can be relatively certain of is that she knows something. We're going to operate on the theory that Polly is alive and out there somewhere waiting to be found. Carol may be able to lead us to her."

Melissa searched his eyes. He tried to show her the

hope, the certainty he felt, but she shook her head. "If that's all she knows—Polly's location—why wouldn't the chief just go get Polly and tell the world that his amazing investigative skills are responsible for solving the case? No one would ever know his wife told him where to look. It's worse than that. I can feel it."

Jonathan couldn't deny that possibility. "For now," he urged, "let's not lose hope."

Melissa laughed but the sound was filled with pain. "This coming from the man who wouldn't give me the slightest inkling of hope that he could ever love me?" She shook her head. "Jonathan, I don't know how I'd have gotten through this so far without your help." She touched his face, just the slightest caress of his jaw. "But I know you too well. You can't love me the way I love you. You said so yourself. I appreciate that you're trying to keep me bolstered now in this awful, awful time. But don't pretend you know what you're talking about when it comes to hope."

She shook her head. "Or that kind of love. The kind that would make a man go against the grain of all he is to protect the woman he loves the way Chief Talbot is obviously doing for his wife."

Jonathan stood. "I can't deny those charges." He crossed the room and stared out the window. He'd never been any good at moments like this, but he had to try.

Whatever his and Melissa's past, whatever their present, a child was missing and by God he intended to do whatever he could to find her.

"Let's go." He pushed aside the unfamiliar emotions she'd stirred and put on his game face. There was a job to do and he wasn't about to fall down on getting it done. That he could guarantee.

She pushed to her feet and reached for her purse. "The chief will try to stop us."

"It won't be the first time someone tried to stop me."

Jonathan opened the door for her. His chest squeezed at the scent of her as she walked past him on her way out the door. He booted the sensation aside and followed her. When this was done, he would go back to Chicago and she could get on with her life.

He hoped she found a man who could feel those emotions she cherished so.

That man wasn't him. He'd known that before he'd answered her plea for help.

She had known it, as well.

CHIEF TALBOT'S HOUSE sat on a side street just off the main thoroughfare. Neat houses lined the street, but only one had a large moving truck parked out front.

Melissa was out of the car before Jonathan could shut down the engine. Every word she'd said to him was true. But in the silence on the drive over here those words had gotten to him anyway. Left him feeling empty and aching.

Strange for a guy who prided himself on feeling nothing.

He caught up with Melissa on the sidewalk. She marched right up to the house and walked through the open door.

"Where's Mrs. Talbot?" she demanded of one of the men who were obviously movers.

The man shrugged. "The owners aren't here."

Melissa turned to Jonathan. "We just spoke to the chief a few hours ago. They can't have suddenly disappeared."

Jonathan hitched a thumb toward the street. "Where are the Talbots moving to?"

Another of the movers stopped his work and scratched his head. "Gatlinburg. Up in northeast Tennessee. We're supposed to have all this—" he gestured to the boxes and furnishings "—up there by tomorrow."

Jonathan and Melissa exchanged a glance. "Has Mrs. Talbot already left for the new house?" she asked.

"Don't know." He nodded toward the door. "You can ask him. He's the owner."

Jonathan turned to face the chief. The shade of red coloring his face warned that he was not happy to find the two of them there.

"You're trespassing on private property, Mr. Foley."

His voice was far too quiet, far too controlled. "We came to see Mrs. Talbot." No point in lying. "We have a few questions about Harry Shepherd for her."

The chief ignored Jonathan's statement and shifted his attention to Melissa. "Now, Melissa, I know you're all torn up and that's completely understandable. But you've got to talk some sense into your friend. When I give an order I expect folks to follow it. I'm doing all I can to find little Polly. But I can't do that if I have to keep an eye on the two of you."

Melissa shook her head. "Sorry, Chief." Tears spilled down her cheeks. "I just can't believe Uncle Harry killed himself and I thought maybe Mrs. Talbot could help me understand what was going through his mind. It's just so awful."

Jonathan had to hand it to her, she'd even fooled him there for a second.

Chief Talbot patted her on the shoulder. "I'll see what I can find out. I'm hoping something Harry confided in her will give us some clue as to where Polly is. Carol has been a good friend to him through all this." He shook his head. "I still can't understand what he was doing. Maybe Price and Rayburn were up to no good and Harry found out. They may have taken little Polly to blackmail Harry. We just don't know yet. But you have my word that I won't stop until I know the whole truth."

He puffed out a weary breath. "Right now, I need your help. This has been real hard on Carol, too. She never has gotten over our little Sherry's death. Polly's disappearance and all that mess over at the river have torn her all to pieces. That's why she moved on up to the new house. She needed to get away from this tragedy to save her peace of mind." He patted Melissa again. "But don't worry, I'm not going anywhere until we find Polly and this case is sewed up. You have my word on that."

"Thank you, Chief." Melissa swiped her eyes. "I know you'll be glad to retire like you'd planned and join your wife."

"Yes, ma'am, but not until my job here is done."

11:18 p.m.

"YOU'RE SURE THAT'S IT?" Melissa peered up at the grand log house. "I can't believe the chief was able to buy something like this up here." Housing prices in the Gatlinburg area were far higher than those down in Bay Minette.

"It's the one." Jonathan shoved his cell phone into his pocket. "According to my sources—"

His sources. He never gave up names. She'd overheard far too many of his conversations back when they were together.

"—the chief has saved a serious chunk of change during his career. He also recently sold the property near the river."

Melissa cringed at the thought of that river. Polly hadn't been found in the water but she could still be out there somewhere.

"I don't remember hearing about that." But then she wasn't one to listen to gossip or rumors. She focused on work, taking all the overtime the hospital would allow. She'd saved quite a chunk of change, as he put it, herself over the past three years. As much as she loved the Shepherd home, she'd always hoped to move on with her life. Maybe go back to Birmingham or Montgomery. Maybe even Huntsville. But with Will, Polly and Harry, the concept just kept fading into the future.

Harry was gone now. Her heart squeezed at the thought. Whatever he'd done the final days of his life, he'd been a good uncle to her and Will for most of their lives.

All the emotions associated with his death would have to be sorted out later…when Polly was home.

Or buried.

She closed her eyes and exiled the thought. Polly had

to be alive. All they needed was someone to tell them where Harry had taken her…and why. That last part wasn't entirely necessary, but it would be nice to know why he'd done this. She could guess, as Jonathan had, but she needed to know.

Jonathan hadn't said much on the way here. She couldn't blame him. She'd said some awful things to him. Most had been true, but she'd been raised better than to say something hurtful.

"Someone's home," Jonathan said, pointing to the massive front windows on the first floor.

Melissa squinted to make out the figure moving around in what she presumed to be the main living area. "That's Carol."

Carol moved about the room, but Melissa couldn't determine what she was doing. Putting things away maybe? Didn't seem likely since the moving truck hadn't arrived. The movers had said they were expected tomorrow.

Carol stopped suddenly, picked something up from what appeared to be a table and placed it against her ear.

Melissa stared harder. A phone. Cell phone probably, judging by its size.

Carol started to move around again.

"She's pacing."

"Looks that way," Melissa agreed.

Carol abruptly stopped once more, directly in front of the big windows. She seemed to stare out into the dark night. Melissa resisted the impulse to hunker down in the seat. She couldn't possibly see them. The tree-crowded drive Jonathan had selected was well hidden.

They'd driven all the way up to the house across the road from the Talbot place and no one had been home. Several newspapers had lain on the porch suggesting the owners were on vacation. Parking at the end of the drive gave Melissa and Jonathan a perfect view of the new Talbot home.

Carol reached up and tugged on something.

"What's she doing?" Melissa murmured.

Heavy drapes glided across the windows, blocking their view into the house.

"That call must've been from the chief." Jonathan checked the road in both directions. "He's probably on his way here."

They had known that as soon as Chief Talbot figured out they had left town he would likely follow or he would send one of his deputies to stop them. Apparently he hadn't learned of their departure quickly enough to stop them en route.

"We should go to the door and talk to her before the chief or whomever he sends gets here." Melissa was terrified they'd come all this way for nothing. If the chief got here he would ensure they didn't get close to the house.

Jonathan turned to her in the darkness. She couldn't see his face but she could feel the tension emanating from him. "You realize that once we set foot on their property, we're breaking the law. The chief isn't likely to let us off with a warning this time."

"I don't care." The law wasn't going to stop her from talking to Carol Talbot. Not unless they locked Melissa away where she couldn't get out.

"Let's do it then."

Jonathan reached under the seat and removed something that he stuffed under his shirt.

"What's that?" She was almost afraid of the answer.

"We can't go in without protection." Before she could argue, he added, "I have a license to carry this weapon. I'm an expert marksman. I'm not going to shoot anyone unless they try to shoot one of us first."

Melissa took a tight breath as she squeezed the door handle. "You think we should just call the FBI or something?" Second thoughts burrowed deep into her brain.

"And tell them what?"

"That we believe Carol Talbot knows something about Polly's disappearance." It might be worth a try.

"And when she says she doesn't, what then?"

Jonathan was right. "Okay, let's go." Melissa opened the door. The interior light didn't come on since Jonathan had adjusted it to stay off.

If they hurried, maybe they could talk to Carol before anyone else arrived.

Jonathan led the way through the darkness, across the road and up the hill upon which the Talbot house proudly sat. It was cooler in the mountains. Melissa wished she had brought a jacket.

"We're going around to the back," Jonathan whispered to her. "There isn't a security system yet, so we don't have to worry about that."

Confusion muddled Melissa's focus again. "How do you know this?"

"I have sources."

"Right." How could she have forgotten?

Jonathan stayed within the shadows of the trees that bordered the big yard. Once they reached the rear of the house, he grabbed her hand and darted toward a clump of designer shrubbery that provided some amount of protection from the landscape lighting.

They stayed put for a few seconds, long enough to assume they hadn't been spotted, then he hauled her all the way to the corner of the house.

Melissa struggled to keep her respiration slow and deep. Her heart was beating so fast she could hardly draw in a deep breath. Jonathan's firm grip on her hand was all that kept her courage in place.

As long as she was with him, she could do this.

Lights were on all over the house. Was Carol Talbot afraid of being here alone?

Jonathan pulled Melissa forward, staying close against the back of the house. At the first window they reached, he listened for a moment, then peeked inside.

When he'd flattened against the house again, she asked, "Anything?"

He shook his head. "Empty room."

They moved forward again, checked a couple more windows. Nothing. When they rounded the corner at the other end of the house, the window was too high for Jonathan to see inside. If they could determine exactly where Carol was, she couldn't pretend not to be there when they pounded on the door. They needed her to know that they knew she was in the house.

"I'll get on your shoulders," Melissa whispered.

He considered her suggestion a moment, then dropped

to his knees. Melissa climbed into a sitting position on his shoulders and he slowly pushed to his feet. She leaned a little to her left to avoid being in full view of the window.

Once he had braced against the house, she leaned a little the other way and peeked inside.

There was a bed in this room, and a suitcase. Melissa stretched her neck to see more of the room without exposing any more of her body than necessary. But she saw nothing else.

The door to the room opened, and Melissa's breath stalled in her lungs.

She knew she should move, should somehow signal Jonathan to lower her down, but she couldn't react. She remained frozen, watching as Carol Talbot entered the room.

The elegant-looking woman walked toward the mattress and patted it as she said something Melissa couldn't quite make out.

Carol repeated the actions, and a child walked hesitantly through the door.

Melissa's heart skipped a beat.

Polly.

Carol Talbot whipped around to stare at the window. That was when Melissa knew she'd said the name aloud.

Carol snatched up Polly and ran from the room.

"She's here!" Melissa shouted. She tried to get down. Her sudden movement toppled both her and Jonathan to the ground.

Melissa scrambled up. "Polly's here!" she cried as she ran around to the front corner of the house.

"Melissa, wait!" Jonathan called after her.

Melissa didn't stop. She couldn't wait. Polly was inside. She was alive.

She hit the front steps in a dead run. Jonathan passed her on the way up and banged on the door. "Carol Talbot, we know you're in there! Open the door!"

Melissa shoved her fingers into the front pocket of her jeans and fumbled to pull out her cell phone.

Jonathan rammed his shoulder into the door. The entire frame shook. "Open the door, Mrs. Talbot!"

Melissa started entering the numbers. 9…1…

Jonathan hit the door again and it burst inward.

Melissa forgot about calling for help. She rushed past Jonathan and headed for the room at the north end of the house.

Jonathan caught up with her, passed her, shoving her behind him as he went.

"Stop right there or I'll shoot."

Carol Talbot huddled in the hallway, Polly wrapped in her arms, her face pressed to Carol's chest. The gun in Carol's hand shook, but its intended aim was unmistakable.

Melissa ceased to breathe.

Jonathan held out his hands in a placating manner. "Put the gun down, Mrs. Talbot."

She shook her head. "No. You're not going to take her."

Polly whimpered. Melissa's chest constricted.

"Mrs. Talbot," Jonathan reasoned, "her parents are waiting for her back home. You need to let her go now and we'll work this out. I'm certain you intended her no harm."

Carol shook her head adamantly once more. "Leave or I will shoot."

Melissa stepped forward. "Then you're going to have to shoot me, because I'm taking my niece home."

Jonathan reached for Melissa, but she stepped beyond his reach.

"Stop!" Carol shouted.

"I'm sorry, Mrs. Talbot," Melissa said, "but you can't keep Polly. I appreciate that you've taken such good care of her. But you have to let her go home now."

Polly cried out, apparently recognizing her aunt Melissa's voice. She wiggled in an attempt to get free. Carol held her tighter, kept the weapon aimed at Melissa.

"Shh, Polly, it'll be okay now," Melissa murmured.

"Leave my home," Carol demanded. "Before I'm forced to do something I don't want to do."

"Mrs. Talbot," Jonathan urged, "think about what you're doing. This whole thing was Harry's idea. You aren't the one who took Polly. You tried to help. That's what we'll tell the police."

Carol blinked. "That's what I told my husband." She tightened her grip on the weapon. "Harry almost lost his mind when William went off to Afghanistan. But when William came home it only got worse. Harry kept saying he had to do something. He took Polly that night. Had Stevie watching her. Everything would have worked out perfectly if that fool Scott Rayburn hadn't gotten in the way. I had to kill him. He was going to ruin everything."

Melissa nodded, following Jonathan's cue. "You had no choice. You tried to protect Polly and Harry."

Carol made a keening sound. "It would have been so perfect. William would have seen Presley for what she was and gotten rid of her, then if he was forced to deploy, Harry and I would have taken care of Polly." Her hold on Polly tightened. The little girl fretted.

"You loved Harry," Melissa said softly. "And he loved you." The kind of love these two had shared had twisted their minds, pushed them over some sort of ledge.

"He was too weak to handle what needed to be done." Carol lifted her chin in defiance. "Now I have to do it. Presley isn't fit to be the mother of this child and William is hardly any better. Sherry needs a real family. One who will love and take care of her."

Sherry. She thought Polly was her daughter.

"Mrs. Talbot," Melissa said, "this is Polly, not Sherry."

Carol blinked as if she didn't understand. In that moment of distraction, Polly darted out of her hold. Carol screamed at her to come back, but the girl ran down the hall to Melissa.

Melissa knelt down and wrapped her arms around the child.

"You won't take her!" Carol shouted. Grasping the weapon with both hands, she aimed it at Melissa and Polly.

Jonathan slammed into Melissa, knocking her and Polly to the floor, just as a bullet exploded from the weapon, echoing through the house.

Crouched over Polly, Melissa heard the sounds of struggling. Jonathan was attempting to subdue Carol. She held Polly close to her chest and scooted away from the danger.

As another shot rang out, Melissa reached into her pocket for her cell phone. Not there. Had she dropped it?

Carol screamed, and the weapon fired again.

She chanced a glance over her shoulder and saw Jonathan fling himself atop the woman.

Melissa jumped to her feet. She had to do something.

She rushed into the closest room, put Polly in the closet. "Stay right here, Polly. Don't move." She closed the door, winced at the child's sobbing.

Frantic, Melissa looked around. There was nothing to use as a weapon… Her gaze lit on the heavy curtain rod above the window.

She snatched it down and rushed into the corridor.

Jonathan had Carol pinned to the floor. "Call for help," he yelled out to Melissa.

She dropped the curtain rod and ran back to the front door to search for her phone. She found it on the steps. She grabbed it and completed the call she had started minutes before.

Once she'd given the dispatcher their location, she rushed back to where Jonathan continued to restrain Carol.

"I'll try to find something to tie her up," Melissa offered.

Jonathan nodded.

That was when she saw the blood.

It soaked his shirt in a long line starting at his shoulder.

Her heart bumped her sternum.

Pull it together.

She ran to the bedroom where she'd seen the suitcase. The zipper gave her hell, but she finally ripped the bag open. Melissa grabbed several items and hurried back to the hall.

Trying not to rough Carol up too much, they got her restrained, with the clothing as makeshift rope.

Melissa hurried back to the closet where she'd left Polly. She lifted the little girl into her arms and hugged her tight. "It's okay now."

Polly sobbed against her chest. Melissa kissed her sweet head, inhaled the baby scent of her silky blond hair. "Thank God. Thank God." It would be okay now.

Except for Jonathan. How badly was he hurt? Polly in tow, she hurried back to the hall. "We should look at—"

Chief Talbot stood in the hallway, his weapon leveled on Jonathan.

Fear grabbed Melissa by the throat.

Jonathan was attempting to talk him into putting the weapon down. Melissa was too terrified to move. If he turned the gun on her he might hit Polly.

"Your wife is going to need your help, Chief," Jonathan offered. "You need to be able to help her. You can't do that if you don't make the right choice now."

Carol lay on the floor bellowing in agony, her hands and feet tied behind her.

Chief Talbot turned to Melissa. Her breath caught.

"I'm sorry." He shook his head. "I thought I could make this right."

With the gun trained on Jonathan, time seemed to stand still.

Then finally Chief Talbot lowered his weapon, bent down and placed it on the floor.

Melissa dragged in a breath.

It was over.

Jonathan took the chief's weapon and ushered him over to take care of his wife. Then he came to Melissa and his arms went around her.

It was really over.

Polly was safe.

The smell of warm blood filtered into her nostrils. Melissa drew back. "You're hurt. Let me look at that."

He didn't resist. They walked outside, away from the chief and his wife and their sobbing. Those two had their own problems to work out.

Melissa settled Jonathan on the front steps with Polly right next to him and inspected the bullet wound.

"It's not so bad," she surmised. "Right in and right out. Based on the location in your shoulder, it shouldn't have hit anything important."

Jonathan looked up at her. "Easy for you to say. You're not the one bleeding."

Melissa smiled. "You'll live, trust me."

He took her hand in his. "I do trust you."

The pain in his eyes was not from the wound; that she knew for sure. "I'm glad you still can after all I said."

"It was all true."

God, she'd said some awful things to him. "I'm sorry. I was...overwrought."

"You told the truth." He squeezed her hand. "But there's always room for change. Even for a guy like me."

She nodded, the movement like the workings of a rusty hinge. Words would not squeeze past the emotion in her throat. It was all she could do to hold back the tears.

"Give me another chance," he murmured.

For three years she had hoped one day he would say those words. "I'm sorry." She sucked in a jagged breath. "Could you repeat that, please?"

He laughed. But before he could, Polly tugged at Melissa's blouse. "I want my daddy."

Melissa laughed and cried at the same time. She scooped the child into her arms. "I will definitely take you to your mommy and daddy, little one."

Jonathan pulled her down to sit beside him. He kissed her cheek and rubbed Polly's pretty head.

They were okay. Melissa felt herself smiling again. They were better than okay.

Blue lights flashed in the distance.

"Those guys should have a first aid kit." She was still worried about Jonathan's injury despite her assessment.

"I'll be fine."

Good grief, she was a nurse. She should be taking care of him, not the other way around. But right now her head was spinning wildly. Her heart was thumping like crazy and she couldn't think.

He lifted her chin, ushering her gaze to his. "Think about my offer, would you?"

She bit her lips together for a moment to hold back the tears. "There's nothing to think about. You're on, Mr. Foley." She narrowed her gaze. "But I'm warning you, you won't get away so easily this time."

He smiled. It reached all the way to her heart. "Don't worry. I'm not going anywhere without you."

Chapter Fifteen

"So this is the real Jonathan Foley?" Melissa bit her lips together to hide a smile as she surveyed the place Jonathan called home.

He quirked an eyebrow at her. He loved it when her eyes sparkled so. "I'm rarely here." But that sad fact was about to change.

Melissa strolled over to the table next to the sofa and pointed to the blinking light on his answering machine. He had fourteen messages. "Are those girlfriends?" She smiled this time but there was a little hesitancy in her eyes. She still needed some reassurance.

Jonathan crossed to where she stood and pulled her into his arms. "My boss or one of my colleagues." He brushed his lips over hers. She gasped. "Probably trying to persuade me not to go."

She searched his eyes, hers full of hope. "You're sure this is what you want to do?"

"Absolutely." He kissed her nose, his body already reacting to holding her near. "My boss hired a new staff when he bought the Equalizer shop. None of the former staff stayed. He's got a couple of really top-notch guys who can handle things until he replaces me. He won't even miss me."

Her gorgeous face brightened with happiness and his heart stumbled. Finally, he'd been able to do what he couldn't three years ago—make her happy. That meant more to him than he could possibly ever hope to articulate.

"Well, let's get you packed!"

She started to pull out of his arms, but he drew her closer. They'd come straight here from the airport. He had to pack up and turn in his keys to the landlord. "Later." He grinned. "We haven't slowed down since we found Polly. I'd like a few minutes with you all to myself."

"Sounds doable." She tiptoed and nipped his bottom lip with her teeth. "We're known for slow and easy in the south."

"Then I'm going to love living in Alabama." He covered her mouth with his own. She melted into him.

The telephone rang.

Jonathan reluctantly drew back enough to take a breath. "Do we really need a phone in Alabama?"

Melissa laughed. "We'll have to negotiate that."

The answering machine picked up and the voice of his former boss from the Equalizers filled the silence. "Your final case has been closed out, Foley. Good luck in your new endeavor." The line disconnected.

"Now—" Jonathan cupped her face "—where were we?"

3:30 p.m.

SLADE CLOSED THE FILE he'd been reviewing. The assignment was exactly the sort of case Dakota Garrett could
handle. Ex–Special Forces. Kicked out of the military
for disobeying orders. Definitely the right man for the
job. No worries there.

He closed the file and turned off the light on his
desk. He locked up on his way out of the brownstone.
He never visited the office unless his secretary was
gone for the day or away on lunch. Never met face-to-
face with his investigators. For now that was the way
it had to stay.

Since Foley had resigned, Slade would need to consider a new hire. None of the former owner's staff had
remained with the Equalizers firm. Not that Slade
wanted anyone who knew the former owner, Jim Colby,
to stay. Still, he needed to keep the Equalizers operational until he was finished here. Staying operational
required staff.

Slade pointed his SUV in the direction of downtown.
He had something to do. The same thing he did every
day at this time. His destination had a transit time of
about twenty minutes, depending upon traffic. Once
at the location, he parked his SUV and then parked
himself at the same table he always chose at Maggie's
Coffee House.

The table provided the best view of the comings and
goings at the Colby Agency. He placed his same order,
medium black coffee, dark Columbian roast. Then he
settled in to observe his prey.

No one at the Colby Agency knew him. Even Jim, the man from whom he'd bought the brownstone and the Equalizers firm, didn't know his name or his face.

Slade Keaton wasn't even his real name.

He hadn't used that sham of a name in over a decade. He never would again.

Slade had taken charge of his life. He'd clawed his way up from rock bottom and now he owned whatever he chose to own, whomever he chose to own.

And not a soul had a clue who he was or what he was up to. Certainly not anyone at the Colby Agency.

But they would know very soon.

Very, very soon they would all know him.

One of them in particular, the illustrious Lucas Camp, would come face-to-face with that long-ago mistake he'd made and quickly forgotten.

And he would pay.

Victoria Colby-Camp had better brace herself.

Her whole perfect world was about to be turned upside down.

* * * * *

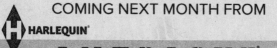

REQUEST YOUR FREE BOOKS!
2 FREE NOVELS PLUS 2 FREE GIFTS!

HARLEQUIN

INTRIGUE

BREATHTAKING ROMANTIC SUSPENSE

YES! Please send me 2 FREE Harlequin Intrigue® novels and my 2 FREE gifts (gifts are worth about $10). After receiving them, if I don't wish to receive any more books, I can return the shipping statement marked "cancel." If I don't cancel, I will receive 6 brand-new novels every month and be billed just $4.74 per book in the U.S. or $5.24 per book in Canada. That's a savings of at least 14% off the cover price! It's quite a bargain! Shipping and handling is just 50¢ per book in the U.S. and 75¢ per book in Canada.* I understand that accepting the 2 free books and gifts places me under no obligation to buy anything. I can always return a shipment and cancel at any time. Even if I never buy another book, the two free books and gifts are mine to keep forever.

182/382 HDN F42N

Name _____ (PLEASE PRINT) _____

Address _____ Apt. # _____

City _____ State/Prov. _____ Zip/Postal Code _____

Signature (if under 18, a parent or guardian must sign) _____

Mail to the **Harlequin® Reader Service:**
IN U.S.A.: P.O. Box 1867, Buffalo, NY 14240-1867
IN CANADA: P.O. Box 609, Fort Erie, Ontario L2A 5X3
**Are you a subscriber to Harlequin Intrigue books
and want to receive the larger-print edition?
Call 1-800-873-8635 or visit www.ReaderService.com.**

* Terms and prices subject to change without notice. Prices do not include applicable taxes. Sales tax applicable in N.Y. Canadian residents will be charged applicable taxes. Offer not valid in Quebec. This offer is limited to one order per household. Not valid for current subscribers to Harlequin Intrigue books. All orders subject to credit approval. Credit or debit balances in a customer's account(s) may be offset by any other outstanding balance owed by or to the customer. Please allow 4 to 6 weeks for delivery. Offer available while quantities last.

Your Privacy—The Harlequin® Reader Service is committed to protecting your privacy. Our Privacy Policy is available online at www.ReaderService.com or upon request from the Harlequin Reader Service.

We make a portion of our mailing list available to reputable third parties that offer products we believe may interest you. If you prefer that we not exchange your name with third parties, or if you wish to clarify or modify your communication preferences, please visit us at www.ReaderService.com/consumerschoice or write to us at Harlequin Reader Service Preference Service, P.O. Box 9062, Buffalo, NY 14269. Include your complete name and address.

HI13R

SPECIAL EXCERPT FROM

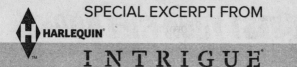

HARLEQUIN

I N T R I G U E

Christmas in Montana is a winter wonderland...until a body turns up in the snow. Now it's up to Tag Cardwell and Lily McCabe to solve the icy murder.

Read on for an excerpt from
CHRISTMAS AT CARDWELL RANCH
by USA TODAY *bestselling author*
B.J. Daniels

"Lily, I have a bad feeling that the reason Mia's condo was ransacked and my father's, too, was that they were looking for this thumb drive."

"Then you should take it to the marshal," she said, handing it to him. "I have a copy of the letters on my computer, so I can keep working on the code."

He nodded, although he had no intention of taking it to the marshal. Not until he knew which side of the fence Hud Savage was on.

"Until we know what's really on this," he said, "I wouldn't mention it to anyone, all right?"

She nodded.

"I need to get to the hospital and see my father, but I don't like leaving you here snowed in alone."

She waved him off. "The plows should be along in the next hour or so if you want to take my SUV."

He wasn't about to leave her here without a vehicle even if he thought he could bust through the drifts. "Are those your brother's cross-country skis and boots by the door?

If you don't mind me borrowing them, I'll ski down to the road and hitch a ride. My brothers and I used to do that all the time when we were kids."

"If you're sure…" She turned back to the papers on the table. "I'll keep working on the code and let you know when I get it finished."

She sounded as if she would be glad when he left her at it. He was reminded that she also had plans to talk to her former fiancé today. He felt a hard knot form in his stomach. Jealousy? Heck yes.

Except he had nothing to be jealous about, right? Last night hadn't happened. At least that was the way Lily wanted it. He fought the urge to touch her hair, remembering the feel of it between his fingers.

"I want you to have this." He held out the pistol he'd taken from his father's place. "I need to know that you are safe."

She shook her head and pulled back. "I don't like guns."

"All you have to do is point it and shoot."

Lily held up both hands. "I don't want it. I could never…" She shook her head again.

"Just in case," Tag said as he laid it on the table, telling himself that if someone broke into her house and tried to hurt her, she would get over her fear of guns quickly. At least he hoped that was true.

Start your holidays with a bang!
Be sure to check out
CHRISTMAS AT CARDWELL RANCH
by USA TODAY bestselling author B.J. Daniels

Available October 22, only from Harlequin® Intrigue®.
Available wherever books and ebooks are sold.

HARLEQUIN®

INTRIGUE®

A MYSTERIOUS DISAPPEARANCE WILL FORCE AN FBI PROFILER TO FACE HIS PAST

There's an alarming vacancy at Bachelor Moon Bed-and-Breakfast. Now it's up to FBI profiler Gabriel Blankenship to investigate the sudden disappearance of the owner's entire family. But the steely agent finds it hard to do his job when distracted by the B and B's gorgeous blonde manager, Marlena Meyers. Damaged by his past, Gabriel has never loved and never wants to. But once Marlena's life is threatened, Gabriel is forced to reconsider his case *and* his emotions.

SCENE OF THE CRIME: RETURN TO BACHELOR MOUNTAIN

BY

NEW YORK TIMES BESTSELLING AUTHOR

CARLA CASSIDY

Available October 22, only from Harlequin® Intrigue®.